Rose Doyle was born into a world still delirious that the war had ended. This may explain why she clings to optimism and a belief that life, no matter what, can be made great. She spent her childhood years in different parts of the Irish countryside, and each summer with her grandparents on the Atlantic coast of Co. Kerry. Her teen years and the sixties coincided with a move to Dublin which, full of energy and irreverence, became her adult home.

Graduating in English from Trinity College, Dublin, Rose Doyle went on to become a successful journalist. She began writing when her two sons were toddlers, and is the author of three bestselling children's books, written following the broadcast of her first radio play. Her first adult novel, *Images*, was published in Ireland in 1993. *Kimbay* is her debut novel in the UK.

ROSE DOYLE
Kimbay

PAN BOOKS

First published 1994 by Town House & Country House
in association with Macmillan General Books

This edition published 1995 by Pan Books
an imprint of Macmillan General Books
25 Eccleston Place, London SW1W 9NF

Associated companies throughout the world

ISBN 0-330-34192-8

3 5 7 9 8 6 4

A CIP catalogue record for this book is available from
the British Library

Typeset by CentraCet Limited, Cambridge
Printed and bound in Great Britain by
Mackays of Chatham PLC, Chatham, Kent

For Ella,
who made it possible.
And for Peter D.,
who shored up my
ignorance.

Acknowledgements

Horse people, everywhere I met them, gave generously of wisdom and anecdote. Those whom I pestered the most, and to whom greatest thanks are due, include vet Peter Dargan, who almost single-handedly rescued me from my imperfect knowledge, Frances Shanahan who kept me on course and in the end checked that I'd stayed there, and Ted Curtin who, with fun, gave me an insight into trainers.

Then there were the three horsemen I met in Sandymount one night. Thanks for enough information for another three books to Peter MnGouran, Michael Keogh and John Boyne.

And thanks to Ella, for the Sunday mornings.

Prologue

It was a most suitable day for a funeral. Winter, under a sky sullen with unfallen snow, lay hard on the graves of the small churchyard and bleakly in the bare trees.

Getting out of their cars the mourners braced themselves. The wind was vicious, the churchyard exposed. They gathered behind the coffin as it was raised onto the shoulders of six men, became a shuffling cortège as they followed it along the path through the graves.

The withered quality of the place wasn't entirely due to the season. Years of neglect had allowed nature become a vandal and Celtic crosses tilted drunkenly, pulled down by rampant ivy. Headstones were everywhere obscured by briars and by the long, brown grass. What had once been a burying place for the great, and sometimes good, had been thoroughly humbled by disuse and the passage of time.

But it was where the dead man had wanted to be buried. It was where his wife, his beautiful Hannah, had been buried eighteen years before, where his parents and grandparents before that had been laid to rest. When he joined his Hannah that day it was likely that Ned Carolan's would be the last interment in the small graveyard.

The ratty February wind, trapped by the stone walls, sniped at the faces of those who'd come to mourn him, whipping away their whispered words. They crept into closer groups.

One of the pall bearers stumbled and, with a low, sympathetic murmur, the cortège came to a standstill. The stumbler was a young man, slim and white-faced. He quickly regained his balance under the coffin.

Thin snow began to fall as they moved forward again, whitening the mound of earth by the newly opened grave.

1

The priest waiting for them was an old man. He coughed, sighing heavily as they gathered around him.

They were a larger crowd than the churchyard could take and were obliged to stand on graves, or lean against headstones, to get close enough to hear the burying ceremony. Some of them, a trio of small, narrow-faced men, gathered in the shelter of the mournful yew tree guarding the new grave.

The old priest's voice was strong and it rose in a clear drone as he began to speak.

'Graveyards are redolent of death,' he said, 'but this one, today, is full too of a sense of the futility of life, of its dreams and ambitions and terrible losses.' He coughed and sighed and the mourners, muttering, shifted their cold feet. 'Maybe it has to do with the manner of Ned's passing. We were together at the races, himself and myself, when it happened. But ye all know that. He was happy that day, full of hope and good humour. He'd had one loser, three winners. Then his heart gave out and he died. There at the track. It was God's will and we must accept his passing. But today is nevertheless a sad day for the locality. A sad day indeed.'

He stopped and, in the silence, there came the sound of a car accelerating fast along the narrow roads to the churchyard. The priest began again, raising his voice in prayer as it came to a gravel-spinning halt at the gates.

'Forasmuch as it hath pleased Almighty God—' The car door slammed and the driver, a tall young woman in red anorak and boots, rushed headlong up the path. '—to take unto himself the soul of our dear brother here departed . . .'

The mourners, with a rustle of recognition, parted to allow the woman take her place by the side of the grave. The priest waited while the young man who had faltered and another man, older and heavier, linked their arms through hers. Standing together their family resemblance was strong.

The priest went on: '. . . We therefore commit his

2

body to the ground; earth to earth, ashes to ashes, dust to dust; in sure and certain hope of the Resurrection to eternal life.'

The young woman and her brothers stood stiff and white-faced as the coffin was lowered into the ground. The sadness in the crowd became resignation.

Chapter One

The telephone message had come to the hotel in Austria where Flora Carolan had been on a skiing holiday with her lover Serge. She hadn't told any of the family at Kimbay that she was going to St Anton and it had taken time to find her. Her father had been dead two days when the message arrived.

They'd been to Austria before, she and Serge, though not to St Anton. Skiing was his sport, along with sailing in the summer, and he'd arranged the holiday as a surprise. Flora would have preferred the sun and sea but knew skiing was the social thing in the early months of the year.

Doing the right thing socially mattered to Serge de Maraville. It came from his background, but Flora suspected he'd have been like that anyway. It gave life definition, he said. Flora agreed with him, up to a point.

But then her growing-up had been less defined and tradition-bound than his. Different in every way, in fact. At Kimbay, the family stud farm, her life had been vigorously free of constraints and obligations while his, as the only son of an old French family, had been a formal affair at the family château in the heart of the Loire valley. The household there had been dominated by Monique, his hopelessly snobbish, strong-minded mother. Sandrine, his younger sister, had fled the stifling splendour of it all as soon as it had been decently possible. Serge, simply because it suited him, had been slower to make the break with its elegantly paced and mannered life.

When he did it was to become a wine distributor. Billaud et fils dealt only in the best of wines. Their customers liked to feel they were dealing with a man who

4

would never drink anything else. Serge's perfect manners and impeccable contacts worked well for the firm and he quickly became a partner. That the company was rapidly expanding was in no small measure due to the easy charm with which he hid a cool, businesslike determination.

In the matter of skiing holidays there was, for Serge, more than the social niceties involved, however. The thrill of downhill speed was in his blood the way horses were in Flora's. She envied him the dizzy heights and each holiday dabbled with the idea of joining him off-piste.

They drove to St Anton. Flora would have preferred to fly, but it was, practically speaking, the best way to make the journey. The trip through Germany had been smooth, but unexpected blizzards made a nightmare of the last hundred kilometres.

Flora, always a bored passenger, brought up the subject of the high slopes as darkness began to obscure the views.

'I think I'll go for the peaks this time,' she said.

Serge, looking for a gap in the almost stationary traffic on the mountain road, didn't answer immediately. When he did he was discouraging.

'I don't think that's such a good idea,' he said. 'You are not ready.'

'I'd like to give it a try, anyway,' Flora said.

'*Ma chère*, I have been skiing since I could walk.' He spoke with tired patience. 'I *know* these mountains, how they can appear and how they really are. It is best if you stay skiing on the lower pistes.'

He turned and smiled his slow, persuasive smile, the smile which had first convinced her that she must get to know this man. A car honked, an open stretch of road loomed and he turned, smile still on his face, to make for the opening. Flora dropped the subject of the high slopes.

Looking up she could see the lights of climbing cars as they appeared and disappeared around mountainous bends. When they themselves got up there, closer to the peaks, Serge would become restless. She'd seen it before. He would fidget, be vague and inattentive, longing to be alone with the snow and downhill speed. He needed it and she understood. She could only go a certain length of time herself without feeling the need for horses, the urge to ride and be around them.

In the dark of the car she sighed and leaned closer to him. He kissed the top of her hair and murmured, '*Ça va?*' She nodded, closing her eyes and hoping for sleep.

Every woman, she thought lazily, should have a Serge. He really was a most civilized, wonderful man. Older than she (he was forty-one), urbane, knowing and past fighting over the small things which didn't matter. He was handsome too, and getting richer all the time. In bed his love was caring in a way that she'd never known with any other man. She was lucky, and she knew it.

'We will be there in less than an hour.' He took a hand from the wheel and lightly touched her cheek.

'Do you want me to drive?'

'*Non, merci.* I would prefer you to sleep.'

Flora lay back in the deep seat of the Citroën, glad he hadn't taken up her offer. Not that she'd expected him to. Serge preferred to be in charge. She didn't mind. It made life a lot easier all round.

Through half-closed lids she studied his profile. She adored his face: strong mouth, chin with a hollow which deepened when he flashed that smile. His mid-brown hair was inclined to curl but he kept it in firmly clipped control. She'd noticed lately where grey was creeping into the sides. She liked it.

Feeling her eyes on him he turned a raised, questioning eyebrow her way.

'What's the hotel like?' she asked him.

'Old. Very good. You will love it,' he assured. 'I brought Monique there once. She approved.'

'No!' Flora gave an exaggerated gasp. 'Your mother left France, stayed in a non-French hotel and *liked* it . . .?'

'It's true,' Serge laughed. 'It was about ten years ago but even now, when I think about it, I am surprised.'

'Does she know we will be staying there?'

'*Mais oui* . . .'

'She'll haunt us,' Flora shuddered. 'She'll spirit herself here to make sure we don't eat cheese after dessert.'

Serge gave a short laugh but his voice was serious when he spoke. 'She is not so terribly *exigeante*, *ma chère*. She is what she is and cannot be anything else. You must understand that she sees all that she believes in fading in her children, in their generation. We have disappointed her, Sandrine and I. Now she just wishes to keep things going, her way, for as long as she is alive.'

Serge's sister Sandrine might be a disappointment to the seventy-five-year-old tradition-bound Monique de Maraville, but Flora doubted that her son was anything but a source of enormous pride to her. True, he had forsaken his *patrimoine*, chosen not to live in the family château and to make his living as a wine distributor. But the two ways of life were not mutually exclusive. They had never discussed it but Flora knew that he would, in the fullness of time, return and run the business from Angers. Monique too expected that he would.

She didn't want to think about the consequences of such a move on their relationship. Brussels without Serge would be unbearable. The Loire valley, on the other hand, was quite beautiful.

But all that was for the future. Now, in the glorious present, they loved one another, enjoyed their every minute together. When the future did occasionally hover in the odd unsure silence, they both, gently, moved on. They would discuss things, make plans, when the time was right. Flora was sure of this. It just wasn't that time yet.

'Your mother will live forever,' she said now.

Serge's affection for Monique was as strong as his many disagreements with her. '*Non*, she will not. But she will not die for several years yet.' Serge brought Flora's hand quickly to his mouth and brushed it with his lips. The bare, feathery touch made her catch her breath and brought a quick rush of pleasurable anticipation for the love they would make later on.

For the rest of the journey she watched the darkened,

snowy landscape and thought about him. She thought, a little, about Monique too.

Madame Monique de Maraville did not approve of Flora and didn't try to hide the fact. She made it clear, with elderly, aristocratic arrogance, that she didn't think Flora a suitable mate for her only son and that she hoped their *liaison* would end. Her objections were mainly to do with her son's companion not being French, a fact which raised for Monique the problems of Flora's unsuitable family and race. The latter she considered *un peu sauvage*, the former a *petit bourgeois* curiosity.

All of this, at first, had seemed to Flora idiotic but amusing. She understood better now, now that she'd come to know something of the ways of the old French families. Marriage alliances, she'd discovered, were catalogued exactly like matings in a horsebreeder's stud book. If Serge chose to marry Flora then her entry into the family would upset the balance of things extremely.

But the question of marriage had not come up. Yet. Serge did not want to repeat his sister's mistakes. Three times divorced, Sandrine lived a jet-set existence in a, so far, disastrous search for the perfect husband. She rarely visited the family château, something Flora found difficult to understand. She herself had adored it.

Perched high above the river in the Loire valley its large, formal salons were filled with old furniture, paintings and porcelain of an exquisite beauty. In the summertime everything was shuttered against the sun but in the spring, when she'd first gone there, it shone green and gold and was dominated by eccentric, terraced gardens. She'd been fascinated by the way their wild, essential nature kept breaking through in spite of the attentions of an army of gardeners.

It was not the sort of background she'd envisaged for Serge when she'd first met him at a party in Brussels.

The party was a boring affair, given by the translating company she worked for. She was about to leave when she saw him, smiling as he listened to an overdressed Belgian

8

woman from the company. She made her way towards them and was introduced.

They had instantly clicked and Serge had taken control. They had left the party together, had dinner in a restaurant run by friends of his. It had all been very easy.

By the third week of knowing Serge Flora had eased Harold, the gentle, English EU *fonctionnaire* she'd been seeing, out of her life. By the fourth she was sleeping with him, thinking of him constantly. He was charming and clever and his friends were charming and clever. Flora loved being part of his world and within months she was in love with Serge the man too.

And now they were to have a whole week together in the carefree world of the Alps.

The heat in the car, the tortuously slow crawl up the mountain, lulled her asleep. She awoke to a blast of cold air and to Serge hunkering beside her open door.

'We are here.' He was invigorated already and beaming. Flora groaned.

'I just want a bath,' she said, 'and to learn to use my legs again.'

It was good to fill her lungs in the clean-aired, mountainy world. The hotel was satisfyingly luxurious and slightly apart from the rest of the resort.

Later, submerged in the deep bath, Flora allowed the bubbly water to soothe and relax the cramp in her limbs. When she came out, wrapped in metres of heavy white towelling robe, Serge had ordered wine and a *bonne bouche* of pâté.

'I thought it too late for a meal,' he said as, stretched in a chair, he watched her pick at the food. 'We will need sleep if we are to be on the slopes early.'

Flora sat on the floor and leaned against him, contemplating the fire which had been lit for them when they arrived. He put an arm around her, pulled her close.

'The forecast is for sunny weather with gusty winds.' He spoke into her hair. 'Not perfect for skiing, but good. There is a lot of newly fallen snow too.'

9

'Wind. Newly fallen snow.' Flora gave a wry smile. 'You're trying to tell me there are avalanche conditions up there, aren't you? And that it will be all right for you on high but not for me?'

'Those are the facts, Flora. The freedom to choose is yours . . .'

They had the wine, and some of the pâté. Before going to bed they stood by the window and watched the white magic of lightly falling snow.

'What a perfect world,' Flora said.

Serge lifted her face to his and kissed her. 'In bed we will make it truly perfect.'

They made love slowly in the darkened room, exploring with hands and with mouths the places they knew would give pleasure. Serge, voice husky, told Flora she was beautiful, murmuring against her breasts, into her hair. Flora laughed softly, loving the smell and touch of him, running her mouth across his body.

When it was over they lay with the curtains open, watching while the last of the snow fell. Unspoken between them there was a glorious, isolated feeling of time suspended.

Sometime before dawn Flora awoke to an incredible silence. Through the window she saw the vague, jagged outline of a distant peak against the lightening sky. The bathroom door opened and Serge emerged, dressed for the slopes. When he leaned over her she allowed him to kiss her sleepy mouth goodbye before turning over to drift into a blissful slumber.

It was after ten, and a good breakfast, before she took herself for a gentle, experimental run on the lower slopes. On the third day, and in perfect conditions, she ventured off-piste with a guide on a moderately high slope. She was flushed and exhilarated when she got back to the hotel.

She was totally unprepared for the sombrely waiting hotel manager. He moved quickly to intercept her as she crossed the lobby.

'There has been a telephone call for you, Madame.' He was a small, fat man and he annoyed Flora with his

10

insistence on calling her Madame. He knew, she was sure of it, that she and Serge weren't married. He had a spaniel's wet eyes and sad smile and Flora distrusted him, only in part because she didn't like spaniels. He spoke excellent American English.

She frowned, unable to imagine who would have called her here. 'Is there a message?' she asked.

'Yes. I'm afraid there is. I took charge of it myself, in the circumstances . . .'

'What do you mean?'

It was only then, as he held up a folded piece of hotel notepaper, that the finger of dread first touched her. But still she didn't think of Ned, or that anything could be wrong at Kimbay. She reached for the notepaper in the manager's soft hand.

'I am sorry, Madame, to be the one to give you this news . . .' He moved with surprising swiftness, and took the paper out of her reach. 'I would hope, if either myself or my staff can be of help, that you will . . .'

Flora, trying desperately to ignore the chill of premonition creeping over her, dropped her hand and looked at him coldly.

'May I have my message, please?' she asked.

'Of course.' The manager, with a small incline of his head, handed her the notepaper. He stood to the side while she read.

The words, at first, meant nothing. Flora read them, blankly uncomprehending. She shook her head to clear it, and read them again. Carefully typed, immaculately punctuated, they said the same thing the second time.

'Dad has died. Sorry to tell you like this. We've had a hell of a time finding you.' It was signed by Fintan, her younger brother.

What did Fintan mean, sending her a message like this? Ollie was older, he should have sent it . . .

But nothing about the message was as it should be. Ned shouldn't be dead. He couldn't be.

*

11

Daisy Sweeney answered the phone at Kimbay. Flora, the receiver jammed so hard against her ear it hurt, almost shouted at her.

'Daisy! I got Fintan's message . . .'

'Flora, thank God! Oh, my poor child . . .' the other woman's strong voice broke and in the silence Flora closed her eyes. 'It's terrible that you had to hear like this,' the voice came on the line again, sounding like a hoarse whisper. 'We had trouble finding you . . .'

'I know. I'm sorry . . .' But why should she be sorry? Ned hadn't been sick. There hadn't been any need to say she would be away for a week. 'For God's sake, Daisy, tell me what happened.'

'It was his heart. Gave out on him at the races.' Daisy spoke quickly. 'He died at the track, before even they got him into the ambulance. It happened on Saturday, Flora. The boys were waiting to contact you before arranging the funeral. You'd best get home right away.'

'On Saturday?' Flora tried to grasp the facts. 'But this is Monday . . .'

'Yes.' Daisy took a deep breath. 'When can you get here?' she asked. 'We need to arrange things . . .'

'I'll leave now. I'll drive to Munich and get a plane. That'll be the quickest. I'll be there tomorrow.'

'We'll bury him Wednesday so . . .'

The words filled Flora with panic and she hung up at once, ignoring Daisy's offer to bring Fintan or Ollie to the phone.

When she was ready to leave she scribbled a note to Serge and stuck it on the bathroom mirror. He was still on the peaks, on the highest slopes. He would shower as soon as he came back to the hotel and would be bound to see the note. It was the best she could do.

Then she phoned for a hired car and ran.

Going down the mountain road they'd come up only three days before she knew she was going too fast. She slowed when she found herself heading for a wall of ice, veered just in time. After that there were more walls and it took forever to get to Munich.

12

At Munich airport there was a go-slow. But there was a seat going on a flight to Paris if she cared to try that route . . . She did, but arrived too late for the flight from Paris to Dublin. It was Wednesday before she eventually got to Dublin, into another hired car and on the road to her father's funeral.

Chapter Two

Flora stood by the grave with her brothers accepting the sympathy and condolences of the mourners. It was the custom. The snow turned to sleet as men offered iron-grip handshakes and turned hurriedly away. Women offered handshakes too, but also words of comfort and unashamed tears. To all of them Flora and her brothers gave thanks and invitations to come back to Kimbay for a drink, a bite to eat. This too was the custom. And it was the way the dead man would have wanted things.

The crowd was big and they stood for an endless time. The sleet turned to rain, washing the last of the snow from the bank of wreaths and bouquets covering the open grave. Ollie blew loudly into a handkerchief and Fintan turned a white, bleak face toward Flora.

'You all right?' he asked and she nodded, gave him a tight smile. The last of the mourners turned away and the gravediggers moved from the shelter of the yew trees to finish their job.

'It's over. Best be going now . . .' Daisy Sweeney, large and red-eyed, touched Flora on the arm. Behind her, on the narrow footpath, her husband and teenage children waited quietly. Shay Sweeney had been Ned Carolan's right-hand man at the stud for almost thirty years. Dully, painfully, Flora became aware of a subdued wretchedness about the Sweeney family. She looked tiredly at Daisy.

'Of course,' she said and moved at last from the side of the grave. Her brothers moved too and together the small group left the churchyard. Behind them the gravediggers began to fill in the deep hole in the ground.

There were three cars in the narrow road outside. Shay Sweeney, after a fierce handshake and nod of his head to

Flora, climbed behind the wheel of one. His twin offspring shuffled uncertainly, before Leah, with a sob, threw her arms briefly around Flora.

'It's terrible,' she said. Her brother, Luke, shook Flora's hand awkwardly. They climbed into the car with their father.

'Now then,' Daisy raised her voice against the wind, 'we'll all have to put grief behind us for the next few hours. There are people waiting back at the house. They'll have to be looked after, decently. No half measures.'

'Is there somebody there to let them in?' Flora asked.

'Melissa stayed behind.' Ollie, wiping rain from his glasses, spoke hesitantly. 'She was too upset to come to the graveyard. We didn't think Peter should be here anyway.' His large brown eyes looked at Flora with myopic apology.

'You can discuss all this with your sister later,' Daisy, firmly, turned Ollie in the direction of the second car. 'All of us standing here, getting wet, is serving no purpose.' Ollie, taller than she and several stones heavier, became in seconds the child Daisy had once worried about and fussed over.

'Right. You're right,' he said and got into the black Golf. Flora slipped the key into the door of the hired car. It didn't turn. She tried again, fingers stiff and fumbling.

'Other side,' Fintan took them from her and pointed to the passenger seat. 'I'll drive.'

It was still vaguely warm in the car. Fintan drove quickly and competently in the wake of the other two cars, now moving ahead of them fast along the country roads. Looking dully through the window Flora thought how different it all was from the last journey she'd driven in a car with a man. There were no snowy mountains in this landscape, no mountains at all in fact. Just rolling, wintry fields, mucky verges, fast clouds in the sky above. And her young brother at the wheel.

'When did you learn to drive?' Flora asked, remembering how, a year before, he'd sworn never to add to the planet's pollution by becoming a driver.

'You mean why, don't you?' Fintan gave a wry grin.

15

'I suppose I do.'

'Actually, it's a when and a why answer. I learned to drive when Dad bought a van for the band . . .'

'He what? But he—'

'—hated our music? No, he didn't. Not during the last year or so anyway. He got interested.'

'And he bought a van for the Lurking Evil? I don't understand . . .'

Fintan, eyes on the road ahead, interrupted harshly. 'Think, Flora. Try putting two and two together. That's what I did. The answer's not hard.'

'He knew . . .' Flora looked at him, forcing her eyes wide to stop the tears falling.

'He knew.' Fintan nodded. Flora saw him swallow.

So Ned had known he had a heart condition. Known how serious it was too. There could be no other explanation for his taking an interest in the Lurking Evil. He'd been behind Fintan's music career all the way, backing and paying for his piano and fiddle lessons. But he'd drawn a puzzled line at his son's commitment to hard rock. Even the cult success of the Lurking Evil had failed to lure him to a concert.

'How long do you think he'd known for?'

'Dunno. Couple of years anyway. I kind of sussed a while ago there was something up . . .'

'You knew? What exactly did you know?'

Fintan flashed her a slightly embarrassed look. He looked so young, Flora thought. None of this was fair. She should be supporting him and instead here he was . . .

'I knew he'd a sense of time running out,' Fintan shrugged. 'The wingèd chariot and all that. Told myself I was imagining it, but . . .'

'*How* did you know? Did he tell you something?'

'Get a life, Flora. He didn't operate like that, as you well know. This thing with the band began about a year ago. His interest in it, I mean. He did stuff that was way out of character, like turning up at a couple of gigs. It spooked me at first but then, when he started turning up at

16

Ollie's place for Sunday lunch, expecting them to play happy families and all that, I started to think about the whys . . .'

'I didn't know about any of this,' Flora spoke slowly. 'Why didn't anyone tell me?'

'I suppose we hadn't really started to face it ourselves. No one expected him to actually keel over and bloody die, Flora.' His voice was harsh again, with grief and with regret too.

'No. I know. I'm sorry . . .' Flora touched his hand on the wheel. 'How had he been recently?' she asked.

'Bit frantic, to tell you the truth. But then he was never much for sitting around anyway. I did the Leopardstown jaunt with him on Stephen's Day and managed a bit of a study of our man at the racetrack. He was acting like there was no tomorrow, throwing fifty-quid bets around, that kind of thing. But for the first time in my life it occurred to me that he was old . . .'

'Well, he was sixty, after all.'

'I know. But he was looking a lot older. I asked him if he was okay. He said he was in better shape than I'd ever be. Typical. Know what I think, Flora?'

'What do you think?' Flora felt infinitely weary, infinitely sad.

'I think he was trying to leave his offspring in good order before he shuffled off. The van wasn't all he bought. He got us sound equipment too. *And* he sussed out Ollie's basic needs.'

'He didn't buy off Melissa by any chance?' Flora's tone was dry.

'Nope. Opposite in fact. He dealt with a little mortgage problem they had, booked grandson Peter into the old school. All a bit odd for a father who used to be heavily into the old self-reliance code for his kids.'

'"The greatest thing in the world is to know how to be self-sufficient,"' Flora quoted. 'He was right, too. But we weren't really, were we? Self-sufficient, I mean. Not when he was alive anyway. He was always there for us . . .'

'Some of us managed it more than others,' Fintan shrugged. 'You look peaky, big sister. Daisy's organized caterers. We'll get you something to eat at the house.'

Flora, looking at him, was aware that Fintan had changed, grown up since last she'd seen him. Nothing to do with his trademark appearance, of course. The drop-dead exterior which ensured him a healthy fan club was unchanged. Of Hannah Carolan's three children he was the most like her, the one people called 'his mother's son'.

He was built like her, slim and slight, and his hair, long and falling on his forehead, was the same blond hers had been. But his eyes were Ned's, grey and clear. Hannah's eyes, large and dark brown, had gone to her other two children.

No, the difference was in behaviour, and far more fundamental. Fintan was acting grown-up. He was being responsible. He was making her feel very unsure, as if she didn't know him any more.

'It's rude to stare,' he flashed her a jerky smile and she saw that he was tired. He touched her arm briefly. 'You didn't miss much, you know. The last few days haven't exactly been a barrel of laughs.'

'How's Ollie? And Peter? Does he realize his grandad's . . . dead?'

'Hard to tell with Peter. You know what kids are. He seems fine. Ollie's . . . Ollie. He keeps smiling, being the good guy. And Melissa's . . . Melissa, the beautiful calculator and light of his life. Next to Peter that is. Enough to put a man off marriage for good.'

Ollie, just a year younger than Flora, had been a tall, handsome, dark-eyed teenager, a gentle loner. He'd been studying accountancy when he met Melissa, small, fat, pretty and desperate for a man. Peter was the result of their mutual dependence and a kind of love. For his sake they'd married at twenty. Melissa flowered in marriage, Ollie floundered. Melissa took to a fitness régime and emerged a beauty. Ollie abandoned accountancy and took to selling houses to support his family. He grew fat, lumbering, unsure. He also fell hopelessly in love with his wife.

18

'Nearly there,' Fintan turned off by an old, and not very straight, wooden sign. On it, in Gaelic lettering, was written Kimbay.

They drove along a wide avenue with wooden fences on either side and a scattering of oak trees, a few poplars. The other cars had vanished behind a curving belt of holly and laurel bushes. They followed and arrived at the house.

There were lights everywhere and, in the darkening dusk, Kimbay's elegant pedigree shone. Its late Georgian architect had chosen the site well and the windows on all sides had views of the farm's land.

Light from the open front door fell across the wide steps leading up and, now, on funeral guests as they arrived.

Fintan turned off the engine. 'I really reckoned the old man.' He glanced at Flora, then away. His voice was immensely sad.

'He was someone to reckon with,' Flora said.

They sat in silence while the last of the guests went into the house and the door closed behind them.

'We'd better go in,' Flora said.

Chapter Three

Flora, stepping into the living room, was assailed by warm waves of whiskey fumes and cigar smoke. The buzz of sound was deep-throated, mostly male. Fintan, without a word, plunged into the throng ahead of her. She shook herself out of the anorak, took a deep breath and was about to follow him when her arm was firmly gripped.

'They'll be all right for a while,' Daisy said. 'Come on down and get something hot into you.'

Wordlessly, Flora followed her broad shape toward the back of the house and the kitchen. She sat at her father's place at the table while Daisy poured tea, added too much sugar and put it in front of her.

'Drink that,' Daisy commanded, 'the sugar'll give you a bit of energy. Good for the shock too. There's a lot of fancy caterer's food in the living room. You can go back for some later. But first things first.'

Flora took a scalding gulp and shuddered. While the sweet heat made its way through her body she looked around the kitchen. It was a chaos of utensils in use and used, of open cupboard doors and a couple of overstuffed armchairs. Peat burned in the old range. Without looking down she knew the crunch under her foot was sugar. Daisy always worked like this, so why not today, of all days? The normality was good. Comforting. When everyone was gone Daisy would clean like a dervish. The result would be scrupulously clean chaos. That would be normal and comforting too. Flora finished the tea.

'That tasted bloody awful, but you were right,' she said. 'I feel better.'

'Time for the rest of the cure so,' Daisy sat opposite her and placed two bottles on the table. 'We'll have a drink and a small chat and then you can attack the business of being civil to that lot up there.'

She poured Flora a whiskey and herself a glass of her own home-brewed elderflower wine. They touched glasses.

'To the man who's gone,' Daisy said. They drank.

Flora took her glass and walked to the wide window overlooking the stables and main yard. The lights picked up the bright red of the horse looseboxes.

'Fintan thinks Dad knew there was a problem with his heart. And that he knew it was bad.' In the yard below her she could see Shay, doing a checking round of the boxes, having a word with a nervous animal. A small boy accompanied him. Peter, she thought, and wondered if Melissa knew where he was. Her sister-in-law was notoriously fearful of the coarsening effects of country or animal life on her son. Peter himself seemed to have no such qualms.

Behind her, Daisy began to speak. 'Ned knew something. I know that now. But then it's easy to have twenty-twenty vision in hindsight . . .' Flora could hear the sigh in her voice. 'He wouldn't talk about it. I asked him. Straight out. He laughed at me, said he planned to see the new century in.'

Straight out is exactly how Daisy would have asked. And with a laugh is exactly how Ned would have responded. If he'd been inclined to tell anyone about a health problem it would have been Daisy, the woman who'd been a mother-figure to his children after their own died.

Daisy had been there for them, constantly, in the terrible months after Hannah's death. When her own twin babies arrived, a year later, they'd had to learn to share her. But even then Daisy had been generous with her time and during Flora's holidays from boarding school it had been Daisy, along with Ned, who'd made Kimbay a home.

Daisy had a way of taking things onto her broad shoulders and, when Flora and her brothers had at last left home, she'd continued to cook in her haphazard fashion for Ned. She had also, after the same fashion, taken to looking after the house and helping with the yard's bookkeeping.

21

Flora, growing older, had come to realize that Daisy, in many ways, was a proud, glorious example of an aging hippie. She must be fifty now, still striking rather than beautiful, her red hair in its perennial, unruly plait. She was too heavy to be statuesque and freckles gave her wide face a childlike quality that wasn't at all an accurate reflection of the woman. Daisy had lived. She had, by her own account, 'been there and done that' many times before, at twenty-eight, abandoning a folk-singing group to marry Shay Sweeney.

Her throaty voice, speaking or in song, was filled even today with the haunting folk memories of her native Kerry. And it was a measure of the closeness of the local community that, after twenty-two years at Kimbay, Daisy was still known as 'the Kerrywoman'. But she'd grown to love this midland county, where the rich, rolling fields were so unlike the rocky, wild place she came from herself. It was a joy to look at it, she often said, 'and to see things growing in good earth and safe from the salty Atlantic winds'. She was brusque, passionate and loyal. Flora thought the world of her.

And Daisy, for all her energy, knew how to be quiet. Like now. Daisy was the only person Flora knew who could create such peaceful silences. The silence between them stretched comfortably, restfully, as she watched at the window, sipping her drink, until Shay began to head back to the house.

'Did you believe Dad when he told you he was fine?' She turned away, went back to the table to sit opposite the other woman.

'Yes and no. I knew there was something wrong. He'd got old . . .' Daisy refilled her wine glass. 'He talked about changes. And he made . . . Flora, I don't know, girl, what was going on in his head or what he was up to. And that in itself was strange because I could read that man like a book. He made . . .' Daisy hesitated.

'What did he make, Daisy?' Flora asked the question gently.

'He made a new will, Flora. Look,' Daisy held up a

large, flat, silencing hand, 'there's no good you asking me. I don't know what was in it. Neither does Shay. He mentioned it to us because he didn't want us hearing about it from someone else. That was all.'

'When? When did this happen?'

'About three weeks ago, toward the end of January.' Daisy's voice was non-committal.

'I'd no idea. No one told me . . . anything. I should have come home for Christmas . . .'

She'd gone to the Loire for that holiday. She'd gone there the year before too. She and Serge had been Monique's only company, Ned had had so many people . . .

'There's nothing to be gained from apportioning blame,' Daisy was brisk, 'and guilt is a waste of time too.' She covered Flora's hand where it lay on the table. 'No one's at fault. He wouldn't have listened to anyone, not even to you. He died as he lived, Flora, a burden to no one. And he left more good than most men behind him. He'd have had no patience with limping along, and well you know it.'

'Yes . . .' Flora would probably have wept then, she certainly wanted to. But the door behind her nudged slowly open and a heavy-eyed black labrador lumbered over to put his head on her knee.

'Dipper, old friend,' her father's dog gazed at her with intense misery as she fondled his ears. He sighed and lay down against her legs.

'He's a bit lost,' Daisy said. 'Doesn't know what to do with himself since Saturday. He's like most of us around here. Come on, Dipper,' she commanded, 'into your seat now . . .'

As the old dog grunted his way into one of the armchairs, Flora stood. 'I'd better go on up and pay my respects to some of our guests before they start leaving.'

Some had already left, thinning the big room out a little. From the door Flora could see her brothers, one on either side of the old marble fireplace, so very different, yet tonight wearing the same tight expressions on their faces. Melissa, beautiful in black, stood a little apart.

23

This was the room they'd used as a family growing up. People suited it, they ~~brought it to life~~. Morning would reveal its neglect but for now, high-ceilinged and glowing in the muted light from the old chandelier, it was at its gracious best. Flora made a slow way toward her brothers, exchanging greetings as she went with Ned's few, distant relatives, with neighbours, with the trio of jockeys who'd been together at the graveyard. A waitress stopped with a tray of drinks and, playing safe and feeling tired, she took a glass of Ballygowan.

She was half-way across the room when she was stopped by an old vet friend of her father's. Jack Thomas was a shambling hulk of a man, white-haired and rheumy-eyed. Flora was fond of him and shook his hand warmly. He had a way with animals which went way beyond anything veterinary training could have taught him, and a way with humans which owed a lot to the Shay Sweeney school of personal relations. His impatience with people, his intolerance of the foibles and everyday follies of his fellow man, were equal only to the same characteristics in Shay.

But whereas Shay had the daily softening influence of Daisy and the twins about him, Jack Thomas had remained a bachelor. The two men had never got on. Flora suspected they were too alike for comfort – but also that Shay had resented the vet's close relationship with her father, the fact that he'd had Ned's ear. Ned Carolan and Jack Thomas had been at school together and had, in their day, been two of the county's 'young blades'. There had always been an ease and trust between them and whenever Ned had gone drinking it had been with Jack Thomas.

'You're looking tired.' He pumped Flora's hand up and down in one fast, furious movement. 'Sorry for your trouble.'

'Thanks, Jack.' Flora knew that, more than most, he would miss her father. She was about to move on when the vet, speaking quite loudly, said, 'Don't suppose there'll be much work for me around here in the future, now your man'll be in charge, more or less.'

'Sorry?' Flora looked at him, puzzled.

'Sweeney. He won't let me treat the animals. Only reason I got near the yard these last few years was because Ned insisted. Kimbay will want a new vet. But there's a few of the mares won't let anyone near but me. You'll have to sort him out, Flora, or he'll cut off his nose to spite his face.'

The penny dropped and Flora shook her head. 'I don't know what I can do about it, Jack,' she said, 'any more than I know what's going to happen to Kimbay. And I doubt Shay would listen to me anyway.'

'Wouldn't be so sure about that.' The vet's eyes, from under bristling white brows, peered hard into hers. 'I'd say he'll be listening to a lot of what you have to say from now on.'

'What do you mean, Jack?' Flora asked the question slowly. Jack Thomas wasn't a gossip. He wasn't an idle listener either. If he said something it was usually based on factual information. But what *was* he saying?

'Just that you're your father's daughter and his first-born child,' the vet glowered and puffed out a grunt of air.

'But I won't be running the stud, Jack. I'm sorry,' Flora said, and meant it.

'Huh.' The vet gave her another close look. 'Don't play cute with me, Flora. I know you too long. I'll bid you good day now.'

He gulped the remains of his whiskey, placed the empty glass in her hand and grunted goodbye. Flora watched him stomp his way to the door, the oiled jacket he wore winter and summer tight across his massive shoulders. He had indeed known her for a long time. Since the time, as a small child, he'd brought her near-dead puppy back to life. She wondered what he thought she was keeping from him and decided, as he pulled open the door and bumbled through, that he was simply becoming more eccentric than ever as he got old.

Ollie looked relieved as she joined him and Fintan. 'Wondered if you were all right,' he said and gave her a

25

brief hug. He looked vaguely around the room. 'People were asking about you.'

His eyes, behind the heavy-rimmed spectacles, were worried. He'd put on weight, too. Flora could see nothing of the boy who'd loved to daydream and whose gentle smile had stopped endless childhood fights.

'I met some of them,' she reassured him. 'Jack Thomas in particular. He—'

'Flora! You poor pet! How *are* you?' Melissa, her perfect face delicately distressed, placed a white hand on Flora's arm. 'How awful to hear on the telephone. But then it couldn't be helped, could it? Not with you so hard to find and everything . . .'

Flora looked at her, marvelling at how guilty her sister-in-law managed to make her feel about being on holiday when Ned died.

'It was bad timing on my part all right, Melissa.' She was aware that her tone was dry, but had never been able to avoid a certain acidity where Ollie's wife was concerned.

'Poor Ned,' Melissa, apparently unaware, sighed. 'Peter's *terribly* upset, you know. He was *so* fond of his grandfather. It's a shame he'll grow up not knowing him . . .'

Flora nodded. Melissa often left her at a loss for something to say. She looked wonderful, a fragile, pale beauty with long dark eyes and a face framed by close-cropped dark hair. She made Flora feel like a draught-horse in the company of an Arab thoroughbred. And, as with most thoroughbreds, Flora was never quite sure how Melissa would perform, when her mood would change.

'It's so very sad,' Melissa spoke in almost a whisper. 'They were just beginning to bond. Ned had started to spend time with us, you know. Peter is – was – his only grandchild, after all.'

'Yes.' Flora marvelled this time at Melissa's ability not only to put the knife in, but to twist it so unerringly. Ned's unsubtle hints, asides about how her mother had had two children at Flora's age, had been half-joking, wholly in

26

earnest. They had caused her frequent stabs of guilt when he was alive. She really didn't need to be reminded today.

'How *is* Peter?' she asked, scanning the room. 'I saw him in the yard. He seemed happy enough . . .'

'In the yard? You saw him in the yard?' Melissa's eyes widened and her voice became thin. 'Oh, my God!' She turned to Ollie, who immediately became more worried-looking. 'How did he get out *there*, Oliver? He knows it's not allowed.' She turned back to Flora. 'Peter's not a country child. He doesn't understand the danger . . .'

Flora, too tired to care, gave way to a rush of irritation. 'It's not exactly a jungle, Melissa. Ollie survived it, after all. So did I.'

'Yes,' Melissa arched her eyebrows. 'But then there's surviving and surviving, isn't there, Flora?' She turned to her husband, quivering with concern. 'Oliver, please go and get him, before something *terrible* happens.'

Ollie, with a hurried kiss to her cheek, almost rushed from the room. Behind his back, Flora caught Fintan's raised eyebrow and sidled quickly over to join him.

'You remember Timmy, and Tobias you know . . .' Fintan introduced her to his companions and Flora nodded, shook hands warmly. Timmy Mulligan was the stud groom at Fairmane, the neighbouring training stables. Tobias Malone was the stud groom at Kimbay, had been for some twenty years. Both were in their fifties, both of them wiry and with narrow, weather-beaten faces. They might have been clones of one another.

Flora grabbed a couple of sandwiches from a passing tray as, with a sigh and faraway look in his eye, Tobias said, 'I'll always remember the day we buried your last boss, Timmy. Old Fergus Donnelly must've been ninety if he was a day . . .'

'He was that, all right,' Timmy agreed, chewing thoughtfully on a cigarette, screwing his eyes against the smoke. 'A decent man. And a bit of a rake, by all accounts, when he was young.' He took a breath of his own smoky air before launching into his story. 'There was an old fella

27

turned up for his funeral, used to be in the breeding business in Tipperary, and he was telling us how himself and Fergus carried on when they were young. "We sowed our wild oats in many a county," says he, "and those were the only times in his life Fergus prayed the crops would fail."'

The two men laughed. Fintan and Flora laughed too, quietly along with them. It was the sort of story that Ned would have told if he could have managed, somehow, to be here for his own funeral.

'Fairmane's new boss looks to me like a man who's sown a few wild oats in his time too,' Tobias Malone said.

'Could have, could have,' Timmy Mulligan was suddenly careful. 'He's a sound enough man to work for.' He turned to Flora. 'I saw him come in a short while ago. You'll find him very straight.'

Flora, with a small nod, excused herself and moved to one of the long windows. It was pitch dark outside, in the way only the unlit countryside can be on a cloudy, moonless night. She was trying to pierce it, break its blackness into the shapes of well known fields, when a man's face appeared in the glass. A long, unknown face which nodded and gave a slight smile. She turned to acknowledge the reality.

'I'm Matt Hopkins.' He was taller than she was. 'We're neighbours. I'm training over at the Fairmane Stables.' He didn't offer his hand; Flora kept both of hers firmly on her glass.

'Nice to meet you,' she said, knowing it was inadequate but not sure what he expected from her. She'd heard about him, of course, from Ned.

His direct gaze took in her hair, moved over her face and fixed on her eyes. If it had been another kind of gathering she'd have said he was contemplating a pass. Coolly, she returned his look. His eyes were a dark blue-grey, his strong-boned face too irregular to be handsome. But there was a sensuality there, a self-willed recklessness. He was the kind of man, she knew, who had a lethal appeal to some women. She was not one of them. The emotional turmoil which went with being the plaything of an arrogant

28

male had never been to her taste. And this man was arrogant, of that she was sure.

He also, if Tobias's gossip was to be credited, had a past. Flora hoped that wasn't all he had, and that he was as good a trainer as Ned, in conversations, had seemed to think he was. It would be good to see the Connolly stables come back to life. The trainer's eyes wandered to the window and came back to her face again.

'Please accept my sympathies, Miss Carolan,' he said. 'Your father will be a real loss. He was the best kind of horse owner.'

'Yes. He was.' Flora lowered her head, ran a finger round the rim of her glass and fought to control sudden tears. The trainer meant it and he was right. Ned's appreciation of the horse was instinctive and complete. He had indeed been the best kind of owner. She wished, though, that she hadn't met this man. Not today anyway. It wasn't the time yet to talk about Ned and horses.

'I'm told you live in Brussels. How was it there, when you left? I've visited a few times. Never quite got a feel for the place.' The trainer spoke lightly, changing the subject effortlessly. Flora gave him silent marks for sensitivity.

'Brussels was fine.' She looked at him. 'It's the sort of town you have to live in to get to know, have a feel for . . .'

'I'll take your word for it,' he smiled, showing white teeth and creating laughter-lines around his eyes. Flora guessed his age at about thirty-two or three. 'I'm unlikely to put it to the test. Do you intend staying around for long?'

The question was casually put, but the answer, Flora sensed, mattered to him for some reason.

She looked away, into the now sparse crowd. 'A few days is all,' she said. 'I've a job to get back to on Monday.'

And Serge to get back to too. God, she was missing him. Especially and suddenly now, standing here with this man asking her about Brussels.

She'd made contact with Serge, between flights on her long wait at Paris airport. He'd wanted to come at once to

Kimbay but she'd told him no, she'd prefer to deal with things alone. What she didn't tell him was that she didn't feel she could cope with the misery of his arriving at Kimbay too late to meet Ned. Later, if ever, would be a better time for him to come. It depended on how often she would come home herself from now on.

Chapter Four

Two days after the funeral Flora was still dazed, aware of a lumpen, sodden feeling where her carefree heart had beaten less than a week before. Life without her father was not a possibility she'd ever contemplated. Death happened to other people, not to Ned Carolan. For a man whose life had been filled with plans, schemes and tomorrows, mortality had never seemed on the cards.

The morning's gallop hadn't done much to help, either. Gently, knowing he must feel the loss of his owner too, she brought Cormac, her father's grey gelding, to a stop. A fine, early mist covered the land and blotted out colour. Viewed from where she'd stopped, on a hill by a solitary tree that was an ages-old landmark, the countryside seemed to weep.

Numbly, unaware of the cold in her bones, Flora began to weep too. She had no idea how long she'd been out. It had been dark when she'd saddled Cormac but now, through the mist, a pale sun was rising over the fields and pastures. There were the beginnings too of a clear day. The kind of day her father would have loved.

Sitting there, her tears subsiding, she from habit began to wind her pale gold hair into the heavy plait she'd worn as a child. Robbed of its protective frame her face appeared defenceless, a lot younger than its twenty-eight years. Her great dark eyes needed sleep, her full mouth looked tired. The tears dried in salty tracks on her cheeks and the damp cold began to penetrate. Still she sat.

Ned wouldn't have approved of her tears. To cry over the dead was, he believed, to cry for oneself. 'Tears are of no use to those who're gone,' he'd used to say, 'they don't need them. Better to get off your backside and do something with the life you've been given to live.'

31

He'd taken his own advice when Flora's mother had been killed in a fall from a horse. Flora had been ten and in her grief had taken to following her father everywhere. She could remember his white-faced stoicism, the doggedness with which he'd begun to extend and build up the small stud farm, the endless, tireless hours of work. He'd never stopped, until now.

He'd run Kimbay as a commercial stud, selling colts as yearlings; most fillies too, unless he wanted to keep one to ensure the continuance of a particular bloodline.

His three children apart, the stud had been his life. He saw it as a stake in life for his sons and daughter, a rooted place to which they could always return. If he'd hoped they would stay to work it he'd never said so. When they left, all three of them, to make other lives elsewhere, he hadn't protested.

Flora had loved growing up here: the yard, the animals, life in the horse-dominated countryside around. It had been a complete and secure existence and she'd been happy, every day. Maybe it had to do with being young, with the careless joy of childhood. Whatever the reason, her memories were still real, and wonderful.

Even so, once she left, went to college and on to travel, she'd found the idea of coming back to live here difficult. It was unimaginable now her father was dead.

She doubted that Fintan or Ollie would come back either. Both her brothers had city-bound careers. Kimbay's future would have to be with the Sweeney, not Carolan, family.

Shay Sweeney had worked Kimbay with Ned for thirty years, longer than Flora's lifetime. He had married Daisy, which had been the 'making of him' according to Ned, when Flora was six years old. Ned's marriage present to Shay had been the gate lodge at the end of the avenue to Kimbay House, and Daisy, with some flair and over the years, had had it extended and made of it a warm, if chaotic, home. These days their teenage offspring were involved in the yard too. They belonged at Kimbay, the four of them. The stud would be in good hands.

It wasn't as if it would be passing completely out of the family, either. Though Shay's mother Nora Sweeney had gone to her early grave without disclosing the identity of her illegitimate son's father, it was unspoken and common knowledge that Greg Carolan was responsible. Ned's wayward uncle, Flora's grandfather's younger brother, had disappeared into the vastness of the American midwest after a feckless youth. He'd never reappeared either to confirm or deny his son.

When, at only twenty-five, Shay's career as a jockey had ended with a shattered wrist, Ned had taken him on to work in the yard at Kimbay. The subsequent present of the gate lodge and the slow building of their working relationship until they were virtual partners, had been his way of tacitly acknowledging his cousin.

Flora doubted they had ever spoken about it. She had been eighteen herself before she'd discovered the relationship – and then only because Daisy, matter-of-factly, had told her. It had explained a lot, not least the bond between Shay, so introverted his conversations were mostly silent ones with the horses, and Ned, open and generous to a fault.

The gelding's patience was not endless, and he shifted restlessly under her. Cormac, in his youth, had been an abandoned, even reckless jumper, the winner of a few worthy steeplechases. With a flash of that early vigour he snorted, turned his head for home.

'Okay, boy, okay. Let's go.' Flora flicked the reins and he made his way lazily downhill. As they reached the flat she pulled him to a halt again. The mist was lifting and she could make out the grey of the winding river, the white-painted wooden fences dividing fields and paddocks. A little further and she could see the bare, wintry woods bordering the lands of the adjoining training stables.

As she watched, a string of horses emerged. They moved slowly, sleek and dreamlike. She counted seven of them before, sensing freedom and open spaces, they broke into a gallop. Her eye was pulled to a flashing chestnut in their lead. Flo Girl.

*

The last time Flora had seen Ned had been the previous summer. Her August trip home had been the one constant in her life. It shaped her year, put things into perspective. With a life and flat in Brussels and a motorway system to the rest of Europe at her door, she could have gone anywhere. But August had been for Kimbay and Ned and home. Always.

'Where's the Frenchman?' Ned had demanded that last August, peering into the hired car as she climbed out. 'Are we not grand enough for him? Or is it that he's afraid of us?'

'He has a home to go to, too.'

Flora had hugged her father, been hugged fiercely in return. Ned's disgruntlement at the absence of her French lover was only half serious. Part of him wanted to meet the man his daughter spent so much time with. A by far greater part of him didn't want to share any of his August with Flora with Serge de Maraville.

There was an added problem. A foreigner who wasn't interested in horses would be, in Ned's estimation, 'a difficult fish to entertain'. Serge, for the three years Flora had known him, had solved the difficulty by spending August with his mother at the family château near Angers.

'You were long enough getting here,' Ned grumbled, carrying all of her bags together up the steps to the house. 'Daisy left some food ready . . .'

'Great. I'm famished.'

Flora, following him, would have preferred a long soak and a glass of wine. But there was the ritual of her return to be gone through and it would be neither wise nor kind to upset it.

The next step would be Ned's proceeding to pour them both large whiskeys. These they would drink while they joked and became gently used to being with one another. Daisy Sweeney's meal, solid and reliably overcooked, would then be eaten to the accompaniment of an update from Ned on stud and local news.

And so it had been, last August as every August. They were half-way through Daisy's hot and unseasonal lamb stew when Ned said, 'I've got a surprise for you, my girl. You're going to love her. That little chestnut filly, remember? No? Well, she turned into a cracker. She's yours, I've named her after you. She's going to make you a rich woman.'

'You'd be wiser concentrating on making yourself a rich man,' Flora said. 'Time you took things a little easier.'

'The easy life wouldn't suit me, and well you know it. No, this filly's for you. She's a winner.'

'Ned, I —'

'No, don't thank me.' Her father smiled, holding up a large, callused hand, not interested in her protests. Flora let it go. It was holiday time and the sun was shining and she'd only just arrived.

'This filly is special,' Ned picked up his fork and attacked Daisy's stew with renewed relish. 'Mark my words, she's going to make history. I know I've said it before but I'm telling you, Flora, this horse is different. I feel it in my bones.'

'Your bones, Ned, haven't been all that reliable in the past,' Flora grinned, pouring herself a glass of the Sancerre he invariably produced for their homecoming meal.

'This is the last furlong, Flora, and Flo Girl is going to make it. You'll be convinced when you see her.'

'Flo Girl . . .' Flora sipped the wine. 'That's nice, Ned. I like it.'

'It's from the same bin as last year . . .'

'The name, Ned, not the wine,' Flora touched his hand. 'I suppose you've put her into training?'

'I have. She's with a fella called Matt Hopkins. He took over Fairmane when old Fergus Donnelly had to sell up two years ago. He's young, he's energetic and, moreover, he's convenient.'

'Hopkins? Never heard of him. Where did he pop up from?'

'Didn't so much pop up as come to land here. Seems he'd been around the world a few times, working as a sort of jobbing horseman or somesuch. Interesting fella.' Her father made the loud, guffawing sound that was his laugh.

'By God, but he's lived. By all accounts anyway. Doesn't talk much about his life himself and that's to his credit. Lets his work with the animals speak for him.'

'He can't have proven himself much so far.'

Flora got up and cleared a place for the cheeseboard Daisy had left on a nearby smaller table. The dining room had a hollow, unused feeling and the air of being newly dusted. She knew that Ned only bothered to eat here when either she or her brothers came home and the fact caused her pangs of guilt. It was a guilt compounded by the general mild dilapidation of Kimbay House. She was filled with visions of Ned, alone and rattling around within its four walls.

'He's got six or seven animals in training, a few of them with decent potential,' Ned said as she put down the cheese. 'And he's hungry, best way to have a trainer.'

'He'd want to have a bit more than an overdraft to make a good trainer.' Flora was ironic. Hungry was Ned's shorthand for lacking money, and she knew of too many instances where his sympathy for broke but committed horse folk had blurred his judgement. Left him out of pocket too.

She cut him a hefty piece of the Kilmeaden they both liked. 'I suppose he's got a good eye, too?' she asked.

'That he has.' Ned ignored the irony in her tone. 'One of the best judges I've seen of a good foal. He's got the gift of reading an animal's legs and wind out on the gallops, too.'

Flora rode with her father to Fairmane later that evening. The sun had begun to set and land and pastures were the gold-green colour of late summer. Animals, cattle as well as horses in the interests of good grass management, ambled and fed as they passed. Ned pointed out various brood mares, indicating which stallion had covered each mare, showing her which yearlings he hoped would sell well.

'There's Nessa.' He stopped, nodded. 'Did I tell you she's Flo Girl's dam?'

'Yes, you did. But I'd forgotten.' Flora was apologetic.

Nessa was the best loved mare in the stud. In her day she'd been a good, middle-distance runner who had won a few races at Leopardstown and Naas. She was gentle-natured, big-eyed and big-eared. Ned was, as a rule, careful about which stallion he brought her to.

'So, who's the sire?' Flora asked as they cantered slowly, side by side, into the more open fields.

'I was keeping that as a bit of a surprise. Didn't want to burden you with too much information all together.' Ned laughed, urged a bit of speed out of Cormac and said, 'Get a move on, we haven't all night,' before galloping ahead in the direction of Fairmane.

Flora, with a resigned shake of her head, went after her father. He looked back, checking, a grin on his open, good-natured face. It was a face which, along with hard work, was responsible for a lot of his success as a breeder. Ned had the appearance of absolute frankness, of being entirely up-front while actually playing poker. In a world in which cards were played close to the chest and where truth was a commodity doled out in strategic portions, this was a definite advantage. He loved to tease, keep people guessing.

Flora, refusing to be drawn into his game, to ask again about the filly's sire, caught up with him and rode silently alongside as they skirted the bank of the river. The peace was immense, the richness of the land they were riding through obvious. The limestone underneath made for a soil and grass rich in minerals and calcium. It was from this the horse population drew its strength and strong bones. Kimbay's 120 acres touched on stud farms and training stables on three sides.

Clearly, in the distance, Flora could see the spire of the church in Dunallen, the village which served the needs of the farming community. She would go there tomorrow, persuade Ned to the Old Nag hotel for a meal perhaps.

The silence stretched and, as Fairmane loomed, Flora acknowledged she hadn't the patience to beat her father at his own game. 'All right, Ned, I give in. What's her bloodline?'

Ned, if he hadn't been holding the reins, would have

rubbed his hands together. As it was he made do with a modest grin.

'Gilla Dacar,' he said.

'Really?' Flora's eyes opened wide in astonishment. 'I *am* impressed. He must have cost you a few bob.'

Gilla Dacar was a champion, a two-times Classic winner. To have him cover a mare could have cost anything up to £100,000.

'How much did you pay?' Flora asked.

'He wasn't cheap. But he was worth it,' her father said. 'Brought Nessa to him just once and the job was oxo. He's quietened down a lot, a great performer now he's in stud. He was a bit of a devil when he was racing as a two-year-old. That's why they called him the Gilla Dacar you know.'

He stopped and Flora, knowing he wasn't going to tell her how much he'd paid for the service, asked instead the question he wanted to answer. 'I don't know. Why *is* he called Gilla Dacar?'

'On account of he was hard to train and get obedience from, same as the Gilla Dacar, the hard gillie, in the old story of Finn and the Fianna . . .'

Flora, half listening as he rambled off into the tale of a myth from Ireland's remote times, wondered why he'd gone for such an expensive stallion. Usually he chose mates for his mares with conformation, courage and value in mind, with the latter all important. Maybe, just maybe and in spite of his protests, he did want to take things easier. It would be typical of him to take a gamble like this as a way of making retirement money.

And it *was* a gamble. Even with a mix of the best blood in the world there was no certainty that the result would be a champion money-spinning racehorse. An animal could still prove useless, or be unlucky, or become injured. No doubt, in his own time, Ned would explain. He obviously wasn't going to do so today.

'. . . He'd too much bloody testosterone in him as a two-year-old,' Ned had moved on to a favourite theory when she picked up on what he was saying. 'That's what made Gilla Dacar hard to train. His sons were all the same, though his daughters were easier.'

They arrived at the back of Fairmane and rode into the yard. Flora, without paying too much attention, noted evidence of money spent on expansion and rebuilding. The trainer-owner was away but the head groom, a crony of Ned's, led them to Flo Girl's box.

Flora remembered her, vaguely, as a foal, when she saw the filly. She had her mother's face, with large eyes and a gentle expression. From her mother too Flo Girl had inherited a golden chestnut colour.

Too golden. Her colour, Flora knew, could prove a problem.

'She's a beauty,' she said sincerely. Then, hesitantly, 'She's . . . bright, isn't she?'

'She's a streak of gold.' Ned dismissed her doubts. 'Brightness didn't affect Grundy, or Generous or Salsabil.'

And of course he was right. But they were champion exceptions that had proved the rule. The discretion of a sober colour, so racing wisdom went, was definitely the better part of valour.

'She's tough, Flora. Tough mentally and physically.' Ned was gruff. 'And she's got courage. You'll see when you get to know her better.'

Darkness was coming on as they rode back. Flora hadn't seen Flo Girl again, either that holiday or since. She'd been uncertain what her father expected of her as the owner and hadn't given it much thought. Ned would look after things. He always did. Apart from which, she was sure he'd his own reasons for making the filly hers.

Now, watching the string, she saw Flo Girl hold the lead as they galloped on. She watched as they became a fast-moving blur, saw them grow smaller, then smaller still until they became busy dots on the green. They crossed a hillock and were gone.

She turned the gelding for home, thinking again about that day in August, wondering now if Ned had known then about the heart condition which had killed him. Not that it would have made any difference. Even if he'd known he would have most likely ignored it. Warnings, signals, pain. They would have been an irritation, nothing more.

Unless. If awareness of his mortality could have moved Ned to do anything it would have been something to do with the horses. Like spending a fortune on a stallion for his favourite mare ... Maybe that's what it was about. Maybe not. Only Ned knew and he hadn't told her, then or since.

Remembering August, times spent with Ned, didn't help the bereft feeling either. Time, people said to her, heals all ills. They'd murmured it on the day of the funeral, afterwards, when they were drinking and remembering Ned themselves. Even Serge, the master of *sangfroid*, had said it, yesterday on the phone.

They didn't understand, any of them, that Ned had been the ballast in her life. As long as he'd been alive, here when she needed him, she'd felt safe. Certain that life was manageable. She wasn't certain of anything any more. How could she be? If Ned could go like that, without warning, then anything could happen.

The lights were on in Kimbay. The working day had begun. There was no place for her here now. She would have to stay for a few days longer, until Ned's will had been read and Kimbay's future sorted out; then she would go back to Brussels, where the distractions of her other life would make all of this easier to bear.

In her room she lay on the bed. Unable to settle on definitives for the future, or even the present, she thought about the recent past, mulling over the crowded events of the days since she'd heard of her father's death.

Maybe somewhere in there she would find a consoling thought, something that would make sense of why he'd been taken as he was, cruelly, without warning and forever.

Chapter Five

While Flora lay on the bed remembering, the sky had become dark with rainclouds. She watched them gathering, breaking up again, moving on. It was cold and she got up to close the window. Her room looked out over fields and paddocks and, as she stood there, a couple of yearlings were led out and turned loose. She felt a familiar, involuntary lifting of her heart as they galloped away free.

She was still watching them when a car came up the avenue and turned onto the gravelly frontage to the house. Ollie got out. He was carrying two plastic bags, his face filled with its usual mixture of worry and anxiety. He'd obviously been to the village, first thing too. Melissa's needs were unending. 'Poor old Ollie,' Flora thought, more with impatience than any real sympathy. 'Why in God's name does he allow her do it to him?'

The front door banged shut and in the hallway she heard Peter's excited voice talking to his father. Fintan's mellow tones joined in before the kitchen door closed on the three of them and all sound faded. Flora, a sudden image of coffee and fresh bread looming before her, pulled on her boots and ran downstairs.

'Any chance of a cup in that pot for me?' Sniffing the freshly brewed coffee she sat at the table beside Peter and ruffled his hair.

'Help yourself.' Fintan shoved the pot her way.

'It'll rot your insides and give you a heart attack,' Peter said gleefully. 'And if you have two cups all your teeth'll fall out.' Dipper, under the table, lay prone at his feet.

'I'll risk it.' Flora continued pouring. 'Where'd you get these fascinating facts, anyway?'

'Boy in my class,' Peter said.

41

'Hmm. Same boy who said reading can make your eyes fall out?'

'No. Another one.'

'Well, if you stick to hot chocolate and TV you should be safe enough.' Flora grinned at him and looked over at his father, busy by the cooker. 'Looks like you've got a consumer watchdog in the making here,' she said. Ollie, scrambling eggs, smiled.

The enforced intimacy of yesterday, which had been the day after the funeral, had brought Ned Carolan's family closer than they'd been for years. They'd spent the day together in the house, receiving callers, talking about Ned, about themselves, about neighbours. The one thing they hadn't talked about was the stud, and what was to become of it. The issue became unavoidable at around five o'clock when Jarlath Maguire called.

The local solicitor's visit had been a surprise, and not only because he'd already paid his respects at the graveyard the day before. Jarlath Maguire was a man to whom time meant money. For him to absent himself twice in as many days from his office in Dunallen there had to be very good business reasons.

There was. He wasted none of his valuable time coming to the point. 'I won't be staying.' He spoke quickly, rubbing his gloved hands together, as Fintan closed the door behind him. 'I called on a bit of business. Your father made a new will. He wanted it read within days of his death, while you were all here. Life wouldn't stand still, he said, just because it had given up on *him*. Decisions would need to be made.' He coughed, a hacking, dry sound, into a pigskin-gloved hand.

Before he could speak again Fintan said, 'Have a drink, Jarlath, and tell us a bit more about this.'

Flora, by the living-room door, added to the invitation. 'Please do, Jarlath. We'd like to hear how Ned was at the time . . .'

The solicitor backed apologetically towards the front door. 'Kind of you, very kind of you both, but time is pressing. The will concerns a number of people,' he produced a sheet of paper from an inside breast pocket, 'you'll all need to be present. Tomorrow, my office, five o'clock if you please. I'll be off now. No, no, stay where you are. I'll let myself out.' He handed the paper to Fintan and, with a bobbing incline of his head, pulled the door open and was gone.

'That man gets loonier every time I see him,' Fintan opened the sheet of paper, 'which isn't very often, thank God.' He glance-read the page and handed it to Flora. 'Round-up of the usual suspects,' he said. 'Not hard to guess what Dad's done with Kimbay.'

Ned Carolan had requested that his three children, grandchild, daughter-in-law and the entire Sweeney family attend the reading of his will. Fintan's guess was that Ned had left the stud to Shay Sweeney, the house to his children.

'Makes sense,' he said. 'None of us are interested in running the yard – and he certainly wouldn't have wanted to see it go down the drain or be sold to a stranger.'

'You could be right,' Flora said, not at all sure that she actually agreed with him but lacking the heart to pursue the subject.

What Fintan proposed was too straightforward by half. Ned had always maintained that straight dealing was no fun, 'no fun at all'. She could hear him saying it, loud and rumbling as if he were in the room with them. The sensation filled her with an inexplicable gut feeling that Ned's will was about to produce shocks for everyone concerned.

Apart from passing word of the reading on to the Sweeneys no one had spoken about the will since then. For Flora it was too raw a subject. She suspected the same held true for her brothers, and even Melissa. Her sister-in-law had been surprisingly, and agreeably, discreet. So far.

The Sweeney family had kept themselves to themselves, Shay and the twins putting in a full working day in the yard. Daisy, who hadn't appeared at all the day before, came noisily through the front door and into the kitchen as Ollie was leaving with a breakfast tray for Melissa.

'Saw you riding out on the gelding earlier on, Flora,'

43

she said. She poured herself a coffee, inspected what had been happening on the cooker. 'You got yourself out for the best part of the day. Looks like rain from now on.'

'Well, at least we've got a roof over our heads. For the moment anyway.' Melissa, followed by a hapless Ollie still carrying the tray, slipped daintily into the kitchen. 'Who knows what this afternoon will bring.'

Ollie put the tray in front of her on the table. She was wearing a black silk kimono with a woollen jumper draped elegantly over her shoulders.

'I always forget how cold this house is,' Melissa shivered as she began to pick at the scrambled egg. 'Though it's warmer here than in that freezing bedroom.'

Flora, giving her a look aimed at lowering the temperature in the kitchen, turned to Daisy. 'I haven't really spoken to the twins,' she said. 'What're they doing with themselves these days?' The question was calculated. Asking Daisy about her offspring was like turning on a tap, a guaranteed distraction.

'Giving trouble, being sixteen-and-a-half.' With a throaty chuckle, and a hard look at Melissa, Daisy settled with her coffee into one of the shabby armchairs. 'Luke, God help us, gets more like his father every day. His longest conversations are with the horses and even then he's not very chatty. He's given up school.' She gave a great sigh and Dipper, under the table, opened an eye to look at her. 'He wanted to be a jockey but all of a sudden he's started to grow. We always thought he'd be dapper, the build of his father. Now he's all arms and legs, doesn't know what to do with himself.'

'And Leah . . .?'

Growing up, Flora had had a vaguely big-sister relationship with Luke's twin. Leah, as a child, had been an almost comical image of her mother. As a teenager the likeness was still there but wasn't comical any longer. Leah Sweeney was becoming a beauty but was, as yet, without the confidence to see what was happening to her. She was tall, with a mane of red-gold hair falling about a high-boned face with green eyes. These basic ingredients were

44

obscured so far by puppy-fat, stubborn pimples and fashion statements like the current, knotty dreadlocks in her hair.

'Leah's . . . Leah.' Daisy sighed again. This time Dipper, in spite of surreptitious protests from Peter, left his refuge under the table and plonked himself dolefully across Daisy's feet. 'You old fool,' Daisy said and rubbed between his ears. 'Leah's got opinions on everything, facts on nothing.' She sighed. 'I've become the cross she has to bear in life. She's still at school, which is something.' She looked across at Fintan. 'She wants to be a singer.'

'You're surprised?' Fintan raised an eyebrow.

'Resigned,' Daisy said.

Leah could sing. Not, however, with her mother's throaty individuality. Hers was more of a sweet, wild tone, with its own haunting quality.

'Can't make a singing career around here.' Fintan, straddling a chair opposite Daisy, watched her face as he spoke.

'That's true. But she's got two years still to do at school.' Daisy looked quickly from Fintan to Flora and in that one, flashing look there was revealed all of the vulnerability of a mother facing the fact that her children would soon be ready to leave her.

'I'll look out for her when she hits the metropolis.' Fintan gave Daisy a playful punch on the knee. 'I owe you one.'

He did too. Daisy it had been who'd spotted his early talent, who'd taken him on her knee at the piano to pick out the notes. She'd sung to him too, and he'd listened, wide-eyed and quiet. Daisy, Flora had always felt, was Fintan's fate. Maybe it was fate too, or kismet or predestination or something, that he should be there now for Leah.

'She's decided on London,' Daisy said, flatly. 'She's applied to places already.'

'Oh. Right.' Fintan frowned, gave a small shrug. 'Hang loose, Daisy, old flower. I'll find a head or two to sort her out there too.'

'I know you will.' Daisy's wide, big-toothed grin lacked heart. 'Well now, I'm off to check on my books and tidy up the office a bit.' She stood, fixing a few unruly locks of hair into her plait. Dipper staggered uncertainly onto all fours and she pointed sternly to the seat she'd just vacated. 'Up you get,' she said and he pulled himself into it. 'He's not much good for anything any more.' She looked at him sadly. 'If I want a bark around here these days I have to do it myself.'

The door had barely closed behind her before Melissa, sharp-voiced, demanded, 'What books is she talking about?'

'Bookkeeping books. For the yard. Fees, wages, food bills, that sort of thing. Daisy helped Dad keep things in order.' Ollie was offhand. 'She does some part-time bookkeeping for the granary the other side of Dunallen too. Brings in some extra cash for the family and gives Daisy a bit of independence from the yard.'

'She does all this here, in the house?'

'Where else would she do it? This is where the office is.'

'It's none of my business, really, but these Sweeney people *do* seem to have their claws on everything. Does it not strike any of you as odd that they appear to be running the place, lock stock and barrel?'

Flora counted to ten as Ollie patiently, gently, explained to his wife. 'They're here, Melissa. All the time. Shay worked with Dad for thirty years. He's fifty-five now so that's more than half his life. Daisy's been here – how long, Flora? Twenty-two years or so, isn't it? We left, all of us. It's just the way it is.'

'Well, I think you've all been very stupid. Not getting something tied up legally before now.'

'Give it a rest, Melissa.' Fintan spun on his chair and lifted Peter into the air. 'Come on, old son,' he said, 'let's you and me go walkabout.'

'You're not proposing to take him into the yard, are you?' Melissa's voice had become shrill. 'He could be kicked. He's not used—'

'But I *like* the horses, Mom.' Peter's young voice sounded weary.

Melissa looked startled and her son, seizing his opportunity while she gathered her forces to reply, left the kitchen at a run. Ollie followed him and Flora, afraid of what she would say if Melissa uttered another word either about the stables or the Sweeneys, left with them.

In the yard she left father and son together and wandered around on her own. Shay, busy with feeding, was brusquely welcoming before leaving her to her own devices. She looked in on some of the mares she knew well, spent time with an early foal. But, painfully aware that Shay didn't really want her there, she didn't stay long.

'Everything all right, Shay?' she asked before leaving.

'Why wouldn't it be?' He looked at her, his narrow face vexed.

'No reason. No reason at all . . .' Flora, uncertain, smiled. 'Just making conversation. See you later.'

'Aye. See you later.' Shay turned to a chart on the wall and, thoroughly dismissed, Flora left.

Walking back to the house she found herself agreeing, and not for the first time, with those who said that Daisy was the only human thing about Shay. He was without doubt one of the most taciturn sods in an industry noted for the type. But he was, too, a bulwark in the yard, the solid force on which, along with Ned, Kimbay had depended. He worked 360 days of the year and she felt as intimidated by him today as she had when she was a child.

There had been a trick she'd used as a child, a way of dealing with him when he'd made her nervous or she'd wanted to coax something out of him. She would simply call to mind her father's laughing story of the young Shay arriving at the gate lodge with his exotic, kaftan-clad new wife and discovering he'd lost the key. Daisy, at first disbelieving, had insisted he force open and climb through one of the then tiny windows. He'd been half-way in when she discovered the door was not, after all, locked. Abandoning him to his fate on the window-ledge Daisy had sailed into and taken charge of her new home alone. She'd been in charge ever since. It was an arrangement which suited them both.

The story had never failed, in the past, to make Shay

seem human and fallible and even funny. Today, though, the memory made Flora feel merely sad.

By five o'clock the day had darkened and rain was driving through the single street that was Dunallen. Parking outside the solicitor's office Flora discovered that she and Fintan were the first to arrive. They sat in the car and waited for the others.

'I feel as if all of this is a dream, that it's happening to someone else.' Flora traced a raindrop, with her finger, as it slid down the windscreen. 'I keep expecting Ned to appear round a corner, keep expecting to hear him . . .' Dry-eyed and aching, she stopped and looked at Fintan. 'I'm having trouble with the for ever and ever aspect.'

'It takes time,' Fintan said and, hearing it now and from him, Flora was able to accept, just a little, that maybe time would work some cure.

'Do you remember,' she began hesitantly, 'when Mom died?'

Fintan nodded. 'Some of it,' he said. 'Not much.'

'Do you remember asking Daisy how long she was going to be dead for?'

Fintan thought. 'No,' he said. 'Did I ask her that?'

'You did. And she said, "Oh, she won't be back at all, she's gone on the most beautiful adventure in life." Which was nonsense but it shut you up. You followed her around everywhere after that, with your mouth hanging open.'

'It was as good an explanation as any,' Fintan said. 'Can't really think of a better one myself. Can you?'

'Not offhand. Not today.' Flora caught a movement in the side mirror. 'The others have arrived.' She opened the door. 'We might as well get this business over with.'

Jarlath Maguire's office was spare. It had a low ceiling with a couple of fluorescent tubes and two narrow windows on to the street. A thin, obliging girl ran about getting plastic chairs for them to sit on while the solicitor himself sat smiling severely behind a black desk.

'Do we have everybody?' He raised a thin, grey eyebrow above the rim of his spectacles. His question hadn't been directed at anyone in particular and for several seconds no one answered. The twins looked self-consciously at one another and Leah, with an acid look at the solicitor, began ostentatiously to count heads. He frowned and focused a look of his own first on Daisy, then Flora.

'You can take it we're all here, Jarlath.' Flora was dry.

'Good. Good. We'll proceed with things so.' He gave a small, sharp cough. 'I'd be obliged, Mr Sweeney, if you could extinguish that cigarette. We don't allow smoking here.'

Shay, who'd refused a seat and was leaning against the wall at the back of the room, took a deep drag and looked coldly at the solicitor. Daisy, sitting in front of her husband, reached behind her with a hand. Shay put the cigarette between her fingers and she stubbed it neatly into a nearby plastic container. The solicitor coughed again.

'Now, if you could all pay attention, please. The reading won't take long.' He looked at his watch. 'I will answer questions when I finish, not before. I do not, however, envisage many queries. The will is quite clear in content and is self-explanatory.' His tone, as he proceeded to read Ned Carolan's will, was neutral, verging on indifference.

The stud farmer's last testament was, as he'd said, quite clear and precise. The stables and yard were shown to be in debt and the reasons for this made clear. In recent years, Ned Carolan had invested heavily in stallion fees. Highest among these was a £50,000 fee for the services of Gilla Dacar. His will declared his belief that the result, Flo Girl, would in time more than repay the outlay. He had made arrangements and paid for her training for the year ahead and suggested that Flora, as her owner, should inject enough of the filly's winnings into the yard to bring it to viability again. But the horse was hers, and the choice was hers too.

There was a small pause as the solicitor neatly turned the page and adjusted his spectacles to begin another. Flora, sitting dumbly by the side wall, felt cold. For the first time in her life she wished she was a smoker. A prop of some kind might help her to think. She shoved her hands into the pockets of her waxed jacket and hunched into its well-worn familiarity. Fintan, across the room by the window, raised a non-committal eyebrow in her direction. Ollie, beside him, stared steadily at the floor. Melissa's lovely features were bored. She yawned behind her hand.

'Now we come to the actual bequests. First of all, there's the question of the yard and land. Mr Carolan has requested – and it *is* a request, that these be worked, for the next two years, on a partnership basis between his daughter, Ms Flora Carolan and his yard manager, Mr Seamus Sweeney.'

Ignoring a collective gasp the solicitor read on. The will, in a mixture of dry, legal phraseology and Ned Carolan's own vernacular, spelled out very precisely what the dead man had wanted to happen to Kimbay.

He had been convinced that Flora and Shay Sweeney, working together, could make the yard viable again. If they agreed then the ten mares were to be split between them, the method of how this was to be done decided by Shay. Yearlings and foals were to become dual property. At the end of two years, the partnership having worked, Flora was free to leave and employ a manager to fill her role. Or she could stay on.

Should the partnership fail, however – and here Ned Carolan recognized the gamble inherent in his plan – then the will empowered Shay and Flora to sell, either to one another or to an outside buyer. The proceeds of a sale to an outsider were to be divided between the two families on a fifty-fifty basis.

All of this depended on Flora's willingness to make the two-year commitment. If she didn't, or couldn't, then the yard and land immediately became the sole property of Shay and Daisy Sweeney. And passed out of the possession of the Carolan family.

The solicitor paused. Slowly and carefully, unmoved by a small cry which disturbed the uncanny silence, he turned a page. Flora suspected the sound came from her but couldn't be sure.

'I would ask you all to bear with me and not to interrupt until I have finished,' he intoned, rather than said, as he began to read again. Flora took her hands from her pockets and sat on them. It stopped her digging her nails into her palms. She concentrated all her energies on what the solicitor was saying.

Kimbay House had been left jointly to Fintan, Ollie and Flora. Both of Ned Carolan's sons received financial settlements – money which had been their mother's and which their father, in spite of the needs over the years, had never touched.

A trust fund had been set up for his grandson. It would pay his school fees and release further monies to him when he reached his majority. Melissa too had been left a small bequest.

Ned Carolan had made Jack Thomas the executor of his will.

The solicitor looked at his watch again as he finished. 'Now I will, of course, answer any questions . . .' He frowned at the furiously smoking Shay and, getting no response, crossed the room to open a window. A blast of chilly early evening air swept into the room. The solicitor went back to his desk and surveyed the occupants with a cold assessing stare. He seemed unaware of the shock effects of the will, immune to the tangible tensions and confusion.

'Everything is quite clear then?' He began to shuffle the papers.

'I cannot believe', Melissa had gone white, 'that a will like that is legal. It's . . . preposterous. What about his grandson? His *only* grandson? Is Peter to have no share in the lands and house which are his family heritage?'

'His father, Mrs Carolan, is a part owner of the house—'

'Part owner! The whole thing's bloody ridiculous! The man can't have been of sound mind when he—'

'I assure you he was, Mrs Carolan.'

'It's unfair and it's unjust—'

'Shut up, Melissa. It's none of your business.'

Faced with her husband's quiet, shocking anger Melissa's rising voice came to a sharp halt.

Ollie turned to the solicitor. 'You've got the facts,

Jarlath, what are the chances of Flora and Shay making a go of it?' he asked.

'About fifty-fifty. If they put their backs into it.' Jarlath Maguire's thin mouth pursed into a ridiculous, disapproving rosebud. 'It's a gamble, obviously. A lot depends on the racehorse, of course, on whether she's any good . . .'

'Is there anything to stop Flora selling the racehorse?' Fintan asked the question casually.

'I don't think there is.' The solicitor sat back, contemplating. 'She owns the animal. In theory, she can do what she likes with it. Your father is merely suggesting she allow it to race as a way of raising monies. If your sister prefers to raise money by selling it, then that's her business.'

'Just thought it might be an alternative for you to think about, Flo.' Fintan looked at the dazed Flora.

'Can we go now?' Shay spoke abruptly from the back of the room.

Daisy glared at him and stood up. 'Courtesy costs nothing, Shay Sweeney,' she snapped and turned to the room in general. 'We'll be off. There's nothing can be decided here and now. Thank you, Jarlath, and good evening to you.'

Driving back to Kimbay with Fintan, Flora marvelled at Daisy's timing. She'd swept from the room with her family in tow, bringing a fraught situation to a neat end.

'Well, Dad's really dropped you in it now,' Fintan said.

Flora gave a small groan. 'I was trying not to think about it,' she said.

'Yeah, well. It won't go away, Flora. You're going to have to think about it, soon. For the sake of the Sweeneys, if nothing else.'

'I know that,' Flora snapped. 'But *my* life is bloody well involved here too, you know.'

They drove the rest of the way in silence.

Drinks in the living room with Ollie and Melissa didn't resolve much either. Peter, who'd been baby-sat by a friend of Leah's, was fractious. Fintan sat him at the piano and they idly picked out notes. Ollie was thoughtful and distracted. Melissa was simply distracted.

'Any words of advice, boys?' Flora, pouring stiff drinks for everyone, asked the question lightly.

'Bedtime, Peter.' Melissa took her drink from Flora and pointed her reluctant son at the door. 'I'll be up in ten minutes. Brush your teeth.' As the door closed behind him she sank into an armchair. 'Frankly, I find this whole business a huge bore.'

'Oh, I dunno, it has its excitements.' Fintan gave a short laugh. 'It's all about sex and money, isn't it?'

Melissa looked at him blankly. 'Joke, Melissa,' he sighed, 'about the breeding business.' Melissa sniffed.

'Look, I need to know how you both feel.' Flora knew she sounded desperate. 'If I don't do this thing, work the two years I mean, the stud effectively goes out of the family . . .' She paused, awkwardly. 'Loses the Carolan name anyway.'

'Yeah, well. It won't be the end of the world if that happens.' Fintan leaned back on the piano stool. 'Keep the head, Flora. You were right, you know, in the car. You've got your own life to think about. Whatever you decide is fine by me.'

'Great.' Flora, helplessly, turned to Ollie.

'Same goes for me, I'm afraid,' he said. He looked, Flora thought, like a horse faced with a choice and no guidance about jumping a fence.

'My decision . . .' She couldn't understand why Ned had done this to her. What he was asking from the grave was too much. Two years of her life, a gamble which mightn't pay off . . .

He'd been a gambler. She wasn't. She couldn't do it.

Chapter Six

The departure of Flora's brothers next morning left a frightening silence in the old house. Flora knew she should have welcomed the quiet, the peace it offered to think through what she must do about Ned's will. All it did was scream of his absence. With the labrador padding at her heels, she walked through the rooms. Something would have to be done about the state of the house, if nothing else.

She didn't go into Ned's bedroom. It wasn't time yet for that.

'It's just you and me, boy.' She bent down, rubbed the dog between his ears. 'We've got the place to ourselves.'

She sat at the kitchen table, watching as the wintry sun crept into the corners of the yard below. It was Saturday and both Sweeney twins were at work mucking out. Tobias Malone led out a couple of yearlings and he and Luke chatted, easy and familiar, as he led them through the yard. It's their world now, Flora thought, there's no place here for me.

She closed her eyes and thought of Serge, comforting herself with memories of the night before's phone conversation. He had been puzzled at first, when she'd tried to explain Ned's will to him. But he'd quickly understood, sympathized with her dilemma. She should not decide alone, he said. He would be there before the end of the week. He checked his diary, decided on Thursday. Flora, this time, didn't tell him to stay away. She felt only relief that he would be with her, helping her decide. It was right that he should be involved – whatever she decided would have to include Serge.

The sun through the window was warm on her closed

eyelids. It made her think of how good she felt sleeping next to Serge's lithe, strong body, how much she liked his face in the morning, his eyes lazily adoring her, his white, slow smile. She felt comfortable with him, never unsure, never afraid. Everything would be different once he got here. It would be easy to make up her mind when he was with her. She wished, suddenly, that he was with her now, that she had not stopped him from coming for the funeral.

'Did you not sleep enough in bed?' Daisy's voice from the doorway jolted her back to reality.

'The sun . . . it's so pleasant.' Flora smiled, glad to see her.

'I brought you these.' Daisy placed a bunch of keys on the table. 'The car keys are there, the safe, the house – you'll need them if you're staying around. Even for a while.'

'Thanks.' Flora lifted the bunch of keys. The car would be useful, now that Fintan had taken the hired car back to town.

'Daisy,' she tried to keep the appeal out of her voice as she looked at the other woman, 'I feel I should go up to Ned's room. Will you come with me?'

Flora hadn't been in her father's room for years and was surprised at how little of him she found there. His bed was made. There were newspapers for the days before he'd died, a pile of them folded open on the racing pages. His dressing gown and slippers were in an armchair, his reading glasses beside the bed. It was neat and functional. The few, faded splashes of colour came from mementoes of Hannah Carolan – a picture on the wall, a straw hat, a jewellery box.

'Things will have to be gone through.' Flora looked at the huge chest of drawers, the wardrobe, an old chest. She didn't move from the door, or touch anything.

'Plenty of time for that.' Daisy walked past her and into the centre of the room. She was wearing a bright shawl today and her plait was wound loosely on top of her head. She placed a hand, briefly, on the smooth bedcovers and turned an infinitely sad look toward Flora.

'He did it for your own good, Flora,' she said. 'It may seem wrong to you, a terrible and unfair responsibility, but

55

to Ned's way of thinking he was preparing you for life without him.'

'You're talking about the will?' Restlessly, Flora crossed to the window. The view was almost exactly the same as from her own room.

'Of course I'm talking about the will.'

'Did he talk to you about it?' Flora didn't turn round.

'No. But I knew that man and I've thought a great deal about what he was up to since yesterday. Listen to me, Flora.' Gently, but with definite urgency, she turned Flora to face her. In the harsh light from the window Daisy's face had a thousand fine lines and her hair looked faded. But her eyes were fierce and strong. 'I want you to think about what I'm going to say while you're making up your mind what to do. I knew your father as a young married man. I knew him as a widower. And I knew him as a father. I knew him altogether for twenty-two years. If he'd a fault it was that he loved his children too much; you especially, because you were his daughter and he was an old-fashioned man.'

Daisy took a handkerchief from the inside of a voluminous sleeve and dabbed a tear as it rolled down Flora's face. 'He wanted you to have a charmed and protected life. He never thought to die before some other man took over his role as your protector. But he saw death coming, I'm sure of it, and he drew up his plan.'

She took a deep breath and looked out over the fields. Flora studied her profile. It was calm, intent. Daisy was very serious about what she was saying.

'He wanted to teach you to let go, Flora, to learn to live without him. Working in the yard he intended as a sort of finishing school,' she flashed a quick, rueful smile, 'a way of teaching you to take life by the throat, stand on your own two feet without a man behind you. Because Shay won't be behind you, make no mistake. He'll be ahead of you, nagging and treating you like a fool. And it'll be up to you, to prove him wrong.'

'Hold it, right there.' Flora could feel the angry flush colouring her face. 'I consider that I've already learned to stand on my own feet. I *am* my own person.'

'You are,' Daisy was placatory, 'indeed you are. But Ned had his own ideas about that and he was worried about leaving you and I'm convinced that this plan of his gave him comfort. There's no good fighting with me, Flora. Just think about what I've said.' Without warning she caught Flora in a smothering hug. Flora clung to her, immersed in the familiar smell of sandalwood from her hair, the warm strength of her arms.

'There now, that's enough of that.' Daisy stepped back, fixing a strand of Flora's hair where it had fallen into her eye. 'I'll leave you to get on with things, do your own thinking.'

Flora thought. Sitting in the armchair with Ned's slippers in her hands, she pondered the truth of what Daisy had said. Mostly she thought that it made a lot of sense.

Ned's two-year plan was by way of a raft, something for Flora to cling to while she found her way in life without him. It was his way of teaching her to take chances with life. Flo Girl was his parting gift, the gamble she must decide whether or not to take. What Daisy had not spoken about was that Ned had wanted Flora to fulfil one of *his* dreams – the one in which she worked the yard, keeping it in the Carolan name.

Because part of his plan, Flora was sure, was that she would become hooked, unable to leave the stud when the two years were over.

'Damn you, Ned.' She spoke aloud, looking around the frugal room, filled with a bleak, trapped feeling. 'It would have been so easy to slip away. I'd have got over you dying, in time. I *have* a life. I *have* a man . . .'

She still had. Ned's will didn't force her to stay. It merely suggested it would be a good idea. And she didn't have to make her mind up, not just yet. She would need a week, maybe two, to think things through.

The house continued to echo silently about her, tomb-like without Ned's outbreaks of laughter. In her own room she wrote a formal note to her employers in Brussels, requesting two weeks' leave, then drove to Dunallen to post

57

it. The fresh air and exercise cleared her head and she felt stronger, more able to weigh things up.

Monday morning, however, brought a caller – and added an aspect to the situation which threw all of Flora's careful considering into confusion. Victor Mangan's visit made it clear that whatever decision she made it would have to be based on far more than personal considerations.

Flora had just come up from the yard, where she'd been attempting to help with routine jobs, when the front doorbell rang. It was an almost welcome diversion. She hadn't been made to feel unwanted in the yard, exactly. She'd simply faced a wall of busy politeness.

The man on the doorstep wore a grey coat with black velvet collar and a wide, apologetic smile.

'Ms Carolan?' he asked and, when Flora nodded, reached out a hand. 'My name is Victor Mangan. I would first of all like to offer my condolences on the death of your father.' Flora took his hand. It was firm and dry, clasping hers briefly. 'And I was wondering too if I might come in and talk to you?' His voice was pleasantly pitched, his accent neutral.

'I'm afraid there really isn't anything I need –'

'I'm not a salesman, Ms Carolan.' He was gently amused, shaking his head. 'I have some ideas about the future of the yard and lands which might interest you. We can, of course, talk here if you prefer . . .'

Flora, silently and taken aback, stepped aside and gestured for him to enter. He was tall, older too than she'd at first thought. Closer to fifty than forty-five, she reckoned, lightly tanned and very good looking. As she closed the door he began, smiling, to open his coat. Rejecting her own need for the warmth of the kitchen she led the way instead into the living room. It was cold there, and very big with just the two of them standing in the middle. Her caller didn't remove his coat and Flora, inexplicably, felt relieved.

'I really do appreciate your seeing me,' he smiled again. He had an easy charm which was hard to resist and Flora smiled too.

'Can I get you a drink?' she asked.

'A coffee would be welcome, if you can manage it.'

'I can manage it,' Flora was tart. 'I've just made some, in fact. If you'd like to take a seat I won't be a minute.'

'I'll come with you. Carry the cups . . .'

'There's no need, really. Do take a seat.' Flora indicated a nearby armchair and left the room.

Neither then nor later could she explain the instinct which had made her confine Victor Mangan to one room, made her determined that he would not share with her the intimacy of the kitchen. Reaffirming her point she closed the living-room door firmly after her, the door to the kitchen too when she got there. He was standing quietly by a window when she returned with the coffee thermos, cups and biscuits on a tray.

'Wonderful views,' he said and Flora, pouring their coffee, nodded.

'Perhaps, Mr Mangan, you'd like to tell me what it is you have to say about Kimbay?' As she handed him the cup his slate-coloured eyes smiled into Flora's and moved, slowly, over her face. Annoyed, she found herself wishing she'd at least taken more care with her hair that morning, not just brushed and tied it with a black ribbon, relic of her schooldays. She wasn't wearing make-up either and Victor Mangan's assessment made her feel exposed, slightly unsure. It also put her on guard.

'Please call me Victor,' he smiled, looking away from her and moving to stand nearer to the fireplace. Following his gaze Flora saw the room as he, urbane and no doubt critical, must see it. He could hardly miss the signs of decay but, equally, couldn't ignore the original wood panelling, Bohemian glass chandelier brought home from their Italian honeymoon by her parents, the ornate mouldings and long, square-paned Georgian windows. His scrutiny ended when he caught sight of himself in the gilt-framed mirror over the mantelpiece.

'Nice,' he said, 'very nice indeed.'

Flora presumed he meant the room. 'Thank you.' She was stiff. 'It needs work. Refurbishing, redecorating . . .' As she spoke she felt annoyed at herself, as if she was being

59

disloyal not only to the room but to Kimbay. She stopped abruptly, allowed a questioning silence hang in the air.

'I'll come to the point.' Victor Mangan sipped his coffee. Flora did not invite him to sit again. 'This room, as you so rightly point out, needs work. I imagine the whole house does.' He was watching Flora's face carefully as he spoke. When she seemed about to interrupt he went on, smoothly. 'It is not my intention to be offensive, Ms Carolan. But I believe this is a house with a future and I have a suggestion to make.'

'Yes?' Flora decided not to help him; not to encourage any more prevarication either.

'I did not know your father, Ms Carolan, but I am aware, in general terms, of the conditions of his will.' When Flora raised an astonished eyebrow he gave a short laugh. 'It's a small country, as living abroad will have made you realize. And the horse world is a confined community. Word gets about, fast. I've been on the look-out for a property in this area and so, obviously, word of the predicament at Kimbay came to me fairly quickly.'

'There is no *predicament*, Mr Mangan,' Flora interrupted.

'Situation then. Point is, and if you're agreeable, I've got a suggestion to make which could be of enormous benefit to everyone concerned. It's got to do with a concept, a dream really, that I've had for some time now. It would create jobs, generate income in the area. This house and lands would make an ideal location . . .' He paused, put his cup on the mantel and faced Flora with his hands in his pockets. As if he owned the place, she thought; as if her silence was assent to whatever plan he proposed.

'This is a stud farm,' she said, 'it already gives employment and generates income . . .'

'After a fashion.' He sought and held her gaze briefly. 'I'll be blunt, Ms Carolan. You're obviously an intelligent woman so you must realize that we are in the middle of a bloodstock and real economy crisis. You don't need me to tell you that the horse industry is in serious trouble. The statistics are there . . .' He spread his hands in an elegant,

60

hopeless gesture. 'Stallion fees are falling. Internationally the industry has been in deep recession since the late 1980s. We can't fight that trend in this country. In the UK alone the yards around Newmarket are closing daily, the whole thing's in such a mess they can't even get the Grand National off to a start . . .'

He smiled, waited expectantly for Flora's answering smile. But a shambolic race start and distressed animals didn't raise much mirth in a woman brought up to care for horses. She looked at him silently, pointedly consulted the clock on the wall.

'Perhaps you could get to the point,' she said.

'Look, I don't relish any of this,' he shrugged slightly. 'But the reality is that breeders can't find buyers and trainers are going broke. The racetracks aren't doing well either, in spite of improved facilities. We're a changing society and small stud farms are a thing of the past. They've got no future. What we need to do,' his voice became harsh with an evangelical zeal, 'is bring wealth into the country, exploit what we have.'

'I see,' Flora's voice was carefully controlled. 'And your plan, your dream, will do this?'

'Yes.' Either not noticing or choosing to ignore her sarcasm he went on quickly. 'I propose to introduce casino-style gambling into Ireland. And this is where it could begin, on this 120 acres of land, with this house as the centre of a magnificent leisure complex attracting customers from all over Europe. There's a vast market out there waiting to be tapped, holidaymakers waiting to be persuaded to gamble while improving their health in our green, clean land . . .'

'Las Vegas on the plains of Ireland?'

'Not at all. I envisage a far wider use of the environment . . .'

'Such as? Compulsory push-ups in the paddocks before a game of craps?' Flora, almost overpowered by her own anger, produced the words like hard, cold pellets.

'Not at all.' Her visitor looked surprised. 'Some horses would remain. There would be riding and a range of —'

'Mr Mangan.' Flora's tone, this time, penetrated his urbanity and he stopped, looked at her in what seemed genuine surprise. 'I won't waste as much of your time as you have of mine. Many of the points you make are persuasive. But they are also deceiving. Times may indeed be lean, social habits changing. But the horse industry is adapting and it will survive. It has before. It's too fundamental to the culture of this country not to. It's been around since the Red Branch Knights raced amongst themselves, since the Fianna in the third century – '

She paused to draw breath, and to hear what she was actually saying. She hadn't known she felt like this, cared so passionately. What Victor Mangan was proposing conceded nothing to the pride and culture of a community which for generations, and in some cases centuries, had lived for horses and horseracing.

But that was a misty-eyed and romantic argument. Good, solid horsesense was what the Victor Mangans of this world understood.

'Kimbay is not for sale.' She was calm. 'Not for a casino site and not for anything else. My father's life work is not for sale either, and the lives of the Sweeney family and others like them who depend on this stud for their livelihood are not for bargaining with.' She stopped, abruptly, aware and ashamed of tears in her eyes.

'It's a sadly emotional time.' Victor Mangan spoke gently. 'I'm sorry, I've intruded. Grief is something we each work out in our different ways. For myself, I've found dealing with the practical a help. I had hoped that, in your case, it might be a help too. I was wrong.'

For all the right-sounding words, Flora was aware of the blinding self-confidence of the man, his belief that how he saw things was how they should be. 'Thank you for calling, Mr Mangan.' She walked ahead of him and opened the door.

He didn't follow immediately. 'All I've offered, Ms Carolan, is an option, something for you to consider,' he spoke slowly. As if I was an idiot, Flora thought and waited stiffly, holding the door open, for him to finish. 'In a few weeks' time you may feel differently,' he shrugged, 'or you may not. I will be going ahead with my plan in any event, elsewhere if not at Kimbay.'

'Good luck to you, Mr Mangan.'

This time he moved, passing her in the doorway with a smiling incline of his head. On the steps outside he turned and offered her his hand again. She took it, even more briefly than before. She had closed the door almost before he turned to go.

In the living room she looked around again. It hadn't changed but she saw it now not with Victor Mangan's eyes but her own, in all its dear familiarity. The beaten, squashy armchairs were comfortable, there wasn't a horseprint or watercolour on the walls without special significance.

She picked up a framed picture of her parents. It had been taken at Kimbay on the day of their wedding. In their laughing faces there was a world of radiant hope. Flora sat with the photograph in her lap. She looked at her mother's face, then her father's. Almost thirty years had passed since that day. For more than half that time Ned, loyally and alone, had lived and worked for the hopes they'd shared. Studying his shining eagerness Flora saw something she hadn't noticed before. She saw his joy at being loved.

'Did you know how much I loved you too?' She ran a finger over his young man's face. 'I never really told you . . .'

She hadn't done any of the things he'd wanted her to do, given him so very little of her adult life. 'But I'm going to now.' She put the picture back in its sideboard niche, smiling at the happy face. 'I'm giving you two years. It's not much, in the scheme of things. But if that's what you want . . . And if it helps stop this place becoming a bloody casino.' She straightened the picture a little. 'Don't you worry about a thing. It's going to be all right.'

It was surprising how sure she felt, she who had been so terribly unsure an hour before. She had no doubts now, felt nothing but enormous relief and a sense of the rightness of what she'd decided. Victor Mangan would never know the favour he'd done her, putting the alternative future of Kimbay so starkly before her. By doing so he had made everything stunningly clear.

It had put two years of her life, Kimbay and her father's wishes into a different perspective. It wasn't such a big thing Ned was asking. In two years Flo Girl's career would have peaked. In two years Kimbay's future would be decided, one way or another. In two years she, Flora, would have played her part in helping Shay to make the place viable again. It would remain, in part, with the Carolan family and she would be able to live with herself.

Serge would understand. She felt sure of that now, too. He spoke often of his own *patrimoine*, his sense of obligation about the survival of the family château. She would explain that this was *her* heritage, her obligation. They would work out a way of being together still, a way which would ensure that Serge got to know and appreciate Kimbay and her world. She would *make* him understand. He might even, perhaps, get to know a little of what Ned had been like.

Chapter Seven

Flora and Shay were dividing the mares.

The problem of how this was to be done had nagged at Flora ever since she'd made her decision. It would need a Solomon to divide them so that she and Shay had animals of equal value — sound, even-tempered, good-looking breeders. Shay knew the horses and so, basically, could make or break her. But only in theory. Because, if their partnership was to work, he couldn't take the best for himself. Nor could he be foolish enough simply to give her the best.

Forget Solomon. The deed would require the cunning of a countryman and the shrewdness of a horse dealer.

Shay was proving to have both. His solution was simple, and simply devious. Ned Carolan would have approved. With the help of Luke and Tobias Malone he had all ten mares brought into the centre of the main yard. Quickly, and without any apparent selection process, he separated them into two groups of five.

'Now,' he turned an expressionless face to Flora, 'you can have the pick of the two lots.'

Flora looked at him. He was absolutely serious. She looked at the two groups of horses, some of them jittery, others calm enough, a couple obviously anxious to get back to early foals. Shay knew them all, she knew virtually nothing of their strengths and weaknesses. A feeling of panic swept over her. This was a first, crucial, test.

And then she began to take stock. The fact that Shay had given her the choice meant that he would inherit the group she rejected. Which meant he had to have matched the groups evenly. As evenly as possible anyway.

The horses were becoming more restive. She would have to choose quickly.

'They won't wait there all morning.' Shay too was becoming testy.

Flora moved closer to the mares and, kismet or fate intervening, saw that she was standing beside Nessa, Flo Girl's mother.

'This lot,' she patted the mare's neck, turned a relieved face to Shay, 'I'll take this lot.' Shay nodded and Nessa's gentle eyes seemed to tease Flora as she was led back to her box.

Daisy had been relieved but not very surprised when Flora had told her of her decision. Flora had kept her explanations brief, mentioning Victor Mangan only in passing. She saw no point in distressing Daisy, or Shay, now that she'd successfully got rid of the developer.

'The will had us stunned,' Daisy admitted. 'We'd no idea how we were going to raise funds to keep it going on our own. Shay knows horses and I know a bit about bookkeeping but that doesn't make us stud owners. I decided I'd keep my own counsel, let you make up your own mind. Except of course,' she grinned, 'for that one little push, when I told you what I thought Ned had been up to in the will . . .'

'What would you have done if I'd said no, gone back to Brussels?'

'To tell you the truth, Flora, we didn't give it that much thought, neither myself nor Shay. It always seemed a likely bet that you'd give it a go. Ned wouldn't have made a will like that if he didn't think so either. Now then,' she patted Flora on the hand, 'a word of advice. You just get on with things in the yard and don't pay heed to Shay Sweeney's moods. He's been like an anti-Christ this past week, your father's death has him upset that much. He'll be all right in time. I'll see to that.'

Flora hadn't expected Shay to garland her with welcoming roses, but their first meeting as partners was better than she'd thought it would be. Within minutes of her conversation with Daisy she went down to the yard

66

to tell him her decision. She found him in the foaling box talking gently to a mare as he examined the udder for milk.

'Everything all right?' The question was instinctive but, remembering his response to the same question only days before, she could have bitten her tongue.

'She'll do. She's always a bit unpredictable.' Shay straightened, gave what looked dangerously like a smile. 'Like all females.' It was a poor joke. But that's what it was: a joke, an effort to make things easy between them.

'I've decided to stay,' she said and Shay, rubbing the mare's neck, nodded.

'That's good.' He was brisk, shepherding Flora out of the box and into the yard. 'You'll want to be filled in on everything so. No time like the present. Place is run much as it always was. We've stuck with the mixed stock.' His sentences were bullets of information. 'You'll have seen the cattle and a few sheep in the fields. Keeps the pastures clean for the horses. You don't have to worry about that, though. It's let for the grazing. The horses are what you and me'll concern ourselves with . . .'

A farm labourer coming in to check the cattle interrupted with a question and Shay, brusquely, told him he was busy. The boy looked at Flora, briefly questioning. It's true, she thought, word travels fast. Even this lad knows what's going on around here. She made her face deliberately bland, stamping her feet in the chill of the yard.

'You're starting off at the busy time of the year,' Shay said.

'I know that,' Flora tried to keep her tone neutral. Did he think her a complete fool? That she'd forgotten everything she'd grown up with, learned from her father? It was the mating season. Sires would have to be selected, between now and mid-June, to cover those mares not already in foal. Yearlings would have to be brought to peak condition between now and the October sales. Mares in foal, and the foals when born, would have to be looked after with special care.

'I've a few minutes to give you a walkabout.' Shay, at

speed, led the way across the yard. 'Things haven't changed much.' The walkabout was quick. In record time, spilling out information in jerky sentences, he covered the main areas of activity around the stud.

The inner yard circled the back of the house and contained the bulk of the looseboxes as well as tack and feeding sheds. Beyond it, through a high, whitewashed arch there was an outer yard and the long, open-fronted shed used for winter shelter. Further out still there was the great storage barn and isolation unit – the last in need of extension and repair.

In the paddock closest to the house Shay came to a stop, leaning on a fence. 'They're in good shape, the animals,' he said. 'We've got six yearlings between us, Flora. There's a filly in that lot of animals you chose – one in my lot too. Myself and Ned bought them out of training last autumn. They're a bit of an unknown quantity, the both of them. Biggest thing at the moment is getting them and the mares covered. I'll give you a word to the wise about stallions,' he was diffident, 'unless you want to go your own way . . .'

'I'd be glad of advice,' Flora said. For the moment anyway, she thought. Until I learn, and that won't take long. She'd no intention of being a lame, or sleeping, partner. 'Breed the best to the best and hope for the best,' she quoted breeder's dictum with a smile.

'That's about the size of it.' Shay, not even trying his wintry smile this time, turned from the fence. 'Day begins in the yard at half-seven, sharp. Every day. No exceptions.'

Flora knew that too. She bit back a response, nodded and said, 'Fine. I'll start tomorrow morning. Shay,' she raised her voice as he turned away, 'I'll be using Jack Thomas as vet to my animals.'

'Thomas? Jack Thomas?' Shay looked disbelieving. 'What do you want bringing that . . .' Words failed him and he stared at her.

'Because I think he's second to none as far as being a vet goes. And as executor of the will it's better to have him

68

with us than against us. You'll just have to put your differences on hold for the next year or so.'

On her way back to the house she stood for several minutes in the busy inner yard. Kimbay wasn't a flashy, glamorous stud. It was clean and solid and old, and nowhere was this more apparent than here. The only touch of flamboyance was the red-painted doors to the boxes. The hinges, she saw, had recently been painted green. A nice touch. Red and green were the Carolan racing colours.

As she stood there, a cat, unhurried and fastidious, high-stepped across the frost which still lay on the far, shadowy end of the yard. Luke appeared through the arch leading a yearling and a stable lad mucked out energetically. No one noticed her, or seemed to. She felt, once again, in the way.

In the house she went through the books with Daisy, found nothing which surprised her and rather less money than she'd thought. She phoned Fintan and she phoned Ollie.

'I'm giving Kimbay the two years,' she said, to each of them in turn. They were positive, pledging support. They were also, she could tell, relieved.

There was a gale blowing through her which hadn't been there yesterday. In a frenzy of organizing activity she resurrected dusty, tired-looking reliables like tweed and Barbour jackets, boots and headgear. She sorted them for cleaning, put on the warmest and cleanest jeans and jumper she could find and telephoned Flo Girl's trainer.

She dialled quickly, tired of hesitation, not wanting to delay any further. The phone rang out eight, nine times, before it was picked up.

'Yes?' The voice was male, impatient.

'Mr Hopkins?'

'Yes.'

'This is Flora Carolan. I'd like to come over to see my horse. Would sometime in the next hour be convenient?' She was aware she sounded curt, even rude. She didn't care. She wanted him to know she meant business.

'Hang on.' The phone was put down and she could hear heavy, booted footsteps ringing across wooden floorboards. She tried to recall the house as it had been when she'd visited as a child. Confused images of large, dark rooms were all that came to mind. The footsteps came thumping back to the phone. 'If you could make it four o'clock I'll be here to see you myself. How does that sound?'

'I'll be there.'

Chapter Eight

Flora almost missed the entrance to Fairmane. She could have ridden over, as she had with Ned, and been sure of finding her way. But a wind had risen and the skies were threatening and the car seemed a safer, dryer bet. The journey by road was longer than she remembered but her father's ancient Mercedes, smelling of dog and animal food, handled well.

The Fairmane entrance she'd been used to had been a nondescript gate with the name in wood. The new entrance, the one she almost missed, boasted high black gates and a black-on-white sign. The avenue up to the house hadn't changed, however. The muddiness, the verges lined with thin bushes and the anxious, wintry trees all seemed familiar. It was shorter than she remembered, though, and she came on the house quite suddenly.

Parking in front she got out and stood to have a look. What could have been a pleasant country house had become tired and sad. There was a great deal of ivy everywhere, far too much of it smothering the windows. If she hadn't known better she'd have said there was no one living there.

The desolate appearance of the house decided her against knocking on the front door. Instead she walked around the back to the yard. It was a world apart from the abandoned-looking house frontage. This time, looking more closely, she saw that here was where the new owner of Fairmane had concentrated his energies. His money too. The entire yard had been expensively rebuilt. Loosebox doors were of hardwood and the buildings themselves had been brought back to their original, natural stone.

She counted a string of horses as they filed through the great iron gates at the other end of the yard. Six. Another four were being got ready to go out. Ten altogether. The trainer wasn't doing too badly, for someone only a few years at the game.

'You're late,' Matt Hopkins's voice, coming up behind her, was cheerful.

'Sorry.' She turned. He wore a slight grin and his features, in the daylight, were darker edged. In the daylight too the eyes which met hers were a mocking, darker blue. 'I misjudged the distance,' Flora said. 'I almost missed your entrance too. You've made some changes.' She nodded at the yard and, with a slightly raised eyebrow, he followed her gaze.

'Yes,' he said. 'The place needed some work.' He was dressed in black: stockman's coat, sweater and jeans. He turned back to her and, under his mocking gaze, her own bright red anorak seemed frivolous and inappropriate. 'Well, glad you got here at last,' he said. 'Your horse has just come in. She's in good form today, so my lad tells me.'

In Flo Girl's box, rubbing her nose and making soothing noises, Flora thought again how like her dam the filly was.

'She's a bit flashy.' The trainer, leaning on the half-door, spoke lazily. 'But she's young. She'll tone down as she gets older.'

'My father always said you could only trust a horse, or man, with a strong head and good face. Flo Girl's got those at least.' Flora turned, found his eyes on her again. 'How's she doing otherwise?'

'She was a bit skittish at first, but she's calming down.' He looked reflectively at the horse. 'She's full of life, interested in everything around her, intelligent, not at all neurotic.' He grinned. 'Best kind of female, in fact.' He left the door and came to stand beside Flora. 'There's something about her . . . I'm going to start working her properly really soon. I could make a very good racehorse out of her . . . Maybe even a great one.'

'Do you have any idea how you're going to do that?' Flora was caustic, but if the trainer noticed he gave no indication.

'Carefully. Very carefully.' He spoke slowly.

'Yes?' Flora was sharp, impatient. The horse jerked her head back and the trainer frowned.

'I'll race her as little as possible this season. She's got strong legs and she's a good mover but she's a bit young. She can do anything she wants to. The trick is to get her to want to.' He shrugged, looked broodingly at Flo Girl. 'I'll race her late in the season at Gowran Park. Then maybe one other race, maybe not. I don't want to overrace her. That way she'll be right for a couple of good wins early next year.'

He looked beyond Flora to where a feeding chart hung on the wall. He put his hands in the pockets of his jeans and crossed to study it, an intent look on his face. 'She eats well,' he said, 'never leaves an oat.' He appeared to be talking to himself.

'Are you trying to tell me,' she kept her voice even, 'that with the training you suggest Flo Girl could win the Guineas?'

'At the very least.' He spoke without turning. 'I think we could enter her in the Budweiser Derby next year too.' If the prospect excited him he did a good job of hiding it. His face, as he turned to consider the horse, was closed, almost bored-looking.

'You *are* serious, I presume?' Flora, lacking the tolerance for teasing, was chilly.

'Absolutely.'

'And you presume too that she has a chance of winning?'

'Absolutely. A more than good chance. Depending on how things go with the earlier races, of course.'

'Of course.' Flora, with a final pat to the horse's neck, left the box. The trainer followed her. In the yard, she faced him again. 'You really think she could be a Classic winner?'

'There's a good chance, yes.'

'Did you discuss tactics for racing her with my father?'

'No. I was waiting until I was more sure of her.' He was watching Flora closely. She pushed a strand of hair out of her eye before replying.

'It may be your practice to decide a horse's career without consultation with the owner,' she smiled chillily, 'but I'd prefer, in this instance, if you discussed things with me *before* making decisions about races.'

The trainer didn't answer immediately. He slowly bolted the half-door, then called over and had words with a stable lad. When he at last spoke to Flora he was curt.

'I was simply being realistic,' his eyes had narrowed, whether in an attempt to hide annoyance or impatience Flora couldn't be sure. 'I know Flo Girl. You don't.'

'Not yet. But I will. And I *am* aware of her breeding.' Anger brought a flush to Flora's cheeks.

'It's the work done with the animal that matters,' his annoyance was obvious now. 'I've been paid by your father to get her to the peak of her ability —'

'And owners shouldn't interfere and have to be trained too.' Flora was icy. 'I'm aware of trainers' feelings on the subject of owner-involvement.' As she spoke the long-threatening skies opened and the first heavy drops of a downpour began to fall. Flora ignored them. 'But I intend staying on to work Kimbay, Mr Hopkins, and how Flo Girl does will be of more than passing interest to me. I *will* be involved —'

'Come inside,' without warning the trainer grabbed her arm, 'no point in getting wet as well as angry.' He began to pull her, running, across the yard toward the back of the house. The rain had become a torrent by the time he shouldered open a heavy ground-level door and pulled Flora inside after him. Only when he'd kicked the door shut did he let go of her arm.

In the hallway she shivered, as much from the pervading gloom as the fact that she was wet, dripping from head to toe.

'Is lighting considered an extravagance around here?' Her teeth chattered.

There was a click and, as light flooded the hallway, the trainer pointed to a half-open door. 'Wait in there,' he said. 'I'll get some towels.' He clattered up deep wooden steps to the house above.

Flora's jacket, proving itself stylishly impractical, was soaked through. She peeled it off and went into the room he'd indicated. It was warm in there, a lot of the heat coming from a crackling log fire in a low grate. She hunkered thankfully in front of it, spreading her hands to warm them while she had a look around. She was obviously in what had once been a below-stairs kitchen but was now the trainer's office. Its two lives were manifest in a shelf, just below the low ceiling, which still held a row of ornate platters, and an oak desk which took up fully a quarter of the room space. Shelves and files covered an entire wall. Behind the desk there was a drinks cabinet and fridge. Matt Hopkins believed, apparently, in compact living.

She stayed where she was, reluctant to wet the only, sagging armchair. Steam had begun to rise from her sweater by the time the trainer's returning steps sounded on the stairs.

'You'd better change too.' He threw a bundle of towels and a sweater into the armchair.

'Thanks.' Flora began to towel her hair vigorously, waiting for the trainer to leave so that she could put on the dry sweater. He didn't move and she raised a questioning eyebrow.

'Pretend I'm not here.' He grinned, and swivelled in the chair behind the desk to face the drinks cabinet.

With a furious jerk she yanked off her wet sweater and pulled on the large, grey alpaca he'd left in the chair. It was gloriously soft, warm against her damp skin. It smelled too, very faintly, of a musky perfume. She shook her hair loose from its collar and looked up to find Matt Hopkins's eyes on her.

She was about to say something caustic about peep-shows and voyeurs when she saw the champagne on the desk. Consoling herself with a basilisk glare in his direction she watched silently as he filled a couple of narrow crystal glasses.

'I thought we should drink to good relations between owners and trainers.' He walked round the desk toward her with the glasses. Too smooth by half, Flora thought, and wondered what it would take to ruffle his confidence.

'Do all your owners get this treatment?' She took one of the glasses from him.

'Not all of them.' He raised his glass. 'To a good working relationship.' They drank.

'To Flo Girl,' Flora said, and they drank again.

With his boot he shoved another log onto the fire and for a few seconds the only sounds in the room were of its crackling. A gust of wind down the chimney made Flora start.

'Storm's not getting any better.' She looked out the window. It had darkened dramatically and rain rushed in sheets across the yard.

'Refill?' Matt Hopkins was beside her, champagne bottle ready to pour. 'That rain's not going to stop for a while.'

'I don't think I should.' Nervously, Flora placed a hand over her glass. 'I've hardly eaten today.' He shrugged, refilling his own and making her feel like a schoolgirl.

'Maybe a half-glass,' Flora held out her glass, 'if we're going to be here for a while . . .' He filled it up.

'So you've decided to stay at Kimbay.' He leaned an arm against the mantel and looked away from her, into the fire. The flames highlighted the planes of his face, giving him a Mephisto-like appearance. He's handsome, Flora thought, and he knows it. He's fully aware he's attractive.

'Just for two years.' Answering his question she toyed for seconds with an urge to tell him about Victor Mangan, alarm him with the prospect of a casino for a neighbour. 'I'll get someone to take over my end of things then . . .'

'. . . And get back to your real life?'

She looked at him quickly. His expression was coolly sardonic, making her flush a little.

'Get back to my *other* life,' she corrected, shaking the still wet hair out of her eyes. His gaze held hers, briefly, before he reached to lift a lock of her wet hair.

'You need to dry that before you go,' he said, and Flora put down her glass and picked up the towel again.

'You're right,' she said, in some embarrassment. What

was the man playing at, offering her a drink then almost inviting her to go? She began a half-hearted second towelling of her hair.

'Here, let me help.' She felt the towel being taken from her hands. 'Needs a bit more energy than that.'

He stood very close while he rubbed her hair briskly and in businesslike fashion. She lowered her head and when it touched his chest she left it there, leaning against him as he rubbed, more slowly now. He stopped abruptly and she shook her hair free of her face. She didn't look at him and for several seconds neither of them said anything, did anything other than stand there, close and warm together.

Flora knew why she was allowing this happen. It was two glasses of champagne, it was their aloneness in this warm, low room. She stepped back.

'I'm sorry,' she said awkwardly. 'I've imposed far, far too much.'

'I wouldn't say that . . .' He spoke softly, smiling, his eyes on hers. Warning bells, whose alarm she'd only half listened to before, rang for Flora. This man was very good at this, a master of seduction. Was she *mad*, allowing herself be used by him? And now he was laughing at her. Laughing . . .

With a cool smile she straightened her shoulders and walked to the window. She sat on the windowseat there. 'There's thunder about.' Her voice was light. She was free. Nothing had happened. And it might have. So easily. 'Why did you buy Fairmane?' she asked, looking across the wet yard. 'You're not from around here, are you?'

'No, I'm not from around here.' He gave a short laugh and Flora turned around. He was looking past her, out of the window. 'I'm a bit of a nomad, really. I ended up here because of your father. I was looking for a place, met him at the races and he put me on to Fairmane. Simple as that.' He smiled at her, considering for a moment. 'He got me my first owner, too.'

He liked Ned, Flora thought. Which might be why he thought Ned's daughter a dabbler, a dilettante who'd decided to amuse herself for a couple of years. Probably thought of her too as a neighbour who might prove flirtatiously diverting, from time to time. Well, he'd find out he was wrong.

'Where did you train before?' She was curt, an owner wanting information. He laughed.

'If you want my CV, Flora, then you shall have it.' He threw himself into the armchair, long legs in front of him as he studied the fire through the flat champagne in his glass. I've trespassed, Flora thought, but I don't care. Let him damn well tell me. I want to know who's training my horse.

'Like you, my father introduced me to horses.' His tone was dispassionate, lazy.

'Your father was a trainer?' Flora was careful not to appear too eager for information. She was good at getting people to talk, reveal themselves. The trick lay in listening, giving them time. She remembered how her old friend Sophie Butler had always insisted that she, Flora, would make a good journalist – which was, in fact, what Sophie herself did for a living. Remembering made Flora decide to get in touch with Sophie. Her lighthearted company would be a boon in the months ahead.

'Yes, my father was a trainer, among other things.' Matt Hopkins smiled. He finds this amusing, Flora thought, and knew he would tell her only what he wanted to.

'He wasn't unlike your father, in a way.' The trainer's voice was thoughtful, as if the idea had just occurred to him. 'Horses were his life. He worked with them wherever he could – this country, England, America, finally in Australia. I went with him. It was a great life.' He stopped. Flora sensed he was withdrawing.

'And your mother? Where did she figure in all of this?'

'She left when I was five. Wise woman, I've always thought.'

Flora, watching him closely, could detect no sign of bitterness or loss. He threw back his head and laughed. 'No need to look so stricken, Flora. Life isn't all happy families, you know. Horses for courses and all that. Some of us are better off outside the fold, not suited to domesticity.'

'Point taken.' Flora paused, wondering if he was talking about his mother or himself. She decided against asking and said, 'But I still don't know what brought you here . . .'

'This is more than the usual information my owners look for.' His tone was light, but Flora felt he was a breath away from clamming up altogether. She pulled back, hoping the tactic would work.

'I'm sorry,' she said, 'I'd no right. I'll go . . .'

They both turned to the window. The sky was lightening but rain still fell in a steady stream. Flora thought she heard a sound in the room above but then the fire crackled and she dismissed the idea. She wondered if Matt Hopkins had heard it too but, when he spoke, it seemed that he hadn't.

'Wouldn't send a dog out into that.' He was cheerful. 'And as for the end of my story, it's this . . .' He came and stood beside her in the window, studying the sky. 'When I was fourteen my father made a bit of money on a horse. He sent me home to the Jesuits to be educated,' he flashed a fiendish grin Flora's way, 'he thought them the "best lads for the job".'

'And were they?'

'They taught me to read and write.' He shrugged. 'When the Jesuits finished with me I went back to Australia. Couldn't settle. Habits of the wandering life too entrenched, I suppose. Worked my way and learned the trade in studs on the continent and in America. Always wanted my own place though.' He stopped, briefly. 'My father sorted that one out for me too by dying and leaving me a surprising accumulation of winnings. So back I came, to Erin's green and rain-washed isle.' He grinned, at the window by now and looking out. 'He'd have enjoyed this place, for a while. Wouldn't have been able to take the weather though, nor to stick around for too long.'

'What about you? Will you stick around?'

'For a while, anyway. Certainly for Flo Girl's racing

79

life.' He began to pace again and stopped, restlessly, in front of a racing calendar on the wall.

'That's a relief.' Flora's voice was dry. He sat behind the desk, seeming not to notice her tone.

'I can make a winner out of Flo Girl,' he said.

'You've trained winners before?'

'Yes. Both here and abroad.' His annoyance at being asked to account for himself was obvious.

'But you need a free hand with her?' Flora left the window to stand in front of the desk.

'Something like that, yes.'

'And you feel I don't know enough to have an opinion on how Flo Girl should be handled?' Flora spoke carefully.

He leaned across the desk. There was no amusement now in his eyes or face. 'I'm in this business to win, Flora. I don't intend being an also-ran. And I'm going to make damn sure that horse doesn't become one either.' He threw a typed sheet across the desk and Flora picked it up. 'That's a list of my owners. They've all been in the horse game a long time. I can discuss things with them and they know what I'm saying.'

Flora went down the list of names, many of them familiar, all of them men. 'I'll try very hard to grasp what you tell me,' she spoke sweetly. 'Always supposing, of course, that I leave Flo Girl in training with you.'

His jaw muscle tightened. 'Your father wanted that horse trained here.'

'Yes. And he wanted me to work Kimbay too. It may not be possible to do both. If I'm to keep Flo Girl she'll have to pay for her keep *and* contribute to Kimbay.' Flora took a deep, steadying breath. 'What I'm saying is that she'll have to win races or . . .'

'. . . You'll sell her?' The trainer's voice was incredulous.

'I may have to.' In the small silence, Flora could hear that the rain had stopped.

'Why don't you cut the crap, Flora!' Matt Hopkins stood and brought a hard, flat hand down on the desk top. His eyes were an inky black-blue. 'You're not really interested in any of this. Taking on the farm is an obligation. Fine. Do your bit. But I'll guarantee you'll be leaving the decisions to Shay Sweeney. And so you should, he's the expert. Flo Girl's obviously an obligation too. So why don't you leave decisions to me? I'm the expert as far as she's concerned. I owe Ned, so I'll train her on a no-win, no-pay basis. All you have to do is get on with what you're good at—'

Flora, disbelieving at first, was filled with a cold fury as he went on. Her words, when she interrupted, were carefully spaced and icily clear.

'And what, exactly, do you think I'd be good at?'

'Playing the county lady, looking pretty in the winners' enclosure.' He raised a sardonic eyebrow. His amused grin had returned. 'Come, come, Flora. It's a fair deal. You can entertain, dolly up the house over there. Ride to hounds. I'll even pay your cap money—'

'Just who the hell do you think you are?' Flora leaned forward on the desk until her eyes were less than a foot from his. Her face was white except for two high spots of colour on her cheeks. '*I'll* make the decisions about my life. Your suggestions are both crude and ignorant. I am *not* the kind of "county lady" you seem to admire. Nor do I wish to join the hunt. Apart altogether from the fact that I've disagreements with it, my mother was killed in a fall during the hunt—' She stopped, gave a small shrug and drew back.

She hadn't meant to say this last. But it was out now. She was about to go on when the trainer, leaning back in his chair, interrupted. His tone was cool, almost laconic, and there was an expression in his eyes she couldn't quite read.

'Grow up, Flora. This is the country, and country ways are harsh. Brutal as nature. You can't have grown up here and not known that. If your mother had died in a car crash would you refuse to drive a car?'

'That's a stupid, fallacious argument.'

'And you, my dear Flora, are a fake.'

'But I'm also the owner of Flo Girl.' She threw the words at him, cold and dismissive.

'Yes. You're the filly's owner.' He shrugged. 'Look, let's try to be reasonable about this.' His tone was patient. As if

81

he was soothing a wilful yearling, Flora thought. 'We both want to do what's right for Flo Girl. And we *both*', he gave her a long look, 'want to carry out Ned's wishes. He'd have wanted the horse to have her day in the sun.'

He was, Flora thought, either very devious or quite sincere, either using Ned as emotional blackmail or truly concerned that her father's wishes be carried out. Unable to make up her mind she played for time, pretended to study the racing calendar.

'Of course, I'll consult with you about her training and races.' The trainer's tone was placatory; patronizing, Flora thought. 'But I should explain that I want horses which will stay with me and develop, not just animals that make it as two-year-olds and are no good after that. Also, I've a schedule and I don't want it buggered up. I don't want Flo Girl buggered up either. I won't be hard on her. It's not my way with horses. An animal has to enjoy working and racing to be any good—'

'Fine.' Flora cut him short. As he spoke she heard the trainer in him, and why he was in the business. Training had an overload of excitement and challenge and insecurity. All of which suited him. 'I'll leave Flo Girl with you for this season anyway,' she said, 'see how it goes, how much of the winners' enclosure I get to see.'

'Your confidence is reassuring. I'll see what can be arranged. Now, if you'll excuse me, I've some things to see to upstairs. Rain's almost stopped but you're welcome to wait it out here. Help yourself to another drink . . .'

'I'll go. But one thing before I do. I'd be obliged if you would use old Jack Thomas as vet for Flo Girl. I have absolute faith in his ability.'

'So have I.' He was curt.

'Good. That's that then. I'm parked to the front of the house – if you've no objections I'll go upstairs and leave through the front door.' He hesitated, for brief but perceptible seconds. 'It would be dryer than going round the house,' Flora explained. She picked up her still damp sweater.

'Of course,' he said then, 'good idea.'

82

Flora, following him up the wooden stairs, caught her breath in the damp cold of the main hallway. She shivered.

'Heating's not in yet,' the trainer walked swiftly to the front door. Flora, curious, looked around.

'Lovely ceiling work,' she said.

'I'll try to save it.' He held open the front door just as, simultaneously, a door off the hallway opened with a crash. A woman stepped through.

'Matt, I've waited and waited.' Her accented voice was high, musical and demanding. 'When are we leaving?' Lustrous black eyes took in Flora before they turned in furious questioning to Matt Hopkins. 'Who is this woman?'

'Flora Carolan,' the trainer made a gesture of introduction, 'meet Isabel Gonzalez.'

Even in the dim light in the hall Flora could see how dramatically beautiful the woman was. Bulky woollens and heavy leggings in no way concealed the willowy length of her body, and not even the gloom could diminish the rich turbulence of hair around the arrogant, high-boned face.

She held out her hand. Isabel Gonzalez ignored it.

'Nice meeting you.' Flora dropped her hand. She smiled coolly at the trainer. 'I'll be in touch,' she said.

She slipped through the door and ran quickly through the rain, down the steps and into her car. Turning, with spinning back wheels, she glanced up at the door in time to see Isabel Gonzalez drape an arm around the trainer's neck as he pushed the door closed.

Chapter Nine

Flora cleaned the car before taking it to the airport to collect Serge. It wasn't easy. Dipper, slinking into the back seat when she'd finished, gave a howl of lonely protest at the absence of scents and things familiar.

'You're a fool,' she told him, 'and you can't come to the airport. You don't have the social graces. Out.' Woebegone, he left the car. Driving away, watching the sad recrimination of his slowly wagging tail in the mirror, Flora almost relented.

The day was crisp and bright with a sharp wind. She had been at home ten days and it felt like a lifetime. Her father was dead two weeks and it felt like a mere breath of time.

The traffic on the busy road to Dublin carried her, unthinking, along. She was glad to be an anonymous, unseen part of it. The week since Monday had turned her life on its head. She had worked in the yard for all of the daylight hours, and often beyond, setting herself a pace she knew she couldn't maintain. She would ease up when she knew what she was doing, got on top of things. So she told herself anyway.

She was wearing, of necessity, what Matt Hopkins would have thought solid, county-lady clothes. Clean jeans, cashmere sweater and hacking jacket had been the only possibilities in a crammed wardrobe. She'd had trouble recognizing that the eclectic, mismatching, impulse-bought clothes it contained had, once, been her way of dressing. Brussels had taught her to select, discern, buy only when sure.

She'd salvaged a few basic items and junked the rest. A

shopping trip to Dublin was going to be necessary, as well as a trip to Brussels to wind up the flat and bring home her clothes.

To minimize the county-lady effect she'd clipped on a pair of dangling silver earrings and shaken her hair loose. Serge would just have to accept this new-look Flora. It was the only model on offer at the moment.

Longing to see him, she arrived early at the airport, then had to sit with a drink in the bar waiting for his flight. Anticipation of the loving warmth of sex made her restless, fidgety. She watched the travelling world come and go, trying not to think how it would be with Serge's arms around her, the pleasure of his mouth on hers. A group of late-teens, nearly men but behaving like boys, sat nearby and distracted her. One of them resembled Luke, red-haired and with anxiety and self-assurance chasing each other across his face. Like Luke, too, he was given to bursts of sudden impatience and within minutes had put himself huffily outside the group.

Luke was proving much more difficult to work with than Shay, or anyone else in the yard for that matter. His resentment was like a weight around him. The stud groom, Tobias Malone, was accepting and businesslike, and the part-time stable lad and lass were amused and careful. All in all, the sheer physical labour of the week had been therapeutic.

A mare of Flora's had given birth, early one morning, to an attractive colt foal.

'Never saw a placid mare but had a placid foal,' Shay said. He made sure the foal's nostrils weren't blocked, helped him find his mother's udder. 'It's not usual for a mare to foal in the morning.' From a distance, standing under the infra-red warming light, he gave the dam a critical once-over. 'Night-time's when it happens, usually.'

'Why's that?' Flora asked the question she knew he wanted asked and Shay gave what, for him, amounted to a speech on the subject.

'Nature's way. Mare knows if the foal is born at night

85

it'll be ready to travel before morning. If she has to move on, that is. It's in the folk memory of the animal. This fella looks a good strong colt. Best to get the vet up anyway.'

'Who was his sire?'

'Knockover. Standing at the Hawthorn Stud. Lovely as a colt. Rangy. A good mover. Won four of his six starts as a three-year-old.'

'Why don't we call his son Overhead, while he's with us anyway?' Flora suggested.

Shay didn't see the joke. He didn't think either that Jack Thomas should be the vet to see the foal. When Flora insisted he shrugged, then absented himself from proceedings when the vet arrived. Flora hoped, but doubted, that all their disagreements could be so amicably resolved.

Leah, hearing Flora had been to Fairmane, had been incredulous. 'You went over there on your *own*? And in *broad daylight*?' She shuddered. 'Are you mad, or what?'

'Or what, I think,' Flora was mild. 'It didn't seem necessary to call out the troops.'

'Well, I hope you know better now.' Leah narrowed her eyes. Her hair, today, looked as if it had had an electric shock. She was dressed entirely in black. 'That man has a reputation second only to Caligula's around here. The old biddies in the village spend their time talking about sex orgies at Fairmane. You should hear some of the stories.' She smirked, her long legs in their black boots stretched across Dipper where he lay on the kitchen floor. 'You'll be part of it now, Flora, now that you've spent an afternoon with him *alone*, and *indoors* at that house.'

'What makes you think I was alone with him?' Flora was arch, mocking.

'There was somebody else there?' Leah sat up. 'Who? Tell me, Flora, please?' Leah held her breath.

'Oh, just some woman.' Flora was offhand.

'So it's true.' Leah let her breath out. 'There *is* a woman living with him. They were saying that, in the village. What's she like? Is she the same one he had staying last winter? Is she blonde?'

86

'Well, in the short time I had to look at her before she hit me with her walking stick—'

'Flora!' Leah almost screamed in anguish. 'Don't *do* this to me. You're the only one who's seen her . . .'

'She hasn't been here long, then?'

'About a week. Now come on, tell.'

'I think he's got Bianca Jagger staying with him,' Flora said. 'I'm sure of it, in fact.'

'Really?' Leah's eyes widened to her hairline.

Flora nodded. 'I'd know her anywhere. Met her once in Cannes.'

'I wonder where *he* met her.' Leah frowned. 'Probably in Deauville or Chantilly or one of those places he goes off to. He sort of comes and goes – you know how dead it can be around here in the winter. Mind you, he manages to knock a bit of life out of this place anyway.' She looked suddenly wistful. 'I must admit that for an almost geriatric he's not half bad looking. I certainly wouldn't throw him out of my bed. Would you?'

'Probably.' Flora's tone was casual.

'Sorr-eee.' Leah giggled. 'Forgot the Frenchman you've got tucked away. Anyway, why don't you bring me with you the next time you go calling? As a sort of chaperone, to protect your good name.'

'Mmm. Wouldn't it be upsetting for you? With his reputation and all that?'

Leah waved an airy hand. 'Don't you worry about me, Flora. I can handle lads like him with my legs in concrete.'

'That's reassuring. But maybe I should just bring Dipper in future.'

'Dipstick? That poor old thing couldn't protect you from horse's wind.' Leah nudged the depressed-looking labrador with her foot. 'You're sure it's Bianca Jagger? She's really *ancient*, you know.'

The first of the phone calls came on Wednesday night, late. Flora was alone in the house and answered expecting it to be Serge. The hoarse, whispering voice was a shock. What it had to say filled her with rage and fear.

'Flora Carolan? Is that you, Miss Carolan?'

'Yes, this is Flora.'

'Aaah . . .' There was a long, sighing sound and she waited. The voice had sounded old. She would give him time. He was breathier when he went on. 'I've been watching you, Flora, riding that big grey horse, in that house alone at night. I've been wanting to talk to you . . .'

'Who *is* this?' A shiver of fear gave an edge to her voice. 'Do I know you?'

There was a laugh. Unpleasant and high. 'The grey horse. You look very . . . appealing on the grey horse, Miss Carolan. But I want to know more about you. I want to know what you're wearing now, this minute. Tell me, what colour are your panties, Flora, I want to—'

'Stop it! Shut up, shut up you filthy pervert! You—' Flora hung up.

For fully five minutes she leaned, shaking and nauseated with disgust, against the wall of the hallway. She felt utterly violated. Obscene phone calls were something which happened to other people. To women in cities, or in suburbs. They didn't happen in the quiet of the hard-working countryside. They didn't happen to her. Or at least they never had before.

But then she'd never been alone like this before, without a man to turn to for support or comfort or help. The realization came, with a painful sadness, that she'd never in her life felt threatened. Only protected.

There must be a way of dealing with it, now that it had happened. Other women coped when ugly things happened to them. She would have to too.

Dipper appeared from the kitchen. He rubbed himself against her with a sympathetic whine.

'Oh, Dippy dog, am I ever glad you're here.' With the labrador at her heels she moved quickly to lock the front door, check the windows, turn on the outside light. Kimbay had never, in her lifetime, had to be made a fortress by night. She felt a desolate, impotent rage at the unknown, unseen, sick caller who made it necessary.

In the kitchen she poured herself a glass of whiskey. He

had known her name and some of her habits. He was watching her. Did that mean that he knew her? Or just that he was a voyeur as well as a dirty, revolting pervert?

She fought an instinct to call Daisy, then an urge to call her friend Sophie in Dublin. Funny how she wanted to talk to a woman about it . . . But there was nothing they could do, even if she did get in touch with either or both of them. She had to deal with this herself. Everything she'd ever heard or read told her that men like him got their sick kicks from the actual call. They rarely followed up with physical activity.

Only now she didn't believe it. Not now it had happened to her.

She rang the guards. The sergeant on duty was friendly, concerned. He would send a car around, have the place checked out. Two garda arrived within ten minutes. Large, deceptively relaxed, watchful, they did a round of the yard and house.

'Just a precaution,' the older one said, 'those boyos never show themselves. If he rings again, let us know.'

'What do you mean, *again*?'

'With sick boyos like that you never know.' His calm had become maddening. 'Hang up if he does ring. Don't entertain any auld guff out of him.' He eyed Dipper doubtfully. 'That the only dog you have around the place?'

'Yes.'

'You might think about replacing him.'

After they'd gone she checked the house again. Disparage Dipper they might, but she was very glad of his heavy old bones across the foot of her bed when she at last lay down. The phone didn't ring again that night.

In the cold light of day she felt better, more confident he wouldn't repeat the call. No one in the gate lodge had heard the guards come and go and Flora didn't tell them anything. Better to let it die, try to forget it ever happened.

Through the arrival crowds she saw Serge coming towards her. He hadn't seen her and she devoured the beloved, familiar lines of his face with an intensity that made him turn instinctively to where she stood. When he held and kissed her it was with more passion than was decent in a public place, and when they parted she looked at him silently, her joy in seeing him too great for any words.

He kept an arm around her as they made for the exit. 'I flew Aer Lingus,' he said. 'I was treated like a child on his first flight.'

'Handsome men always get the best treatment,' Flora laughed; his confidence enveloped her as it always did, making her feel, for lightheaded minutes, as if the events of the last fortnight had never happened.

They stepped through the door and into the biting wind. 'Welcome to springtime in Ireland,' Flora said.

Driving into Dublin they chatted easily, and of nothing much. Serge made observations about its citizens and their environs with a detached curiosity. 'Are there no rules about jay walking?' he asked and Flora, used to Dubliners' anarchy in regard to traffic lights, assured him there were.

The Friday afternoon traffic was more than usually chaotic. It made Flora tense. By the time she'd driven through the centre of town she had completely lost her earlier sense of euphoria and started to worry. Serge wasn't staying long, only until Sunday. How was she going to tell him that she was not, as he assumed, going back to Brussels in a couple of weeks?

She wished, with a despairing frustration, that she'd worked something out. Doubts crowded in, fears she'd kept at the back of her mind until now. Serge might *not* understand. For the first time she acknowledged the terrible possibility that she might lose him. She'd chosen Kimbay, and to do what Ned wanted, with so little thought for Serge and their relationship. She hadn't even consulted him, for God's sake . . .

'You are worried, drifting away from me,' Serge rubbed the back of her neck gently. 'But you are still beautiful. More beautiful than ever.'

Flora blew the horn as two youngsters stepped off the kerb in front of her. They gave her the finger sign and she ground her teeth.

'*Ma pauvre petite*. Perhaps we should stop and discuss

90

why you are upset.' Serge was mild. He stroked her white knuckles on the wheel. 'To talk about it would be the best thing.'

'You're not too . . . tired?'

'*Non*. Of course not. I would like to know.'

Serge had always listened when she needed to talk. Suddenly, she couldn't wait to tell him. 'I'll find us a pub. You have to experience an Irish pub anyway. Sooner's better than later.'

They were on the quays. Flora slowed the car, changed lanes so as she could turn off. Sooner was a better time to tell Serge too.

The pub was low and dark and full of a lively buzz. They found seats near the back and Serge said he would try a Guinness. While they waited for its head to draw Flora fiddled with the beer mats and asked desultory questions about Brussels.

'So,' Serge took the mats out of her hand, 'tell me what is wrong. It is more than your grief for your father.'

And so Flora told him, awkwardly at first but then with passion as she tried to convince him of the necessity and reasons for her choice. He *had* to understand, see how important this was to her. And he *had* to be involved. Otherwise . . . otherwise she might lose him. The thought brought on a sick feeling of panic. She grabbed and held his hand, tight.

'I can't just walk away,' she said. 'I need to be here. If the racehorse wins races then the money will go back into Kimbay. If she doesn't then I'll sell her. Apart from all that I want to put in my two years, keep the Carolan interest in the yard. If I left and the Sweeneys had to sell and the place became a casino I just wouldn't be able to live with myself.'

She stopped. She had explained enough. Serge would have to try to understand. If he loved her, he would.

Opposite, studying the creamy head on his perfect pint, he was silent for an age. His face was impassive, but then he was good at hiding his feelings. He sipped the pint at last, grimacing slightly. Still he said nothing.

91

'Serge . . .?' Flora, looking at him, saw an expression of bewildered incomprehension fleetingly cross his face.

'I should have been here, with you for this terrible time,' he said. 'It was unfair of your father to make such a will.'

'It wouldn't have made any difference, Serge, even if you had been here. Things would have happened like this anyway. It's fate, destiny . . . It is my *patrimoine*.' She was only half joking. Heritage and obligation were things Serge had always seemed to understand.

'Your father has bound you with a moral obligation.'

'I suppose he has.' Flora spoke slowly. 'But I don't mind. I did at first but I know now that I'm doing the right thing. You'll understand better when you see Kimbay.'

'I cannot imagine you a *fermière*.' He shoved away the pint and signalled a passing barman. 'It is another Flora. I suppose she was there all the time but I did not think about her.' He ordered a Pernod.

'I'd nearly forgotten her myself,' Flora said. 'But horse-breeding is a special kind of farming . . .'

Serge cut her short. 'I do not think you will be able to put the grown-up Flora behind you so easily. 'You have grown sophisticated in your tastes. This existence will not suit you for long, *ma chère*.'

'It doesn't have to suit me for long. Only for two years.'

The Pernod arrived and Serge, with a frown at the measure, asked the question which went to the heart of things like an icicle.

'How can you and I, *ma chère*, Flora, keep our love alive, over two years of separation?'

She was anxiously eager. 'We don't have to be separated, not all the time. I've been thinking about what Victor Mangan had to say. The air and the life really *are* wonderfully healthy at Kimbay. There's already a computer system there and I'll install a fax. You could come and live here for part of the time, get away from city life for a while . . .'

Serge looked at her in genuine astonishment and she felt, for the first time ever, the hugeness of the cultural gulf between them. 'You must know I could never live like that.'

He sounded, Flora thought, offended. 'So far from everything.'

'This *is* the twentieth century.' Flora allowed herself a flash of annoyance. 'And we're not talking about the last frontier.'

'I could not live here. It would not be possible.' It was a statement of fact, not an arguable point.

Flora swallowed. 'Then we will have a commuting relationship. I'll come to an arrangement with Shay that will allow me to spend some of the winter months in Brussels. And in the summertime you can come for the races and parties. We can make it a wonderful two years.'

'Perhaps.'

They left soon after that. Flora, filling a silence in the car, took on the role of guide as they drove along. 'Goffs,' she nodded into the dark as they neared Kimbay, 'where more than half of Ireland's thoroughbred horses are sold. How am I doing? You getting a picture of this fair land?'

'I'm getting a picture,' Serge said.

Daisy had lit fires. They blazed in the living room and in Flora's bedroom and filled Flora's heart with gratitude.

Earlier in the day Flora had stripped her bedroom of its more girlish decorations and filled the gaps with greenery and an exotic rug from Fintan's room. Serge pronounced it *charmant* and in one swift movement dropped his bag and reached for her.

'Brussels is nothing without you,' he said and Flora laughed softly into his neck as he kissed her hair, lifted it, nuzzled her ear, made a slow way toward her mouth. They kissed gently, as if they had all the time in the world. When she felt his tongue part her teeth Flora wound herself closer, feeling the power of his shoulder and back muscles as he held her to him.

'Come,' Serge pulled away, lifted her into his arms. 'We will make use of your virgin bed.'

Slowly, and with infinite care, he undressed her on the bed. Just as slowly, his eyes never leaving her body, he took off his own clothes. When he lay beside her Flora was aching for him, trembling as he took her in his arms again. This time, when they kissed, it was a statement of intent.

Later, they went out to eat. Flora wore the one black wearable dress she'd found in the wardrobe and piled her hair loosely on top of her head. The dark-beamed restaurant was quiet, suiting their mood. They ate well and spoke little, enjoying the peace which comes after lovemaking, not thinking about tomorrow. Everything, Flora felt sure, was going to be all right. They couldn't throw this away.

When tomorrow came she brought Serge on a tour of the stables, proudly showed him her first foal. Leah, doing her weekend shift in the yard, bounded over to be introduced.

'What do you think of him?' She cast a sly look at Serge then back at the foal. 'He's a lovely little fella, isn't he?'

'He is . . . healthy looking,' Serge said.

'Don't you like horses?' Leah was frankly curious. Serge smiled.

'To ride on, yes. I do not care much for the business of breeding them, or even of looking after them. I prefer to leave that to others.'

'You don't know what you're missing.' Leah looked shocked to her marrow. 'Flora could tell you a lot about the joys of mucking out. Couldn't you, Flora?'

'Maybe you could go one better, Leah, and demonstrate?' Flora suggested and Leah tossed her head.

'See you around.' She grinned at Serge. 'We work a seven-day week here so give me a call any time you want that demonstration.' She looked appreciatively at the sharp blue sky. 'Great morning for a ride.'

The fields had miraculously lost their winter sludge and come to life with a searing new green. Flora and Serge rode for an hour and ate ravenously in the kitchen afterwards. Daisy called, gave Serge the once-over and clearly liked what she saw. The approval was mutual but it was next day, just hours before he left, when Flora realized this.

They were walking, after a lazy morning in bed. Serge was wearing a jacket of Ned's, boots belonging to Fintan. I have never, Flora thought, actually *liked* a man as much as this one.

'Do you understand any better now?' They had come to the river. She asked the question as they began to walk along its bank. She didn't look at him. Her eyes, she knew, would betray the anxiety she'd begun feeling that morning again.

'*Mais oui.*' He sighed. 'It is easy to see why you care so much for this place. And the wonderful Madame Sweeney and her family – I understand how you must feel for them too. But you are grieving for your father and have made an emotional decision. I hope it is the right one.'

'I hope so too,' Flora said.

'I will think of you like this, when I am in Brussels.' Serge touched her hair where it blew lightly in the wind. 'I will miss you. I wish this thing had not happened to part us.'

'So,' Flora stopped, looked him full in the face, 'we are to become commuting lovers?'

He nodded. When he started to say something she stopped his mouth with hers, kissing him gently. 'Who knows,' she pulled back, 'we may find it a very good thing to have happened.'

Later, driving to the airport and already starting to miss him, she prayed she was right. In two years so much could change. In two years Kimbay would be a different place, one way or another, and Flo Girl would have been proven a racehorse. Or not.

She supposed that she, Flora, would have changed too. Exactly how, she couldn't imagine, and didn't try.

Chapter Ten

The weeks passed and the season began, slowly, to change. Primroses shot up and the darker yellow of daffodil rings around the trees started to appear in some fields. The days got longer, a little less cold. It all helped Flora deal with the bouts of grief when they came. Made it easier too to live without Serge.

Her life had become the hard-working one of the stud farmer. It was said of breeders that one third made money, one third broke even and one third lost money. She determined to become part of the first group. She chose sires with a mixture of instinct and knowledge, and transported the mares driving the jeep and towing a horsebox. It meant being away from Kimbay for the best part of a day each time but the trips invigorated her. They also helped get her known, and accepted.

On St Patrick's Day she brought Nessa to be covered by a stallion called Fir Bolg, whose looks she fancied as much as his pedigree. 'This one's for Ned,' she told the mare as she was taken away to be teased. She crossed her fingers that all would go well.

The outing left her feeling reasonably confident that the mare might be in foal. She had no way of knowing for sure, and wouldn't even have an indication for at least twenty-one days, but the covering went well and with what seemed almost like enthusiasm on Nessa's part.

She deliberately didn't visit Fairmane, but she did telephone. The trainer invariably assured her that Flo Girl was 'coming on fine' and that he would be in touch. For the moment, and because she was too busy to do anything about it, she ignored the brush-off.

'There's no good burning yourself out in the first few

months.' Daisy, waiting for her one evening when she returned from a trip, was grim. She stood in the kitchen doorway, frowning at the sandwich and glass of wine Flora was making her dinner. Flora knew she was working on a big account for the granary – but she knew too that she would never work this late. Daisy was keeping tabs on her, treating her like a child.

'Have you no home to go to?' Flora was short. 'It's way past office hours.' She pulled a face as she bit into the sandwich. 'Damn bread's gone stale.'

'What do you expect? It's been there over a week. This'll have to stop, Flora. You're gone to skin 'n' bone. Time you got a decent bit of food into you, organized yourself to do a weekly shopping trip.'

'God, Daisy, what brought this on?' Flora dumped the sandwich and opened the fridge. There was milk and some tomatoes. She chose the milk and filled a glass.

'What brought it on is the fact that I've enough to do without having to visit you in some anorexic ward. You'll be no use to either the yard or yourself if you keep going on like this.'

'Have a glass of wine, Daisy, and calm down. I'm not sixteen any longer, you know.'

'Indeed you're not sixteen. You're old enough to know better.'

'Pax, Daisy, and point taken.' Flora made a peace sign. 'I'll stock up. Did you wait around just to tell me this?'

'No. I've been trying to get hold of you for days.' Daisy deposited a collection of telephone memos on the table. 'Most of these you've seen. Don't tell me you haven't. They're neighbours and they mean well. It's time you either accepted their invitations or told them you've become a nun. I'm not making any more excuses for you.'

Flora picked up the memos. The invitations were to dinner, for drinks – even a brunch in one case. She'd already seen all of them.

'I don't suppose you'd . . .' she began but Daisy shook her head.

'Not a snowball's chance in hell,' she said. 'Ring them

yourself. Make your own excuses. Though I think you should accept at least one or two.'

'It's too soon.'

'Rubbish. Your father wouldn't have wanted you living like this. He'd no time for mopers and I agreed with him.'

'That's not what I'm doing.' Flora's protest was genuine.

'Well, that's what it looks like.' Daisy shrugged herself into the coat which had been lying across her shoulders. 'I'm going now. But before I do I want you to promise me you'll come to the hunt ball at least.'

'Will you leave me alone if I do?'

'I'll try.' Daisy grinned and it was arranged. Flora would take her father's place in the Kimbay party for the local hunt ball.

After she left, Flora reluctantly thought about the more general point Daisy had been making. She should, she knew, make a social effort. It was just that she couldn't bear, yet, to become part of the neighbourly life that had been her father's. The Sweeneys apart, she would rather have the company of people who had nothing to do with Kimbay. One person would be enough. Someone she could talk to about ridiculous things like life and love and the pursuit of happiness . . .

She wanted the company of Sophie Butler. She needed the benefit of her old friend's shrewd brain to bounce things off, her infallible suss of situations. And she wanted, very much, to experience again Sophie's glorious, uncomplicated joy in living.

Flora thought about Sophie as she got ready for bed. She hoped her friend hadn't changed. She wanted her to be the Sophie who'd arrived late for the first lecture of their first term at Trinity College Dublin. To be the same, shamelessly exuberant young woman who'd fallen into the bench beside Flora as the lecturer was getting into his stride about the destructive effects of blind passion in Racine. Sophie could have given the lecture herself. But she didn't. She merely destroyed the concentration of every male, including the lecturer, in the hall.

It wasn't that she was beautiful. Sophie, more than anything, fed fantasies. Her lips were too large and soft and her body too angular to fit any convention. On that day in October she'd been wearing a sweeping coat of green velvet and thigh-high boots. Her hair had been Titian-coloured, which was reasonably close to its natural state.

Sophie's affairs had all been characterized by abandon, insecurity, midnight dramas and broken hearts. The afflicted had fallen like ninepins but Sophie had emerged carefree from all encounters. She'd got a good degree to boot.

Afterwards, when everyone split up, Sophie had gone to New York. She'd drifted into journalism there, working on magazines. She and Flora had kept in touch for a while. But then, life and distance intervening, contact had been broken. But not affection, and never friendship.

The last Flora heard Sophie had been working for a Dublin magazine. God knows what she was doing now — unless the unimaginable had happened and she was a kept woman. Flora had already tried, and failed, to get in touch with her. Sophie had moved on, left her apartment and the magazine. She'd abandoned the attempt, but now she would try again, this time through Sophie's mother. Mary Butler should have some idea where her daughter was to be found, although, knowing Sophie, there was no guarantee. Mrs Butler was a fussy, discontented woman, impossible to shut up. It would take energy and time to deal with her but Flora would do it, tomorrow. She would buy in some decent food too.

She took time off the next day and shopped, going mildly wild in the small supermarket and deli in Dunallen. She was heading for the car, feeling equipped for a siege, when she almost bumped into Matt Hopkins.

'Planning a party?' He rebalanced the melon threatening to topple out of the bag in her arms. 'Am I on the guest list?'

'No party. Just stocking up.' She was curt, annoyed at how defensive he made her feel.

'Let me give you a hand.' As he spoke he caught the

underside of the bag and lifted it from her arms. 'Where's your car?'

'There's no need, I can manage.' Flora found herself trotting to keep up with him. He was wearing black denim and he needed a haircut. 'I'm in the car park behind the hotel.'

'Still driving Ned's car?' He stopped at the entrance, scanned the parking lot and saw the elderly maroon Merc for himself. Flora opened the boot and he hefted the bag inside.

'Care for a drink?' He nodded toward the hotel and, when she hesitated, gave a small shrug. 'Drive carefully,' he said and opened the driver's door for her.

'Thanks for your—' Flora began but was interrupted by a voice hailing the trainer from the back of the hotel.

'Matt! I've been waiting *hours*. And now I find you skiving off in the car park . . .'

'Oh, Christ.' The trainer swore quietly under his breath before turning with a smile to greet the woman approaching through the cars.

'You forgot,' she accused without acrimony, 'didn't you? You forgot all about our date.'

'To tell you the truth, yes.' He grinned down at her and she shrugged good-humouredly.

'Story of my life,' she said and turned a round, creamy-skinned face of startling prettiness toward Flora. 'He's heartless,' she said, 'heartless and vain and cruel.'

There's many a true word, Flora thought, spoken in jest. Aloud she said, 'You may be right. But no one's perfect.'

'You won't mind if I grab him from you now, then.' The sleepy, green-flecked eyes which looked up at Flora were childlike, as was the woman herself. To Flora she looked like a voluptuous doll; tiny, fair, tousle-haired and dressed in the brightest Barbie outfit in the wardrobe. She was nothing like the Latin beauty in residence at Fairmane. Matt Hopkins's taste in women was obviously eclectic.

'Be my guest,' Flora said and looked at the trainer in time to catch a flash of irritation cross his face. 'Thanks again, Matt, for your help.' She included them both in a smile as she slipped behind the wheel. This time she didn't look back as she drove away.

At Kimbay she went about the second task she'd set herself for the day.

'Flora, my dear! How lovely to hear your voice.'

Flora was surprised how wavery Sophie's mother sounded. She listened for a while to a litany of health complaints, reflections on the government and worries about Tom, Sophie's father. Not for the first time she wondered how the coupling of Mary and Tom Butler could have produced the extravagant and independent creature who was Sophie. There were no other children. Terrified, perhaps, at what they'd unleashed on the world, Tom and Mary had drawn a halt after Sophie.

Flora, gently as she could, interrupted Mrs Butler. 'I wanted to contact Sophie,' she said, 'can you give me a number for her?'

Mrs Butler made a throat-clearing sound and followed it with a large sniff. 'She's married, you know.' She sounded at once disapproving and melancholy.

'No, I didn't know.' Flora was shocked. She felt, almost, a sense of betrayal too. Sophie, to put it mildly, was not the marrying kind. Or at least she hadn't been. Her opposition to marriage had obviously changed. Of all their crowd at college she had been the one most adamantly anti what she'd called 'that man-made institution'. Marriage, she'd maintained, was for those who needed it – and she didn't. She couldn't see the point. Those who knew her couldn't see the point for Sophie either.

'About a year ago,' Mrs Butler sighed deeply. 'A most unpleasant little ceremony it was, in London. We didn't go, of course, neither Tom nor myself. Not when she was refusing to marry in The Church.'

Flora could hear the capitals, the enormity of the social disgrace Sophie had brought upon her parents. She resisted an urge to ask Mrs Butler how, since she hadn't been there, she knew Sophie's wedding had been unpleasant. She moved instead onto safer ground. 'Whom did she marry?' she asked.

'Some person who works as a cameraman on films. His name is Robert. Robert Gardner. We haven't been told much about him but his name doesn't sound Irish to me. Not Catholic either.'

Insult compounding injury, Flora thought. Mary Butler was proof that prejudice and bigotry were infinite in variety and as lively in the Irish middle classes as they were amongst the old French bourgeoisie. She would probably get along fine with Monique.

'Where do they live? Do you have a phone number?' She asked the question more assertively this time.

'Oh, they live here, in Dublin,' Mrs Butler said and Flora felt a wave of relief. 'They've an apartment in the city centre. Not the sort of place we'd ever want to visit anyway. The violence in the town is terrible, you know. But of course you wouldn't know, living down there in—'

'Do you think I could have the number?'

'All right, dear, all right. I'll get it for you. Don't go away.' The phone went down and Flora waited. The number, neither beside the phone nor readily in her head, was obviously not one Mary Butler dialled very often.

Flora tried it immediately. She was surprised and gratified to get her friend straight away.

'I don't believe this!' Sophie's throaty laugh was unchanged. 'I was thinking about you yesterday, Flora. Your gorgeous little brother and his band crossed my orbit . . .'

'Hands off, Sophie, he's too young and he's not your type,' Flora laughed.

'They're never too young and they're all my type. But don't worry, I didn't get close enough to actually talk to him,' Sophie said but didn't, Flora noticed, mention the restrictions of marriage. 'Where are you, anyway?' she asked, 'Can we meet?'

'I'm at home. At Kimbay. And yes please, Sophie, let's meet.'

'How long are you going to be around for?'

'Indefinitely.'

'Oh? What's wrong?' Sophie's voice sharpened. 'The Brussels gravy train run into a siding?'

'Something like that. My father died, Sophie.' Bleakly, Flora listened to the shocked silence on the phone.

Sophie's voice, when it came at last, was quiet. 'God, I'm so sorry, Flora. When did he die?'

'About six weeks ago.' Six weeks and three days actually, but Flora was trying not to count. 'He left me a half-share in the yard. It's a bit complicated but the bottom line is I'm working at Kimbay.'

'You're stud farming?'

'Yes.' Flora, remembering the glamour and world travel they'd promised themselves, gave a small laugh.

'Well, I'm married,' Sophie said the words with finality.

'Why?' It was all Flora could think to say.

'Seemed like a good idea at the time.' Sophie's light tone told her nothing. 'Look,' Sophie rushed on, 'why don't I come down there this weekend? I'm not working and Robert's away. Sounds like we've a lot to catch up on.'

They arranged it. Putting down the phone Flora felt a mixture of gladness and anticipation. It would be good to see Sophie. It would be interesting to see how, and if, she'd changed. Saturday would reveal all.

Flora was in the yard when Leah appeared there after school and saddled up Jumbo, the hacking horse she'd been riding for years. She was flippant and dissatisfied-looking, a sure sign she'd had a run-in with Daisy.

'Wanted me to start studying *seconds* after I arrived home. I told her to get a life, that my brain's been addled enough for one day. You'll have to talk to her for me, Flora. She'll listen to you.'

'Wouldn't dream of it,' Flora shook her head.

'Thanks a lot, friend.' Leah was morosely sarcastic. 'Must say, though, you've got plenty to say in car parks in Dunallen . . .'

Flora groaned. 'God, but people have little to talk about.'

'Well, if you want to have secret meetings with your trainer and his *secretary* then you should do it under cover of darkness. You might stand some chance of going unnoticed that way.'

'It wasn't exactly what you'd call a meeting – more an accidental encounter.'

'Doesn't matter. Truth's boring, Flora. The old biddies want something to get their teeth into and you're the flavour of the month. What did you and Marigold talk about anyway? She can be a real ding-bat.'

'Marigold – you mean the little blonde?'

'The same. Soon to be secretary at Fairmane. She's more than just a pretty face.' Leah adjusted her hat and gave Jumbo a rub to remind her the ride was still on. 'She knows how to look out for herself, does our Marigold. *And* she's gone through what passes for eligible males in these parts like a dose of salts.'

'She's very pretty,' Flora conceded.

'She's fun, too,' Leah was magnanimous. 'Still,' she sighed deeply, 'it's sad to see the fall of a man like Matt Hopkins. I'd hoped for greater things from him. Even that he might take note of my humble self. Maybe an older man is what I need. It won't last,' she brightened, 'the children will put him off. Can't see him bothering—'

'Children? What children?'

Leah made an impatient face and grabbed Jumbo's bridle. 'Marigold's children. She's got two. A boy and a girl. Lovely kids, but wild as hares.'

'She can't have! She's practically a child herself.'

'Huh. Might look like one but she's definitely a mother. She married Declan Kennedy. Do you remember him?'

'Who could forget him?' Flora was dry. Declan Kennedy was the spoilt, ne'er-do-well son of one of the wealthier local families. One view held that he was charming but feckless, another that he was a petty crook. Flora wondered which had prevailed. 'How did the marriage work out?' she asked.

'It didn't. He buggered off when Marigold was preggers with the little boy. The word was that the guards were keen to have a chat with him.'

So, Flora thought, the petty crook had prevailed. 'And Marigold?'

'She stayed on in the Kennedy house. Old Mrs Kennedy does a *lot* of babysitting.' Leah swung herself into the saddle.

'But what does Marigold know about being a trainer's secretary?'

Leah grinned down. 'Enough, I'd say. She's a bookie's daughter. Course, her secretarial duties may not be everything. She may be a replacement for Bianca Jagger too. She left a couple of weeks ago, *whoever* that South American was. Probably had enough of the cold.'

'You're remarkably well informed about local events.' Flora was admiring.

'Not much to do around here but talk about what people do.' Leah's dissatisfied look had returned. 'Wait'll you're home a bit longer – you'll be gossiping too.'

She jerked the reins and Jumbo, at an easy pace, moved off. Flora watched them and wondered how a set of twins could be so utterly different. Leah would go, hit the world like a cracker, as soon as she finished school. Luke would stay on, make horses and, hopefully, Kimbay his world.

By Saturday Flora was experiencing an inkling of what Leah had meant about the joys of gossip. For days without a break she had been talking, thinking and dreaming horses. She craved conversation about anything else – gossip would have been fine, but a hands-on conversation about life, love and the pursuit of happiness would be even better. Sophie couldn't come a minute too soon – and if she could persuade or bribe her to stay a week, or two, then Flora would do so.

It was mid afternoon when Flora, standing restlessly at a window, saw a car arrive up the avenue. With a lifting heart she ran, opened the front door – and stopped short on the top step. The person getting out of the car was Victor Mangan. He waved, immaculate in a silvery grey raincoat, and came slowly up to greet her.

'I was passing,' he grinned widely, 'and thought I'd call.' He had a gold tooth she hadn't noticed before. Too ostentatious by half, she thought.

'Do come in,' she said politely before she turned, silently fuming, to lead the way to the living room. She managed a social smile when she offered him a drink.

'Brandy. A small one.' He grinned and Flora wished he wouldn't. The tooth was really a no-no. She poured his drink and one for herself too. 'I fibbed when I said I was just passing by.' He didn't sit down and for that much Flora was glad. 'I really came to see how you were.'

'That was kind.' She tried to keep sarcasm out of her voice. Tried too to feel better about him. It took all kinds to make a world – even property developers had to live.

'So – how are you? And how's life on the farm working out?' He gestured with his glass in the direction of the fields outside.

'Extremely well,' Flora said. 'Much better, in fact, than I'd anticipated.' She hesitated. 'I'm enjoying it.'

'You made the right decision then?'

'*Please*, Mr Mangan, we've covered this ground before. I'm expecting a friend and I don't —'

He held up a hand. 'I was wrong, and I'm sorry. And please call me Victor.'

'I'm sure you'll find an alternative location for your casino, Victor.' Flora smiled sweetly. 'Maybe you could get vacant possession of the Hill of Tara?'

'And have kings turn in their graves? Ambiance all wrong.' He shrugged, finished his drink. 'Look, why don't you and I have dinner? We could talk – and not just about the farm. We could', he smiled into her eyes, 'get to know one another.'

Flora, disbelieving, took a step away from him. He uses a sun lamp, she thought, and he takes me for a complete fool.

'I'm sorry,' she said. 'This is the busiest time of year on a stud. I don't have time.' She took the still-unfinished glass of brandy from his hand. 'In fact I must leave you right now.'

His smile didn't falter. 'Let's make it a working lunch, then.'

'Look, Victor, I'd rather not. We don't have anything to talk about.' She smiled icily. 'I'm really not interested.'

106

'Shame. I'd rather thought we'd find *something* in common. Still, since you're obviously a woman who knows her mind I won't push the issue. My offer stands,' he produced and handed her his card, 'so if you change your mind, about *either* of my offers, please call me.'

He had been gone an hour before Sophie arrived. This time, when Flora heard the car on the gravel outside, she checked its occupant from the window before rushing to let Sophie in. They stood on the steps, old friends sensing the changes in one another, each of them wanting things to be immediately all right, be as they'd always been.

'You look great,' Sophie fell on Flora with a hug. 'The ice queen in mufti. How *are* you? Has it been terrible?'

'I'm fine, fine.' Flora linked her arm, urged her into the house. Sophie had, she saw, quite a large bag with her. A good sign. 'Tell me how *you* are? You don't look a day over thirty.'

'Watch it. I'm still a year younger than you.' Sophie laughed, kicked the door shut behind them with her foot. 'Country air might suit you, my pet, but that's my quota for today.' She shivered. 'Everything where it used to be? Armchairs still that way?'

In the living room she prowled, firing questions, remembering weekends spent at Kimbay when they'd been at college. Flora, from one of the armchairs, watched her, answering when she could get a word in. Sophie's particular kind of beauty had, if anything, become more compelling with the years. Her hair, in a mass of ripple curls to her shoulders, was darker than it had been and she was wearing a leather pilot's jacket and leggings in a shade of cranberry.

'Sit, Sophie,' Flora said at last and Sophie sat, legs curled up and head thrown back in a way she'd always had. She looked languorous and sexy – and she wasn't even trying. Lazily she poked with her foot at the dozing labrador.

'Good to see you're still here too,' she said.

Flora got glasses, opened a bottle of a red Bordeaux '82 and put it between them. It was what they'd always used to drink and she'd got a case of it for the weekend.

'So, you got married,' she said.

'Yup. And you didn't. Wise woman.' Sophie was wry, her real feelings impossible to gauge.

'He must be special,' Flora said, 'to have won you to the joys of monogamy.'

'*Was* special,' Sophie corrected and gave a short laugh. 'And it was monogamy for one, as it transpired. Bizarre as you may find it, my pet, it's muggins here who kept the pact, played the faithful spouse.'

'Oh . . .' Flora digested this, a first in Sophie's love-life. Her friend had been notoriously the one to find a new love, usually before casting aside the old.

'It's all in the name of good clean fun when you don't make promises,' Sophie's grin was crooked. 'It's sort of different when you commit . . .'

'Why did you marry him?' Flora was genuinely curious.

Sophie hugged herself and sat forward. Her wide violet eyes were unblinking as she spoke. 'I went out of control,' she said, 'lost the head – and the heart. Primitive stuff, I promise you. In my own defence I must tell you that Robert's beautiful and funny and smooth. He's so smooth he's almost convincing. He makes advertising videos and he's away a lot. Flirtations are the name of the game, and those I can live with.' She took a steadying breath and slumped back into the armchair. 'A full-blown affair's something else.' She shrugged. 'And that, it would appear, is what Robert has been having since a few weeks after we married.'

'He told you about it? Does he want to leave?'

'I don't know what he wants to do and no, he didn't tell me. She did. She called to the apartment a week ago, gave me the benefit of her pain and guilt. Silly cow. But I haven't a bull's eye what Robert wants to do. He's so twisted he probably doesn't know himself, except that he'll want to have his cake and eat it.'

'Where is he now?'

'Italy, for another week at least. I could pretend nothing's happened, of course, get on with things.' She grimaced. 'Only I can't see myself doing that. I'll probably attack him the moment he walks through the door.' She toyed absently with Dipper's ears. 'It's more than the cheating, though.' She was thoughtful. 'He's just not the person I thought he was when I married him.'

They sat quietly for a while, pondering the age-old truth of marriage disillusion. Then they talked again.

'Funny thing is,' Sophie said, 'I always thought you'd be the one to marry. You always picked such *nice* men to get involved with.'

'I'm involved with a more than just a nice man at the moment,' Flora admitted.

'Oh?' Sophie looked around the room as if she expected Flora's man to materialize in a corner.

'He's not here.' Flora heard the wistful note in her own voice. 'He's French and he's wonderful and I hope to God I don't lose him because of Kimbay . . .'

'Sounds like you might be in love?' Sophie said. 'Are you?'

'Yes,' Flora said.

'So – he's moving here, right?'

''Fraid not. We're going to commute . . . sort of.'

'Mmm. Interesting. Hope it works out for you. He's worth it, is he? This anxiety you're so obviously putting yourself through?'

'Yes, Sophie, he's worth it.'

Flora described Serge, told anecdotes which brought him to life for her friend. Then she told her about Kimbay, why she'd decided to stay. Sophie didn't understand but it didn't matter. It was great just to be talking to her, hearing her objective and witty view of things.

The day grew short outside and darkness ended it. Still they talked. Flora got up once to get them food and Sophie a couple of times to get them wine. Even when it became completely dark they didn't turn the lights on, and in the flickering shadows thrown by the fire found even more to say to one another.

Sophie had abandoned a regular income and thrown herself upon the waters of freelancing. It was working well, she said, so far. 'It's a hard graft,' she said, 'but it's fun too.

My New York contacts are good, I send them a lot of stuff.'
She nibbled critically at a piece of cheese, wrinkling her
nose. 'I have come to believe,' she pointed the cheese at
Flora, 'that men, on the whole, are a pack of rats. They're
cheats and they're users and most of all they're cowardly.
They bring nothing but grief to women and I've gone right
off them. But,' she bit into the cheese and this time stabbed
a finger at Flora, 'let me tell you something, old friend.
Women are changing. They *know* now they deserve better.
I've changed. *I* know I deserve better. Men are wonderful
when it comes to amusement and pleasure – and I intend
keeping them in that pocket of my life from now on.'

'That's not exactly a dramatic change,' Flora giggled,
'that's where you've always had them.'

'You're right,' Sophie waved a dismissive hand, 'but
before it was instinct. Now I've experience and knowledge
behind me and I realize I was right all along. And if you,
my old friend, have any sense at all you'll pay heed to what
I've learned.' She stretched and reached for the wine. 'Let's
get drunk, Flora. Rotten, mouldy, stinking drunk . . .'

Chapter Eleven

A few weeks after Sophie's visit, just before Easter, Shay went to the Newmarket sales. A week of pressing horseflesh, discussing trends and fancies, was the only thing which could persuade him to leave Kimbay. He'd gone every year that Flora could remember and she'd never given it much thought. But then she'd never had to take charge of the yard in his absence before.

'The total immersion helps him put the winter behind him,' Daisy confided after he left. 'He'll be easier when he comes back. More agreeable.'

Flora hoped so. Shay had become taciturn to the point of being mute and she guessed that the reality of Ned's death was getting to him. The changes it had brought to his life were, if anything, greater than those to Flora's own. For thirty years Shay had been the calm, measured influence at Kimbay, the straight-man foil to his boss's volatile personality. All that had changed with Ned's death. Shay was having to adjust to working with Flora – a woman, and one who had only a fraction of Ned's savvy and real knowledge. Probably even more unsettling was the reality that responsibility for Kimbay's future now lay a firm 50 per cent in his hands.

Flora's relationship with Shay was beginning, in small measure, to mirror his partnership with her father. A bank loan had been necessary to see the stud through until October and the yearling sales at Goffs. Shay, with much muttering, had made it clear that he felt uncomfortable about the actual trip to the bank.

Flora had gone instead and, with the help of figures worked out with Daisy, had negotiated a deal which gave them both leeway and generous terms. Shay had been ungrudging in his appreciation, and the beginnings of a pattern to their relationship had gradually emerged. Flora would be the public face of Kimbay, Shay the private one. It would suit them both and work well for Kimbay – if it could be maintained.

Between them, too, Flora and Shay had organized a tight schedule for the week he would be away. Tobias Malone had been persuaded to add extra hours to his day and a part-time stable lad had been taken on. Leah, off school for Easter, would be working full-time in the yard for the week.

Shay had been gone three days when Tobias came off his moped and badly sprained his ankle. He came hobbling into the yard on a crutch next day but Flora insisted he go home. There were only a few days left until Shay returned. They would manage until then.

That same day the yard had visitors. Flora was working out feed allocations when Luke came to tell her. 'Don't know either of them.' He was curt. 'They say they're interested in buying a yearling but my father never sells from the yard. They want to see you. I said you wouldn't sell either.'

'Did you?' Flora made a mark on the chart. She didn't look at him. 'I'll decide things like that for myself, Luke. Where are they?'

'Outside,' he jerked his head. 'Leah's keeping an eye on them. I think you should tell them to come back when my father's here.'

Flora studied his young, resentful face. 'Why should I do that?' she asked.

Luke, meeting her eye, was cool. 'Because he'll know how to deal with them and you won't.'

'I might surprise you.' Flora, eyebrow raised, handed him the feeding schedule. 'Get on with this, Luke, will you?'

Outside, she saw the two men immediately. They were standing just inside the yard, one of them smoking. Walking toward them she took a closer look but couldn't recall having met either before.

112

'Can I help you?' she asked. She was several inches taller than the man who reached out a hand in greeting. Under a straggle of white hair his face was square and red-veined. His smile was open.

'Tom Kelly,' he said. 'I knew your father. Sorry about his passing.' He made a benediction sign over the yard with a square, red hand. 'Looks like you're doing a grand job here, Miss Carolan.'

'Thank you.' Flora looked questioningly at his leaner, tall companion.

'This is Con Merrigan,' Tom Kelly introduced them, 'my right hand in matters of horse dealing.' Con Merrigan nodded, stubbed his cigarette underfoot. He wore a belted tweed coat and leather gloves and looked like a man intent on business.

'Might as well get to the point,' Tom Kelly rubbed his hands together. 'It's like this, Miss Carolan. I'm looking for a nice yearling. Nothing fancy, I'm not buying for myself but I'm not buying for one of the sheiks either.' He gave a short guffaw of laughter. 'I just want something with four good legs that might make a decent miler. I'm told you might have something ready for sale here.'

'Your information's not altogether accurate.' Flora pulled a regretful face. 'We've a few we're getting ready for Goffs but we're not keen to sell yet. I'm sorry.'

'That's a terrible pity. You wouldn't like to think about it? My buyer's an impulsive man and he's in the mood to get himself a yearling right now. It'd be a handy thing for you to turn a few bob on a colt before the sales.'

'But I'd prefer to do business at Goffs. Maybe I could meet you there?'

'My man won't wait that long. I can do you a turn today, give you a good price and take a colt off your hands.'

'I'm sorry,' Flora shook her head, 'I think I'll wait for the sales.'

'At that rate I'll keep the chequebook in my pocket.' Con Merrigan spoke for the first time. He had a clipped, not unpleasant voice. 'Fine yard,' he looked around. 'I see you've got a few empty boxes. Would you be interested in boarding a mare for me?'

Flora hesitated. Keeping a mare on a board-and-lodging basis would bring in some cash. Not a lot, but some. 'Depends,' she said.

'It would only be for a month or so, I'm having work done at my own place and she's uncomfortable there at the moment.' He smiled his serious smile around the yard. 'She'd like it here. You'd be obliging me greatly if you could see your way to doing it. I'll pay in advance, cash, so as not to put you to any expense.'

Flora made up her mind. 'Why not?' she said, and they made arrangements for the animal to be delivered next morning. She allowed herself a feeling of satisfaction. Boarding wasn't something her father or Shay had ever been keen on but she could see no reason why not to, in this case. The box was empty, it would bring in some money and she would do the extra work herself.

Con Merrigan's mare, a fairly undistinguished-looking grey, arrived early next day. Flora let her loose in a paddock where she ambled off happily. Only Luke had been openly disapproving about the arrangement. Boarding, he said, was more trouble than it was worth. Flora would prove him wrong.

She had just got back to the yard when Matt Hopkins, at a quick stride, arrived from the front of the house. 'G'day, he called, 'just making a neighbourly call. Everything all right?'

Flora nodded, resisting an urge to ask him if he'd have asked Shay the same thing. No point being too touchy about things. 'Fine,' she smiled, 'absolutely fine. You do know Shay's away?'

'So I heard. How's it feel to be in charge?'

'Busy,' Flora said, 'it feels busy.'

Leah, watching from across the yard, mimed a swoon. Flora frowned, wishing she would stop.

'I'm taking up too much of your time.' The trainer was brisk, mistaking her frown for impatience with him. 'Just dropped over to tell you that Flo Girl's coming along fine.

114

I'm still thinking of entering her at Gowran Park at the end of August. How's that sound to you?'

'Sounds good. I like Gowran Park.'

'I have your approval, then, to go ahead?' His tone was dry.

'Please do.'

'Good. I'll have a word with Luke then and be off. Any idea where he is?'

'Walking out one of the yearlings. Should be back soon. When would be a good time for me to come over and see Flo Girl?' This time it was the trainer who frowned in concentration.

'I'm coming and going a bit at the moment, but call any time,' he said. 'Introduce yourself to Lorcan McNulty. He's my stable jockey and he's doing very well with Flo Girl. Could be the man to ride her, eventually. Be seeing you.' The labrador lolloped after him as strode across the yard.

Watching him, Flora thought how ill-contained his impatience was – and how well he got on with animals. At the arch he turned and told the dog to stay. Dipper, disconsolate, sat and followed the trainer with his eyes.

'That dog has no bloody loyalty.' Flora whistled him back before returning to work. She was short minutes into mucking out a box when the trainer reappeared at the door.

'That grey mare out there has a dirty nose.' He was harsh. 'Get her out of the paddock. And for Christ's sake don't let her back into the yard. She'll infect the whole place.'

'Oh, God, no!' Flora stared at him in shocked disbelief. 'She can't have – I didn't notice – '

'You weren't looking, and you should have been. Certainly Luke should have noticed her, or Tobias.'

'Tobias is ill and Luke hasn't seen her yet.' Flora felt sick. 'I took her in as a boarder this morning.'

'You *what*? Without checking her out? Good Christ, Flora . . .'

'Right, so I was wrong,' Flora snapped, 'but I'm going to get her right out of here.'

Swiftly, a frantic plan already forming in her head, she grabbed her jacket with the keys to the jeep. She knew only too well that a dirty nose could be the beginnings of a viral 'flu or cough which could spread like wildfire to every horse in the stables. If it happened it would be her fault.

The grey mare was still alone in the paddock where she'd left her. She was docile, allowing herself be loaded into the still hitched-up horsebox at the back of the jeep without trouble.

'Where are you taking her?' The trainer helped her close the horse in.

'Back where she came from.' Flora was brief. Anywhere away from here, was what she thought.

It took forty minutes to find the address Con Merrigan had given her. The large, showy modern bungalow wasn't what she'd expected. Its pseudo-Spanish arches and wrought iron were not, somehow, the style of living she'd pictured for the reserved Merrigan. Spinning up the white gravelled driveway she noticed a small, reassuring paddock.

The yellow front door was opened to her second ring by a lank-haired, vexatious-looking woman in an overall.

'Mr Merrigan in?' Flora was crisp.

'No one of that name living here.'

Flora put her foot in the door as the woman began to close it. 'I was given this address by a Mr Con Merrigan. And I've brought his mare back.'

The woman peered past her at the horsebox and pulled her lips into a thin pucker. 'There's no Merrigan here, I told you,' she said, 'and no horse either. It was sold and taken away this morning. Man who took it away's probably the Merrigan you're looking for.'

'Who sold it?' Under the woman's scathing curiosity Flora was beginning to feel more and more like a fool.

'The Donovans sold it, since they owned it. They own this house too. They're gone to Dublin for the day so you'd best come back tomorrow and talk to them. I've my work to do.'

'What was their horse like?' This time Flora put her hand against the door to stop the woman closing it.

116

'Grey-white,' the woman snapped. 'Lonely old divil of a thing.' Her eyes were cold. 'They never rode it. Only had it for show.'

'Look, there's been a mix-up,' Flora said. 'It's their mare in my box. I'm going to leave her in the paddock. Here's my number. They can phone me when they get back. I'll explain then.'

The drive home, without the grey mare, calmed her down. At Kimbay Luke's righteousness was balanced by Leah's genuine understanding – and relief in the knowledge that the mare had not had contact with any of the other animals while she'd been at Kimbay. She'd been spotted in time, it was unlikely her infection would spread.

Flora, crossing her fingers, put the episode down to experience.

She was almost asleep when the phone rang that night. Listening as it pealed through the empty house, she willed it to stop and buried herself deeper under the bedclothes. But it rang on, and on, until she knew she would have to pick it up.

'Must be those Donovan people, or Merrigan.' She padded down the stairs, her father's dressing gown doing a bad job of keeping her warm. Dipper stayed where he was, refusing to bestir himself from the foot of her bed.

'Hello.' She knew, as soon as she picked it up, that answering had been a mistake. The approach was different but the voice was the same as before.

'Flora, my dear Flora,' he gave a sniggering whisper, 'did I get you out of your bed? All tucked up and alone, were we? Tell me, Flora, what you wear —'

With a silent scream of disgust she slammed the receiver down. Shaking, she gathered the dressing gown tightly around her and sank down against the wall.

'Why me?' Her voice echoed back to her in the hallway. 'Why is he picking on me? I can't deal with this . . . It's too horrible . . .' Shivering, she rocked to and fro. She was still shivering when she got up and made her way to the warm kitchen.

117

'The lousy, sick bastard.' Anger gave her back some courage. She waited until her eyes became accustomed to the dark before she made some tea. She certainly wasn't going to turn on the light and put herself on view to anyone watching outside.

Fear receded but disgust stayed, and her sense of violation. She stood, in the shadows to the side of the window, and looked down into the yard. There was a lot to be done. There could be 'flu in the yard. She would need her strength in the morning.

'I am *not* going to let this get to me.' In the dark kitchen she swore resoundingly at her persecutor and felt a lot better. 'I'm not going to live my life in fear because of some sad, sick pervert. I'm on my own and I've got to learn to deal with things like this. I'll figure out a way to cobble him – spread the word that I'm not intimidated, to begin with.'

Feeling resolute, and as if, somehow, she'd taken charge of another bit of her life, she reported the call to the guards in Dunallen. She couldn't quite bring herself to take a knife to bed with her, but she did slip a heavy poker under her pillow. She slept fitfully but her resolve didn't weaken.

The ride to Fairmane next day was just what she needed after her sleepless night. She arrived at a busy time and when she asked for the trainer was told he was in the office. She tied up Cormac, and after an instinctive, and hard, look at the office window, made for Flo Girl's box on her own. She wasn't sure exactly what she thought to see at the window. Marigold could hardly be expected to work in view of the yard.

At the door of Flo Girl's box she stopped. The trainer was inside, rubbing down the filly. As she watched he gave the horse an affectionate pat. 'Good girl,' he said. 'You're going to be a bit of all right.'

Flora stepped back, then clunked the sole of her boot loudly on the cobbles as she approached the door again. 'Morning,' she called. 'Security's fairly open around here. I've been making myself quite at home.'

'I've got cameras everywhere.' The trainer's brows came

118

together. His low voice was furious. 'Sensors too, at the gate and along the avenue.'

'I didn't mean . . .'

She shrugged, turned back to the horse, cursed silently to herself. What the hell possessed me to say that, she thought. She bit her lip to stop herself saying any more. Of course he was security conscious. Any trainer or stable owner with valuable animals took precautions since Shergar. The kidnapping of £10 million worth of thoroughbred stallion had caused a seismic shock in the bloodstock industry. No one, least of all a trainer as ambitious as Matt Hopkins, could afford to be casual since that February day in '83.

'Flo Girl's looking well.' She strove for a friendly tone. Only the day before he'd done Kimbay a service and she'd just insulted his security arrangements. 'Thanks again for yesterday,' she said. 'The mare didn't actually come into contact with any of the others so we're probably all right.'

'Did you sort out with the owner why he dumped an infected animal on Kimbay?'

'Well, the situation was a bit strange.' Flora told him about leaving the grey mare, and her phone number.

He smiled, eyes mocking, when she'd finished. 'What an innocent you are, Ms Carolan. Don't expect to hear from either of those parties again. That animal was dumped on Kimbay deliberately. That's why they waited until Shay was out of the way. They knew you'd fall for it.'

Flora flushed, deeply and painfully. 'But why', she had trouble getting the words out, 'would anyone want to infect the yard?'

'God knows,' the trainer was impatient. 'Figure it out yourself, Flora. It's a competitive industry. An infection in the middle of the breeding season would make Kimbay mares unwelcome with stallion owners. Or it could be someone with an old grudge against Ned. These things happen all the time. It's your job to be on the alert, especially at this time of the year.'

'But he gave me the address, Con Merrigan did. If he knew the mare was infected why would he do that?'

119

'Because your friend Merrigan is long gone and not at all worried about you returning the mare. It's money well spent, as far as he's concerned. And the Donovans will have figured something's wrong and won't want to be involved.' He slapped his thigh impatiently with his hand. 'Look, Flora, this is all very interesting but I've a busy morning ahead. Lorcan's going to work Flo Girl with a couple of others over six furlongs. You can watch if you like.'

'I'd like,' Flora was subdued. She felt, perversely, both grateful for his help and annoyed that she should be obligated to him. Though maybe she shouldn't feel *too* obligated. He'd been at the right place at the right time and could hardly have ignored the mare's dirty nose.

'Do you think they really wanted to buy a yearling?' she asked.

'Without a doubt. Probably thought they could wheedle something out of you there, too.'

They went together to where they could view the horses racing and watched as Lorcan McNulty on Flo Girl slowly went ahead and galloped into a comfortable lead. Flora's heart warmed to the willing, sparky filly as she went steadily up a hill and without losing pace took the last furlong. Beside her she sensed the trainer's excitement. His hand touching hers was a shock.

'She runs one hell of a good race.' His good humour had returned and he was buoyant, smiling into her eyes.

'Does she always run that well?' Flora looked away, back to where horse and rider were returning across the fields.

'Better, sometimes. She'll be a mile-and-a-halfer, do the Curragh distance no problem.'

'Let's hope you're right, and that she doesn't break a leg or anything.'

As soon as she'd said it Flora could have, again, bitten her tongue. But it was how she felt; dreamily hopeful but very, very cautious.

Chapter Twelve

He'd written the letter on the back of a menu. This seemed, to Sophie, appropriately callous. What Robert had brought to her life by way of fun and good sex had been invariably ruined by a ruthless selfishness. His goodbye letter, dashed off as he dined with his current love, was simply typical.

So typical that as she read it she realized that she had, in fact, been expecting it for some time.

She shifted a pile of magazines, most of them Robert's, and threw herself onto the two-seater leather settee which had been his sole contribution to the apartment's furnishings. She'd never liked it but, like a lot of other things in their marriage, she'd done nothing about changing it. The settee was all style and hard lines and offered no comfort. Very much a metaphor for marriage to Robert, in fact. He'd been married before. Sophie wondered if he'd brought a settee to that marriage too . . . But it was the only seating they had and so she tucked her legs under her and read the letter again.

It wasn't long. The fun had gone, he wrote. They'd made a mistake. Both of them. He didn't know what *she* wanted out of the marriage but he, 'sure as hell', didn't want what they had. Robert was fond of phrases from American films. The next couple of lines read like a B movie script. 'It's over, sweetness,' he wrote, 'time to wrap up the good times and move on while the memories are still okay. Maybe, in time, we can meet as friends. I'd like that.'

Of course he'd like that. She'd be a sort of insurance policy, a bit on the side for lonely days.

He'd added a PS. It told her more about his reasons for going than anything he'd written in the main letter. 'I'm leaving the country anyway,' he wrote, 'off to Florida for a three-year stint with a film company there. Clean start all round, Sophie, okay? Keep the settee, and anything else, to remember me by. I'll be travelling light.'

He was vermin. A moronic shit. He was a retarded adolescent who knew nothing about life or what it was to care for someone. He hadn't even come to terms with the fundamental rule of relationships – which was that you cared, even a little would do, for the other person as well as yourself. She hoped the alligators got him in Florida, though she thought it likely that even they would find him indigestible.

Sophie fumed on, refusing to cry. The death of love didn't surprise her. She'd never, until Robert, expected it to last. In Robert's case she had foolishly thought love would endure for some time. She certainly hadn't ever anticipated him being the one to walk away. But he had, and she had become a statistic. She was a deserted wife.

'Teach you to fly in the face of your deepest instinct and conviction, Sophie my girl,' she told herself. She made a torpedo of the letter-menu and nose-dived it across the room. It landed, upright, in the empty grate. 'Tried hard, didn't like it. That'll be my defence against marriage from now on. It's back to basics with me – so goodbye Robert and hello again to serial monogamy.'

She felt the tears begin and closed her eyes, letting them seep from between her lids and down her cheeks. They weren't just for Robert. She was crying too for that brief period of naive stupidity when she'd believed love would conquer all, believed in and completely trusted Robert. For a while there too she'd been convinced that male chauvinism, if not dead, was certainly on the wane. She'd even hoped for equality in her marriage. Now it was back to the merry-go-round. But this time she wouldn't get off. Men, from now on, would remain sex objects and for amusement. It was the way they'd treated women for centuries and someone had to redress the balance, sometime.

After a while she poured herself a long gin and tonic

and sat with it in the window, looking down at the street below. The apartment was in Temple Bar, the burgeoning left-bankish area of the city. Life in the streets went on twenty hours a day, sometimes all of the twenty-four. Sophie liked it that way. The apartment was hers, her only investment ever, her one wise move.

Now that she had it to herself she would persuade Flora to visit for a few days. Their weekend together had been good. Sophie would have stayed longer if she hadn't been rushing back for a call, which never came, from bloody Robert. Flora needed to be put wise on marriage, which seemed to be the direction she was headed with the Frenchman. Which might not, of course, be a complete disaster. It had been Sophie's experience that the married French male handled the subtleties of marriage better than either his Irish or British counterpart. Whatever, it was something she and Flora could discuss. She would invite her soon.

She hadn't told Flora quite everything about her own life. She hadn't told her about the cocaine tripping she'd been coming off when she met Robert. She'd told her nothing either about the reality of her high-living days in New York, how it had caught up with her, almost fatally, and was the real reason she'd come home.

Sophie had faced her choices, starkly, on the morning she'd woken and discovered that she'd lost an entire week of her life. Lost it in a strange bedroom and with a strange man who giggled when she asked him about the inexplicable cuts and bruises covering her body. She still had nightmares in which she developed AIDS.

In the shattering, drug-free week which followed she'd faced the fact that she couldn't resist the underside of New York. As long as she stayed it would continue to suck her in until, eventually, it would destroy her. She would end up a knicker-wetting bag lady, wandering friendless through the grimier boroughs of the city. She bought a one-way ticket and came home.

It had taken her a year to settle, find her feet, stop

being fidgety. She'd been half-way there when she met Robert. And now he was gone. Another episode over, as he might say himself. Time for a little therapy.

In the kitchen she found a carving knife. It was Robert's, she didn't cook. Slowly, and with infinite care, she began to shred the leather settee. It took forty-five languorous minutes before she was satisfied enough to stand back, admire its complete destruction with pleasure. She went to bed then and to sleep, accepting, as she drifted off, that Robert was probably right and it had all been a lousy mistake. Thank God for work, she thought, and for economic independence and for the fact that they hadn't had children.

In the morning she phoned Flora. 'Leave those wretched animals for a couple of days,' she said, 'and come up to town. We can shop and eat and look at people. Be hedonists . . .'

She was surprised, and very glad, when Flora said yes immediately. She would come on Saturday, but could only spend the day.

They met early, and had breakfast in Bewleys. Flora hadn't been there for an age and over-indulged on the cherry buns. 'I shouldn't have done that,' she groaned. 'I need to buy a ball or evening gown and I'm bloated as a whale now. You don't mind if we traipse around a bit, do you? I need to get some other things as well.'

'Why the evening clobber? You planning a posh party?'

'Not exactly. I'm going to a hunt ball. We country folk are quite stylish, you know. I want to look decent and all my proper clothes are in Brussels.'

'Hmm. We've all heard about hunt balls, Flora my pet. Stylish is not the word most commonly used about them. Debauched is more usual. So's wild. However, if you say stylish then I'm sure that's what *your* hunt ball will be. Let's get you a frock.'

In Grafton Street they stood deciding where to go. 'Smooth stylish?' Sophie asked. 'Or modish and under-stated? What're we looking for, exactly?'

'Something I'll like,' Flora said. They began with

Brown Thomas, going slowly through the different fashion outlets in the grand old department store.

'Do you have a partner for this outing, or do hunt balls ignore boring social niceties?' Sophie asked as Flora tried and rejected dresses.

'Yes and no. I'm going as part of the Kimbay party. My father went every year and I feel I should, this year at least, put in an appearance and maintain the tradition.'

'Who'll be going along? Shay and Daisy?'

'The twins too, for the first time.' Flora struggled into a long black lycra tube. 'In fact the party seems to be growing by the day. The twins have got themselves partners and a trainee-jockey friend of Luke's wants to tag along too. And now Daisy tells me that Matt Hopkins usually joins the Kimbay party.' She grimaced and shook her head at the tube. 'Won't do. Too night-clubby.'

'I'd have thought, from what you told me of your trainer chappie, that his time was spent in pursuit of Latin ladies.'

'Obviously likes to slum, now and again. Probably intends using the occasion to make contacts, that sort of thing.'

'Why, Flora, you're becoming cynical.' Sophie was genuinely surprised. 'Never thought it would happen. You'll have to introduce me to this trainer. Satisfy my curiosity.'

They made their way out to the street again and did some desultory window shopping. Which was how Flora found a dress she *had* to have, and paid more than she should have for a froth of chiffon which bared her shoulders and fell in cascading multi-colours from her hips.

Sophie, as Flora tried the dress, considered her critically. 'The bones have it.' She tilted her head. 'Age brings them out, you know. You've never looked better and in that dress you'll rock the county.'

She meant it too. Flora, in the chiffon, was a vision of creamy gold elegance. Her cheek and jaw bones had become more defined and she'd lost the vaguely self-conscious slouch her height had once given her. Her great, dark eyes were warier than they'd used to be but that, Sophie

125

thought, was not a bad thing. Flora had been too unquestioning of the world by half.

They celebrated the dress in the Baily, a one-time haunt which brought on a fit of sighing reminiscences. Sophie recognized a bad poet, wistfully loitering by two long-limbed girls, and felt a rush of *déjà-vu*.

'I feel old today,' she admitted. 'Must be the effects of being dumped.'

Flora had just lifted her drink. She put it down again. 'Dumped?' She said the word hesitantly.

'Dumped. As in cast aside, no longer wanted.'

'Robert's gone?' Flora guessed.

'Into the mists of time. Become history.'

'Christ, Sophie, why didn't you tell me sooner?' Flora looked aghast and, to Sophie's horror, full of sympathy. 'When did this happen?' she asked.

'About a week ago,' Sophie was abrupt, 'and please don't look so tragic, Flora. I'm fine. He's fine, worse luck. It was all a stupid mistake and not worth wasting our precious time talking about. We are now going to have lunch.' She finished her drink. 'Hurry up. I'm taking you to a place you're going to love in Dawson Street. I'm paying and I've booked, so come on.'

Sophie was right about the restaurant, though neither of them ate very much. Journalist friends of Sophie's invited themselves to their table and Flora laughed several times in a way Sophie remembered but hadn't heard her do for a long time. Afterwards they did some more shopping, practical jeans and shirts for Flora, crushed velvet and a hat for Sophie.

'I enjoyed today.' Flora, exhausted, lay with the reviving comfort of a glass of Irish on a futon in Sophie's apartment. She eyed the tattered remains of the leather settee. 'Should I ask what happened here? Or is it meant to be like that?'

Sophie, head tilted, considered the settee. 'Now that you mention it, there is a certain symmetry to it. Yes, you could definitely say it's meant to be like that. It was Robert's and I hated it. The futon is to replace it.'

126

'I see.' Flora grinned. 'I take it reconciliation is not on the cards?'

'Not if he was the last man on the island.' Sophie pulled off her ankle boots. 'And, Flora,' she looked her friend in the eye, '*please* don't let's talk about him. I mean it.'

Flora knew she did. 'Fine,' she said.

While Sophie micro-waved an apple tart and made coffee Flora took time to look at the apartment. There was a curious, unlived-in air about the living room but she liked it nonetheless. It was bright, the walls were eau-de-nil and the curtains made of white muslin. The floorboards were polished and the only pieces of furniture, apart from the futon, were a bookshelf, tv and music centre.

She wandered through the other rooms, and in them found Sophie's imprint. The room she worked in had an ordered chaos which had Sophie written all over it and the bedroom, absolutely without evidence that a man had ever shared it, was happily strewn with clothing and cluttered with everything else she owned.

'We could never agree on what to do with this room,' Sophie, briefly, explained as they ate. 'I've got great plans for it now.' It was her last, if oblique, reference to Robert.

'When I'm rich and my horse is winning money I'll buy myself a place near here,' Flora said.

'You're sure she's going to win, then?'

'Not sure – but she's shaping up. Just as well. We've been having problems at the yard. Nothing major, just a series of small things. It would be nice to have some money to cushion the effects.'

'What sort of things?' Sophie looked up. It seemed to her that Flora was more worried than she pretended.

'Well, that storm earlier in the month damaged the isolation unit and we had to have repairs done. It needed the work anyway. Then, just this week, a stable lad left without warning. Didn't give much of a reason, either. We've got a very sickly foal at the moment too and a yearling's somehow managed to injure a leg.' She sighed. 'All small things, but . . .'

'Have another drink.' Sophie bounced up from the cushion she'd been sitting on.

'No. I'm off.' Flora finished the coffee and uncrossed her legs. 'Please, Sophie, don't make it harder. I *can't* stay. Too much to do in the morning. Tell you what, though – why don't you come to the Curragh tomorrow? I'll meet you there at, say, 2.30 p.m.?'

'Me? Go to the races?' Sophie wrinkled her nose. Flora was becoming altogether too involved in this old-new world of hers. 'My knowledge of horses, as you know, is limited to the fact that they've got four legs and a tail. I've never been to the races in my life.'

'Go for broke then, have a new experience. You might even back a winner.'

'But all that fresh air.' Sophie shuddered.

'Please,' Flora said. 'I'd like you to come with me.'

She meant it, Sophie could tell. 'Okay,' she agreed, 'for the experience then.'

Flora had been gone more than an hour before she remembered she hadn't given her the intended lecture on marriage and the Frenchman. There would be other times. And Flora, anyway, hadn't mentioned him all day. Which fact could mean something, or nothing at all.

Sophie, next day, didn't feel at all like going to the Curragh. A raw, northerly, rain-carrying wind blew through the city streets. God alone knew what icy effect it was having on the plains of Kildare. But she'd promised, so she wrapped herself in scarves and a military-style greatcoat and hoped for the best.

Still wondering why she'd said she would come she pulled into the car park only fifteen minutes after the time she'd agreed to meet Flora.

She was waiting. 'You made it.' She shoved binoculars into her friend's hand. Disgustingly, classically right for the day in suede jacket and trousers, she didn't seem to feel the cold at all.

'Dear God, Flora, I don't know what I'm doing here,' Sophie moaned, looked at the darkening clouds, down at the binoculars. 'It's bloody freezing. I suppose it's too late to change plans, make for a local hostelry?'

'Much too late.' Flora was brusque. 'Come on, it'll be fun.'

Sophie gathered her coat against the wind and followed Flora through the main hall, on to the upper stand levels and her father's box.

'*This* is a box?' Sophie sank faint-voiced into one of the numbered, pull-down seats. 'I'd hoped we'd be all closed in and comfy, preferably looking at things through thick glass. Still,' she brightened, 'we must be thankful there's a roof over our heads, at least.'

Flora handed her a racecard. 'Study that. This is not a simple spectator sport. You're supposed to take part, inform yourself, move around, look at the horses, listen to what the punters are saying. It's a show and a parade with a huge dollop of excitement called a race every half hour or so.'

'Enough, Flora, enough. You're beginning to sound born-again.' Sophie, leaning forward, peered down at the damp, high-spirited crowd gathering to meet the winner of the last race as he was brought in. When the next race was announced they left the box and made their way to the parade ring to view the runners. It was there, as glossy, proud, thoroughbred horseflesh displayed itself in all its arrogant splendour, that Sophie at last caught something of the fever of the racetrack.

'They really *are* quite wonderful looking, aren't they?' she breathed.

'Quite wonderful,' Flora agreed, grinning. 'Who're you going to put your money on?' She tapped the racecard, nodded at the parading horses.

'I'm going to rely on instinct,' Sophie said loftily. 'Always the best thing in matters of chance.'

She watched the horses going round for a few more minutes but, ever a student of human nature, found herself increasingly fascinated by the slight, perched figures of the jockeys on their backs. She found it hard to imagine

129

that, within minutes, they would be thundering over turf at God-knew-what speeds. And yet there they sat, calmly expressionless and frighteningly fragile-looking.

'Right,' she announced, 'I'm putting my first fiver on the jockey in green and blue, on the dark brown horse.'

'He's a bay.' Flora looked briefly at Sophie's choice. 'Dark brown horses with black manes and tails are called bays. He won't come anywhere. Take my word for it. Why don't you try—'

She stopped and Sophie, following her gaze, saw that her friend had been distracted by the entry into the ring of a tall, black-haired man in a long raincoat. He pulled a horse aside and spoke to the jockey and looked, from where Sophie stood, to be not bad looking at all. Certainly worth closer inspection.

'Who is he?' she asked. 'Come on, Flora, give. You can't keep all the nice-looking ones to yourself.'

'My horse's trainer,' Flora was scanning her racecard, 'and I didn't realize he'd a horse in this race. How *could* I have missed it. Here he is. Dark Boy.'

'So *that's* the local Lothario.' Sophie gave a small whistle.

'I can't introduce you now,' Flora caught her arm. 'He's busy and we've got to place our bets.' Sophie, with a wistful glance at the crowd swallowing the trainer, followed her to the bookies.

They watched the race from the box. Flora's horse won. Matt Hopkins's Dark Boy came in a close second and Sophie's bay trailed the field to finish second last.

'Instinct only works if applied with intelligence.' Flora grinned maddeningly and Sophie allowed herself be led to the Santa Claus bar to spend the winnings.

Matt Hopkins was at the counter when they got there. Flora touched his arm and he turned round.

'Congratulations,' she said. 'Your Dark Boy ran a good race.'

'Not *my* Dark Boy.' The trainer smiled and Sophie was struck by the contrast between his dark hair and brows and the cobalt blue of his eyes. 'Martin here is his owner.'

The tall, snowy-haired individual standing beside him smiled, nodded graciously at both women in turn. 'Let me buy you a drink, ladies. It's not every day I've a horse comes this close to winning.'

He ordered champagne and they found a table. Martin Ryan was seventyish, benign and clearly in love with the first horse he'd ever owned. Sophie shed her coat and scarves and lay back in the low seating. She shook her hair loose and studied Matt Hopkins through half-closed lids. As a male specimen, and in purely abstract terms, he was *very* good to look at. Up close she liked the way his eyes crinkled when he smiled. He was smiling a lot, including her with his eyes. She definitely liked the look of him. She smiled back.

'His first race of the season too.' Martin Ryan rubbed his hands together. 'You were right, Matt, to go for this one.'

'Bad luck that he didn't win. Just lost it on the last furlong,' the trainer said.

The barman arrived with the champagne on ice and, while their host began slowly to work the cork free, the trainer leaned toward Sophie. His eyes had a speculative look she was well used to. 'Any winners today, Miss Butler?' he asked.

'Sophie,' she said, 'and not yet.' She spread her arms. 'I was hoping for beginner's luck but it didn't happen.'

'Perhaps I can advise you . . .'

There was a small pop as their host gently removed the cork from the champagne. He filled four glasses and handed them round. 'To Dark Boy,' he said and they drank. They toasted the horse's luck in his next race too and, at Martin Ryan's insistence, the horse's trainer; 'a man who knows what he's about'.

'I train to win.' The trainer gave a half-smile, as if afraid he sounded pompous. Flora obviously thought he did. Her smile, looking at him, was cool.

'Dark Boy will have a win next time out.' The trainer made the remark confidently, first to Martin Ryan and then to Flora.

'Here's to all the Dark Boys of the world,' Sophie raised her glass and Flora, raising hers, added, 'And to golden girls.'

Sophie felt a touch of claustrophobia as the crowd pressed good-humouredly around them. Hands were clapped on the trainer's and owner's backs, voices told Flora they were glad to see her at the track. A race was announced and the crowd thinned.

Matt Hopkins finished his drink. 'Enjoy the afternoon.' He nodded at Flora, who smiled. 'Honey Bee in the four o'clock's your sure thing for the day,' he told Sophie, then grinned. 'You can buy me a drink with your winnings next time we meet.' He was a head above the rest of the crowd as he made his way with Martin Ryan out of the bar.

'Well, well, *well* . . .' Sophie gave a low, appreciative whistle. 'Interesting lad, your trainer. Lovely bod, obviously not poverty-stricken either.' She helped them both to the last of the champagne. 'You were right about the races, Flora. There's a lot of excitement around here.'

'Sophie, you're hardly out of the frying pan.' Flora raised a mildly protesting brow.

'True. But I've always liked the warmth of the fire, you know that. And my marriage bed was so very cold, and for such a long time.'

'How long since you slept together?'

'Mmm. Two months, at least. I'm due some fun. Overdue.' She gave a low, purring laugh. 'There's a case to be made, Flora my pet, for gathering rosebuds while ye may, seizing the hour, all that kind of thing.'

'There's a case too for giving yourself a bit of space, using time alone to take stock, all *that* kind of thing.'

Sophie reached behind her for her coat. 'It's getting stuffy in here.' She smiled good-naturedly. 'Let's look at some more horses. Think I'll put a fiver on that horse in the four o'clock, might be lucky this time.' She put an arm through Flora's as they made their way down to the racetrack. 'It'll be a test of Mr Hopkins's judgement.'

Honey Bee came in third. The horse Flora had backed,

132

a dignified grey, ran a better race and finished a furlong ahead in second place.

'Well, your trainer's not perfect, obviously,' Sophie lowered the binoculars. 'Now that I don't have to buy him a drink maybe I'll put him on the back boiler. For a little while.' They were in the box. She pulled her collar up against a sniping wind. 'Can we go now? I think I've had enough for my first outing.'

In the car park they said goodbye, promising to keep in regular touch.

'I could get to like this sort of country life.' Sophie gave Flora a hug. 'I might even find myself a little retreat somewhere near here.' She gave a mock shudder. 'But not yet.'

Chapter Thirteen

There never seemed time to rest. Mares, when they foaled, did so in the small hours of the morning and broke Flora's sleep. A stable lad went sick. A valuable early foal, born to one of her mares, jumped out of the paddock and badly injured himself. Her body set up a protesting ache against the long hours, the constant vigilance demanded by it all.

Still, she felt more confident about her role in the yard. She suspected this had to do with the hard work involved and the truth of the adage about being thrown in at the deep end. She had become more determined than ever that neither she nor the yard would sink.

The adage about work expanding to fill the time available came to her too. She would prove it by taking time off soon, allow things go on without her while she went to Brussels. Her apartment and life there needed to be sorted out. Serge rang all the time, never demanding but always gently suggesting she jump on an aeroplane. He'd been away himself, on longish trips to the US and Hong Kong, and Flora was consoled by the thought that, even if she'd been living in Brussels for the past months, she would have seen very little of him.

The two weeks of sheer grind and repetition preceding the hunt ball made it seem, suddenly, a wildly exciting prospect. Since buying the dress Flora had put the event out of her mind. Now, in the week leading up to it, she found herself caught dizzily in the general anticipation.

She also found herself with a partner. Serge, three days before the hunt ball, decided he would fly over for it.

'I hope it is not too late,' his tone said he didn't really think this a possibility, 'and that you can get me a ticket. I cannot come until Saturday, and I must leave on Monday early. But we will be together for two days – and I will learn something of the life you are living there.'

'Serge, you're a darling. I'd *love* you to come.' Flora felt a quick lightness of heart. He would love her dress, she was certain of it. Serge noticed, was a joy to dress for. They would dance and talk and enjoy one another at the ball. Afterwards too. Serge coming would make the night perfect.

'You must not come to the airport, *ma chère*,' he insisted now. 'You will need rest, time to prepare yourself for the *bal*. I will hire a car and be with you in the late afternoon.'

'I'll be counting the hours,' Flora laughed.

This became a reality in the days which followed. A great impatience to see Serge gripped her and she found herself checking her watch, noting the hours as they passed.

But the gods weren't playing fair. Friday dawned grey and overcast and by mid-morning the edges of a coastal fog had drifted inland and were eerily inching across the fields of Kimbay. By mid-afternoon Dublin airport had begun announcing flight diversions and cancellations.

The fog was expected to continue overnight and flights for the following twenty-four hours would be affected. Yes, Flora was told when she telephoned, it was likely that tomorrow's flight from Brussels would be late. No, they couldn't say *how* late.

Serge himself, when she phoned him, was philosophical. 'It is unfortunate,' he said, 'but it will only mean a few hours' delay.'

For Flora, keyed up to see him, he might as well have said months.

It had been arranged that the Kimbay party would meet at seven for drinks at the house. Its number had grown to ten and Flora had spent lavishly to provide generous quantities of drink and finger-food. Shay was stunningly grumpy about the whole thing and registered irritable disbelief when she stopped work at midday to help Daisy prepare things in the house.

135

'He wouldn't go at all last year.' Daisy, piling food morsels onto plates, shook her head in furious resignation. 'But I told him he'd better make the effort this year or I'd remove myself from his bed.'

'You didn't!' Flora gave a yelp of laughter.

'I did. And I meant it. A woman has to be persuasive if she's to get things done in this life,' she shook the knife she was using in Flora's direction, 'just you remember that, Flora.'

By five o'clock the word from the airport was that the Brussels flight would arrive around seven. Which meant Serge should get to Kimbay about two hours later.

Flora, soaking in the bath, was jolted out of a reverie that was dangerously close to real sleep by Leah's voice and Doc Martens pounding up the stairs.

'Flora? Are you there, Flora?' She stopped outside the bedroom door, knocked loudly. Her voice was pleading. 'Please be there.'

'What's wrong? Has something happened?' Flora, pink from the bath and full of alarm, pulled open the door.

'Everything. Everything's wrong.' Eyes bright with tears, words pouring out of her, Leah rushed past Flora into the bedroom. 'They know how important tonight is to me. I wanted everything to be right, just this once. But they're doing nothing to help and they're going to be late and it's all going to be the usual mess . . .' She stood in the middle of the room, balldress over her arm and a jangle of frustration to the roots of her tangled, just-washed hair.

'Calm down, Leah.' Flora, assured that no one was actually dying, found her dressing gown and got rid of the damp towel. 'Right,' she was businesslike, 'what exactly is all the hysteria about?'

'I thought *you'd* understand.' Leah, sinking exhaustedly onto the bed, was sulkily unrepentant. '*They* don't, my *mother* doesn't . . .'

'Understand what?' Flora, patient and prepared to listen, sat on the bed beside Leah. She'd got through her own teen years in relative peace, angst sorted out in long late-night boarding-school huddles. But then she hadn't had a mother, least of all one like Daisy, to react against. It had become obvious to Flora that all of Leah's anxieties had their root in a horror that she would grow up to be like Daisy. Which she probably would.

'It's my first ball, like being a debutante,' Leah's voice rose despairingly, 'and *look* at my hair. It's like a mattress.' She looked suddenly and totally miserable. 'They don't care. Luke's got two creepy friends of his down in the cottage, sneering and jeering. They think they're hilarious but they're actually total pains. And my mother's not even back from the village yet and God knows what she's going to look like tonight and my father's still out in the yard . . .' She shook a fiery head. 'They're a mess, they're always a bloody mess. Can I get dressed here, Flora, have my bath? Can I, please?' Her eyes were glitteringly bright and as Flora sat down beside her, a tear fell, then another. Gently, she pushed a clump of the girl's bright hair back from her face.

'Of course you can get ready here. Have your bath straight away. You'll feel better.'

Leah took a long time in the bathroom and emerged relatively calm. Flora, in the meantime, had brought them up a tray of wine and snack food. If she was being cast *in loco parentis* then she was going to do it her way. Idly, as she poured the wine, she wondered if her responsibilities in the yard had given her a gravitas she'd lacked before. She was not, usually, the sort of person others leaned on. More the reverse in fact; she was usually the one to do the leaning. She handed Leah a glass, feeling that she quite liked her new role.

'Thanks.' Leah took the wine, contrite but mutinous still. 'Sorry about barging in. They made me so *mad*. Just for this one night I wanted them to be *normal*. I wanted them to be ready and welcoming when David arrives.' She took a gulp of the wine. 'But of course they won't be. Daisy'll be all over the place, as usual.'

'David . . . I thought he was a convenience?' Flora looked at the girl thoughtfully, realization dawning. Leah's date, the young man she'd disdained as merely a necessary

137

prop for the evening, was what this was all about. He mattered to her. Leah was smitten.

'Well, he *is* a convenience. But I like him.' Leah flushed puce and sniffed. 'You don't imagine I'd have beaten Daisy up to get a dress like this,' she shook the long, thin piece of burgundy crushed velvet at Flora, 'and paid for the tickets myself if I didn't like him.' Her eyes overflowed again. 'And now they're going to make a show of me and he'll think I'm a fool.' She caught a running tear with her tongue.

'Oh, get a life, Leah.' Flora stood up. 'He'd certainly think you a fool if he could see you this minute. Finish the wine and we'll get dressed. I'll see what I can do with your hair.'

'I pinned a note to the door telling him to come on up here.' Leah flushed again, her face full of a sly embarrassment. 'I sort of knew you wouldn't mind.'

A second glass of wine made Leah giggly and Flora *very* relaxed. She was enjoying Leah's company. This, she thought, is how things should be in this house. It needs more people. It wasn't meant for one person, ever. She wished Serge would change his mind, come to live for a while. She wished too that Fintan and Ollie would visit more often. They'd only come a couple of times, and briefly, since Ned's death. She'd asked them to come to the hunt ball but they'd made excuses. An empty house was worse than an empty bed. Something would have to be done, she wasn't sure what. The front doorbell rang at two minutes to seven.

'Oh, God! It's him.' Leah made for the window in the weaving trot enforced by the tight burgundy. Briskly, all at once her mother's daughter again, she pushed it up and shoved her head and bare shoulders into the freezing air outside.

'David, is that you?' she called and, her eyes confirming the presence below, yelled, 'I'll be right down.' She slammed the window shut and turned. 'Do you realize, Flora, that you're wearing one earring?'

'Yes. I need to find the other. Let's have a look at you before you go down . . .'

They stood side by side, critically appraising one another in the standing, three-sided tailor's mirror Flora had had since a child. Leah was a vision, transformed and nearly beautiful. Her still damp hair had been controlled with gel and fell in dark russet curls over her bare shoulders. The crushed velvet, more of a slip than a dress, changed her from skinny to slinky and some of Flora's eye-shadow had made her face huge-eyed. She turned sideways and groaned.

'My behind's sticking out,' she said. She gave Flora a quick hug. 'Thanks a mil. You were great – and you look great, for someone your age . . .'

A well-aimed slipper from Flora just missed her as she fled through the door. After it shut behind her Flora carried out her own critical appraisal.

Night-lighting suited the chiffon dress and the weight she'd lost in the last few weeks meant it hung better too. It skimmed her breasts and hips, fell in soft folds against the length of her legs. With Leah's help she'd piled her hair loosely on top of her head and the effect had encouraged her to wear a necklace and earrings of her mother's. They were of old silver with lapis lazuli and would be perfect once she found the second, matching earring. It turned up just as the doorbell rang again.

Daisy, wrapped magnificently in the pale musquash she kept for 'state occasions', swept into the hall at the head of the men in her family, Luke's date, who was a tiny blonde in green taffeta, and Luke's trainee-jockey friend, Kevin. 'You look grand,' she told Flora. 'Did the misfortunate David find his prima donna?'

'He's here.' Flora led the way to the living room. David, curly-haired and assured, stood as they came in. Leah, aplomb apparently restored, remained lolling on the settee and introduced him to Flora with a casual wave. Formally welcoming him, Flora wondered what about him excited Leah. He was good-looking, with an entirely bland smile. Nothing more. The ways of the heart were indeed strange, the ways of the teenage heart strangest of all.

The tiny blonde, whom Flora now recognized as a part-time stable girl called Dymphna, obligingly helped with the drinks. Luke in a tuxedo looked self-conscious, adrift. He'd lost his yard bravado and seemed a lot younger than his twin. His friend Kevin vied for Dymphna's attention and seemed anxious to be off. Daisy, when she shed the coat, was revealed to be wearing green velvet, matching exactly the combs which caught back her hair. Shay was the biggest revelation of all. In a tuxedo he looked like Fred Astaire. Flora, for one mad moment, expected him to dance. What he actually did surprised her almost as much. He accepted a drink, smiling, then stood with his back to the fire and raised his glass.

'To absent friends,' he said and they all drank. In the quiet following the toast a pair of headlights swept briefly across the windows. A car door banged outside and Flora went to answer the front door.

'Hope I'm not late?' Matt Hopkins, coatless and smiling in the light over the door, made a mock salute.

'Not at all.' Flora stepped aside. In the hallway he thrust a narrow box into her hands.

'Oh . . .' She looked down, surprised and unprepared for the beauty of the primrose corsage. 'You didn't need to—' she began but he shrugged, smiling.

'No need to feel compromised, Flora, you're not exclusive. I managed to get one for each of the Kimbay women.'

Flora saw then what she hadn't noticed before – three more slim boxes in his other hand. Obviously, he'd even included Dymphna, whom he didn't know. Nice move, she thought. Thoughtful and charming. She tried not to feel cynical, or to wonder why, as she said, 'Thank you, Matt. It's quite lovely,' and began to lead the way to the living room.

'They're to be worn,' his touch on her arm was light but it stopped her, 'not just admired. Let me put it on for you.'

Wordlessly, she allowed him take the corsage. He had put the others on the table and she watched his hands, long and brown-fingered, as he opened the box. Gentle hands, tonight. Clever, dexterous hands too. They opened the box in seconds.

'Now, where would you like to wear it?' His eyes on hers were laughing. They moved from her face to her bare shoulders and the front of her dress, to where it lay across her breasts. Flora stepped back. The man was a consummate flirt – which would be fun if he weren't so vain and presumptuous with it.

'It'll have to go on my wrap. This dress fabric's too fragile to hold . . .'

'Your hair, then.' Before she could stop him, protest even, his hands were in her hair and he was fixing the primroses. Expecting the imminent collapse of the hairstyle, she stood furiously still, aware of how much taller than her he was, of his Italian-cut gun-metal tux and pink shirt. And of how deliberately, provocatively sexual he was being. The man didn't seem able to stop himself.

'There.' His hand touched her cheek and he stepped back. Her hair had not fallen down. '"Blossom by blossom the spring begins . . ."' He quoted the words quietly, not looking at her, before he picked up the other three corsages. Wordlessly, she followed him into the living room.

His primrose offerings were joyfully received by the others and Flora felt a stab of guilt. It could be that he simply sought to please. He liked women, all women. And why not? Perhaps she should be less defensive about his flirting, even about his presumption.

The party became cosier. It was almost eight o'clock. They should leave soon for the Nag's Head. The thought occurred to Flora that they might be waiting for her and she looked, eyebrows raised, at Daisy. Daisy understood, instantly.

'Maybe you should check once more with the airport, Flora, before we decide what to do.'

The airport said the plane from Brussels had landed. On time, an hour before.

'Serge should be here in less than an hour.' She stood just inside the door, holding it open. 'I'll follow when he arrives. No sense in everyone being late.'

Shay stood immediately and Daisy glared at him. 'There's such a thing as indecent haste,' she snapped and

141

picked up the musquash. 'We'll go – but someone should stay with Flora. Luke, I think you should.'

'I'll wait, obviously.' Matt Hopkins cut across Daisy and nodded reassuringly to Luke. He dropped into what had always been Ned's seat by the fire.

'Please, I don't need *anyone* to wait with me. There's no need –'

The trainer interrupted Flora's protest too. 'I don't mind.' He stretched his legs lazily. 'We can finish our drinks, and talk. The time should pass quite pleasantly.' He looked very comfortable in her father's armchair.

When the others had left he took a cigar from an inside pocket. 'An occasional indulgence,' he held it up, 'do you mind?'

Flora shook her head. 'Not at all.' She watched while he sliced the cigar, slowly lit up. His presumption was getting to her again. She wished he'd gone with the others, that she was sitting quietly, alone, waiting for Serge. He didn't know the roads. She hoped he would be all right.

'Care to come back from wherever you are and join me?'

Flora blinked. The trainer's face, seen through a pall of bluey smoke, seemed piratical. 'Sorry. Just wondering how long it will take Serge to get here.'

'And what have you concluded?'

'Another forty minutes, less maybe.'

'Then I've certainly time for another whiskey. Maybe some ice this time?'

The ice-bucket was empty. 'I'll get some,' Flora said. She took her time in the kitchen, checking the yard below, talking a little to Dipper, asleep in his chair but jerking occasionally and moaning as if having a dream. 'Poor old thing,' she rubbed between his ears. 'You miss Ned.'

'We all miss Ned.' Matt Hopkins leaned against the door jamb. Flora said nothing for several seconds. She was having trouble with a sudden lump in her throat. He had no right to intrude, touch feelings which were still so very raw. She got the ice from the freezer.

'We should go back to the living room,' she said.

'Why?' He looked around the kitchen. 'I like it here.'

He'd brought the whiskey bottle with him and Flora poured their drinks. They drank and Flora looked at him in the shaded light as he hunkered to pat the dog. An unaccountable feeling of desperation crept over her. She shouldn't be here, in the kitchen, alone with him.

She fought an urge to rush headlong out and kept her eyes on his face as he bent down, on his hair as it fell over his forehead, on the shape of his mouth, the gentleness of his hand on the dog. Sex and sex appeal had so much to do with what a person seemed to be – and Matt Hopkins at that moment seemed kind and human and not at all presumptuous. She reminded herself that it was not a crime to want someone, that betraying someone you loved was the criminal part. It was easy to desire a man, especially an attractive one. It was harder by far to love. And she had love, precious and loyal and driving through the night to be with her. The feeling she had with Serge was a winner. Matt Hopkins was a wild card and she didn't want to play.

'So – am I judged and found wanting?' The trainer looked up, sardonic smile in place again.

'Not at all . . .'

'Not found wanting?' He was incredulous.

'Not judged.'

'That's a relief.' He raised his glass and moved closer, away from the dog in his chair. 'You look beautiful tonight,' he said.

'Thank you.' She was curt. He was pushing things again. She looked at her watch and he shrugged, sipped his drink in silence. The clock ticked loudly and the old dog snored. Flora wanted to say something. Anything. But words would have added to the intimacy, made it unbearable. She tried to think of her father, of how Ned had been in this kitchen. She couldn't. He'd slipped away from her. For now anyway.

'Ned enjoyed the ball last year,' Matt Hopkins said and she thought, for a heady moment and before common sense prevailed, that she must have spoken out loud. He moved away from the dog.

'Did he?' Her question was automatic.

'Definitely did. He was the life and soul. Great dancer.'

'I'm glad.' Flora turned her head away, looked out the window.

'Do *you* like to dance, Flora?' He hadn't moved but he seemed closer. She should never have allowed this intimacy develop. On the other hand, maybe she was making too much of it all.

'Love to,' she said.

'Great.' He went to the radio and fiddled. He seemed to know where everything was. When he found a piano concerto he turned up the sound. 'Dance, please, Ms Carolan?' He made a mock bow and held out a hand in invitation.

'We won't hear the doorbell when Serge arrives.' Flora could hear the panic in her voice. The trainer put a hand on her back, drew her to him and lifted her hand to dance.

'Of course we will.' He did some steps to the music, taking her with him to the centre of the kitchen. His hand on her back pulled her close against him. He whirled her round and looked down into her anxious, upturned face. 'You don't dance as well as Ned,' he said. 'Not as relaxed. He knew how to let go.'

'Maybe he wanted to let go.' Flora spoke stiffly. And he had nothing to lose, she thought, like control of the situation, for one thing. Matt Hopkins was humming to himself, out of tune. He whirled her again, smoothly, powerfully. He tightened his hold.

'Enjoying it?' His eyes taunted her.

'I prefer the cut and thrust of the dance floor.' Flora felt the table behind her and stopped. When she looked up Matt Hopkins's face had become very close. His head came down and he put his mouth to hers. Shocked, she allowed the pressure rest for a few seconds. She wasn't sure at what point the gentle nature of the pressure changed, when or how exactly it became a hungry, greedy kiss on both their parts. She yielded and clung to him, feeling his heart beat as wildly as her own against her breasts. He tightened an arm around her and with his other hand tumbled her hair

144

so that it fell loose. The primroses dropped to the floor. He was kissing her in a way that demanded more, said things could not stop.

And Flora, suddenly, regained control.

'No.' She broke the kiss, spoke against his mouth. 'This is *not* a good idea, Matt.'

He let her go at once, stood back. 'Maybe you're right.' He looked rueful. 'Bad ideas can be fun though . . .' He picked up the corsage, looked at it thoughtfully before handing it back to her. 'You shouldn't worry so much, Flora.' He picked up his drink again and leaned against the sink. 'It doesn't do any good, you know. Life, as they say, is a game of chance, a risky venture at the best of times.' He gave a short, wry-sounding laugh. 'You can multiply that wisdom to the power of ten when you talk about the horse business. Look, you're doing a good job here, Flora. I don't have to tell you that, do I? You know it yourself, instinctively. You were bred to it. What you have to do now is learn to relax, go with things.' He raised his glass to her and drank. Flora sipped from her own.

'That was quite a speech.' Still shaken, she spoke curtly. 'Does it mean you've revised your view of me as a hat-stand for the racetrack?'

'Certainly does.' He was unabashed. 'You're a worker. Looks like your pedigree survived the rigours of life in Brussels.'

Her anger at his patronizing attitude was a cold, hard thing inside her.

'Anyone ever point out to you, *Mister* Hopkins, what a self-righteous bastard you are?'

'Nope. That's not one I've been told.' He looked deliberately thoughtful. 'Other flaws I hear about regularly. Bastard, for instance, is a frequent contender. But I've never been called self-righteous.'

'Well, now you know. And while we're on the subject,' Flora's fury had gathered momentum, 'does your idea of "going with things" mean I should submit to your seduction routine or to your plans for Flo Girl? Or both?'

145

Though she couldn't be sure, she thought she saw a flash of anger in his eyes. But the familiar, tauntingly amused look was there when he spoke.

'Put like that, and since you obviously feel so strongly, maybe I should drop one and continue negotiations on the other—'

'Good idea.' Flora, interrupting, was crisp. 'I'll discuss Flo Girl's future with you during the coming week.'

'Ouch.' He sighed, gave a small shrug. 'Can we at least be friends?'

'I think that's possible, yes. Neighbours should be friends. But friendship would be a lot easier if you could accept that not every woman who crosses your path is up for grabs. I'm not.'

'Ouch,' he said again. 'Point taken.'

'And now, if you'll excuse me, I'm going to repair the damage to my hair.'

She had almost finished, almost got it the way it had been when the night began, when she heard Serge arriving up the avenue. She put the primroses in water on her dressing-table. They didn't deserve to die just yet. It wasn't their fault they'd been part of a seduction power-play.

Chapter Fourteen

The Old Nag was unrecognizable. In its normal, everyday existence it was a gracious mid-nineteenth-century house which functioned with elegance as a twentieth-century hotel. But for tonight it had thrown restraint, and style, to the winds and opted for untypical extravaganza. The light from a thousand multi-coloured bulbs gave a meteoric brillance to its normally sedate, ivy-covered walls and a vast yellow banner proclaiming the occasion had been draped between two of the garden's oldest beech trees. Foot-level spotlights along the long avenue shone on a seemingly endless stream of noisily crowded cars.

Stepping into the warmth of the seething lobby with Serge and Matt Hopkins it seemed to Flora that the entire county, along with several bordering ones, had given way to an unbridled urge to have a good time. The place throbbed with the laughter, conversation and general insouciance of the old, young, elegant, debauched and hopeful of the population for miles around. Young women, bright as flamingoes, competed for the attention of glassy-eyed young men. Old men with sharp eyes watched the young women and talked horse business out of the sides of their mouths. A waiter moved among them, banging an unheeded gong as he announced dinner.

'It is not so different from such celebrations in the country-side in France.' Serge sounded disappointed. 'Except per-haps that in France people would be preparing to go home by now.' He smiled, his arm around Flora, and she laughed.

'The night hasn't begun yet,' she said. It was ten o'clock, and he was right, in France she had been amazed at how early people went home to their beds. 'Things here could stagger on until dawn,' she told him.

147

A fragrant woman stood close to the trainer. She stroked his lapel with a long, orange-tipped hand. 'Matthew, darling, how *lovely* to see you.' Her voice, full of purring laughter, came from deep in her throat. Her strawberry blonde hair tumbled about her face, hiding it. Flora couldn't tell whether or not she'd ever met her before.

'Louisa!' The trainer lifted and kissed her hand. 'I'd no idea you would be here.' The woman giggled softly and whispered in his ear. He grinned, nodded and excused himself to Flora and Serge. 'See you at the table,' he said and, with her arm through his, melted with the woman into the crowd. Serge touched Flora's shoulder and she turned, smiling at him.

He looked handsome tonight, his white dinner jacket setting off the light tan he'd picked up on his trip to the States. He had been tired when he arrived, but civilized as always.

'Airports are inhuman places,' he'd kissed Flora lightly, 'fit only for insomniacs. And you', he took her face in his, 'are *vraiment séduisante* tonight, *mon ange*.'

He'd showered and changed quickly, been remarkably invigorated by a couple of apéritifs from the bottle of pernod Flora had bought with him in mind. Toward Matt Hopkins he had displayed gracious appreciation for keeping Flora company. Which was, she thought, either clever or naive of him. She had never known him to be naive.

The waiter pounded the gong in their ears. 'You must be ravenous,' Flora said, 'perhaps we should head for the table too.'

They went with the crowd, slowly drifting now in the direction of the huge dining-ballroom. The waiter followed, harrying them ineffectually and suffering lighthearted insults for his trouble.

At the ballroom door Flora heard Daisy's call before she saw her, wildly beckoning from a table too close to the stage. She stood, a mauve and green masthead, making sure they were headed in the right direction. When they were half-way across the room she sat down.

Flora held Serge's hand, introducing him here and

148

there, as they threaded a way between the round, linen-covered tables. The centre of each was piled high with fresh spring flowers – though without, Flora noticed, a primrose in sight. Refracted light from the overhead chandeliers glanced off the crystal and silver place settings and on the stage a lone pianist played gentle melodies to which no one was listening.

'So you got here.' Daisy held out a hand to Serge. 'You're welcome.' She gestured to the seat beside her, gracious as an empress receiving at court. Serge took her fingers, lightly kissing the air above them before sitting where he was told between Daisy and Leah. Flora sat in the place left for her between Shay and a distant-looking David. They'd finished the melon entrée before Matt Hopkins, smiling and apologetic, took his place.

'Had to see a man about a horse,' he said. Dymphna threw back her head and laughed, a loud, hyena-like sound that ended in a snort. Luke winced, flushed and fiddled with his glass. The laugh, Flora guessed, had been a shock to him. Certainly, it had never been heard during the daylight hours Dymphna spent at the yard.

A waitress began serving them lamb cutlets with green-gage sauce. 'I can't eat this,' Leah's low cry was anguished. 'I asked for vegetarian.' She looked pale and agitated and, though it was warm in the ballroom, hadn't taken off her woollen wrap. Flora hoped the two glasses of wine hadn't been a mistake, that they hadn't led to her downing too much since then.

'Bring her a salad.' Daisy, without expression, handed back the meal. 'A *large* salad.'

Leah threw a miserable, ignored look David's way. He was already, with relish, eating the lamb.

'You've no objections to meat, then?' Flora asked him.

'None. Should I have?' His tone and expression were surprised.

'Well ... no reason why you should, exactly,' Flora said, 'just wondered if you shared any of Leah's convictions.'

'Certainly don't.'

Flora, after a thoughtful look at his handsome, spoilt face, dropped all effort at conversation.

'You do know that you're all devouring what was a living creature just days ago?' Leah's voice rose above the buzz of other talk at the table. 'An animal with feelings, that people thought was cute. Then they *murdered* it —'

'And now we're going to salivate while we eat its sensitive flesh. Why don't you shut up, Leah?' Luke plunged his knife into the meat in front of him.

'You're an *animal*.' Leah was almost tearful. Luke snorted, then laughed outright.

'Then you should be nicer to me, since animals are what you care —'

'Stop it, both of you. Stop it this minute.' Daisy was flint. 'You are not at home now. This is a social occasion.'

Dymphna giggled and Luke glared at her warningly. She didn't laugh. Leah's salad arrived and she turned with a small sniff to Serge. 'Do *you* realize that what you're eating was a living thing once?' She ignored Daisy's furious glare.

'Yes. But it does not bother me,' Serge assured her. 'I do not see corpses on my plate.' He raised an eyebrow. 'It is not usual, surely, for a country girl to be vegetarian?'

'Maybe not. But I'm an iconoclast, a trail-blazer.' Leah gave a wobbly grin. Serge, with a smiling shake of his head, resumed eating.

'I am lost to your cause,' he said. 'If I was hungry enough I would kill for a steak, *saignant*, of course.'

Flora, hiding a grin, turned to Shay. 'Anyone ever tell you, partner, that in a tux you look like Fred Astaire?'

'Yes,' he was serious. 'Daisy did, once.' He pushed his half-finished meal away. 'I've been thinking, Flora, and Matt here agrees with me, that you should be the one to take the yearlings to Goffs in October.'

'To the sales?' Flora, catching her breath, felt a rush of sheer excitement.

'Luke'll go with you, lead them round the ring, that sort of thing. But you'll be in charge. Only way you'll ever learn the business.' He lit a cigarette and, as a cloud of smoke rose between them, Flora let her breath out again.

'You're right,' she said, 'and I'd love to do it. You're sure you don't want to go yourself?'

'Ned usually did that kind of thing. Best if you take over. No point both of us being there, right, Matt?'

'One of you should be enough,' the trainer agreed.

Flora, toying with her lamb, resisted an urge to ask what business it was of his. The sale of the yearlings at Goffs would account for the major part of Kimbay's income for the year. Now it was to be her responsibility. Her appetite deserted her and, as Shay had done minutes before, she pushed away her unfinished meal.

'The grey should make a tidy few bob.' Shay, oblivious to signals from Daisy, created a canopy of smoke as he spoke. 'He's the one you should concentrate on getting right from now on. His half-brother's winning races this season already.'

David's chair, the other side of Flora, moved back from the table. 'Excuse me,' he said to the table in general and, to Leah, 'be back in a while.' Leah focussed on her meal. Her face was an ashen colour.

'Pathetic philanderer.' Luke, without looking up, spoke in tones of disgust. Flora prayed that Dymphna wouldn't laugh. She didn't.

The noise level in the ballroom rose, became more uproarious. By the time coffee and petits fours reached their table, the atmosphere had become Bacchanalian. A five-piece jazz combo appeared on the stage, the tables were pushed back from the dance-floor and, amid much whooping and hollering, a first, brave couple took to the floor. The woman, in a glittering gold fishtail dress, was Marigold.

'Dance, Daisy?' Matt Hopkins asked and Daisy, nimble and beaming, got immediately to her feet. The floor began to fill up and Flora took Serge by the hand for her first dance with him for far, far too long a time.

Dancing together, close and slow, she realized she was enjoying the night more than he was. His face wore a smile but, sensitive to his mood, she noticed when he glanced at his watch and how he tried to hide his lack of interest when

151

people stopped to chat. She wasn't surprised when he asked if they could leave.

'Think you could take another half hour?' She tilted her head in teasing appeal.

'Twenty minutes?' he bargained, and they agreed.

They were leaving the floor when a breeder friend of her father's hailed Flora. 'Have a drink.' He pulled out a chair at his table, a second for Serge. He poured two very large whiskeys. 'A word of advice, Flora, about selling the yearlings . . .'

Flora, acutely aware of Serge's impatience, didn't ask how he knew about something she'd only just discovered herself. This was a man who knew about selling. It would be idiotic not to listen, for a few minutes anyway.

'You'll have to start getting those yearlings ready months beforehand.' The breeder stabbed the table with a finger. 'Tomorrow's not too soon to start sorting out the geese from the swans, so to speak. You'll have to get to know the animals that'll need help with showing and the ones you can expect to make reasonable money . . .' He talked on and she listened, learning from him what she should do to make the most of each colt and filly. 'Another thing you should do,' he frowned at their untouched drinks, 'is trot those yearlings of yours out for viewing at a coffee morning a few weeks before the sales. Ask along a few dealers and agents as well as some straight-talking friends . . .'

'It's all good advice,' Flora said to Serge as they left.

'*Enfin.* So now we can leave?' he asked.

'I'll get my things, tell everyone we're off.'

At the table Leah sat alone. Her face was frozen in a tragic mask and her eyes were bright with unshed tears.

'Perhaps it is her diet?' Serge murmured as they drew near.

'I don't think so,' Flora was thoughtful. 'I think it's her heart. I'll have to talk to her.'

'If it is her heart there is nothing you can do. Her young man is ill-mannered. She would be better to find

152

another.' Serge's shoulders, inside his perfectly cut jacket, shrugged elegantly.

'It's not so easy, when you're nearly seventeen,' Flora said. 'It's not so easy at any time.'

'There are plenty young men here and she is a pretty girl . . .'

'I didn't mean she couldn't find another,' Flora was reproving. 'More that she doesn't want to. She cares for David. I think she might even imagine she's in love with him, at the moment.'

'The heart recovers. She must learn that. Better to learn now, then she will have learned the lesson for life.'

'I'll tell her. I'll tell her the wisdom comes from you.' Flora's tone was hurt and Serge laughed, deep in his throat. He put his lips to her hair.

'Do not play the *coquette, ma chère*. You know I would never recover from you.'

'Of course you would,' Flora said, and knew she was right. The idea frightened her and she tightened her grip on his hand. 'We'll leave straight away.'

At the table she picked up her bag and wrap. 'We're leaving,' she told Leah, gently.

'You're wise.' Leah was arch. 'This is a huge bore.'

Flora, looking around for someone to keep her company, saw Luke dancing with Marigold, looking happier than he'd been all night. Two tables away she spotted Shay in deep conversation with an individual who might have been his clone.

'Why don't you ask Jumping Jack Flash to dance with you?' she nodded in his direction.

'Don't want to dance.' Leah's eyes widened and became absolutely desolate as she looked across the room. 'Flora,' she blurted, 'can I come with you? I don't feel well.'

Flora followed her gaze and saw David in a clinch on the dance-floor. 'Sure,' she said, 'get your things.'

In the car Serge was quiet, Leah loudly and loquaciously self-pitying. 'Ditched. At my first dance. And for a tart from Dublin who just *happened* to turn up tonight and

153

whom David just *happened* to have known in the past. And no one danced with me. Not even Matt Hopkins. He danced with my mother and he danced with Marigold. He'd even have danced with the caterwauling Dymphna if that blonde with the nails hadn't taken him off with her.' She stopped to draw breath and to peer at the dark, passing countryside. 'I suppose I should look on the bright side of things. I at least got away before Daisy's stage performance. Did you know, Flora, that she sings every year?'

'No.' Flora, concentrating on the road ahead, had begun to feel tired and a little flat.

'Well, she does.' Leah sighed heavily as the car stopped outside the cottage. 'That's me finished with men, for ever.' She climbed out. 'I've decided to become a nun. I'll be joining a contemplative order. I've tried the world and it is *not* a pretty place. 'Night, Flora, 'night Serge.'

Flora's flat feeling persisted as she lay in bed with Serge. From nowhere, unaccountably, there came a flashing, uncomfortable memory of Matt Hopkins, their kiss in the kitchen. She should never, she told herself, have allowed it happen.

'We knew it would not be easy,' Serge touched her mouth gently, picking up her mood. 'But we are together now. Be happy, *ma chère.*'

Looking at him, his eyes warm as he leaned over her, she felt as if the woman in the kitchen earlier was some stranger, a part of herself she didn't know. She would never allow her free to betray Serge again. Reaching up she traced his features with a finger.

'I *am* happy. Very happy you're here.'

They made love silently, almost as if they were afraid words would destroy the frailty of the moment. And they made love slowly and lingeringly, all the time conscious of time lost, of more separations facing them. They pleased each other in the ways they were familiar with, happy with each other's pleasure, putting everything else aside and finding again the closeness which had always given them so much joy in each other.

Afterwards, lying lazily in one another's arms, Flora asked, 'You didn't enjoy the ball, did you?'

'It was interesting.'

'Aha! I was right. I knew you didn't.' She looked at him. 'There were times when I didn't feel a part of things myself.'

'That is not true, *ma chère*. You were very much a part of it – you made tradition beautiful tonight.' He touched her breast, made a small circle around her nipple. 'But soon you must take time to come to Bruxelles. You have friends and a life there which misses you. As I do.'

'I'll come next month,' Flora said. 'For as long as I can.'

Drifting to sleep later Flora felt herself floating, at peace. Everything's all right, she thought drowsily, everything's all right again.

The morning brought wide open blue skies. There was the odd stray cloud, but not a sign of the day before's fog. 'Blast you,' Flora said to the day, and weather, as she struggled, later than usual, into the yard. 'You'd have saved me an awful lot of hassle if you'd stayed fine yesterday.'

Serge left before dawn on Monday. Even as the car lights disappeared down the avenue Flora was missing him, looking forward to the trip to Brussels. But she felt relaxed. Things, she reminded herself again, were working out fine. Just fine.

155

Chapter Fifteen

The skies over Brussels were grey. In that way, at least, things were the same. Flora, circling the airport on an early flight from Dublin, wondered how the city, and her life and friends there, would seem after all that had happened in the past months.

When she'd first moved to Brussels she'd felt the constancy of the overcast skies like a leaden weight. She'd sorely missed the turbulent clouds of home, the mercurial winds which made for ever-changing skies. In time she'd got used to it, and to a lot more. She'd had to. Brussels was very different to the sort of life she'd known before, completely unlike Dublin and with nothing at all in common with Kimbay. Its Belgian citizens she'd found serious and unfriendly. They cherished order and strove for it and in the attempt lost out on *joie de vivre*. Its international citizens, and there were many in this bureaucratic heart of Europe, were seriously fun-loving and infinite in variety.

In Brussels she had eaten in some of the finest restaurants in the world and viewed some of the ugliest buildings. She'd enjoyed the best of company and been terrifyingly bored by a stunning conformity. The paradoxes had appalled and fascinated her, and for a long time she'd had a kind of love-hate relationship with the Belgian capital.

When Ned died she'd been there five years and the hate part had been on the wane. She'd even, vaguely, been thinking of buying her apartment.

The plane came slowly down through the heavy cloud and landed at Zaventem. Flora had insisted that Serge not meet her. She wanted the day until evening alone, to have time to orientate herself, make the apartment habitable again, contact her landlady.

She joined the, mainly male, passengers as they disembarked and enjoyed, briefly, the impersonal mood of the airport before picking up a taxi. The driver was Flemish and growled when she gave him directions in French. She ignored him, wishing he'd leave his feelings about his country's language and political differences outside his taxi. He drove fast through the familiar mazelike motorways and industrial landscapes surrounding the airport, got them quickly onto the road for the city.

She was glad to be back. She needed this distancing from Kimbay, from all of the changes which had taken place in her life. There had been a great deal of activity but not much time for reflection during the fifteen weeks since Ned's death. She intended using the holiday to put things into perspective. Hopefully.

One thing, at least, she'd cleared up before leaving. Her obscene caller would not, she felt sure, be bothering her again. His last call had come, as always, as she'd been drifting into sleep. She'd known it was him the second she lifted up the phone.

'Alone, are we?' he'd sniggered, confident and pleased with himself. 'Alone in that lonely hallway with our knickers off . . .'

Flora had been precise, conversational almost. 'Why don't you fuck off?' she asked. 'Back to whatever filthy sewer you crawled from . . .' She paused, and in the silence she thought she heard him catch his breath. Before he could say anything she went on, 'And *don't* phone me again, you creepy little rat. I've got a whistle here that will blow your bloody ear off if you do.'

When she listened again she found the phone had gone dead. 'Should have done that the first time he rang,' she told the mournful Dipper.

But she wouldn't have been able to, then. The months between had toughened her up. She was learning, every day, a little more about the untapped Flora, discovering reserves and strengths she hadn't known were there.

That had been two weeks ago and her caller hadn't phoned since. She'd had an alarm system fitted to the house,

157

too, not unlike the one operating in the yard. It went against the grain and was not something Ned would have approved. But times were changing and this was how *she* needed to do things. It made her feel a lot safer.

The taxi came to Avenue de Tervueren and she watched the passing parade of high, ornate old mansions with the same pleasure they'd always given her. The rape of the city in pursuit of office space had barely touched Leopold II's wide and wonderful avenue. Between the fat, leafy trees lining its sides she caught watery flashes of distant lakes and, beyond those, glimpses of dense and lovely woodlands.

The avenue's grace and elegance compensated a little for the ravages ongoing in other parts of the city, for the confusion of glass and cement towering over the delicate lacework of medieval spires and the belching traffic on six-lane motorways crossing ancient and narrow cobbled streets.

The great arch of the Cinquantenaire loomed ahead, then disappeared as the taxi sped into a tunnel. Minutes later they were out into daylight again, skimming along the side of the park and pond in front of Flora's apartment. The taxidriver took his money in unforgiving silence, his pinch-lipped dignity unassailable.

The apartment was less stuffy and unused-feeling than she'd expected. She opened the windows and walked through its rooms, touching and feeling the things which had mattered to her when she lived there. The antique Indian low table she'd picked up at a *marché aux puces*, a nineteenth-century tapestry she'd bought while on holiday in Spain, her collection of French and Italian obelisks, at least half of them presents from Serge. They were pretty objects, some of them beautiful. But they might have belonged to someone else. Even as she touched and looked at them she was aware of a feeling of detachment – not just from them but from the apartment and the life she'd lived there.

In the bedroom wardrobe she found one of Serge's jackets and in the bathroom a set of his toiletries. The prospect of seeing him dispelled, briefly, the feeling of isolation.

She was sitting in the leather seat by the window, vaguely planning her next move, when the doorbell rang.

The concierge, when Flora opened the door to her, was agitated. 'Oh, Mam'selle Carolan, it's you!' she crossed herself twice, quickly. 'I heard a noise. I thought it was a thief, or worse. But then I thought no, not in the morning. That would not be the time for a thief to do his business. So I came up . . .'

She stopped, wringing her hands, her tired brown eyes worried behind small spectacles. Flora was not fooled. Madame Lupis missed nothing. Her ground-floor apartment was arranged so that she had a constant view from the window, and her ears so acutely tuned that not even a letter dropped in the foyer without her hearing. She had a cantankerous husband and avoided his attentions by occupying herself totally with her caretaking duties.

'Come on in,' Flora stepped aside. 'I should have let you know I was coming. How have you been?'

Madame Lupis had not been well. She had had a problem with her back and a grandchild was in hospital. Monsieur Lupis had been ill too. Flora, translating this, decided he'd been hitting the bottle again.

'So – when will you be returning to live?' Madame Lupis blinked nervously and tidied her already immaculate hair. Flora, in a letter, had told her only that Ned had died, nothing about what she was doing. She looked around the apartment now, regret mingled with sadness.

'I won't be coming back. I will be staying in Ireland for a while. So . . .' She spread her hands, letting the situation explain itself. Madame Lupis's sad eyes became moistly sympathetic.

'So terrible,' she said, 'your life taken from you like this. It is always the woman who suffers, who must make sacrifices in the family.'

'It's not like that,' Flora said, startled. 'I'm doing something I want to do. I like —'

159

'That too is what women always say.' The concierge shook her head and sighed. 'Believe me, I know, I understand.'

Flora gave up, made an arrangement to see her landlady later in the week. There would be no problem with the apartment, Madame Lupis assured as she left, already people had been asking about it. Flora felt an unreasonable chagrin, as if her life in the apartment had already ended.

But that was how Brussels operated. People came and went all the time and were immediately replaced – not only in apartments, but in the lives of those left behind. It would be naive to think things would be any different in her case.

To stock up a little Flora went to the local market. From the stalls she bought flowers, as well as some fruit and cheese. In the pâtisserie she bought croissants and bread. She had a coffee in the *taverne*. None of it brought back the feeling of belonging, made her any more comfortable with her old life. The solution, she felt sure, lay with friends. She needed to get in touch, find out how things were for the people who'd meant most to her. She would telephone Alison Boyd.

Alison had been, for Flora, the quintessential Brussels expatriate inhabitant. She was English, with three children and a claim to the same number of constant lovers. Her accent, after twenty years in Brussels, was an odd mixture of French inflections and the Yorkshire vowels she'd grown up with. Her divorced French husband had left her rich enough to have empty days to fill and she squealed with delight when she heard Flora's voice on the phone.

'We'll meet. Immediately. For lunch. Where do you want to go?'

'Why not somewhere in the Place Sainte Catherine?' Flora was suddenly hungry for food, the centre of town and some hot gossip. They named a restaurant in the fashionable old fish market area and Flora changed into a stone-coloured linen suit. Her car started without trouble, but by the time she arrived at l'Heure Rouge she was suffering from the panicky claustrophobia driving in the city always brought on.

'Look at you! So healthy and so *thirsty*-looking.' Alison, without pause for breath, ordered a second *apéritif maison* for Flora. Her lively, birdlike face was impatient as Flora, after three brief, Brussels-style kisses, sat opposite. 'Tell me everything,' she commanded.

'All in good time.' Flora looked around, enjoying the fashionable crowd before turning back to her companion. 'You're looking well.' She smiled.

'I try.' Alison touched her hair, raised fine eyebrows. She wasn't at all beautiful but took pains with herself, and spent her ex-husband's money on being unforgettable. Her platinum hair, in a butchered look that was new, highlighted her small grey eyes. She had a boy's body, slim and lithe, and her constant smile revealed neat, orthodontically perfect teeth. 'I've gained a kilo this winter,' she sighed. 'I really shouldn't eat today. But because you're here . . .'

They ordered from the *menu gastronomique*, starting with a salmon terrine.

'Now, talk.' Alison filled their wine glasses and Flora told her, in brief outline, how her life had been since she'd left. As she did it seemed more and more ludicrous to expect Alison to understand. The disparities between their lives were too great. Their common ground had been tennis, shared friends, some gossip. She wasn't surprised when Alison crisply interrupted at the only point which interested her.

'What are you going to do about the gorgeous Serge?'

'*Do* about him?'

'Don't toy with me, my girl,' Alison wagged a ring-encrusted index finger. 'Are you going to marry the man, or what?'

'Or what, for the moment,' Flora shrugged. 'I don't have much choice, do I? He's here, I'm there.'

'True. You want to think this thing through carefully, Flora. I don't know what the score is over there, but this place is alive with rampaging women . . .'

'Yes, I know,' Flora grinned, deliberately mis-understanding.

'Excluding me.' Alison pulled a face. 'He's not my type.

161

I married a Frenchman, remember? Pompous, self-important race. Wouldn't be caught dead, not to mind in bed, with one these days. But not everyone's so discerning.'

She was silent as the waiter served them with home-cured ham and a three-vegetable mousse. When he'd gone Flora, an edge to her voice, said, 'Alison, if you're trying to tell me Serge is having a thing with someone then I don't want to know. That's his business.'

Alison tilted her head, looked at Flora thoughtfully through half-closed eyes. 'I don't think he is, actually. Having a thing, I mean. But you should bear the possibility in mind when making your calculations.'

'Calculations?'

'About whether or not to marry him.' Alison was impatient. 'And don't tell me, Flora, that it hasn't come into your reckonings about this future in which you're going to make money out of horses.'

So Alison *had* been listening, after a fashion. Flora frowned, took a few minutes before answering. Alison, wisely intuitive, didn't push her.

'Frankly, Alison, marrying Serge hasn't come into the reckonings,' she said eventually. 'Not in any real sense anyway. I'm doing what I'm doing because I feel I have to. In the strangest way Serge has become peripheral, these last months. But I don't want him to stay that way and I don't think I could go on without knowing that he's there for me, even if it's in the background. As for marriage . . .' She hesitated and shrugged. 'I'd just assumed it would happen. I still do.'

'You're taking a chance, that's all I can say. But then not so big a chance.' Alison gave a wry smile. 'You're the sort of female who'll always have some nice man in attendance. Question is – will you get the one you want, this time?'

'We'll háve to wait and see.' Flora smiled uneasily. Alison was not noted for her discretion and the conversation had become far too personal. They declined desserts and the waiter brought them coffee. Alison's face took on a faraway, dreamy look.

'It could be,' she said, 'that you've already worked out the ideal arrangement. Marriage has no mystery, you know.' She sighed, cast a glance over the dark elegance of the restaurant. 'It leaves no illusions between people, just encourages a complicity to fool one another. Better by far to remain lovers, at a distance. Stay as you are, Flora. That's my advice.'

Flora didn't tell Serge about her lunchtime conversation with Alison. Which did not mean she wasn't thinking about it, or about the risk she was taking of losing him. It had made her edgy and unsure, feelings which were compounded by her realization, as the week went on, that Brussels and the life she'd led there had lost their appeal for her.

There was no one thing which pinpointed the discovery. It certainly had nothing to do with Serge, or how they were getting on. Their times together were wonderful, made special by the knowledge that next week they would again be apart. They laughed a lot, made love with care, talked thoughtfully. Their trustful ease made Flora wonder if Alison didn't have a point. Being lovers at a distance had its compensations. For the moment anyway.

It was from other people that she got the sense that Brussels was no longer what she wanted. It came from a creeping boredom with friends she'd once enjoyed and the knowledge that the months away had put a distance between her and this life which could never be bridged.

It began when she and Serge dined *chez* Maus. Flora had always liked the Mauses, a Belgian couple with a great deal of old money which they spent on an elaborate house with white walls and parquet, pediments and marble fireplaces. They entertained with style and lavishly. Food at the dinner party was superb, as always. Flora, enjoying a simmered mixture of baby artichoke hearts, *morilles* and other mushrooms, found herself drawn into a conversation about the healthy body.

'You have to experience pain,' Pierre Maus told her, 'it is no good otherwise.'

'And you must never give up.' The American woman

163

opposite Flora was adamant. 'It has to be done every day, minimum one hour but twice that time is best. Mostly I play tennis or go to the gym. What do you do?'

'I used to play tennis,' Flora said, 'but now I work.' A blank expression crossed the other woman's face and Flora hastily amended, 'For pure exercise I ride.'

'Not bad,' the woman conceded, 'but not great for the rear end. You need to do some work in the gym, honey, to keep the old cellulite in control.'

'I'm sure you're right.' Flora, agreeing, stifled a yawn. She'd had this conversation, or variations of it, many times before. She'd been interested before. She wasn't interested now.

On the last day of the holiday she spent an almost blissful day with Serge in the Ardennes. They walked through wooded uplands and, as the day got shorter, made their way along a river back to the steep, narrow valley in which they'd left the car. The sun shone in a clear, untypical sky.

'We should have come here days ago,' Flora sighed in satisfaction.

'Would you have been less restless, *mon ange*, if we had spent more time in the country?'

He'd noticed. Flora was silent for a while. When they reached the car she spoke again.

'I've got out of the habit of having time on my hands. The life I lived here seems . . . pointless. I've grown out of it . . .' she paused '. . . but not all of it. You don't seem pointless at all, my love.' She kissed him lightly on the lips.

Serge moved away from her and looked thoughtfully back the way they'd come.

'Your green freedom has changed you,' he said. He picked up a stone and took careful aim at a boulder in the river fifty yards away. He missed. He was an excellent marksman, usually. 'You will never return to live in Brussels, Flora.'

'No, I won't come back to live in Brussels.' Flora felt sad. She was, she knew, closing a chapter in her life.

'Perhaps it is just as well things happened this way.' Serge took aim with another stone. This time he didn't

164

miss. He turned, put his hands on her shoulders and pulled her close against him. 'I had not planned to live my life in Belgium either. My mother complains a lot about her age, about death. It is time to think about returning to France.'

They didn't talk then, or later, of the implications for their relationship. But for Flora there was peace, and a certain security, in the knowledge that they had both arrived at a crossroads. She was sure of his love. The way ahead, together, would be worked out in time.

Serge waited until her last night before giving her another bit of news. They were standing on the balcony of her apartment, sharing a drink and enjoying the nostalgia of the moment. This would be their last viewing of the pond together, the last time they would listen to the ducks cackling crankily in the dark.

'I am going to the US for ten weeks.' He played with her hair. 'To New York and to Boston.'

'Ten weeks! That's nearly three months! You've never gone for so long before . . .'

'No. But business has never been so good before and there are opportunities which cannot be missed.'

'Two months. It's not that long.' Flora stood very still. The words didn't work. It *was* very long. A feeling of desolation swept through her. The Atlantic was huge. He would be so far away if she needed him. Might as well say out of touch.

'I will be back at the end of July and will come straight to Ireland.' His arms went around her and he tilted her face so that she was looking at him. 'Now it is your turn to understand something *I* must do.'

'And I do,' Flora assured him. 'But it doesn't mean I won't miss you.'

She packed the last of her belongings next day, ready for shipping home. She signed the last of the landlady's forms too and said goodbye to the melancholy concierge. Just before she left she rang Alison and other friends with promises that she would be back to see them.

Five years of her life was disposed of in a shockingly short time but she didn't, as yet, feel any regrets.

Chapter Sixteen

Sophie, leaving the doctor's surgery, walked blindly for ten minutes before realizing she was headed away from where she'd parked the car. She stopped, took several deep breaths, then leaned against some railings and closed her eyes. The feeling of panic subsided a little.

When she opened her eyes to take stock she saw that she'd walked the length of Rathgar Road, almost to Rathmines village. It was lunchtime and busy, the sun spilling over the pavements and creating a modest carnival mood. The village offered an infinitely more inviting prospect than the alternative of retracing her steps to pick up the car and drive home. She didn't feel in any shape yet to go back to the apartment, sit in its memory-sodden rooms and try to sort this thing out. What she needed was anonymous, agreeable, unquestioning surroundings while she tried to get used to what she'd just been told. A pub would do just fine.

A miserable May had given way to a glorious, shining June and it was one of a string of beautiful days. She passed through a group of lunch-break workers, noisily lounging at pavement tables, and went into a likely looking pub. It was dark and almost empty but she stayed there anyway, hugging a glass of wine and picking at a cheese sandwich. Her thoughts went on chasing themselves around her head, reminding her of the Indian analogy which compared the mind to a chattering monkey.

Shit, she thought, this can't be happening to me. Not now, not when everything was beginning to come together. She finished the wine and gave up on the sandwich. The pub was chilly as well as dark and the silence made her jittery. I can't think here, she decided, too damn morbid.

The contrast, when she emerged into the sun, made her

feel immediately calmer; more positive, too. She found another pub and this time sat with her glass of wine at a pavement table. There, in the sun, she went over the conversation in Dr Clare O'Grady's surgery. She knew it wouldn't change, or even solve, anything. But it might somehow give her a fix on things.

The irony was that she hadn't suspected a thing. Maybe if she'd had even an inkling the shock mightn't be so great. She'd been fine, no different to the way she always felt, before she'd gone along for her routine check-up.

She was fussy about things like that; particular about keeping her body in shape with exercise and a once-a-year examination for signs of undue wear and tear. A couple of weeks ago, as she always did, she'd popped in to give Clare samples for the usual tests. She liked the reassurance of having everything checked at the same time.

Even so, she'd thought it a sort of a sick, or at the very least silly, joke when Clare – quite casually – had said, 'You're pregnant, Sophie. About eight weeks gone. But I suppose you suspected as much.'

The shock, at first, took Sophie's breath away. Then common sense, and scepticism, came to the rescue.

'I can't be,' she was emphatic, 'and of course you're joking . . .'

'I most certainly am *not* joking, Sophie.' Clare O'Grady was quite sharp. 'Surely you—'

'It's a mistake. They've sent you back the wrong test results. Someone else . . .' Sophie held out a shaking hand for the lab report and the doctor, reluctantly, handed it to her.

'There's no mistake, Sophie. But if it'll make you feel better I'll double check. When did you last have a period?'

And that was the question, age-old and dreaded by women since God was a child, which chilled Sophie's heart. She couldn't remember. She'd never been regular and, with Robert and frequent sex gone, she had no reason to pay heed. 'I don't know,' she said dully. 'How could it happen? I was so careful.'

'I can't help you there.' The doctor sighed. 'There's always a reason.'

'My marriage is over. Did I tell you that, Clare? My marriage is over . . .' Sophie's voice rose, she could hear it herself. 'The bastard I married is gone, vamoosed, skedaddled. And now you tell me—' She choked, unable to get the words out, and threw the report chart onto the doctor's desk.

'Okay. That's enough.' Clare O'Grady was firm as she filled a glass with cold water from the thermos on her desk. 'Drink this and we'll look at the situation together. I'm sorry about the marriage, Sophie. It'll make things difficult.'

'Difficult—' Sophie choked at the understatement. 'Difficult! Jesus, Clare! Have you any *idea* what this means to my life?'

'I do,' the doctor was gentler. 'But you're healthy and young, and earning money . . .'

'But I don't *want* a baby!' Sophie's bitter cry ended in a sob. 'And I certainly don't want *his* baby. I wouldn't know what to do with it. I'd be a lousy mother.' She got up and walked to the surgery window. Outside, in the long back garden, the sun shone through the leaves of old trees. It created a dancing mosaic on the spot where two of the doctor's grandchildren played on a swing.

'I've never wanted children,' Sophie was quieter. 'There are enough in the world already and there are women more capable of mothering than me who're willing to produce more. We don't all *have* to be mothers, you know.' Looking at the garden, at the golden day and happy children, she found it impossible to comprehend that life was growing inside her.

'It's inconceivable.' She tried a joke but the doctor, when she turned around to her, didn't smile.

'You'll have to make plans, Sophie,' she said.

'Bit late for that. I should have had myself sterilized. To make things *not* happen you have to plan, too.'

'That might have been difficult,' the doctor consoled. 'You'd have been considered young for a decision so final. People do change their minds, you know. All the time.'

'I won't. I don't want it now and I won't want it any

more in seven months' time. You'll have to refer me somewhere.' The words came in a bewildered rush.

'I can't.' The doctor shook her head. 'You must know that, Sophie. The law doesn't allow me to.'

'The law! To hell with the law! What does the law know about me, about my life? Christ, what am I going to do?' Distraught, Sophie sank onto the chair by the desk and stared blankly in front of her.

'Go away and think about it, Sophie,' the doctor said. 'That'll do for starters. Do you have anyone you can talk to? A friend? Someone in the family, perhaps?'

Sophie laughed then, and picked up her bag. 'Definitely *not* someone in the family,' she said. 'The last time we got together was for an aunt's funeral. The peace didn't hold while we were putting her into the ground.' She left after that, her mind in a kind of fugue, and started walking.

Around her people began drifting back to their offices. After another glass of wine it became vaguely clear to her what she should do.

To begin with she would talk to Flora. Babies weren't a subject they'd discussed a great deal in the past. Motherhood had seemed such a distant prospect for either of them in those days. But Flora would surely understand. It was quite likely she felt, as Sophie did, that it wasn't a woman's automatic duty to procreate. She might even be practically helpful, know of a discreet clinic in Brussels Sophie could go to.

The decision perked her up. She even, as she walked back to the car, enjoyed the heat of the sun a little. But the fragile buoyancy popped, like an air bubble, when a wave of unaccustomed nausea came over her an hour later in the apartment. 'It's not fair,' she held her stomach, 'it's not bloody well fair.'

Flora was welcoming when she phoned and invited herself to Kimbay for a few days. 'Why not stay a week?' she asked. 'It's quiet here, nothing much happening at the moment. And with the weather so good . . .'

Sophie allowed herself to be persuaded. It took a couple

169

of days to wrap up the job she was working on but by Thursday she was packing the car, heading down the quays and out of town.

She wore a straw hat and red-flowered *crêpe-de-chine* dress and looked anything but pregnant. She didn't feel pregnant either, apart from the odd bout of nausea.

She hadn't been outside the city since her one brief visit to the racetrack. Even to her urban eyes the countryside looked good, and utterly changed in the few months since then. The roads were bleached in the sun and the ubiquitous green had been livened up with great multi-coloured bursts of flower. Trees and hedgerows drooped with impenetrable masses of leaf. I could get to like the rural existence if it behaved like this more often, Sophie thought, and hummed a little with the car radio. She drove slowly, getting lost once in the narrow roads which wound the last few miles to Kimbay. It was late afternoon when she arrived, hot and fairly tired.

Kimbay too looked different, lush and peaceful and very much in command of itself. There was no one about and she felt uneasy with the quiet stillness. Unfriendly looking horses grazed in a field quite close to the house, others stood under an old tree and swished their tails at flies. In the distance a voice called and a dog barked. Closer to where she stood, almost at her feet, the busy, clicking legs of a grasshopper broke the silence.

'All very idyllic and picturesque,' she muttered, 'but a bit of human company wouldn't go amiss.' She pulled her bag from the car and turned to look at the house. It too had changed since the last time she'd seen it. The wisteria that Flora had promised her would be 'a sensation' in the summer came pretty close to being just that. A good half of the front of the house was covered in bunches of its rampant, grape-like blue flowers. In the garden by the side of the house a sea of wild colour had sprung up but it was, as far as Sophie could see, empty of human habitation.

The front door was open but the hallway, when she got there, was empty. 'Good to see the old Irish custom of leaving the house open to burglars alive and well.' She spoke aloud to herself as she dumped her bag and swatted a persistent fly. 'Bugger off,' she said and then, louder, 'anyone at home?'

The fly droned in her ear and she took a swipe at it with her hat. She called again and opened the door to the living room. The darkening sun on its worn carpet emphasized both its shabby gentility and its emptiness. She crossed to the dining room. It looked as if it hadn't been inhabited for months.

She was standing in the hallway, battling with annoyance and the worry that she might have got the day wrong, when the door next to the dining room opened. Daisy, tent-like and smiling in a loose green dress, beckoned her into the office.

'Thought I heard something,' Daisy said. 'Hope you haven't been waiting long.' She was wearing earphones and had obviously been keying something into the computer on the desk. 'Take a seat,' her gesture took in the room, 'I'll be with you in a jiffy.'

Sophie, after moving a stack of newspapers, sat looking around the room. It might have been handsome once; the ceilings were certainly high enough to give grandeur; but at the moment it was a chaos. She thought of Wilde's chaos, 'illumined by flashes of lightning', and wondered if it applied to Daisy's way of working.

'That's that, then.' Daisy took off the earphones and a heavy mass of hair fell forward. 'You look tired. A glass of my elderflower wine is what you need.' She caught and expertly wound her hair as she spoke. 'Flora will be here shortly. A yearling's gone down with an injury.'

'Oh. Anything serious?' Sophie followed her to the kitchen.

'Could be. We'll know when she gets back. She's had to take him over to the vet's surgery so it can't be too good. He gave him a shot of tetanus here but it looks as if he'll have to be stitched.' Daisy put the wine and glasses on the table. 'You can have tea, if you prefer.'

'The wine will be lovely,' Sophie slipped off her sandals and sat at the table. Daisy poured the wine. 'Do the horses hurt themselves often?' Sophie asked as she sipped. 'Flora mentioned an accident the last time I spoke to her.'

'Well . . . there's been more than the usual share this year. Today's fellow tried to jump a fence and nearly impaled himself. He ripped the skin on a hind leg between hip and hock.'

'Ugh, sounds horrible.' Sophie pulled a face.

'He's a bit of a jumper,' Daisy explained, 'but something must have excited him.' She frowned. 'He's a valuable animal, too. Best yearling we have in the yard at the moment —' She stopped as Sophie, hand pressed to her mouth, bolted for the sink and proceeded to retch. Daisy was beside her in seconds, comforting hand on her shoulder. 'Get it up now, that's the girl.' She reached for a towel. 'I shouldn't have given you any of that wine. It's not everyone can take it.'

'Sorry.' Sophie, white-faced, straightened up. 'Disgusting thing to do. Must be the heat, the car journey . . .' She buried her face in the cold, damp towel then took several deep breaths. 'I'm fine now,' she said.

'You don't look fine to me,' Daisy peered at her. 'A cup of tea is what you need. Best thing is for you to go up for a bit of a lie down. You're in the room opposite Flora. I'll bring you up the tea.'

In the bedroom Sophie lay with the curtains half closed. It had started already. This betrayal by her body was what she could expect, what lay ahead. And how in God's name was she going to get through a week at Kimbay if she couldn't drink Daisy's wine? She groaned and buried her head in the pillow. She was asleep when Daisy brought the tea, was unaware of her closing the curtains and covering her with a cotton spread. She missed too the thoughtful look the older woman gave her before leaving the room.

She woke to find Flora sitting on the bed.

'How're you feeling?' Her friend smiled, but looked tired herself.

Sophie stretched and threw her legs over the side of the bed. She wriggled her toes, testing. 'Fine.' She grinned. 'Everything seems to be working.' She crossed to the

172

window and opened the curtains. The evening sun flooded the room. 'I've hardly been the ideal houseguest so far, have I? How long did I sleep? And how long have you been here?'

'About an hour is the answer to the first question and I've been here less than a minute. Sorry if I woke you.'

Flora was wearing a denim shirt, and damp tendrils of hair straggled from an alice band. Her sun-tan didn't at all disguise the wan look about her face.

'You didn't wake me,' Sophie assured her. 'Anyway, you look far more of a specimen for concern than I do. Have you been burning the candle – or is it all these injured animals? How's the fence-impaled horse?'

Sophie sat at the dressing table and began to reapply her make-up carefully. From the bed Flora watched her silently. 'The horse will recover,' she said. 'But what about you, Sophie? You *never* get sick.'

'I don't, do I?' Sophie's reflection arched a comical eyebrow. 'But I certainly made up for lost time today, didn't I?'

'Daisy thinks you're pregnant.' Flora held her friend's gaze in the mirror. 'Are you?'

Sophie didn't answer. Applying mascara she closed a lid and broke eye contact. Flora waited. When she had finished both eyes to her satisfaction Sophie turned round. 'Yes,' she said. 'I'm pregnant.'

Flora straightened up. It was as if someone had poked her with a pin and Sophie knew instantly that her friend had thought Daisy was wrong.

'I was going to tell you anyway.' Sophie turned back to the mirror and began to tease her hair. 'Tomorrow, or the day after . . .'

'Is that why you came down?' Flora was gentle.

'Yes. The news was a bit . . . unexpected.' Sophie gave a short laugh.

'Is Robert . . .'

'Oh, yes. Robert's the father.' Sophie laughed again, almost gaily. Flora started to get up and she waved her to stop. 'Don't, Flora, please don't go all soft on me.' She stood up from the mirror and walked to the window. When

173

she spoke it was with her back to Flora and in a toneless voice. 'I don't want commiserations or sympathy or, God forbid, congratulations. I just need you to listen, to understand how I feel, help me sort out what I'm going to do.'

'Fine.' Flora sat down again. 'But how in God's name did it happen, to you of all people? It was hardly an immaculate conception, was it?'

'More like the wages of sin.' Sophie leaned her forehead against the glass of the window. Her voice was calmer, reflective even. 'I've had time to think and I've figured what happened. It must have been the psychological thing of being married to Robert that put me off guard, made me less careful than usual. I don't know how else to explain it.' She began to pace, restlessly, as she spoke. 'That last time you and I met, after I'd got the letter, remember? Well, Robert's departure to the sun was delayed and he phoned. He wanted a few things from the apartment. He was supposed to arrive during the day but the sod didn't turn up until nearly midnight.' She laughed, shortly. 'And of course he was drunk and sentimental and randy. I should have changed the locks, but then there are a lot of things I should have done in my time and didn't. I'd had a few glasses of wine and he just walked in and one thing led to another . . .' She shrugged, stopped pacing. 'I'm not talking about rape here. It was the long goodbye, as he'd have said himself. One for the road. Our love-making was never one-sided. In that department, at least, we always got things together. But I'd come off the pill, to give the old bod a rest from oestrogen dosing, so we used a condom. And the rest, my pet, is history. So,' she stood facing Flora, 'where do I go from here?'

'You tell me,' Flora said. 'You only want me to listen, remember.'

'Right. Well,' Sophie began pacing again, 'I'm about nine weeks gone. Which doesn't leave me a lot of time to get organized. I can't have it. Married, I'd find it difficult. In the limbo land I'm in now I'd find it impossible. Maybe in five or six years' time, when the old biological clock begins the countdown, I'll feel differently. Though I doubt it. I'm not the mothering kind. I'd make life hell for a kid. Can you imagine it? Me, a mother?'

'It's difficult to imagine all right.'

'Some women are born to it. I'm not one of them. Plus I've an unreliable source of income and a flat in the centre of town that would be totally unsuitable. And now that he's finally gone I don't want Robert having any rights in my life. Like coming to visit his kid and hanging around.' She stopped, flattened her hands on her hips and pulled a wry face. 'And I can't bear the idea of getting fat, all wobbling cellulite and swinging breasts . . .'

'Well,' Flora plumped up the pillows and leaned back against them. She closed her eyes. 'That about covers the negatives. Any positive thoughts on this unhappy event?'

Sophie, in a rush of worried concern, saw how tired her friend was. But her need to be rid of how she felt drove her relentlessly on and she put the thought aside for the moment.

'None that make any difference.' She was blunt. 'So I've decided it's better for everyone if I terminate. Trouble is, I never, ever thought this would happen to me and I don't have a clue about where to go or what to do. I could fly to London next week and find a clinic there, I know that. But I thought that if you knew one in Brussels I could go there and you could come with me . . .'

Flora opened her eyes and sat up. She started to say something but Sophie held up a hand.

'Wait, I'm not finished. I'm frightened, Flora. I really do feel it's best if I don't have this baby but the thought of the actual abortion frightens me. I'm worried too about the psychological effects afterwards. The old guilt trip and all that . . .' She hesitated. 'I don't want to be on my own.' She abruptly stopped talking and pacing and, like a clockwork doll wound down, fell into the armchair by the window.

'Seems to me,' Flora left the bed and crossed to stand over her, 'that you pretty well know your own mind on this. You're lucky to be so sure.'

'Wouldn't you be?' Sophie sounded curious.

'No. I'd be full of doubts. I'd probably have the baby,

because I'd never be sure that not having it was the right thing, or justifiable. But then that's me and I'm discovering that life is a greyer matter than it used to be.'

'What do you mean?'

'Not so black and white, is all. Look, Sophie,' she knelt in front of her friend and took one of her hands, 'I'm not being unhelpful, but I really don't know of a clinic in Brussels. Belgian law on abortion is not a lot different from Irish law, you know.'

'I see. It's all right, Flora, forget it. It was just an idea.' Sophie seemed to have got a lot smaller in the chair. Flora stood, caught her by the arms and pulled her to her feet.

'Get a life, Sophie, this victim mode isn't you. All I'm saying is that you should consider your options, if only for the sake of your peace of mind afterwards. Look, stay here for as long as you like and take the time to think about it. If you still want to go ahead then I'll go to London with you. I promise.'

'I thought you'd be absolutely with me. I'd no idea you felt like this.'

'Which is why you chose to talk to me, right? You didn't want doubts, or advice.' Flora put an arm around her. 'Better now than afterwards, Sophie.'

'I'm not so sure about that.' Sophie nearly managed a laugh. 'But I'll give it a week, no longer. I can't stand decisions hanging over me. And the longer it goes on the harder it'll be, in every sense.' She gave a long, shuddering sigh. 'I'm glad I told you. Makes it easier to handle, somehow. One week, Flora, and I'll be sticking you to your promise.'

Chapter Seventeen

Sophie made an effort to get involved in the life and workings of Kimbay. She did it because of Flora and a real desire to understand what her friend was up to. But she took an interest, too, because all knowledge was grist to her journalistic mill, and because being involved helped keep her mind off her own problem. A rest from thinking about her 'condition' would, she felt sure, help her see things more clearly.

The injured yearling came back from the vet on her first morning at Kimbay. He was a large, arrogant-looking grey and he gave Sophie a distinctly cool look.

'He's got guts.' Flora patted him fondly. 'I was terrified we might lose him. I'm depending on him to make us some money at Goffs. He needs care, but he's going to be all right.'

'He was really that bad, then?' Sophie was unconvinced. 'I must say, Flora, I don't like the way he's looking at me.'

Flora laughed. 'He's not a gentle animal, I'll grant you. But if only you'd seen him yesterday you'd understand. His skin was hanging down in tatters and he just stood looking at me when I went up to him. He walked like a lamb back to the yard, though he must have been in terrible pain. The vet had to put him out to stitch him up. Still, as you can see, it really wasn't that bad when it was all cleaned up.'

'I'll take your word for it.' Sophie shuddered and looked away from the vet's handiwork.

As the day went on and she saw something of the work in the yard Sophie found herself envying Flora the purity of her affection for the horses. Life, she thought, must make wonderful sense when it was centred on the horse-breeding cycle. She said as much to Flora, who laughed uproariously and told her to take a walk.

Sophie did a lot of walking in the days which followed. Sometimes she went with Daisy, who liked to take an hour during the day and walk by the river. It was the week of the longest day in the year and of the hottest June days in living memory. In dread of the sun on her pale skin Sophie wore a wide hat while Daisy bared practically all and cultivated freckles. They didn't talk much since this would, somehow, have been a transgression of the peaceful intent of the walks. Instinct told Sophie that Daisy would think the baby good news, would never understand her desire not to have it, and so she didn't mention the thing most on her mind. But they developed a companionable ease anyway, one which matched the lazy days.

Afterwards, when that summer week was a memory, Sophie would wonder if perhaps she *should* have talked to Daisy. It probably wouldn't have changed anything, but then again perhaps it might. Maybe, if she'd talked to Daisy, she might have taken more care. Or at least have thought a bit more about things.

But life, as she had always known, was inclined to go its sweet and nasty way no matter what.

On Sunday, when Sophie had been at Kimbay three days, Flora decided they would go to the races at Punchestown. Sophie put on a striped silk dress and nearly wept when she saw what her slightly swelling stomach did to the pattern. She changed into a Daisy-like creation in muslin and felt comfortable, if nothing else. She slipped on a pair of hooped earrings and caught her hair back with a scarf.

'It's an ethnic look,' she explained crossly when Flora raised an eyebrow. Flora herself wore a sleeveless white linen dress and belted it in a way that made Sophie grit her teeth.

Sophie immediately liked the intimacy and cheerful mood at Punchestown. The heat was intense but the crowds, all of whom seemed to know one another, circulated constantly and seemed not to notice. Flora studied the horses and racecard with a nail-biting intensity that exasperated Sophie.

'We're supposed to be here for fun,' she said.

'Right,' Flora tapped the card, 'put something on number three in the next race and on five in the one after that. A couple of wins should liven things up.'

The first horse won, the second came a poor third. Sophie made her own choice for the next race and lost again.

'I need a drink,' she said, 'and I need to sit somewhere cool. Can we go to the bar?' The bar was in a tent and not at all cool. But the wine was chilled and they sat with a bottle of Chablis, fanning themselves in desultory fashion.

'Is that horse of yours ever going to see a racetrack?' Sophie sipped the Chablis. (She'd discovered, to her relief, that Daisy's elderflower wine, as well as Daisy's strong tea, were the only beverages which brought on the nausea.) Mention of Flo Girl seemed to make Flora restless. She frowned, crossed and uncrossed her legs.

'She has her first race in August. In Gowran Park. And here's the rub,' she turned a rueful smile on her friend. 'All winter I wanted that filly to race but now that the date's drawing near I'm getting cold feet. Suppose she hates it? Or throws a nervous fit, or breaks a leg?'

'Supposing she wins?' Sophie grinned.

'Thanks, Sophie, that's just what I wanted you to say.' Flora was refilling their glasses when a voice, genial and slurred, spoke behind them.

'Flora Carolan! Be the holy, it *is* you! Thought I saw you earlier.' One of the roundest men Sophie had ever seen pulled a chair up to their table. 'And who,' he asked, 'is this beautiful filly you have with you?' He looked at Sophie with rheumy blue eyes. Scarce red hair lay damply on his forehead.

'Hello, Gus.' Flora took his outstretched hand and introduced him to Sophie as Gus Fitzgerald.

'Knew this lassie's father well,' Gus explained to Sophie. 'A decent man.' He blinked the rheumy eyes at Flora. 'Sorry to hear the way things are working out at the yard. Bad luck's a terrible thing when it hits a place. But if you keep the head down and get on with—'

'What *are* you talking about, Gus?' Flora, leaning forward, spoke sharply. 'Things are fine at Kimbay. What do you mean about bad luck?'

Gus fumbled with a fob watch and shot a blinking look at its face. 'Just something I heard,' he mumbled. 'I'll have to be off now.' He winked at Sophie. 'Put a few bob on Love Spot in the last race. He'll pay for the wine.'

'Gus,' Flora's voice was threatening, 'what were you talking about just now?'

'Something I heard, that's all.' Gus pushed his chair back from the table. 'I meant no harm, Flora. From the open way people are talking I thought you must know yourself what's being said.'

'Well, I don't,' Flora snapped. 'What people, and what's being said?'

'People in the business.' Gus waved a red, freckled hand around the tent. 'There's a lot of talk about bad luck hitting Kimbay. Accidents, losing staff, 'flu in the yard, that sort of thing. Happens sometimes, when there's a change in the running of things. Just as easy changes back. Sometimes.' He smiled. Sophie supposed it was meant to be a sympathetic expression. It was merely ghoulish.

'Listen to me, Gus, and listen hard.' Flora tapped him on a fat knee with her index finger. 'You go back and tell those people, all of them, that Kimbay's never been in better shape. I don't know who is spreading the rumour but the facts are that we didn't have 'flu in the yard because, *luckily*, a dirty animal was spotted in time. The colt who had the accident is coming along fine and the staff member who left was no great loss. We've a better team without him. Anything else you want explained?'

'A misunderstanding, Flora, that's all it was. A misunderstanding.' Gus mopped his brow with a large, checked handkerchief. 'Don't be getting yourself upset over nothing.'

'You're right, Gus, it was nothing.' Flora was sheer ice.

'Just rumour and gossip-mongering. Sure I can't buy you a drink before you go?'

'No, thanks all the same, Flora. I might catch you at the Derby next week.' Gus heaved himself out of the seat. 'Take care now. And don't forget,' he shook the checked hanky at Sophie, 'Love Spot in the last race.' He wove a way through the crowd, mopping his brow and greeting people as he went.

'Someone will hang for that man one day,' Flora said.

'You certainly stopped him in his gallop,' Sophie gave a low chuckle. 'I felt like applauding your little speech there. Most impressive, Flora, this new, tougher you.'

'Needs must . . .' Flora took a long drink of her wine.

'Who is he, anyway?' Sophie asked.

'He's a messenger. All I've done is shoot the messenger.' Flora shrugged. 'Better, I suppose, than doing nothing.'

'Messenger?' Sophie wrinkled her pale brow.

'Gus Fitzgerald was *meant* to tell me all that gibberish.' Flora was thoughtful. 'I'm sure of it. He suffers from chronic verbal diarrhoea. Can't keep anything to himself. Giving information to Gus is the quickest known way of ensuring it gets to the entire county.'

'Aha!' Sophie clapped a hand to her head. 'So that little scene was all about unnerving you? Getting you worried about what people are saying?'

'Something like that. Question is why, and who put Gus up to it?' Flora looked around the tent, coolly. Sophie had never seen her like this. She was like a military campaigner assessing the enemy. 'Thing is, Sophie, the credibility of the yard could be destroyed by rumour. Once word gets about that a stable is having problems it becomes easy enough to destroy it. And the bad luck thing is particularly insidious in a business where good luck is a real commodity!'

'Mmm. The gentle vicissitudes of country life.' Sophie looked at the bantering drinkers around them, at the flat caps and colourful tea dresses, the general camaraderie. 'Any truth in the rumours?' she asked.

181

Flora didn't answer immediately, and when she did her voice was less sure. 'That's the problem, Sophie, there could be. It sounds absurd, I know, but it's occurred to me once or twice that someone might be trying to create mischief in the yard. I mentioned it to Shay and he pooh-poohed the idea, said I was imagining things. He's probably right. Problems arise in yards all the time. It's the nature of the business to be unstable.'

'But why would anyone want to create mischief?' Sophie asked. 'Or, and it's probably the same question, *who* would want to?'

Flora shook her head and her eyes darkened. She seemed to be thinking out loud when she replied. 'Who knows? A competitor who wants to see the yard on its knees? Someone who'd like it split up so's they could move in? Someone with a grudge against Shay – or Ned or me? Someone,' her face was grim, 'who thinks women should be background ornaments, not running yards.'

'Quite a few possibilities there,' Sophie said.

'There's another,' Flora wasn't finished, 'and it's more specific.' Sophie could see intensity and anger building in her as she went on, speaking quickly. 'It's occurred to me that Victor Mangan might have something to do with all of this. It would be risky, even foolish of him, to try to sabotage the yard. But he's a man used to getting what he wants and Kimbay is top of his current want list.'

'Take it easy.' Sophie was very calm. 'This is heavy stuff, Flora. You're making serious accusations here. It could be, as you said earlier, that what's been happening is all part of the cut and thrust of the business.'

'I *know* that.' Flora nervously, jerkily, pushed her glass around the table. 'But I've been giving it a lot of thought. And if I'm right and there *is* someone working against the yard then I'd be a fool not to do something about it.'

'True. But if you do something and you're wrong then you're in worse trouble. In court for slander or defamation . . .'

'I'm not that sort of a fool,' Flora snapped. 'If I only knew, for sure, that there was someone behind things then

182

I could sort it out, deal with it discreetly. It's this not knowing that's driving me mad. I'm full of suspicions, Sophie, doubting everyone – and that's not like me. You know it's not. I hate living like this.' She stopped. She was trembling, her eyes wide and bright with unshed tears. 'It's got to the stage where I'm afraid to trust my judgement about people. I'm so unsure about everything . . .'

'That's obvious.' Sophie was dry. Flora's fingers were drumming a tattoo on the table and she held them, stilling the frantic movement. 'Listen to me, Flora.' She was firm and very serious. 'You're too close to all of this, too involved with the yard. Think about it – you've never in your life had this kind of responsibility and now, only months after your father's death, you're right in there at the deep end. Could be that you can't see the wood for the trees, that the yard problems really *are* your average growing pains . . .'

'You're saying I'm paranoid,' Flora said dully.

'Heading that way.' Sophie was cheerful. 'Look, the Brussels trip didn't help much, from the sound of things. Why don't you come back to Dublin with me next week for a few days? We can see a film, meet people. It'll do you good. And it's a quiet time in the yard, you said so yourself.' She gave a lopsided grin. 'I could do with the company myself at the moment.'

'Maybe I will.' Flora was hesitant. 'I could see the boys – Fintan and Ollie, I mean.' She pulled a wry face. 'I'm told by Daisy it's not politically correct to call grown men boys any longer.' Her face had become a deep pink as she spoke. 'I've even, at times, had suspicions about them. They haven't been in touch, been particularly supportive. They stand to gain, you know, if my stewardship of the yard fails.' Her eyes, when they met Sophie's, were ashamed. 'Sickening, isn't it, how suspicion eats away at the soul, at trust?'

'Confront it, then; talk to them. Anyone else on your list of suspects, while we're at it? I'm not in there by any chance?'

'Not at the moment.' Flora's voice had lost some of its shaky quality and she gave a half-laugh. 'But I could work up to it, the way I'm going. I *have* entertained suspicions about my neighbour and trainer, though.'

'The gorgeous Matt?' Sophie looked incredulous.

Flora shifted uncomfortably. 'Not without reason,' she defended herself. 'He's accused me of being a dilettante, told me I'd be better off leaving the running of things to Shay. Women,' she was tart, 'have a very confined and specific role in his life.'

'Doesn't seem a good enough reason to me.' Sophie waved off Matt Hopkins as a suspect. 'But then I rather fancy him so my judgement's hardly sound.'

When they left Punchestown a half-hour later it had been agreed that Sophie would stay for the Budweiser Irish Derby, to be run at the Curragh the following Sunday. Flora would go back to Dublin with her the day after. The trip, at the very least, would give her a chance to get out of jeans and T-shirt for a few days.

In the sunny days which followed, Sophie staved off panic attacks about her own problems by watching Flora at work. She saw how she pushed herself, doing jobs she could have delegated, checking and rechecking small and big things about the yard. And she noted how she took responsibility for the injured colt, telling Shay she wanted to learn and rejecting an offer of help from the sulky Luke. She watched over him constantly, keeping him quiet lest he pull the stitches out. Twice a day she washed the wound with peroxide and dressed it. To Sophie's dismay some of the stitches came out anyway – though the result was merely to drain what poison remained.

By Wednesday Sophie had become bored, and thoughts of her own dilemma had begun crowding her head again, ruining the fragile, stand-off peace she'd been building. 'A diversion's what you need, Sophie my girl,' she told herself, and came up with a plan for a picnic.

'We're having a picnic tomorrow,' she announced on Thursday morning.

'Who's having a picnic?' Flora was only mildly surprised.

'We are – you, me, Daisy. Anyone else around here who cares to come. The bloody horses, too, if you insist.'

'You're going to organize it?' Flora hazarded an uneasy guess.

'I am.' Sophie was airily confident. 'It'll all be happening in the garden from three o'clock onwards tomorrow.' They were in the kitchen, dark and sunless at that hour of the day, and she shivered. 'It's like a morgue around here. A bit of excitement will do us all good.' She poked the dozing Dipper with her foot. He didn't move. 'See what I mean?' she demanded.

'Fine. Sounds great.' Flora patted the labrador's head as she left the kitchen.

Sophie couldn't cook. Breakfast was the limit of her culinary skills. But she was nothing if not resourceful. A kitchen shelf, to her surprise, produced a cookbook which produced a picnic menu. In Dunallen, later in the day, it proved easy enough to acquire the ingredients for smoked salmon mousse, chicken drumsticks in honey mustard, potatoes with basil and a green salad. She bought a case of the Sancerre Flora liked and, with great magnanimity, since she'd discovered that even the smell made her queasy, a case of beer too. In the late evening, as the heat of the day died, she surveyed the garden and decided on a corner where wild woodbine and climbing roses scrambled for space on the walls. Thoughtful now, she stood enjoying the lingering scents as the sun slowly set. She went inside when Flora came to look for her.

It was almost midnight, and Flora had gone to bed, when Sophie on impulse phoned Matt Hopkins. He was gruff at first but became amused, friendly, when she told him who she was and invited him to the picnic. He'd like to come, he said, would drop by for an hour or so around four o'clock.

'Now that, at least, should prove diverting.' She put the phone down slowly. 'Just what we need around here.'

Next morning dawned cloudy. 'Murphy's bloody law,' Sophie groaned at breakfast, 'if anything can go wrong it will.'

'Rain may hold off,' Flora studied the sky through the kitchen window, 'though there's thunder promised.'

By mid-morning Sophie herself could tell there was a storm coming. She could see it in the low, heavy cloud gathering beyond the viewing hillock, feel it in the clammy air and in the strange stillness. There would be thunder, as Flora had said, lightning too most likely. Sophie swore profusely to herself and the old dog, as she made the final preparations for the picnic.

The weather held, nervously, and just after three her guests began drifting into the garden. Shay had a quick beer and left.

'That's his duty done,' Daisy said resignedly. But Shay had set the mood and Luke and a couple of stable staff grabbed some food and followed him back to the yard. By four o'clock, when Matt Hopkins opened the wooden side gate and sauntered across the garden to join them, the picnic had wound down to Flora, Daisy, Leah and Sophie.

'I thought I'd be neighbourly and ask him.' Sophie grinned at Flora's surprised face. She sat up and waved to the trainer. 'Blessed art thou amongst women,' she said as he lowered himself onto the grass beside her.

'That's all very well,' he smiled lazily, 'but does a man stand a chance of getting food around here?'

He was deeply tanned and wearing a white T-shirt with black jeans. He had, Sophie thought, an unfair number of natural advantages. He was the essence of male desirability *and* he would never become pregnant either.

'Help yourself.' Flora, smiling, gestured at the food. 'What'll you have to drink?'

'The wine looks good.'

Flora reached behind her for the cooler. The action emphasized the lithe lines of her body and Sophie was all at once desperately aware of her own changing shape. She seemed to have grown even in the week since her talk with Flora – and still she'd not decided on a plan. 'Why me, God? Why not some woman who *wants* a child?' She groaned inwardly as the trainer's eyes coolly followed Flora's movements, went on frankly studying her as she poured his drink. Sophie held out her own glass to be filled.

'Sure?' Flora looked at her uncertainly.

'Absolutely positive,' Sophie said and Flora, with a quick look at her face, poured. Sophie knew she was becoming tipsy but was quite enjoying the sensation. Drink in hand she leaned back on the cushions, deftly rearranging her silk blouse into flattering folds. 'I was hoping you'd have the inside track on Sunday's Derby winner.' She raised her eyebrows and gave the trainer a teasing look.

'Few real champions in the field this year.' He briefly stopped piling a plate with food and smiled warmly at her. 'But there are several really good mile-and-a-half colts running.' He began eating with concentration, like a man genuinely hungry.

'Couple of high-class fillies running too.' Leah, who'd been suspiciously quiet all afternoon, sounded indignant.

'You're right.' The trainer pushed his plate away. 'But for my money one of the colts will have it.'

The conversation became more technical than Sophie cared for and, suddenly tired, she closed her eyes. She awoke to Daisy and Leah arguing about a party Leah wanted to go to, and in time to see Flora and Matt Hopkins disappear round the side of the house. It had become heavily overcast.

'Party's over, I see,' she said drowsily. 'Sorry about dropping off. It's this heavy weather.'

'It's the wine.' Daisy briskly poured herself another. She glared at Leah when she pertly held out her glass for a refill. 'You can start clearing up here, my girl,' she said. 'It *might* get you some credit points.'

'Where did Flora and Matt go?' Sophie asked.

'Matt wanted to have a look at the injured yearling.' Leah, sulkily, began stacking plates.

'I'll do that in a little while.' Sophie stood up. 'I just want to stretch my legs first.'

Feeling stiff, and oddly restless, she picked up her glass and headed for the yard. The picnic hadn't yielded even the minor excitement she'd hoped for. Maybe Flora and Matt Hopkins could be persuaded back for another drink before things finally broke up.

In the yard she didn't see them immediately and was

about to abandon the idea when Luke, leading a horse, called, 'Hey, Sophie, coming for a ride?'

'Why not?'

She didn't mean it, but he came toward her with the horse anyway. She put the glass on a windowledge beside her and considered the idea. She'd only been on horseback once in her life, but this was a friendly looking animal. It was a pale sandy colour and had nice brown eyes.

'You're sure?' Luke, beside her now, looked uncertain. 'I was only teasing, you know, because I haven't seen you ride all week.'

'Course I'm sure. Never felt more positive about anything,' Sophie replied gaily. 'Lead me to my mount.' As she spoke a few tentative drops of rain began to fall.

'You don't want to ride in the rain.' Luke looked relieved.

'Oh, but I do.' Sophie caught him by the arm and gave a laughing, coaxing smile. 'It'll be fun. And I want some fun, Luke.'

Luke, blushing slightly, his face a mixture of anxiety and the desire to please, cupped his hands to help her up. Sophie put her foot in his hands and awkwardly heaved herself onto the mare's back.

'She's called Fast Sally,' Luke said, 'but she's about as much speed as a tortoise left in her. Just take her round the yard. You sure you know what you're doing?'

He handed Sophie the reins and the mare moved off slowly towards the arched gate leading to the paddocks and fields. Sophie, instinctively tightening her thighs against the animal's flanks, wondered briefly how she could ever have thought this would be fun. Fast Sally began to move more quickly. She was almost trotting when Sophie, with a small panic-stricken cry, dropped the reins and caught frantically onto her mane. Behind her she was aware of Luke calling, of Flora coming out of a box just ahead with Matt Hopkins. The gate loomed and, beyond it, the wild green of the countryside.

Everything happened then, at once. The mare, sensing freedom and a gallop ahead, began a slow canter toward the gate. Sophie, with a wail of sheer fear, threw herself along her neck and clung on for dear life.

She might have made it, hung on until she reached the softer landing of the grass outside, if Murphy's law hadn't again taken a hand. A clap of thunder struck directly overhead and the mare veered, stopped suddenly and dropped her head. Sophie's grip on her neck came unstuck and, slowly and sickeningly, she was propelled out over the animal's head onto the cobbles of the yard.

The bright lights made Sophie want to keep her eyes closed. They were warm but not reassuring. She knew instinctively that as soon as she faced them, left this comfortable stupor, things would become unpleasant. She was lying on a bed and a voice was calling to her, telling her to wake up.

She knew she would have to, eventually, when she'd rested a bit more. When she could cope with the light. But something in the voice, a desperate pleading as it said her name over and over, wouldn't leave her peace. Groaning, she slowly forced her lids apart.

The whole of the room was bright – ceilings, walls, curtains. All pale. It was small too. She took it in at a glance.

'Oh, thank God! Oh, Sophie . . .'

The voice changed, became relieved. Its owner took one of Sophie's hands and she slowly turned her head and saw Flora, huge-eyed and strained.

'Flora.' She smiled and it felt as if her head was splitting open. 'Jesus,' she muttered and closed her eyes again. And began remembering. 'I fell, didn't I?' She didn't open her eyes as she asked the question.

Flora's hand squeezed hers. 'Yes,' she said. 'You fell.'

Hot tears formed behind Sophie's closed lids and seeped through, down the sides of her face and onto the pillow. She hadn't the energy to wipe them away. Holding Flora's hand she fell into sleep.

Later, they told her she had lost the baby. The jolt from the fall had been too severe, too shocking. A doctor tried to give her the medical details but she didn't want to know.

It was over. The unwanted living thing within her was gone. She didn't want to think about it, so how it happened didn't matter. When the doctor told her there was no damage, no reason why she couldn't conceive again very soon, she looked at him in shock. He sent for a nurse and went away.

When Flora came again Sophie was ready for her. 'It's not the way I'd have chosen to end it,' she said.

'I know that.' Flora was gentle.

'I don't suppose it felt anything.' Sophie felt the tears on her cheeks again. She seemed powerless to stop them. 'It's not as if there was conscious life, or anything. Not at nine weeks.'

Flora stayed a while longer and then left. Sophie didn't sleep much. Miscarriage apart, she had broken ribs, severe bruising and a concussion which needed monitoring. Painkillers eased the physical pain but the strange, frightening sadness couldn't be prescribed for. She could have dealt with it if she'd understood its cause. It wasn't as if she'd wanted to have the baby, had been dreaming about buttons and bows and tiny feet pattering. God, no. There had been nothing like that. She had been quite definitely going to terminate. It was obviously her hormones acting up.

She didn't make it to the Derby. But there was always next year. Life went on, even after death.

It was Tuesday before the hospital released her and Thursday before Flora drove her back to Dublin. She still felt stiff, quite sore in spots, and the sadness had been replaced by a vague sense of loss.

Chapter Eighteen

Sophie still ached, and her ribs were strapped up. None of it affected her determination that Flora should be helped to make the most of her stay in town. Sophie had been more moved than she cared to admit, even to herself, by her friend's loyalty and understanding during what she now thought of as her 'pregnancy predicament'. She owed Flora. She was going to see that she sorted through a few things before going back to the farm.

'Ring Fintan,' she brought the phone to Flora in bed the first morning, 'and after that ring Ollie. It's time for a bit of Carolan bonding. Go on.' She put the phone into her hand as Flora hesitated. 'Arrange to meet them. We'll plan the rest of the week around whatever you set up.' She hovered, making sure Flora did as she was told.

Fintan was spontaneously glad to have his sister in town. He'd be right over, he said.

'It's nine o'clock, a.m.,' Flora pointed out. 'Thought you didn't function before three p.m. at the earliest.'

'I don't. But I haven't been to bed yet. See you in half an hour.'

Flora dressed. While she waited for Fintan, Sophie redirected her back to the phone. 'The other one too,' she said.

Flora called Ollie. He had a client with him, he'd been meaning to phone, could they meet on Monday?

'You're not free over the weekend?' Flora asked, disappointed.

''Fraid not.' Ollie sounded embarrassed. 'Saturday I'm taking Peter and a couple of his friends out for the day and Sunday Melissa's coming home from a trip to London.'

'Fine, I'll take my place in the queue,' Flora laughed

lightly. 'Monday will be my treat then. We'll have dinner – Melissa too, of course.'

'I'm really sorry –' Ollie began, but she interrupted.

'I should have let you know I was coming up to town. I'm staying with Sophie – you remember Sophie? I'll bring her along. How's Peter?' They chatted, briefly, and Ollie went back to his client.

'I just don't feel part of their lives,' Flora, grinding coffee beans, confessed her discomfiture to Sophie. 'Their friends and interests and how they live – all of those things have happened to them while I've been away. I almost feel as if I'm intruding.'

'Intrude then, if that's what it takes,' Sophie said. 'Tell them you'd like to feel they're behind what you're doing at Kimbay. Confront your wormy feelings about why things are going wrong.'

'Look, Sophie, I feel really stupid about some of the things I said that day at the races . . .'

'Stop worrying. That's between you and me, right?' Sophie took the beans from her, poured water over them into the pot. 'A lot of your niggling worries are the product of being cut off. You've isolated yourself, Flora, and it's time you did something about it. Bonding with the boys,' she grinned, 'is as good a way as any to begin.'

Sophie popped out for croissants and missed Fintan's lightning visit. He'd looked wrecked, Flora confessed, but had left tickets for the Lurking Evil's late show the following night.

'The Rock Garden,' Sophie looked at them, 'that's just round the corner. Should be fun.'

'He wants us to meet for a drink beforehand. I said okay.'

They met at The Norseman, Sophie's local. It was a close, muggy night and most of the pub's customers were drinking outside in the narrow, pedestrianized street. Fintan, pint in hand, was leaning against a wall waiting for them.

'You look far too healthy.' He greeted Flora with a hug, narrowly avoided spilling the dark brown liquid on

192

the white shirt she'd worn for the evening. 'This good old polluted, metropolitan air suits you.'

'Doesn't seem to be doing you much harm either.' Flora hugged him back, carefully, her eye on the pint.

'Sophie . . . ah, Sophie!' Fintan stood in mock admiration. 'Lust-figure of my youth. Fantastic as ever.' He shook a regretful head. 'The dreams I had about you when I was but a virgin lad on the farm. Give us a kiss.'

Sophie kissed him, on the lips but chastely. 'If only I'd known, Fintan.' She sighed. 'You're adorable but it's too late. I'm into older, bankable types these days. You know, grey suits and all that.' She ran her hand over his chest, bare under a leather waistcoat, and sighed again. 'Sex appeal just isn't enough any more.'

'But I've got a big, warm heart too.' Fintan held a hand to his chest and leaned forward. 'If you ever change your mind, Sophie, fancy a bit of unsuited, unwaning lust, I'm your man.'

Sophie laughed and, wincing, held her ribs. She was wearing a silk metallic shirt and dark blue cigarette trousers and had convinced herself the soreness was all in her head. It was too, until she laughed.

'Hey – is this a private party or can anyone join in?' Flora helped herself to a long drink from her brother's glass. 'I'll have one of those, Fintan, since you're buying. I think we'll go inside, too, find some seats.'

Sophie, the soreness fading but feeling tired, shot her a grateful look. In the comparative dark inside, sitting with their drinks, Flora explained briefly why they needed seats. 'Sophie had a bit of an accident at Kimbay. Fell off a –'

'Don't remember you as the riding type.' Fintan raised an eyebrow. 'You okay?'

'Fine, thanks. And you're right, I'm not a rider. That's why it happened.' She felt a sudden small chill and folded her arms over her chest. Flora quickly changed the subject.

'Kimbay's looking great at the moment,' she spoke lightly, 'why don't you visit, Fintan? I'd sort of hoped', she tried for a diffidence that didn't quite come off, 'that you and Ollie might keep more in touch.'

193

'Yeah, well . . . I've been busy. And I didn't want to interfere.' Fintan looked embarrassed. 'Truth is, after the – funeral I kind of got involved in a lot of things. Seemed like a good idea at the time. I kept telling myself I'd check you and Kimbay out. Only there wasn't a right time, no point when I didn't feel a bit raw. But it's cool now, Flora. Things are okay.' He raised his drink. His eyes were apologetic. 'I'm glad you're here. How's about if I bring the guys in the band down to Kimbay for a few practice sessions?'

'No, thanks.' Flora laughed. 'There's enough talk as it is –' Sophie saw her almost bite her tongue as she said the words. So too did Fintan.

'Talk?' His eyes narrowed and Flora, reluctantly and briefly, told him about the rumours and problems at the yard.

'Doesn't sound much fun.' Fintan was thoughtful when she'd finished. 'The world can be a shit when you're trying to get something up and going. Believe me, I know.' He gave a rueful grin. 'You think the horse industry's tough? You should try the music business. Only advice I can give you is watch your ass and give me a shout if there's anything I can do.'

'Thanks.' Flora was quiet, two spots of colour on her cheeks. 'I might just do that – next time I need help with a bit of extra mucking out.'

They talked in desultory, relaxed fashion for a bit before Fintan said he would have to be off, get tuned up before the show.

'How's the band doing?' Flora put the question each time they spoke and invariably got a laconic response. This time Fintan was disposed to be chatty.

'Things are working out,' he said. 'The live show's good, you'll see for yourselves later on. We're getting together a second album, too. I've got things I want to say and the music's saying them for me.' He became self-mocking, rueful. 'I'm aiming for enough zeros at the end of my bank balance to be able to make the music I want, not just play for the money.'

Flora was thoughtful after he left. Sophie worked on her, teasing and provoking to draw her out, but it wasn't until they'd left the pub and were making their way to the Rock Garden that she revealed what was on her mind.

'I haven't given them a thought, Sophie. My brothers lost their father too. Fintan and Ollie are working out their lives and dreams and aspirations and all I can think and worry about is myself and what I'm doing. I'm not much of a sister, am I?'

'Oh, I dunno. I'd say you're about average. No point in martyring yourself. You're listening now. You're bond—'

'If you say bonding once more, Sophie, I'll scream.'

They entered the dark stone-and-ironmongery decor of the Rock Garden. Within minutes of finding themselves a vantage point, the Lurking Evil, with an exhilarating surge of sound, spun onto the stage. It wasn't just a show, or a mere performance. It was, Sophie hissed, an event. The Lurking Evil were edgy and physical, hitting their audience with music and message in equal measure. And they were playing to the converted, a crowd who loved the band, but for whom Fintan was the focus.

'He's two people,' Flora's voice in Sophie's ear was filled with awe. 'He's Fintan and he's that – demi-god.'

'He's doing all right,' Sophie agreed. 'More than all right in fact.'

Sophie eased herself back into work. The rent had to be paid and the demands of a deadline kept her mind occupied. By the time Monday's evening dinner date with Ollie and Melissa came round she'd begun to believe there really would be a time when the events of the past weeks would be a memory.

'I *never* eat here.' Melissa was petulant. The restaurant was Sophie's choice. Flora was paying. They had ordered and were waiting for their food.

'I come here quite a lot.' Sophie was mild, unable to fathom Melissa's peevishness. The restaurant was good and it was fun. It was the fashion place to eat at the moment and she'd wanted Flora to see it.

'The food's awful. I had a dreadful experience here six months ago,' Melissa tapped Ollie's arm, 'do you remember?'

'Remember what?' Ollie, startled out of his conversation with Flora, looked nonplussed.

'When I got the food poisoning? This was the restaurant.'

'Oh? It was?' Ollie looked momentarily uncomfortable, then patted her hand. 'Lightning never strikes twice,' he reassured and turned back to his sister. 'I'd meant to go down so often,' he said, 'but the weeks slipped by.'

'Why don't you bring Peter down for a weekend during his holidays?'

'Peter has his summer school,' Melissa was charmingly apologetic. 'He adores it, wouldn't miss it for the world.'

'Surely a few days . . .' Ollie began.

'I don't think it would be a good idea.' Melissa poked suspiciously at her salad as it was put in front of her. 'Flora's too busy. I doubt she'd have the time to look after him.'

'I'd *like* to have him,' Flora said shortly.

'I've just spent a week at Kimbay myself,' Sophie said. 'It's another world, the horse business, isn't it?'

'It certainly is.' Melissa was tart.

'Melissa's not keen on country life.' Ollie gave a barely perceptible shrug as he explained to Sophie. 'Prefers the pavements under her feet.' He concentrated on his lamb with lime.

'We've that in common,' Sophie grinned, 'though I must say there's a certain charm about the countryside in flower and good weather. I could just about be persuaded to spend more time at Kimbay.'

'How are things working out?' Ollie's brown eyes fixed on his sister.

Flora, very calmly Sophie thought, gave him a brief outline of events on the stud farm since February.

'This gossip; do you think it's serious?' Ollie's round face looked worried. He'd stopped eating.

'It's serious all right, but it'll go away in time. Maybe I shouldn't have told you, but I thought you'd be interested.'

'Of course I'm interested. I think it's bloody awful that you have to put up with this sort of thing.' Ollie fixed his eyes on those of his sister. 'Flora, if you need me to I'll come down. Just tell me when.' His eyes glinted behind his spectacles and he closed a fist on the table. He looked, Sophie thought, like an angry Michelin man.

'Oh, for God's sake, Ollie,' Melissa sounded wearily exasperated. 'This is the end of the twentieth century. We're talking about a bit of country gossip. If you go blundering down there looking for brotherly revenge you'll only make things worse.'

Ollie, deflated but holding his dignity, doggedly finished what he had to say. 'I'm with you, Flora, and I mean it about giving me a shout. Any time.'

'Thanks, Ollie.' Flora was gentle. 'If I do it'll be in the next few months. They're going to be crucial. Flo Girl races in August at the maiden in Gowran Park. If she wins it's money for the yard. And in October I sell the yearlings at Goffs.'

The rest of the week until Friday went gently and lazily for Flora and brought a slow build-up of work for Sophie. Flora saw a good deal of her brothers, bridged a lot of the gap her years away had created. She headed back to Kimbay early on Saturday, buoyant and ready, she said, to deal with any number of Gus Fitzgeralds.

The apartment seemed terribly, isolatingly empty after she'd gone. Sophie paced a bit, thinking about Flora and Kimbay objectively now that her friend had left. An instinct, fed by a basic nosiness and honed by her journalistic training, told her that Flora's fears of sabotage attempts on the yard could be more than simple paranoia. She could be wrong, suffering slightly from paranoia herself, but Sophie had a feeling there was something to her friend's suspicions. Fintan and Ollie had never been contenders – but it would do no harm to carry out a bit of gentle investigative work on Victor Mangan. Just in case.

Even if there was nothing linking him to Kimbay it

was possible she might turn up something else on him. Someone like Victor Mangan was bound to have irons burning in many fires. Nosing around always turned up interesting facts, on something.

Chapter Nineteen

The summer became fitful once June ended. There were still some bright and glorious days but they were invariably followed by rain in torrents and sometimes gales.

It was on one such day that Flora decided the time had come at last to sort out her father's bedroom. Cleaned out and redecorated it could be used for guests. Ned would not have wanted it to become a mausoleum.

Which was what it looked like when she stepped inside. Daisy, carefully thoughtful, had stripped the bed of its linen and covered it with the plaid bedspread he'd favoured. Flora hadn't been in the bedroom since her one, brief visit in the days after the funeral. No one else had either. During his life Ned's bedroom had been his one area of privacy. It was the space he'd shared with Hannah and where he'd spent all of his solitary nights after he became a widower. To invade it immediately after his own death had seemed, somehow, indecent. But now it was time. Flora would have to store his personal things carefully, restore the room to the living.

Opening the heavy curtains didn't do much to brighten the room. Outside, the clouds were massed and dark and a heavy summer shower beat a bleak tattoo on the window. The wind lashed a piece of wisteria against the glass, reminding Flora that she should get it trimmed back a little.

The bedroom said nothing, and yet everything, about her father. It was functional and uncluttered. She walked around slowly, touching those things of Hannah's he'd always left on view. The pale blue satin dressing gown on the back of the door felt cold. The delicate watercolours on the wall were dusty. Two silver filigree perfume bottles, side by side on the heavy oak dressing table, were discoloured and the straw hat on the chest of drawers was faded-looking. Running her fingertips over the yellow and purple silk flowers filling its brim she remembered it with an aching sadness. She blew on it and a blanket of grey dust lifted into the air.

Standing there, wondering where to begin and knowing she must if the lump in her throat was to go away, Flora felt her mother's presence more than her father's. The room he had slept in all those years was Hannah's room. It had been his quiet, lonely way of keeping her with him.

The desk near the window was the single piece of furniture she associated completely with her father. On her rare visits to him in this room he had invariably been sitting there, working on something or dreaming through the window. She sat at the desk. It had a roll top with the key hanging on a cord by the side. She turned it in the lock and looked at the surprisingly neat piles of her father's papers, the firmly closed rows of drawer doors. For an hour she worked her way solidly through documents, receipts becoming memories as she saw how he'd kept a frugal note of sales but boldly asterisked and commented on his purchases. If ever she wanted to write a history of Kimbay it was here, all noted in her father's carefully kept records of failure and success.

The rain had stopped, and as a struggling sun fell across the desk she stretched and stood up. Ned's room was to the back of the house and, looking down into the quiet yard, she thought of the countless times he must have stood in this same spot, studied this same scene.

She turned back to the desk and saw that the last drawer she'd opened contained letters tied with a black bootlace. She took them out gently, sensing they were different, nothing to do with horses, land or business. The bundle was small. She counted five letters, all with English stamps. They were postmarked 1963. Before I was born, Flora thought. She carefully untied the bootlace.

The first letter she opened had an address in Highgate, London. It was written on blue paper and the handwriting was large and looping. Generous was the quality which came to Flora's mind as she began to read.

'My dearest, dear Ned', it began. 'Life is strange and lonely here without you. I think perhaps you have ruined me with your love, destroyed forever my ability to live happily alone. How could you do this to me? Just when I was getting used to it all, had pulled myself together again.'

Flora put the letter down. She shouldn't be reading this. It was private, the love and shared secrets of two people who were dead. They should be allowed the dignity and peace of that long sleep together. It wasn't right to pore over the confidential exchanges of their lives.

But the two people were her parents and the written words were those of a mother she'd never had a chance to really know. She began to read the letter again, letting it lie where she'd left it on the desk. It was as if, by not touching it, her violation was somehow less.

But I'm not sorry, Ned, about anything that has happened. You've made me love you, isn't that what the old song says? And I do, I do. Very much. It's not the same as that other love. It's altogether different. Your love, and what I feel for you, has given me light and hope again when I'd thought for so long that those things were in the grave with Sean. It was a happy Stephen's Day that I met you, at the races at Leopardstown.

When I think how sharp I was with you, how right you were with your tip for a winner and how stupid I was not to put something on that friendly looking grey . . .

I won't make a mistake like that again, Ned. I'll never again look the kindness or goodness of your gift-horse in the mouth. Which is my way of saying, yes. Yes, I will marry you, Ned.

There now. You have it in writing. And you have it from my heart. We will be good for each other, Ned. We will be kind and loving to each other. And we will be happy for long, long years. I'll give notice to my job here tomorrow and be home in a month.

Living here these past two years has been good for me, put a decent distance between me and everything that

201

happened. I'm glad I came but I'm more glad now to be going home. To you. I'll stay with my mother until we can organize things. She'll be pleased to have her only daughter back. She'll be interfering and maddening too but we'll have to put up with that. She means well.

And Ned, can we please do things quickly, quietly? I don't want us to get engaged because I don't want ghosts of the past resurrected, either by my mother or other 'consoling' souls. One engagement in a lifetime is enough for anyone. Anyway, the price of a ring would feed a foal for the winter. See how committed I am to your enterprise already? And I'm not even a gambling woman.

You were hardly gone before I started missing you. Write to me, Ned, a long letter. It doesn't matter if it's all about the horses. Just as long as it's a letter from you. I love you. I will love you forever. Your Hannah.

On a separate page there was a PS: 'When the freesia you gave me died I bought others, in exactly the same lovely purple and yellow colours. I'm never going to be without them on my mantel where the smell and sight of them will make me feel close to you always.'

Flora caught a tear with her tongue. The loving warmth of the letter, the references to an earlier sadness in the writer's life, the brimming hope . . . It could have been written by a stranger. It was hard to find, anywhere in its flowing words, the hard-working, beautiful mother she remembered.

Flora touched the notepaper gently, and began putting her mother's story together in her head. Clearly, Ned Carolan had not been the first love in her life. There had been someone called Sean who'd died. Her mother had even been engaged, intended marrying him. Then, somehow, it had ended and she'd gone to England to start a new life. She'd come home for Christmas and that was obviously when she'd met Ned Carolan – at the Leopardstown races. It didn't sound either as if she'd been overly impressed with him, that first meeting.

But Ned had never been a man to take no for an answer, to let a dream go once he saw it within grasp.

There was no point now entertaining qualms about

reading the rest of the letters. Flora *had* to know what had happened about Sean, what the beginning as well as the end of her mother's story was. She went through the letters. The one she'd read was the last one written. She selected the first, postmarked six months earlier, and began to read. It was short, simply thanking Ned for a lovely day in Dublin, an enjoyable evening in the Theatre Royal. In it Hannah said she doubted very much that she would be home again in the near future but said she would be pleased to see Ned, should he ever come to London.

Ned had gone to London. The other three letters charted the speedy development of their love affair over the six following months.

Ned had been sure, never doubting their love from the very beginning. In that short year he had broken through Hannah's guard and persuaded her to let love grow. His method had coupled sheer, dogged, persistent sincerity with a huge understanding of the woman he wanted to marry. He had not wanted to own her, merely to love and care for her. He'd been willing to give up his infant but growing stud farm for her, willing too to 'cross the pond' that was the Irish Sea and to seek work in an English stables. Love, for him, was wanting the other person's happiness before his own.

Hannah had had reason to be cautious. The letters didn't say a lot about Sean but what they did say was enough. Sean Dowling had been engaged to Hannah Russell for two years. He had broken the engagement just six weeks before their wedding day. A month later he had been killed in a car crash. His companion, the woman he had been involved with while he was engaged to Hannah, had been badly injured and died later.

In the drawer where the letters had been Flora also found a brief newspaper announcement of her parents' wedding. She'd known the date anyway. Ned had always, every year, celebrated it with a bottle of Tullamore Dew. Checking the dates Flora saw that they had married two months after Hannah's letter accepting Ned's proposal.

She put the letters and cutting back where she'd found

them. Then she closed the drawer and locked the desk, slowly.

By the chest of drawers she picked up the straw hat, blew the remaining dust from the silken purple and yellow freesia. She put it on her head and studied herself in the mirror. It was too small, and a residue of dust made her sneeze. She put it back where it had been for years.

Ned and Hannah had been happy together. She knew that. The pity was that their marriage hadn't been for the long, long years they'd anticipated in their letters. She stood for an age in the window, looking over the rain-drenched, luminescently green fields. The telephone ringing downstairs brought her back to the present.

The caller was Ollie, saying he would drive down on Sunday with Peter for the day. Flora couldn't persuade him to stay overnight but was glad he was coming anyway.

Leah, fuming and aggrieved, appeared in the kitchen as Flora was having a coffee.

'The outer limit has been reached.' She looked dramatically dissatisfied. 'I cannot take any more.'

Flora waited, silently, while Leah poured herself a coffee. This had to be something to do with Daisy. She did not, today, feel like getting involved. But Leah was determined.

'Daisy's decided I'm not to have a holiday this summer.' Her aggrieved tone was almost tearful. 'Just decided. No question of a discussion. It's a heads-down-and-belts-tight year for the Sweeneys, she says. Depends which Sweeneys you're talking about, of course. Luke Sweeney gets to go sailing for a week with his crummy friends in Cork. Attila the Hun had his yearly fix at Newmarket and Dayglo Sweeney doesn't want to go anywhere anyway so she's not suffering. Which means, as usual, that it's —'

'Chill out, Leah,' Flora yawned, 'and while you're at it try to be fair. Shay would go off the deep end if he missed Newmarket and Luke's organized himself a free holiday. Obvious thing is for you to do the same. You must have *some* money saved, surely? And don't you have a friend you could stay with for a week or so?'

'Yeah. Plenty of them. All within a radius of ten miles of here.' Leah walked up and down the kitchen, face a tragic mask. 'Might as well move into one of the looseboxes for a fortnight.'

'The horses deserve better.' Flora was dry, her patience wearing thin.

Leah dropped into a chair by the table and looked at her with huge repentant eyes. 'Sorry, Flora, I'm being an old cow. Again. I'll get over it,' she sighed melodramatically. 'I always do.'

'I've just had an idea.' Flora looked at her thoughtfully. 'I'll make a call which might, just might, come up with a holiday for you. Any chance you'd make me a sandwich while I'm on the phone? I haven't eaten since breakfast.'

Leah, with a look in which resignation did battle with hope, nodded.

Behind the closed doors of the office Flora dialled. Sophie answered on the second ring. She didn't hesitate when Flora asked if she'd have Leah to stay for a while. 'Love to have her,' she said, 'if only to get my hands on that hair of hers. It needs —'

'Keep your paws off her hair,' Flora warned. 'I don't want Daisy's wrath blistering the back of my neck for months to come. Will Friday be all right to send her up to you?'

'Lovely. Just so long as she doesn't expect me to babysit her. I'll give her a key so's she can come and go.'

Leah, when she heard, was expansive in her appreciation and joy. She hugged herself and chortled, then she hugged Flora and shoved a robust-looking sandwich her way. 'You've saved my life and sanity.' She was beaming, when her eye fell on an apron hanging on the back of the door. Her face darkened. 'Daisy won't allow me go. I know she won't.'

But Daisy gave wholehearted, and relieved, approval. On Friday morning Leah caught the bus in Dunallen. 'The break', said Daisy that afternoon, 'will be good for both of us. Leah and myself I mean. We need some space from one another.'

Enjoying their quiet, non-combative *café à deux* Flora thought this a case of optimism flying in the face of reason. She nodded agreeably.

The sun shone for Ollie's visit with Peter and the day slipped by pleasantly for everyone at the yard. Even Shay forgot himself enough to give Peter a riding lesson.

'He must be sickening for something,' Daisy said. She was on a rare visit to the yard.

'Why did you marry him?' Flora asked.

Daisy was wearing a loose, Indian-style dress with sandals and looked like a friendly amazon. The question was one Flora had always wanted to ask but she was surprised when Daisy answered.

'The first time I saw that man,' Daisy's tone was indulgent and she gave a rueful smile, 'he was sitting alone in a pub watching me sing. I knew, looking at him, that we'd end up together.'

'Sixties soothsaying?'

'No.' Daisy watched her thin, wiry husband as he patiently led the small boy on the horse up and down the yard. 'I just knew,' she said. 'I felt waves of peace when I looked at him. I still do. He balances the world for me.' She turned to go. 'You need balance in love. Especially if you decide to marry your love. You'd do well to remember that, Flora.'

Flora, when Daisy had gone, thought that, although Daisy and Shay's affection for one another was palpable, there was very little visible peace in the Sweeney marriage. Balance, obviously, meant different things to different people. She would have to work out what it meant for her.

These were busy racing months and Flora spent a few Saturdays at the racetrack. Matt Hopkins was running a couple of horses in England and she saw him hardly at all. She knew Flo Girl was doing well, could see this for herself on the mornings she managed to watch the Fairmane string on exercise gallops. Even at a distance the filly radiated a fire and energy, looked every inch a competitive racehorse. Flora visited the Fairmane yard a couple of times too. She felt a sort of nervous pride as she patted and indulged in a close-up study of Flo Girl.

Matt Hopkins called one evening after she'd been to the yard. The filly was 'on course' he assured Flora. He felt his judgement about the timing of her first race was 'bang on', said he was more certain than ever that she had a more than even chance of winning at Gowran Park at the end of August. Flora hoped he was right.

The long days and holidays brought a calm to relations at Kimbay. Luke, who'd been subdued for a while by the Sophie incident, returned from his sailing trip in a benign mood. Its glow, for the first week anyway, included Flora.

Serge phoned often, and in good cheer, from the US. His trip was paying handsome dividends, he was glad he had made it. He would be in Ireland towards the end of July, which was perfect, Flora said, since it meant they could spend time in Dublin at the Horse Show.

Leah returned from Dublin with her hair cropped to above her ears and an earring in her nose. She appeared in the office doorway as Flora and Daisy were checking the breeding details of the yearlings to be sold in October. Flora took one look at her and held her breath. If she could have found a way of disappearing quietly through the window she would. Daisy, beside her, gave a short, strangled gasp.

'Sweet Jesus.' The gasp became a straight-from-the-heart groan. Mother and daughter eyed one another for a tense, silent, thirty-second lifetime. Then Daisy, opening her arms, stood up. 'Come here and give me a bit of a hug,' she said, 'I missed having you to fight with.'

Leah, caught in her mother's arms, looked like a long, bony child. 'The nose-ring doesn't work,' she muttered, 'it keeps falling out. And sometimes my nose bleeds.'

'We'll do something about it,' Daisy promised. 'Maybe a different kind of ring . . .'

'No. I've changed my mind about it anyway.' Leah stepped back and, none too gently, removed the ring.

'If you're sure?' Daisy said. 'Because I can —'

'No.' Leah was firm. 'It was just an idea. A sort of experiment.'

A deliberately provocative one, Flora thought, to which Leah had expected Daisy to react negatively. But Daisy hadn't. It could be that in her tolerant reaction, and their week apart, there was the basis for a new relationship between Daisy and Leah. Or at least some change.

Daisy, encouraged by Leah, took herself off for a week's stay at an alternative health therapy centre. She justified the expense by saying that the knowledge gained would help cut the doctor's bill the following winter. She came back convinced she could run a better centre herself.

'The place was full of crackpots,' she said.

'You must have felt at home then,' Leah said and Daisy laughed.

'Suppose I did,' she said.

The dates for the Dublin Horse Show, circled on the kitchen calendar, came closer with a lazy speed. Serge rang to say he'd managed to make himself free for the entire week and Flora booked them rooms in a Ballsbridge hotel for the last three days of the show. Her clothes had arrived from Brussels and she took time, and a lot of pleasure, sorting them out and deciding what to wear for the week of Serge's visit. As well as items which would give her a reasonable, working-day *chic* for the time he would be at Kimbay, she needed a wardrobe which would see her through days at the Show and nights on the town.

For Dublin she chose loose, floral-printed dresses for daytime, one to be worn with matching palazzo pants. She would wear them with either a navy or cream straw hat, both with deep brims. For evenings she decided on the decadence of an antique lace blouse and, alternatively, the lavish effect of a Valentino dress she'd splurged on and rarely worn.

Serge brought gifts and New York stories.

'You sound as if you fell in love with the place.' Flora felt a surge of envious longing for the excitement of it all.

208

'It was an experience I will not forget,' Serge kissed her, 'and next time you will come with me.'

After three days at Kimbay they left for Dublin and the heady, end-of-the-week excitement of the Horse Show. Flora was glad they'd had their quiet, acclimatizing time together. Once in the thick of the Horse Show and ancillary activities there was little time for reflective talk. The days went quickly, in a frenzy of fun and friends. Sophie was able to meet them only briefly, which disappointed Flora. Serge grumbled a bit, complaining the Irish were *chauvin* and thought the horse an animal of their own creation.

'Not quite,' Flora laughed, 'we just breed the best. Look at this for instance . . .' It was Thursday and they were watching the puissance. Flora's nod was directed at the horse emerging to compete his round in the competition. The silence about them became intense and in the charged air she spoke almost in a whisper.

'Just wait until you see him jump. He's born to it, magnificent ability. Gets it from his mother, of course, along with his even temper. She was an Irish draught mare.'

'And his father?' Serge's dramatic whisper matched hers. 'He gets nothing from his father?' The horse sailed effortlessly over the optional first jump.

'Oh, yes.' Flora's eyes followed the animal on to the next jump. She sighed with satisfaction as he went over without fault. 'Grace. Beauty. Speed. He gets those from his thoroughbred sire. It's the breeding of the draught mare with a thoroughbred which puts the Irish jumper in a class of its own – Oh, God no . . .' Flora groaned, along with the entire arena, as the horse in the ring hit a pole and charged on, out of control, to balk at and finally shy away from jumping the high wall.

'His even temper seems to have deserted him.' Serge shook his head. 'Perhaps he has inherited more of his thoroughbred father's disposition.'

'Not at all,' Flora was tart, 'he's just got a stupid rider.'

They left the jumping enclosure soon after and made their way through the crowd for a cocktail date. As well as

209

the puissance it was ladies' day, and competition for attention was as feverish outside the jumping ring as it was inside. High fashion black and white, as well as a lot of red, dotted the crowd. Hats, practical and bizarre, had been brought out to compete in the best dressed lady stakes. They met Melissa, wearing red. She was bright-eyed and charming and captivated Serge.

'*Bonne chance*,' he kissed her as she moved on, anxious to be seen by the judges, fearful that she might be overlooked in her absence. 'I am sure that you will win.'

'Follow me,' Flora said when Melissa had moved out of earshot, 'I'm going to show you something of what the Show is really about.' She led the way to the veterinary paddock behind the stables, to where horses were being paraded in front of would-be buyers. 'You are looking at future champions,' Flora said. 'Some will make international jumpers.'

'Interesting.' Serge shrugged. 'They look very fine, *ma chère*. But perhaps we could return to the bar or, if you insist, to the jumping.'

'I thought seeing this side of things might help you understand what my business was about.' Flora felt herself becoming angry. 'Round out the picture for you, so to speak.'

'It does that, and now I have seen it.' Serge took her arm. 'Besides, with your beautiful hat you should be where it can be seen by the judges.'

'I don't *want* to be seen by the judges.' Flora, stiffening, withdrew her arm. 'I want to know what's going on, what animals are being sold . . .'

'Please, Flora, not today,' Serge sounded weary. 'This week is ours, our time to be together.' His voice became cold. 'You are going too far with your devotion to your business. I'm sure your father would not have worked while at the Horse Show.'

'He didn't come to the Horse Show,' Flora snapped. 'He thought it was all "show", that most of the people here didn't know one end of a horse from the other. Like Melissa.' As soon as she said it she knew she sounded bitchy. In Serge's raised eyebrows she saw that he thought so too. 'I think he was wrong,' she went on quickly. 'There's a great deal that's good and positive and exciting about the Show. And I don't intend to follow Ned's criteria slavishly for —'

'Good. So now you have seen these horses and now we can leave.' Serge was coolly angry.

But for Flora the issue had become something she wanted Serge to understand. She had always understood and made time for his work needs. He must see that she needed the same from him now. She caught his eye, ignoring the anger she saw there, and stated her case as rationally as she knew how.

'The commodity I deal in, Serge, is horses. They are as important in the market place as wine. Good ones are part of a multi-billion world market. If I don't succeed in putting the yard and my concerns with the business behind me when I'm with you it's because I expect you to understand that I have to be alive, at all times, to what is going on. No, don't interrupt, please.' She held up a hand, waving it slightly as he tried to speak. 'You, Serge, don't even try to put work behind you because you don't think you should have to. In common with most men you think you've a God-given right to mix business with pleasure. While you've been here, during our time together, you've had the business papers sent to the room every morning, you've sent half a dozen faxes in three days and there hasn't been a day this week you haven't been in telephone contact with Brussels —'

'It is imperative that I keep in touch.' Serge's coolness matched her own. 'And these things take only minutes out of each day.'

'Of course. You're absolutely right. I'm not at all suggesting you abandon contact. That would be ludicrous. What I *am* saying is that what's sauce for the goose should be sauce for the gander.' Serge looked startled and Flora, realizing she had lost him in the proverb, laughed. He looked affronted and she went on, explaining more gently now. 'What I'm saying, Serge, is that if it's all right for you to be like that then why is it not all right for me? Why should I not mix work with play? Is it because I'm a woman?'

Serge looked thoughtful. He leaned against a railing and folded his arms over his chest. He looked patrician, and righteous.

'Yes,' he spoke calmly, without apology, 'it is because you are a woman. Women are the civilizers. We need them to keep us decent, to remind us what the real values are . . .'

'Don't patronize me, Serge. Who is "we"? Do you mean men? Are women to exist merely to keep men decent, remind them how to be human? Is that what you're saying?'

'Of course not,' Serge frowned, 'I was speaking of women's value to all humankind, to themselves and to children as much as to men.'

They parted to make way for a young girl leading two ponies. The incident gave Flora pause, time to cool her anger a little. When she spoke again she was quieter. 'I have come to believe, Serge, that men also have a responsibility to help maintain the balance in life.' She gave a small smile. 'We're all in this together.'

'Of course we are, *ma chère*.' Serge's tone was light. 'And we each have different things to give.'

They were silent for a while, making their way back to the jumping arena. Flora felt as if a huge chasm had opened between them but knew she couln't go back on what she'd said. It was Serge who gave her the opening that built a bridge, of sorts.

'I had no idea you felt so strongly about these things,' he said.

'Nor had I,' Flora confessed. 'But then I had no reason to care until now. My job didn't matter to me before.'

'And now it does.' Serge sounded fatalistic. 'What does this mean for you and me? Does it mean we will for ever have this long-distance relationship?'

'No!' Flora felt a rush of panic. 'I'm not saying that. I just want to make a go of Kimbay, that's all. I need your support. You must help me, Serge, you must understand.'

'I do.' He took her arm and turned her to face him. 'I am only human, Flora, and I would prefer you to be with me, all the time. But if this is how it must be, then *ainsi soit-il*. But I think we must have a different arrangement.'

'An arrangement?'

'Yes. And I have already thought of one. It is something I am saving for the end of the week. A grand gesture.' He gave a wide, self-deprecatory grin and the tension between them fell away.

'Now,' Flora demanded, 'tell me now.'

But he was teasingly adamant, refusing to be budged even by bribes of an ice-cream and, later, by her more fundamental, love-making cajolery.

They went late to the Show next day, breakfasting in bed and feeling comfortable together, happier than they'd been all week. It was the last day of Serge's holiday. Tomorrow he would leave for Brussels, get to work there on the results of his US trip. It was also the day of the Aga Khan Trophy, the week's pageant event.

The Irish team were favourite to win and a light breeze helped keep temperatures in the wildly partisan crowd at a vaguely controllable level. Even so, the tension was knife-edge when the last Irish horse appeared to try for an essential, faultless round. Held breaths created an eerie silence as horse and rider went through the minute-and-a-half jumping circuit, were released in a roar of spontaneous triumph as the pair rose cleanly into the air over the last parallel and cleared the fence.

The celebrations that night were riotous and everywhere and, half-way through the evening, Serge good-humouredly declared he'd had enough. Flora drove them out of town, along the coast road to Dun Laoghaire. They strolled the mile-long length of the west pier and in the darkening night watched the city's lights come on to create a fickle, flickering frieze around the bay.

'A city with a bay has a certain advantage.' Serge put his arms around Flora from behind and held her tightly. He spoke into her hair. 'It can look so very romantic.'

Flora turned in his arms, looked up at him. 'Kiss me then,' she demanded, 'you've got your Frenchman's reputation as a romantic to live up to.'

'As a lover,' Serge corrected her. 'Frenchmen are the great lovers. Romantic is something different . . .'

He kissed her, still teasing at first but as Flora moved with him, murmuring love against his mouth, he nudged her lips open with his tongue. They stood for a long time, savouring the excitement of the longest of kisses.

Flora slipped her arms under his jacket and Serge pulled away, gently. 'I want to take you to bed.' His voice was husky, 'We can discuss the difference between romance and love there. All night if you wish.'

'I do wish.' Flora laughed and caught his hand. 'Let's go then. It's a long walk back.'

'But, first,' Serge did not move, 'there is something to be arranged . . .' He hesitated, looked at her with a serious smile. Something in his eyes made Flora catch her breath. They were serious as his smile and very, very loving. She nodded, her mouth too dry for words. She was unaccountably trembling. 'I want us to become engaged, Flora. I would like you to marry me. Will you?'

'When?' It seemed the only sane answer. The trembling stopped. Of course she would marry him. When was the problem, when was the difficulty. Her eyes were bright, looking at him.

'When you are ready. When it is right.' He cupped her face in his hands. 'For now it will be a promise only, a pledge to our future.' He took his hands from her face and reached with one into a pocket. When he took it out again it held an ornate ring-box. He opened it and Flora, unprepared for the beauty of the exquisite ring inside, blinked.

It was a ruby, encrusted in diamonds and set in white gold. The effect was of ice with a glowing heart and she knew, without a moment's hesitation, that it could have been made for her. She said nothing as, with infinite care, he removed the ring from the box. Just as slowly he lifted her left hand in his and slipped it onto her third finger. It nearly fitted her.

'I love it.' Flora looked at the ring, held her hand in front of her. 'It's a most beautiful ring.' She twisted it on

214

her finger, silently wishing for all that it seemed to promise. 'Where did you get it?'

'It was my mother's, and her mother's before that. You will be the third generation of women to wear it.'

'Monique . . .' Flora couldn't stop looking at the ring. 'How does she feel about the ring becoming mine?'

'Monique, when all's said and done, is a pragmatist. She is pleased for us.'

Flora doubted this. But she leaned happily against Serge, murmuring into his chest. 'You must have been very sure I would say yes.'

'No. I merely hoped.' He laughed and she looked up at him, disbelief big in her eyes. 'It seemed right,' he amended. 'The ring is a small thing but it will be a bond when we are apart.'

The hotel room was awash with flowers, great, sweet-smelling massed bunches of them everywhere. There was champagne too, on ice. Flora laughed, clapped her hands and threw her arms around Serge's neck. 'It really never occurred to you that I would refuse, did it?'

'Not unless you were crazy, *ma chère*, and you are not that.'

Chapter Twenty

Wearing a ring, Flora discovered, changed more than her own perspective on her relationship with Serge. In what she now thought of as the 'pre-ruby days' Serge had been referred to, variously, as her 'beau' or her 'Frenchman'. He'd been viewed as a distant dalliance who made occasional walk-on home appearances. Now, especially at Kimbay, he took on substance and a worrying reality.

'It's totally beautiful.' Leah pored over Flora's finger. But her immediate concern was clear. 'Will he be living here? Only he didn't seem all that keen on horses to me.'

'We haven't decided anything yet.' Flora was offhand. She should have prepared herself for this conversation, especially this question. It was what everyone was going to ask her and she had no answer. So much depended on the year ahead, on the sale of the yearlings at Goffs, perhaps most of all on Flo Girl. 'Nothing's going to happen for a while yet anyway,' she added.

'Ah – so you haven't set a date? Is this going to be one of those forever-and-a-day Irish engagements?' Leah grinned, seeming to relish the prospect. She was wearing a black, oversized T-shirt and leggings, part of a wardrobe acquired on her Dublin holiday. She threw herself into an armchair opposite Flora. They were in the living room and Flora had been enjoying a rare enough read before Leah arrived.

'No, it's not.' Flora was firm. 'Once the winter's over we'll make arrangements.' This was news to her as much as it was to Leah. But it made absolute sense. She would put it to Serge.

'Can I try on the ring?' Leah asked and Flora handed it to her. 'Oh, God! I should have known,' she gave a whimper of disgust as it stopped at her second joint. 'My farmyard paws are just not meant to wear aristocratic jewels. If *my* day ever comes I'll have to get a blacksmith to design something for me.' She closed her eyes and turned the ring round on her finger three times. 'Old custom,' she opened her eyes, 'meant to ensure you get a husband. I know I've sworn off men but at the same time it's always best to cover your ass on these things. I might change my mind someday.'

Daisy was guardedly happy for Flora. 'He's a nice man,' she gave her a brief hug, 'and I suppose it's time you thought about starting a family. Him having a bit of money is no harm either.' The question about where they would live hung, unasked, in the air. Forestalling it Flora said to Daisy exactly what she'd said to Leah. It seemed to satisfy.

Shay was forthright, coming to her in the yard and formally shaking her hand. 'Best of luck to you,' he said, 'you've done right, picking a man outside the business. He won't be interfering.'

For the first week or so Serge's name continued to crop up in conversation at Kimbay. It was as if everyone felt they had to pay due regard to Flora's commitment to a future partner. After that, in the manner of a nine-day wonder, interest waned and the remarks ceased. Sophie, on a weekend visit before going off on a month-long working trip to Holland, was magnanimous and happy for her friend.

'You need someone, living the way you do,' she said. 'And I must say, I liked what I saw of him at the Horse Show. Upright. Suave. Reliable. Just what you need.'

Flora examined her expression for irony and found none. Sophie was simply in a pragmatic mood about marriage, and men. And she was, Flora thought, right in many ways. Flora *did* need Serge. Not by her side, exactly. Just having him out there, a loving safety-net, was enough.

She left the ring, for the most part, on her dressing table in its box. It wasn't the kind of thing you wore mucking out looseboxes or even exercising the horses. None of the de Maraville women had exposed it to such labours and she wasn't about to be the one to put it at risk.

The date of Flo Girl's maiden race came suddenly and

terrifyingly close. Flora was attacked by nervous apprehension of all sorts – dread, excitement, anticipation – and took to visiting the filly every other day. Sometimes she caught her on the gallop and was reassured; other days she came upon her contentedly munching grass, relaxed in the dark gold late-August sun. At those times she looked like any other lithe, athletic, well cared for thoroughbred. Flora, watching her like that, had to remind herself how like the wind Flo Girl could be when she really moved, what a glorious streak of chestnut speed she was on the gallops.

Matt Hopkins had decided that his stable jockey, Lorcan McNulty, would ride Flo Girl. Watching them together Flora knew he was right. The jockey pushed himself as much as the horse and Flo Girl repaid him with trust. When Flora asked him about the filly he was direct, vigorously positive.

'She'll be all right. She's more relaxed than myself when I race her on the gallops. She gets a bit excited when I put the saddle on but that's it – she calms down once we move off.' His child's face creased into a grin and he rubbed the filly down. 'We'll show them a thing or two at Gowran. Won't we, Flo?'

Because she called mostly in the afternoon Flora kept missing the trainer. Shay had told her he'd had 'a spot of bother' with a couple of horses, he didn't know what exactly. Flora nervously tried not to let the knowledge get to her. Things had settled down at Kimbay, she was learning to accept swings and balances. Matt Hopkins's problems wouldn't affect Flo Girl. She could see for herself that the numbers in training at Fairmane were growing. She was not going to worry about it.

Three days before the race she rode over on a mid-morning visit to the stables.

'Matt's out,' Marigold told her. 'He's working your horse and a few others. He should be back soon. Why don't you wait here?'

'I'll wander out, see what they're up to.' Flora smiled. Marigold worked mornings and this was the first time she'd actually met her at Fairmane. 'Looks like you've plenty to do.'

'*Please* stay.' Marigold was pleading. 'I'm just taking a break and the company would be nice. It gets bloody boring here on my own.' She held up the percolator. The fresh coffee smell was too much for Flora and she laughed.

'I'll have a quick cup,' she said.

Marigold immediately produced two mugs. 'No biscuits, I'm afraid,' she said, 'I'm dieting.' She patted a slim waist and grinned. 'You'd go to seed in a place like this in no time if you weren't careful.' She was wearing a chemise top and short skirt and seemed to Flora like a tiny, bright flower.

'How're the children?' Flora still found it difficult to reconcile Marigold with motherhood.

The other woman shrugged, smiling. 'They're fine. Children are survivors, I always think. Mine have survived me.' She gave a tinkling laugh and handed Flora her coffee. 'Lucky I've this job. It gets me out of the house in the mornings, keeps me sane. And my mother-in-law helps, of course.' She pulled a face. 'The kids keep her out of mischief too.'

'Sounds like the perfect set-up,' Flora said.

'You think so?' Marigold, for a brief, bleak moment wasn't smiling any more. 'You should try it.'

'I'm sorry,' Flora said, 'I didn't mean to —'

'What I'd much prefer to talk about is *your* news.' Marigold bounced her golden curls. 'When can I see this fabulous jewel I've heard so much about?'

'I don't see a lot of it myself, these days.' Flora was embarrassed. 'Call over any time if you really want to have a look.'

'I might do that. I've never been to Kimbay. Funny that, isn't it?' Marigold looked thoughtful. 'Maybe I will drop over,' she said again. 'Some day. Are you nervous about Saturday?'

'Well, yes. Trying not to be, though.'

'She'll be all right,' Marigold said confidently. 'Matt

sweats over the horses. Mad ambition, you know.' She giggled. 'Which isn't to say he's put the rest of his life on hold. Wish I could manage my love-life as well as he does. He's got the beautiful Isabel phoning from Spain and at least two "good friends" closer to home. I suppose it's got to do with energy and management, not things I'm much—'

'I suppose it has.' Flora, annoyed at herself for having got into a gossipy conversation about the trainer, put her mug down. What Matt Hopkins did outside training Flo Girl was none of her business. She didn't want to know. 'Thanks for the coffee,' she said pointedly.

'Any time,' Marigold was unabashed. 'Good luck on Saturday.'

Flora found the trainer easily enough. He was leaning against a fence, at a point which gave him a clear view of the exercising horses. There were three others along with Flo Girl. 'Morning, Flora.' He was brisk, unsurprised when she rode up. He didn't look at her. 'Flo Girl's working well today. See for yourself.'

She dismounted and stood beside him. His gaze stayed fixed on the galloping horses as he beat a tattoo on the fence with a whip. He wore a slight frown, hadn't shaved and looked tired. He looked, Flora thought, as if he was burning the candle at as many ends as Marigold seemed to think.

'No problems, then?' she asked.

'None.' He turned to her briefly, seeming puzzled. 'Why do you ask?' He had stopped beating the tattoo.

'No reason,' Flora said. She wished she didn't feel so nervous about Saturday. She wished Shay had kept his mouth shut. Quite suddenly she couldn't stand not knowing what had happened to Matt Hopkins's horses.

'Shay said you'd a bit of bad luck with a couple of horses.' She spoke quickly. 'Everything all right now?'

His eyes didn't leave the moving horses. 'Everything's fine, Flora. And you needn't worry. Flo Girl is still in the best hands.'

220

'I wasn't questioning that. I was simply—'

'Yes you were, questioning.' He gave her another sideways look, his eyes a chilly blue in his suntanned face. 'It could be argued that you've a right to, so I'll tell you what happened. One of my last week's runners pulled a muscle. Another, the week before, got a load of gravel in his off-fore hoof and developed a blasted infection.' He was holding the whip in both hands and she could see the white of his knuckles. 'The result, Flora, is that I'm being extra vigilant. Nothing's going to happen to Flo Girl.'

'It never occurred to me that it would,' Flora lied. 'I can see for myself how well she's doing. I'm sorry. I . . .' She stopped. He wouldn't want to hear what she was going to say. It was all history now anyway.

'What is it?' He looked genuinely curious and her sense of fair play told her she owed him an explanation.

'I let myself become rattled a while ago by some talk about Kimbay. I was afraid this might be more of the same. I was out of order.'

'I heard the talk. I paid no attention. You shouldn't have either.' His eyes were cold upon her, and absolutely unreadable.

'I know that now.' She looked at the horses without seeing them.

'Listen to me, Flora,' his voice was flat, expressionless. She didn't turn round. 'No one's going to get near Flo Girl as long as she's in my yard. Take my advice and forget all this crap about bad luck. You make your own luck. Work hard and know what you want to do. It's as simple as that.' He stopped and she turned to him.

'Yes,' she said.

'Flo Girl's happy and she's doing well. I'm told her owner's happy and doing well too.' He smiled. 'Congratulations, Flora.'

For brief, confusing seconds Flora couldn't think what he meant. Then her mind jolted away from the horses and she flushed, realizing. 'Thank you, Matt.' She knew she sounded stiff but it didn't matter. She'd already lost his attention. He'd turned away and was beating a tattoo with the whip again. A muscle throbbed in his cheek as he narrowed his eyes, became absorbed in the galloping horses.

'I've taken too much of your time,' Flora said. 'I'd better go.'

'Fine.' He didn't turn round. She was on Cormac's back, turning him, when he called to her. 'I don't want you to worry about Flo Girl,' he said. 'Win or lose, she has a future.'

'I hope so,' Flora said and rode quickly away.

It rained next day, and the day after. Flora, sick at heart, watched the skies for signs of a break in the heavy, lethargic cloud. She listened on the hour to weather reports. Neither activity held out much hope for a drying period before Saturday. Flo Girl didn't like soft, wet ground. Unless it cleared and dried the odds would be stacked against her on Saturday.

On Friday morning the clouds broke and a lively wind blew up. It might, just might, be okay. Flora was listening to the long-range forecast when the phone rang. She picked it up in the hall and Marigold's voice tinkled in her ear. 'Flora? Matt asked me to call. Said to tell you he'd been thinking about your conversation and has got someone in to sit with Flo Girl tonight. An anti-nobbling watch he called it. Whatever you said to him really made him jumpy.'

'Oh . . .' Taken aback, Flora muttered her thanks.

Marigold didn't seem about to hang up. 'Hope she wins tomorrow,' she said.

'Will you be there? At Gowran Park, I mean?' Flora asked.

'God, no. I never go to the races. Betting's a mug's game and what's the point otherwise? Anyway, I've a lovely new chap and I don't plan to spend our time together with a cast of thousands hanging around.' She laughed. '*Bonne chance*, though.'

Flora, before going to bed, decided on a terracotta jacket and sand-coloured trousers for Flo Girl's day at the races. Nothing too attention grabbing; let the filly herself do that. Later, in bed, she tried to read. When this failed to

222

bring on sleep she tried listening to music. But not even the soothing songs of the Auvergne, reliable comfort in times past, could do anything to stop the nagging anxiety about the race. By midnight it was raining again. Flo Girl would be racing in less than fifteen hours. The ground was going to be hopelessly soft.

Serge had phoned earlier to wish her luck. As always in August he was in the Loire with Monique. The gardens were wonderful, he said, full of colour and sun all day long. 'Next year you will spend August here,' he told her. 'You must arrange for Flo Girl to race during the other months.' Listening to the rain as it pattered on the window Flora, longingly, agreed.

When she did at last fall asleep, at about twelve-thirty, Flora's dreams were filled with chestnut horses. They raced along a seashore, ivory manes and tails lifting in the wind, toward a tide which ceaselessly retreated before their hooves.

She awoke in the muggy gloom of pre-dawn. Groaning she tried to get back to sleep, burying her head under the pillow to blot out light before the ringing telephone infiltrated her consciousness and brought her to the side of the bed. She checked her watch. It was five o'clock.

'Oh, my God, what's wrong . . .?'

She reached for her dressing gown, pulled it round her as she stumbled for the door. She couldn't think and didn't want to. Nobody made calls at this hour unless something was terribly wrong. Dipper, padding beside her down the stairs, began to whine. He leaned against her legs as she picked up the handset.

'Flora? What in God's name kept you?' Matt Hopkins's voice, rough with tension, shocked her fully awake. 'Flo Girl's gone. I need your help.'

'Gone?' Flora's mind raced and couldn't comprehend. The filly couldn't be *gone*. He'd had someone guarding her. Desperately wanting a logical explanation she asked, 'Gone where?'

'If I knew where . . .' She could feel the trainer's frustrated fury down the line. She felt only shock herself, so far, and waited for him to go on. 'We don't know where she's gone, Flora. She got out of her box. Looks as if she was turned loose. I'm fairly sure she hasn't been kidnapped, taken away.'

Flora, feeling about for the chair, found an empty space. Someone had moved it again. She wished people would leave things where she could find them.

'Flora? Are you there, Flora?' His voice was sharp, impatient.

'Of course I'm here. You say Flo Girl's loose? How can you be sure she hasn't been kidnapped?' She sank to the floor pulling her knees up and leaning against the wall. Dipper, whimpering, tried to lick her face. She pushed him away.

'Ground's wet. No signs of wheels anywhere near the yard.'

'But you had a watchman . . . Marigold said . . .'

'He didn't turn in. Look, we're wasting time. Lorcan's already out looking for her. I've phoned Shay. Can you saddle up and get out there too?'

That she was the last to know her horse was loose struck Flora immediately. 'I'm on my way,' she said and hung up.

The rain had stopped and it was getting brighter by the minute. Flora rode quickly, her eyes narrowed and alert for any movement, any shape or disturbance of the quiet landscape which might be the racehorse.

There was nothing. Nothing in the open fields or by the hedgerows or in the wooded area when she rode through it. She reached the top of the hillock and reined in. The river wound below her, dull metal coloured in the breaking light. She followed its course with her eyes, back to where it circled the Fairmane yard. And then she saw them; a man on a horse leading another, riderless and golden coloured, toward the stables. She gave a sob of relief and allowed herself a long, unburdening sigh.

The lightheaded feeling lasted until she rode into the Fairmane yard and saw the three men in a huddle outside

Flo Girl's box. It was Shay who turned as she dismounted and went toward them.

'Could be worse,' he said. 'Looks like she just went for a bit of a run and then settled down to graze.'

'She's not hurt?'

'Nothing we can see. Matt's phoned the vet. She seems all right but it's best to get him to run his rule over her.'

'My apologies, Flora.' The trainer spoke for the first time and Flora turned to him. She wouldn't have believed he could look so ashen. 'I don't know how it happened but by Christ I'm going to find out. Had to be someone who knew the place, how to get by the alarm system . . .'

'The watchman?' Flora prompted as he stopped. His unshaven face gave his anger an intimidating dimension. Briefly, the thought came to her that she would not like to be on the receiving end of his wrath.

'Was meant to be old Tom Curran. When he didn't turn in I went looking for him, tracked him down about eleven. He was arseholed. I took the watch myself until two. Then I went to bed. It was a set up.' He paused. '*I* was set up.'

His rage, and its impotence, were as palpable as the unspoken need in him to lay hands on whoever had freed the filly to run wild. Beside him Lorcan McNulty was hunched into a miserable knot. Shay alone seemed in control, reasonably sanguine.

'Doesn't mean she can't run a good race today,' he said.

'It's sure as hell not going to help her be at her best.' The trainer spoke through his teeth.

'She's tough,' the jockey found his voice. 'She's a trier. She's not going to sit down. She stood and waited for me when I rode up. She wasn't interested in running amok.'

'So it was you who found her?' Flora asked.

'It was. She hadn't gone far. She's no fool.' The jockey's small face was pinched-looking in the early light. He turned to the trainer. 'If I'm to ride I'll need sleep. I'm serving no purpose here anyway so I'll be off. You know where to get me if Jack Thomas has anything to say.' They watched him go, looking like a determined twelve-year-old as he crossed the yard.

'He wanted to stay the night with the filly and I wouldn't let him. Christ Almighty!' The trainer exploded with an intense ferocity. 'I made the job easy for the bastards. Might as well have left the door open for them.'

'It happens.' Shay's cool tones interrupted him. 'It's a lesson learnt, man.'

'At the expense of a damned good horse.' The trainer's voice was relentlessly furious. 'It won't happen again. Not to me,' he looked at Flora, 'and not to any horse in my charge.'

A familiar rattle and hum announced the arrival of Jack Thomas's Volkswagen at the side of the house. Flora and the two men waited in silence while he came toward them, cigarette glowing in his mouth, perennial tweed coat flapping. He grunted when he came abreast and went straight on and into Flo Girl's box.

'Bugger'll set fire to the straw.' As Shay made his growling prediction the vet's cigarette came flicking out over the door of the box. Watching it sizzle and die on the cobbles of the yard Flora could hear his low voice talking to Flo Girl as he checked her over. Morning was well broken now and the rain-washed sky held the promise of a clear day. She tried not to wonder if it mattered any more.

The vet appeared in the door of the box. He stopped to light a cigarette and walked slowly toward them. Flora almost screamed with impatience.

'She's right as rain,' the cigarette hung from his lower lip, 'there's no reason why she shouldn't run a good race. None of this should have happened, of course.' He squinted through blue smoke at the trainer. 'She could have had an accident, anything. Daresay you're aware of that yourself. No need for me to labour the point.' Wordlessly, he handed Shay a cigarette, then the matches. Shay, with a grunt of thanks, took them and Jack Thomas went on. 'There's a bad egg in this somewhere. Be in everyone's interest if you were to find out who was behind it.'

The morning stayed fine. The day was still rain-free at

two o'clock when Flora drove into leafy green Gowran Park. The mood was easy, the noise level high with excitement. The ground, according to both experts and punters, was soft.

Flo Girl's maiden race was at three-fifteen. It was over six furlongs and there were fifteen runners.

Shay, disquieted by Flora's high-strung tension, had left for the track mid-morning. Leah had driven to the course with Flora but disappeared in search of a friend as soon as they got inside the grounds. Flora, longing for Sophie's company, made her way to the owners' and trainers' viewing stand. Her nerves were taut as piano strings and she found herself calling up image after reassuring image of Flo Girl on the gallops. When Ollie's large and smiling figure rose from the stand to greet her she fell on his comfortable neck with relief.

'God, but I'm glad you're here,' she hugged him.

'Tried to rattle up Fintan, but he's on tour.' Ollie gave her an awkward, smiling pat on the shoulder. 'I did manage to extract a few bob from him to put on Flo Girl.'

'I'll be putting a tenner on her too. What are her chances of winning, Flora, honestly now?' Melissa, stunning in a white suit with thin black stripes, appeared from the seat beside Ollie.

'Melissa.' Flora air-kissed her cheek. 'Nice of you to come – and her chances are excellent. Though they were better yesterday.' They sat and she told them what happened in the night. Ollie was quietly furious when she finished, Melissa predictably scathing.

'Obviously someone left the door open and all of this about the horse running away is a cover-up,' she said. 'You're very naive, Flora.'

Startled, Flora looked at her. 'I really don't think it happened like that, Melissa. Someone *did* set her loose.'

'Maybe. But it sounds to me like you've a bee in your bonnet about people getting at you, Flora. Point is, she's here now and I'd like to see your horse.'

Flora, controlling a flash of anger, led the way to the parade ring. She was *not* going to be persuaded that she

227

was imagining things, or was paranoid. She would take care and be very, very watchful about everything to do with Flo Girl, and Kimbay, from now on.

It came to her too that, in an odd way, the night before's incident had given her extra confidence about Matt Hopkins's guardianship of the filly. It wasn't just that he cared for Flo Girl, though he patently did. It was more a question of the affront to his ego and vanity. He would not want something like last night's humiliation to happen again. Once was just about understandable. Twice would make him look a fool. He would never allow that.

In the parade ring Flo Girl looked undeniably flamboyant. But she circled with a cool which was a match for the demeanour of the calmest grey. Lorcan, perched like an underfed robin on her back, looked pale but fierce.

Matt Hopkins came to Flora as the race was called and the horses began to leave the ring. 'I walked the course.' He looked grim, angry still. 'Ground's a bit soft.'

Flora, with no desire to rub salt in his obvious wounds, managed a rueful smile. 'Given the rain we've had I'm sure it's more than just a bit soft,' she said.

'Look, Flora, it's best to be pragmatic about this.'

He gave her a close look, as if testing her reaction before saying what he wanted to say. Flora returned his inspection steadily. She wasn't going to help him any more.

'Flo Girl needs this racing gallop.' He spoke quickly. 'It's the only way we'll find out more about her. She's up against a hot favourite of Weld's, and Lorcan's happy enough too not to give her too hard a race. We don't want to do her any harm.'

'So we're not talking about a win?' Flora tried to keep the bleak disappointment out of her voice. She'd known anyway; all the signs had been there. Hearing it said aloud still wasn't easy. Clearly, in the air, there came the announcement that the horses were loading into the stalls.

'None of it'll matter in a few minutes.' The trainer was crisp. 'Looks like we've got lift-off.' He took her arm. 'We'll miss it if we don't get to the stands.'

Slipping with the trainer into a space in front of Ollie

and Melissa, Flora discovered she wasn't tense any longer. She was filled instead with a sense of calm expectancy. It was only a race, she told herself, life would go on afterwards. This burst of philosophical acceptance wouldn't last, she knew. But it was timely and reassuring.

The crowd fell silent and the starter began the race. She raised her binoculars. The stalls went up and fourteen of the horses charged forward, racing at first in a tight group, then spreading out across the field as they found their pace. The one horse left in the stalls was Flo Girl. The others had already begun to break their start-up grouping when she made a late, flying start from the stall.

Flora, still with a deadly calm, kept the binoculars clamped to her face and watched in silence as the filly began an impressive run up the inside. It wouldn't be enough. Nothing she could do now would be enough. The filly could never pick up on those crucial, lost initial seconds. She looked wonderful, though, moving faster than Flora would have ever thought she could on the soft ground. Lorcan was playing her just right and she was showing her mettle, running a courageous race. She would not disgrace herself. She wouldn't win either.

She was still running on the inside but was in the thick of the other runners now. For a few tormenting seconds Flora lost sight of horse and jockey. Then the bunch broke up and she saw them again, saw Flo Girl make for a gap in the runners and get through. She soared away, close on the tail of the favourite. Flora's calm had gone. Her hands on the glasses were clammy, her teeth uncontrollably chattering. Beside her the trainer stood still as a rock.

Then the horses were coming to the finishing line, the favourite running a great race, Flo Girl hard and unflagging on her heels. The crowd stood and roared a lusty appreciation of a close-run finish. On the waves of its excitement the first two horses passed the finishing post. They were so close that Flora, initially and against her better judgement, allowed herself to believe that her horse had won.

She hadn't. She'd come second and she'd more than proven herself.

Flo Girl, steaming and blowing in the winners' enclosure, was being held by her dazedly delighted jockey when Flora got there. Drained and relieved, and as yet unable to take it all in, she rubbed her nose gently. 'You were brilliant,' she told her, 'and you were wonderful. You've earned your keep.'

'Another furlong and she'd have won,' Matt Hopkins's voice behind her was measured. She looked up at him, saw the excitement in his eyes where he couldn't control it. Around them other voices were agreeing.

'Brilliant race, great potential,' said a sports reporter as a photographer took a picture of Flora with her horse and jockey. 'To be left in the stalls and come up on the inside like that . . .' he shook his head in wonder. 'Only a special animal could do it.'

'She's a trier,' Lorcan's grin was getting wider all the time, 'doesn't like to be beaten. I'd say she's always going to be like that. She'll never let herself be left behind.'

'How hard did you have to push her?' the reporter asked.

'Hardly at all. I shouted at her a few times and she pushed a bit more. She's clever. She knows what she's about.'

'Ned was right about her.' The trainer turned to Flora. 'This one's a winner.'

It was only then that Flora felt the first, naked pleasure of owning a really good horse. She wanted to laugh aloud, throw her arms around Flo Girl, her jockey and trainer. Instead, she did what she knew her father would have done. 'Champagne's on me,' she said.

But in the bar, with excitement high and the mood jubilant, Flora's spirits took a plunge. She fixed her smile and laughed at all the right moments but everything in her cried out for quiet, the peace of aloneness at Kimbay. I'm tired, she thought, I've been keyed up for weeks and last night just finished me.

'You do realize, Flora, that she's got definite Classic potential?' Matt Hopkins touched his glass to hers. Flora nodded, smiling, smiling. He looked at her curiously. 'I'll talk to you at another time,' he said, 'but I think we should take a chance on the Moyglare Stakes next month.'

Flora nodded again, brilliantly smiling. A young woman, laughing and flirtatious, came between them and took the trainer's arm. 'You promised you wouldn't stay all afternoon,' she said and he patted her hand.

'Be right with you,' he said, and to Flora, 'we'll talk next week.'

Flora smiled and nodded her way through the crowd. Once outside she ran without stopping to her car. She drove fast, and by the time she remembered Leah was almost at Kimbay. Her first instinct was to turn about, go back for her. Then she thought no, Shay's there to give her a lift, or Lorcan McNulty – even Matt Hopkins might manage to squeeze her in.

The first thing she would do when she got to the house would be to phone Serge. Driving up the avenue she planned how she would tell him. She would be offhand, casual – which wouldn't fool him for a minute. He would be glad for her and the news would go a long way towards vindicating her decision to take on Kimbay. He would see even more clearly now why she needed to be here, be involved. He might even come over for Flo Girl's next race.

Then she would get some sleep. God, how she wanted to sleep.

Chapter Twenty-One

'You might at least have told me you were leaving me high and dry.' Leah, hair damp after a ride in the next day's persistent drizzle, stood furious in the door of the feeding shed.

'I'm sorry.' Flora looked up from mixing oats with horsenuts and soya-bean meal. 'To tell the truth I forgot about you.'

'Forgot!' Leah looked disbelieving. 'How could you *forget* about me?'

Flora grinned. 'Seems incredible, I know, but that's what happened. By the time I became aware of the silence in the car I was almost home and I decided to have faith in your proven ability to look after yourself.'

'That was really friendly of you.' Leah had decided to be hurt. Her face took on an aggrieved expression.

'Well, I was right, wasn't I?' Flora weighed some nuts. 'Here you are, safe and sound and in fighting form.' She bent over the mixing. 'Look, Leah, either come in and help or buzz off.' She was sharp. 'You're blocking the light standing there.'

Leah, with a peevish toss of hair grown unruly again and frizzy now that it was drying, left the door and buried herself in feed mixing. 'You didn't care. You weren't even worried.'

'Careful with those nuts,' Flora frowned, 'they're too expensive to spill about the place. And of course I wasn't worried.'

Leah sniffed. 'Just as well I had one friend, at least, who was willing to see that I got home.'

'Aha! So that's it! What is it you want to tell me, Leah? *Who* brought you back?'

'Well . . .' Leah hesitated, looked under her brows at Flora. 'You're wrong if you think there's anything between Lorcan McNulty and myself. For one thing he's too small for me. We're mates, that's all.'

Flora looked at her in genuine astonishment. 'I didn't – it hadn't occurred to me.' She looked thoughtful for a moment and then grinned. 'But my, my – methinks the lady doth protest too much.'

Leah flushed and gave a half-hearted glare. 'It's not that I fancy him, or anything. He's just kind of easy, nice to be with. You know . . .'

'I know.' Flora smiled. 'So, tell me, what did you and this mate of yours talk about?'

'This and that,' Leah began and then, throwing caution to the winds, opened up. 'He's so interesting, Flora. Not a bit like the dickhead, moronic, half-baked—'

'Not in front of the horses, please,' Flora interrupted.

'Yes, well he's got plans, ideas about all sorts of things. Jocks aren't usually like that, you know. He's not going to stay around this place for ever either. After Flo Girl he plans to move on, ride all over the world.'

'He should, too,' Flora said, 'he's a good rider. He's right to want to get around. What does his present employer think about his plans?'

'Matt? He's all for it, too. Though I'd say myself that he'll miss Lorcan. In a funny sort of way he treats him like a son. Course by the time Lorcan takes off Matt will probably have a son of his own.'

Flora looked up, startled. 'Matt has plans to get married? He's planning fatherhood?'

'Planning marriage anyway. According to Lorcan at least.'

'Matt told Lorcan he was getting married?' Flora was experiencing a sense of shock and wasn't quite sure why. It was probably because Matt Hopkins had always seemed such an unlikely candidate for either matrimony or monogamy.

'Don't know as I'm inclined to tell you any more.' Leah looked teasingly arch. 'Lorcan was talking to me in confidence, after all.'

'You're right.' Flora stood and briskly rubbed her hands on a cloth. 'Time we stopped gossiping. There are animals waiting to be fed.' Resolutely, she picked up two lots of feed and began across the yard. Leah, carrying two others, trotted quickly after her.

'No need to overreact,' she sniffed. 'I'll tell you anyway, just to keep you in the picture. It seems Marigold was trying it on with Matt, you know the way she does, and he was having none of it. He told her, nicely and all that, of course, that he was working on becoming a one-woman man. So there!'

'Sounds like a plan of some sort all right.' Flora pulled open the door of Nessa's box. 'Though fatherhood would seem a bit down the line.'

Flora met with the trainer a few days later to discuss Flo Girl's racing future. The Moyglare Stakes, to be run at the Curragh in mid-September, was a group one race. If she won it . . .

'She *could* win, couldn't she?' she asked.

'Absolutely.' The trainer was curt.

They were standing in the yard. It was late morning and he looked vaguely formal in jacket and cords. He was obviously preoccupied and Flora wondered if it had anything to do with his desire to become a one-woman man. She wished the woman luck, whoever she was. She would need it. Matt Hopkins was a high-risk love venture if ever there was one.

'You're agreeable to giving it a try, then?' he asked.

'Why not? It won't do her any harm, will it?'

'None at all. And if she wins . . . well, you need never race her again. Winning a group one will make her very valuable as a brood mare.'

'I realize that.' Flora was tart. 'But, equally, if she wins, she'd be worth trying in the Guineas next season, wouldn't she?'

'I'd be more ambitious than that for her. I'd push her to the Derby. I've always thought she had the potential. But we've a winter to get through before then, and the Moyglare too. I'll enter her.'

234

Two days later the post brought a surprise, and a crisis decision. Flora, answering the door to the postman, looked at the envelope with Serge's handwriting for a while before sitting on the steps to read it in the sun.

Serge wasn't a letter writer, usually. He put pen to paper only when all other forms of communication failed. Flora tried to ignore a feeling of trepidation as she tore the envelope open.

The letter was short and loving. The enclosures were the problem. Flora looked at them with a leap of the heart which became a groan when she saw the dates.

'Dear God,' she closed her eyes and groaned with fervour, 'please make my life simple again. Make it the way it used to be.'

'Talking to ourselves now, are we?' She looked up as Daisy's voice broke into her self-communing. 'I met the postman going down the avenue. I suppose he's the cause of this attack of piety?'

Wordlessly, Flora handed her the envelope. Daisy glanced through its contents and sighed. 'Frenchmen know how to treat a woman, no doubt about it,' she said. 'What's the groaning about then?'

'Look again,' Flora said, 'and look at the dates this time.'

Daisy did as she was told and made a tut-tutting sound. 'I see what you mean. Bit of a clash there.' She handed back the envelope. 'It's the sort of problem I wouldn't mind having, though.'

'Oh, Daisy, it's not funny.'

'It's not a tragedy either. God Almighty, Flora,' Daisy gave an exasperated snort, 'I'm worn out with the dramatics round here. If it's not Leah it's yourself. Look, sit there in the sun a while longer and decide what you're going to do. And while you're at it remember it'll make no difference how the horse runs whether you're there or not. How the man you're engaged to marry will feel if you turn his invitation down because of a horse is another thing.'

She swept on into the house, sandals flapping and long skirt fanning the air as she passed. Flora, hurt and feeling that

235

Daisy's attack wasn't quite fair, looked again at the tickets and hotel bookings which had arrived in Serge's envelope.

In her hand was a plane ticket to Paris for the weekend of the Longchamp Prix Vermeille Escada, a reservation for a private box at Longchamp and a booking for a room at the George V for two nights. Serge had written that he would have arranged for them to go to the Prix de l'Arc de Triomphe were it not so close to the Goffs sale dates. A Paris break would set her up for the sales, he wrote, was just what she needed before the arrival of winter. It would be good for them both and it would introduce Flora to the wonders of French racing.

Serge had only once been to Longchamp himself but had professed himself shocked when Flora, so close to horses all her life, admitted that she had never been to the French racecourse. He'd obviously put a lot of thought and effort into making the arrangements.

But he'd chosen the weekend Flo Girl was due to race at the Curragh in the Moyglare Stakes.

Flora would have to go to Paris. Daisy was right. Not to go would endanger their relationship, kept together with such fragile links as it was. She needed Serge. She couldn't go on without his support, the knowledge that he was there when she needed him. 'I can't *not* go to Longchamp,' she told herself. 'Flo Girl will have to race at the Curragh without me.'

Her decision didn't cause the upset she'd anticipated. Matt Hopkins was offhand. There would be other Flo Girl races to watch. She'd enjoy Longchamp. The French knew how to put on a show, he said, and the racing was damned good. Lorcan told her not to worry, things would be fine. The filly herself continued in fine form.

No one, it seemed, considered her vital, or even necessary, to her horse's final race of the season. But Flora found it hard to kill off the feeling that she was betraying a trust, walking out at a crucial point in the filly's career.

It wasn't until she was in the air over Dublin, aware of and turning Serge's ring on her finger, that she for the first time felt the beginnings of a pleasurable anticipation of what lay ahead. Below her the airport green gave way to the grey of city housing and then to the wide blue of Dublin Bay as the plane banked, turned and headed on course for Paris. She sat back and began to relax.

The French capital was *en fête*. In the glowing early autumn the City of Light flaunted the wonder of its wide boulevards and the arrogant beauty of its *bâtiments*. Flora, driving to the hotel with Serge, felt herself being pulled simultaneously by its vibrating glamour and the sheer, noisy aggression of its street life. She determined that later, after they'd checked into the hotel, she would persuade Serge to spend an hour or so at a pavement café, just looking. Anywhere in the Place Dauphine would do, with the river and Nôtre Dame and *tout le monde* as backdrop.

She looked sideways at Serge as he muttered a *merde*! while artfully, in swift darts and frustrating stops, getting them through bunched traffic. At the Arc de Triomphe a taxidriver engaged him in battle, intent on making him complete the circuit again. Serge calculated, biding his time on the inside until, an unwary opening presenting itself, he surged through, headed off the taxi and drove onto and down the straight of the Champs Elysées. The incident reminded Flora of Flo Girl's careful inside manoeuvring and dash through the bunch for second place in her first race. But the thought was fleeting and she said nothing about it to Serge.

'It's great to be here,' she said and meant it, 'and it's great to be with you.'

He gave her a quick, warm look before focusing again on the capricious traffic. She touched his face with a finger and he smiled without looking at her. He said nothing and neither did she. There was nothing to say, then.

For the short rest of the journey Flora lazily reflected on the weekend of being cared for which stretched ahead, on the security and pleasure of spending it with a man who smelled of Givenchy, wore a suit whose tailoring was impeccably continental and who belonged, in every way, to this city.

They talked later, in their room with its pale, rose-coloured walls in the George V Hotel. A waiter brought them chilled wine on a silver salver, they toasted one another and Flora told Serge about Flo Girl's race the next day.

'It's her make-or-break race.' She kept her tone light. 'After tomorrow I'll own a very valuable horse or, at the very least, one with possibilities.'

'And I have taken you away from all of this excitement.' Serge's tone was rueful.

'Yes, you have.' Flora went to where he stood by the fireplace and ruffled his hair, put a finger through the curls going grey at the sides. She touched his mouth with hers. 'I am, as you see, a willing victim. I'm here and I'm putting her out of my mind until tomorrow evening. I'll phone then. But for now . . .'

They made love, and she forgot her determination to sit at a pavement café. Outside, the golden afternoon dulled to early evening and the city caught its breath before the serious business of its night life began. In the semi-dark Serge was gloriously familiar, his kisses and warm touch filling her with longing.

'Let's just stay in this room for the weekend.' She leaned over him, laughing. Her hair fell on either side of her face and he caught it, pulling her gently down to him.

'You are so easily seduced,' he smiled at her, 'or is it that you are afraid to see racing as it should be? To compare Irish racing with the best in the world?'

'You foolish Frenchman,' Flora gave his ear a sharp nip, 'I can see the best of racing any time at home. But Longchamp has novelty value.' She lowered herself on to him, and he touched her breasts again, feathery movements across her nipples which made her catch her breath. 'First things first,' she murmured as she felt his need match her own.

'As you say, *mon amour*,' Serge's voice was husky, 'first things first.'

Afterwards, while Serge showered, Flora lay among the pale pink sheets and studied a pair of medieval lovers cavorting, forever young and wanton, on a wall tapestry of lushly woven threads. Barred street lighting crept through the shutters into the still, luxurious silence. She hardly thought at all of Kimbay, or of Flo Girl.

They went early to the Bois de Boulogne next day. The racecourse was carnival-like with flags, music, flowers and showpiece fashions from three continents. Flora had dressed in palest, silvery blue, a slim, bias-cut dress whose subtlety held its own with the very serious dressers swarming the Longchamp meeting.

In the open-air champagne bar they went through the list of runners, spotted famous and infamous faces, owners, trainers and even the odd jockey. Flora missed the irreverent sideshow provided by the on-course bookmakers at home, but the prize money was dizzyingly high and generated another kind of excitement as they placed their bets with the tote. They had a lunch of *crêpes de volaille* with a *salade verte* in their box and then the races began.

The day's buzz lasted through the first two races – a win for Flora, none for Serge. But as three o'clock and Flo Girl's race came closer Flora's iron intention to play cool, not to phone Kimbay until the end of the day, began to suffer melt-down. Acquaintances of Serge joined them for part of the afternoon and she smiled and nodded and sipped champagne and watched another race. Eventually, sick with apprehension and resolve foundering, she slipped away to telephone the Sweeney cottage. There was no reply. The phone rang emptily and she cursed the insouciance which had made her tell people she didn't want to know the result until evening.

They stayed until the last race, Flora only twice slipping away to the telephone, once even trying Fairmane. When the meeting was over and they were cruising back to the George V Flora gave thanks that the racetrack was in the city, that they weren't faced with a long drive through snarling, post-race traffic.

In their room she pounced on the phone, indecently hasty, all pretence at cool gone. This time it rang twice before, thank God, thank God, it was picked up at the other end.

'Yes?' Shay. It was Shay.

'It's Flora. What happened?'

The silence lasted a single breath. 'She won,' Shay said then and Flora sank onto the bed, the phone so tightly against her ear it hurt.

'She won,' she whispered after him.

'She did. By a good length. Ran a great race.'

She wanted more detail, wanted to hear everything, but knew it would be like getting teeth from a hen to get Shay to commit himself to further conversation on the phone.

'Is Leah there?' she asked.

'No. Bit of a party on in the Old Nag. They're all at it. You'll be home tomorrow, then?'

'Yes. Tomorrow evening.'

'We'll see you then.' The line went dead. Flora held onto the elegant George V handset until she felt it gently taken from her hand by Serge.

'Your little gold horse has won her race, then?' He hunkered down in front of her and Flora nodded.

'*Eh bien!*' He grinned widely. 'Maybe now she will someday be good enough for a French racecourse.'

They ate that night in Fouquet's on the Champs Elysées and danced later in a nearby club called le Calvados. Flora drank a lot of champagne and thought about the party going on in the Old Nag. She wished she could somehow transport everyone here so she could be with them for the celebration. She said as much to Serge and he laughed, nuzzled her ear.

'It is better that we celebrate alone,' he said.

She felt a stab of resentment and quickly tried to bury it. The thoughts came anyway. Serge, surely, must realize that Flo Girl's win was a triumph for Kimbay, her trainer, her jockey, everyone concerned. It was an occasion for sharing, and as the horse's owner she should be there, be a part of it all. She hoped he would grow to understand better in the future. It would make their shared lives very difficult if he didn't. She would have to explain, but later. Not now. It wasn't the time and it certainly wasn't the hour.

They danced in silence for a while and Flora felt her resentment evaporate in plain tiredness. Serge had arranged all this, gone to endless trouble. She must remember that. Floating champagne-dizzy in his arms, she said, 'I am the luckiest woman in Paris and you are the most beautiful man here.'

'*Merci, ma chère.*' He kissed her. 'I am lucky too.'

Chapter Twenty-Two

Autumn was in the air. Flora could smell it in the mornings when she rode out, see it in the slow bleakness creeping daily over the landscape. Hedges were thinning, trees beginning to fall bare and the fields taking on the naked, spare look that went with a lack of foliage. As the days shortened the air got colder and animals of all sorts settled into the natural slowing down of things. All this at just the beginning of October.

The community around Dunallen moved, too, with the rhythm of the changing season and began preparing itself for a cycle of new activities. The hunt was one of these.

Flora, adamant that she did not want to take part, hoped feverishly that she would not be approached to join. Such a hope was, she knew, based on a shortsighted optimism. Ned had for so long been an enthusiastic member that it was unlikely she would escape an attempt to persuade her into the ranks. He was dead almost eight months now. Time, they would say, for her to take his place. But she hadn't paid her cap money, nor made any advances. It must be clear that she had no intention of turning up. But she awaited the call and it came.

Charlie Quinn, Master of the Dunallen Hunt for as long as Flora could remember, arrived in the yard on an afternoon when one of her mares had proven not to be in foal. Disappointed, angry with herself for failing to notice earlier, Flora was in no mood for his brusque insistence.

'Numbers are down, Flora,' he shook his head heavily, 'we'd like you to ride with us. By way of taking Ned's place, so to speak. He's sadly missed. He'd have liked you to —'

'He'd have wanted no such thing, Charlie, and you know it.' Flora was impatient, and sharper than she'd meant to be. 'He understood my feelings about the hunt and he respected them.' She heard herself as if from a distance, hardly crediting she was talking like this to the hunt's master. She'd lived her young life in subdued fear of him, hardly daring to raise her head above a notional parapet when he was around. He'd been both adversary and some-time friend of her father's, the bogey-man figure of her and the boys' childhoods.

There was a great deal of local sympathy and under-standing of Charlie Quinn's gruff and forceful ways. It allowed him to get away with a lot of bullying. He farmed several hundred arable acres of land and had raised four sons alone after his wife left him for the more genteel charms of an art historian. Two of the sons had in time gone out into the world but two had remained to become, with their father, the hard core of the Dunallen Hunt.

He wasn't as big now as he'd been then, but Flora stood at an instinctively safe distance from him anyway. Watching how his ruddy face darkened at her tone, a surge of memories almost overpowered her. He obviously hadn't lost his tendency to anger quickly. She didn't want a shouting match, not here, not in the Kimbay yard.

'Come on into the house, Charlie,' she issued the invitation as gently as she could, 'and have a drink. Maybe we can understand one another inside. Or at least listen better.'

'Good idea,' he said at once and walked ahead of her, leading the way as if he were the host and control of the situation lay in his hands alone.

Flora, following, gave a small, resigned smile. He had always been thus. Always his own worst enemy. Funny how she understood now what she had only feared before. Watching his huge lumpen shoulders and heavy neck she remembered how, as children, she and the boys had dreaded his visits. He had treated them in much the same way he'd treated his own children, or so she'd imagined, lining them up and setting them questions on horse lore. He would bellow answers and corrections before they could properly reply, thumping the floor for emphasis with his blackthorn walking stick. Other times, banishing Ned and announcing he would be 'uncle' for the afternoon, he would set about testing their horsemanship. With hard, unsympathetic eyes he would then oversee them taking jumps and generally working animals.

He was always critical, always harsh, fond of telling Ned that he was sparing the whip and spoiling his children. Flora and her brothers, with the instinctive understanding of children, had been aware that his visits were an effort to redress the balance of what he perceived as Ned's too soft treatment of his offspring. As the farmer saw it, he and Ned were both men whose wives had left them. His view seemed to be that it had been deeply careless of Hannah Carolan to fall off a horse and leave Ned to care for their family. His occasional 'toughening-up' visits to his friend's children were, for him, a duty. Ned, for his part, thought the farmer's treatment of Flora and the boys robust but well-meaning.

Looking at Charlie Quinn now, ahead of her going up the back stairs to the kitchen, Flora saw how he'd aged. His sandy-red hair had thinned and his nose become grotesquely bulbous. The ruddyness was far too red and the broken veins on his weatherbeaten face were livid and copious. For the first time ever she experienced a strange pity for him. She'd heard recently that his sons wanted him to hand over control of the land to them. If this was true it would make the hunt, and his stewardship, even more important to him. It would be all he had, in a way.

In the living room she poured him a large rum, remembering it was what he liked. He downed it in a gulp and she poured him another.

'Please, Charlie, sit down.' She indicated an armchair, and when he was seated uncomfortably at its edge, she sat opposite. 'I'm sorry I can't ride to the hunt,' she began but he held up a hand.

'Don't be hasty now, Flora. Don't make up your mind too fast. Give it a bit of thought and you might find you feel differently.'

'I *have* thought about it,' Flora said. 'I don't —' ·

'Now, now,' he shook his great head, 'I know your

mother dying the way she did put the hunt in bad odour with you when you were a child. But you're a grown woman now. Time to —'

Flora, taking a deep breath, interrupted him firmly. 'It's not that, Charlie. Or at least that's only part of it. It's more that I'd find it hard to be a wholehearted member. I don't feel right about hunting, per se. No, please hear me out.' She left the armchair and began to pace. 'I know you'll give me sound, traditional reasons why I should feel otherwise about fox hunting and, believe me, I do understand those reasons. It's just that I don't agree with them. I feel that horsemanship can be challenged without killing the fox and that there has to be another way of keeping fox numbers down.'

When she sat down again she held her breath, watching the farmer as he struggled with his desire to explode, tried to deal calmly with his disagreement about everything she'd said. The strange pity welled in her again and this time she understood it better. Her pity was for his confusion, and his loss. Here was a man unable to deal with change and who saw change happening all around him. His security and sense of self lay in the traditional country way of life and he was afraid to begin understanding anything else. Probably because he feared there would be no role for him in a new way of doing things. His bullying days were over. She knew it.

'It's worked well for long years now,' he began, and she reached out and touched his hand.

'I know it has, Charlie. The hunt will go on, too, I'm sure of it, but in a different form. And without me, I'm afraid.'

He whirled the remains of the drink in his glass and said nothing. She thought about topping it up, then thought better of it. Too much rum might be a disaster, maybe bring on a row about the morality or otherwise of the hunt. She knew all the arguments and didn't want to get into it. She really did see the validity of the country-person's view. It had been her father's view and, no doubt, her mother's too.

Foxes were a pest and their numbers had to be kept down. The hunt, to some extent, saw to it. Other arguments were more subtle. The hunt was an instrument of social advancement, it afforded an opportunity to be aggressive without hurting anyone but yourself, the chase was a test of riding skills and brought people together, got them cheerfully out of their houses during the dark months of winter.

'I'm sorry you feel like this, Flora.' Charlie Quinn emptied the remains in his glass. 'You were a long time away of course. A long time with the Europeans.' His voice was strained with resignation.

'I was,' Flora said and left it at that. Let him think, if it made him feel better, that she'd been corrupted by city and foreign ways.

With a heavy grunt, and the aid of a blackthorn stick, the farmer pulled himself out of the armchair. Flora wondered if the stick was the one he'd had all those years before. She thought about asking him, but thought better of that too. He no doubt imagined her half-mad as things stood. Questions about his walking stick would confirm his suspicions.

'The hunt'll go on.' He thumped the floor with the blackthorn. 'We'll be there if you change your mind.'

'If you were to organize a drag hunt I might go along.' Flora went with him to the living-room door. He stopped.

'A drag? Organize a drag, is it? Have you taken leave of your senses, woman?' He drew himself to his full height. His voice became strong and his argument, as he made it, was expressed with considerable dignity and passion. 'You're in a minority, Flora. Nobody in this part of the country disagrees with the hunt. If you intend staying around you should pay heed to how your neighbours and the people you'll be living with feel about such things. Excusing your presence,' he cleared his throat noisily, 'but the argument against it is a load of bollocks. Same as with coursing. At a coursing meeting you'll have about twenty of the rent-a-crowd outside and about 20,000 inside taking part. It's nature. If you let a dog off he'll kill a rabbit. It's

246

nature they're protesting about. Same crowd object to fur coats – but what're their shoes made of? We were all hunters and trappers before technology.'

As he spoke, voice unwavering in its fierceness, he stamped along the hallway to the front door. He pulled it open and turned again to face Flora. 'The amount of cruelty involved in the hunt is negligible. As for those protesting about jockeys whipping the horses – more balls! Jockeys love their horses and they treat them well. I've never met a jockey didn't love his horse. The three or four skelps a fellow might give an animal round the arse at the height of a race are nothing when put in the context of the horse's life as a whole and the fine treatment it gets daily.' He drew a huge breath and stepped outside. 'You think about what I've said, Flora, and maybe you'll change your mind.'

'I doubt that I will,' Flora held out her hand, 'but could we shake on our differences? Agree to respect one another's view? Be friends, maybe?'

Slowly, with a slightly shocked look on his face, the farmer extended his hand and they shook, briefly, on it. He didn't meet her eyes as he sketched a small salute and turned to go down the steps.

She closed the door on him with relief, glad that the business of the hunt had been dealt with at last. It was less than a week to go to Goffs sales and her waking hours were devoted to the three colts and filly she hoped to sell there. She'd done all she could to prepare them, including having the local blacksmith work on their hooves. 'No foot, no horse,' Ned had always said and she'd come to believe he was right. She'd even held the coffee morning as suggested by the breeder at the hunt ball. The feedback had been most useful. It was time now for her to give them their daily practice walk, a circuit of the paddock today, since it was hard and dry.

Next day near disaster struck. It would have been complete disaster if the injury had been to the grey yearling she hoped to sell for real money. But it was one of the others, a lively bay, which limped across the paddock the following afternoon. It was the slightest of limps but couldn't have happened at a worse time. Flora brought him in, not even allowing herself to look at the troubled leg until she'd got him inside the box.

When she examined the wound, holding her breath as if this would prepare her for the damage, she saw a jagged cut on his foot. Even that quick look told her it would need stitches, though not many. It was not deep and he stood quietly while she examined it further.

'How in God's name did you do that?' She put the foot down, shaking her head at him in despair. He was a nice-looking animal and he looked at her, big-eyed and mute. He'd have done well at the sales – she doubted she could sell him now, not with a blemish. It would cure, in time. It wouldn't even affect his spirit or health really. But it wouldn't cure quickly enough for Goffs. A blemish, a thick fetlock, could take £5,000 off his value at sale. And if it swelled he would have a permanent blemish. She rang for Jack Thomas.

The vet stood shaking his head after he'd examined the cut. 'Auld fool must have got it going through the gate or something,' he said.

Flora thought it more likely it had happened during horseplay, but didn't contradict him. He could be touchy enough. The bay was one of the more energetic yearlings, forever cavorting about, throwing up his feet, playful. What she said to Jack Thomas, hopefully, was, 'It's really only a bad scratch, isn't it?'

'You're always the optimist, Flora.' Jack Thomas looked again at the yearling's fetlock. 'It's more than a scratch.'

'But it'll drain, won't it? The open part of the wound is to the bottom. That means it'll drain.'

'It'll drain all right. But he won't make it to the sales. Not this time, anyway. I'm sorry, Flora.'

One animal less to sell increased the necessity to do well with the other three. Flora cursed, furiously and helplessly, and her tension quota increased.

She left the yearlings safely in Goffs the day before the sales, depositing the paraphernalia essential for the day's work too. Headcollars, rugs, brushes, polish for hooves and linseed oil for coats were just basics for good grooming. She'd no intention of losing money, maybe as much as several thousand guineas, because of something wrong with the appearance of a perfectly fit and able animal.

Driving to the Kildare Paddocks next morning she convinced herself the omens were good. The overnight clouds had rolled back to reveal a startlingly blue sky. Beside her Luke quietly dozed, apparently unfazed by the fact that he would be walking the horses in the parade ring. Ever since the Sophie incident a peace of sorts had existed between him and Flora. Flora could only hope the day ahead wouldn't stretch it past its limit.

Out of habit she drove around the complex, past the great sales theatre and rows of looseboxes, to park on the grass at the back. It was cold when they got out of the car and a nippy wind cut sharply across their faces. Flora was glad she'd worn boots and a fleece-lined jacket. Crows cawed aggressively overhead as she and Luke walked the muddy route to the row of boxes she'd rented for the day. Kimbay's name, in gold and black above each door, looked confident enough when they got there.

'Looks like we mean business.' Luke grinned.

'We do.' Flora tried to match his up-beat tempo, but knew she'd failed when he threw her a vaguely supercilious look. Damn him, she thought, I should have insisted on bringing Leah to do the walking. She at least wouldn't have indulged in this macho cool. But Leah was too tall, would have made the yearlings look small. This was one job where Luke's lack of inches would be an asset.

Flora was stroking the grey, talking quietly to him, when Luke came into the box ten minutes later. He spoke jerkily, cool suddenly gone. 'Pat Morgan wants to see him.'

'Now?' A leading bloodstock agent wanting to see an animal before auction could mean something. Or it could mean nothing more than curiosity.

'Right away. He's outside.' Luke slipped the bridle onto the colt.

'Who's he buying for?'

'Japanese, looks like.'

249

Flora knew the agent, but not well, and stayed by the box as Luke led the colt up and down for him to view. The agent's impassivity was matched only by that of two Japanese men watching from the end of the yard. Japanese buyers, and their money, were welcome at the sales but, given a choice, Flora would have preferred an animal of hers to find an owner nearer home. A continental or UK buyer would mean she could keep in touch with his career, see how things went for him after he left her.

But a sale is a sale. She saw the agent have a brief, quiet word with Luke, saw Luke give a nod as impassive as anything the agents or his buyers could manage, then walk the colt back to his box.

'Just thanked me. Said he'd talk to his buyers.' Luke rubbed down the grey.

'Would you like tea?' Flora asked and the boy nodded. She made tea in the small, draughty room beside the boxes. There was no point her going over to the sales ring yet. She drank hers too hot and cleaned up before Luke had finished his. She checked the animals again. She studied the catalogue, criticizing punctuation aloud for Luke's benefit. She suggested more tea.

'Christ Almighty, Flora!' Luke exploded. 'You're making me nervous. God knows what you're doing to the horses. Why don't you go over to the sales ring, see what's happening?'

'You don't think it's too early for that?' Flora was humble, knowing he was right and that she could upset the horses.

'Go, Flora.' Luke was firm. 'There's nothing more to be done for now. I'll send someone over if I need you.'

The noon start of the auction proper was a good forty-five minutes away, and there was as yet only a thin scattering of bodies in the blue seating around the ring. Walking along the overhead balcony Flora tired to gauge the day's mood; see, if she could, what buyers were about. Nothing she saw told her anything. She just didn't know enough, wasn't familiar with things.

250

She came upon a group of spotters, laughing and conspiratorial. Fintan had worked as a spotter and she knew they would know the score. She could hardly ask them, though. It would be as much as their jobs were worth to tell her anything. They were all young, clean-cut, dark-blazered and looked as if they'd strayed from a city broker-age firm – which was probably where most were headed anyway. For the sale they would be positioned around the ring to 'spot' buyers and indicate their bids to the auctioneer.

She leaned over the balcony for a while, watching the crowd as it thickened. The grey colt, listed 20 in the catalogue, would be the first of Kimbay's yearlings to come up for sale.

The mood below her quickened and, without warning, she was assailed with sudden and terrible uncertainties. She wished Shay had come with her. He'd have known how things were shaping up, been able to read the signs.

But – so what if he could? The small voice of her growing confidence piped up as unexpectedly as the doubts of seconds ago. The die is cast and the yearlings are here, it said. You're the one got them ready and you're the one going to oversee their sale. Shay's ability to read the signs would make bugger-all difference to what's going to happen from now on.

She gritted her teeth and decided to enjoy things. She would leave the fate of the Kimbay yearlings in the lap of the gods. She'd done everything else.

She moved down to find herself a seat, saw some familiar faces do the same thing. A few she knew personally, but others were familiar only from the social columns or their eminence in the worlds of business and politics. In the discreet talk and accents around her she picked up an idea of the numbers of nationalities present – certainly there were Arab, American, Italian and British buyers about, as well as the earlier Japanese. With five minutes to go she found a seat.

'Look at them – all friends. Even the most introverted

251

bastards are talking to one another today.' Jack Thomas, wheezing and panting, edged his bulk into the seat beside her.

'Hello, Jack.' She looked at him in surprise. 'You buying or just looking?'

'Looking, dammit. Saw you sitting alone. I'll go away if you prefer to stay that way.'

'No, please stay,' Flora said quickly. 'You can fill me in on what's happening, give me the inside track, so to speak.' No harm in knowing, she told herself. The information would be useful for next year.

'The hidden agenda, you mean.' The vet gave a black laugh. 'It's there all right, the chicanery and everyone trying to be smarter than the next one. It's a way of life with them, that's the long and short of it.' He shook his head. 'Amazing what the prospect of a sale will make a man do. Who he'll make up to for information.' He gave her a sly, sideways smile. 'Women must be different. Don't see you making up to any of them.'

'I'm talking to you,' Flora said reasonably.

He ignored this. 'They're right, you know, to come out of their corners for a day like today. You have to talk to people because you never know who you're talking to.' He fiddled with a pack of cigarettes and with painful reluctance put them back into his pocket. 'You never know who'll be useful. You should remember that, Flora, talk to more people.'

The auctioneer appeared in his box over the ring and, after the various procedural announcements, the first of the day's yearlings was led in.

'Too bloody small for my liking, that filly,' Jack Thomas muttered. He consulted the catalogue. 'Getting late in the year when she was born, she's a bit young. Sire's good enough, though. Bit of healthy black print in the catalogue.'

Flora found his commentary, pedantic and salty as it might be, a welcome diversion. 'I like the look of her myself,' she said as bidding began for the filly in the ring. 'She's elegant.'

Jack Thomas's 'tsk' of exasperation made her immediately wish she'd said nothing.

'Jesus Christ, woman, they're not buying dolls here. She's a sweet little thing, I'll grant you that. But it's doubtful she'll make a racehorse. There, she's gone,' he grunted as the hammer came down on 18,000 guineas. 'Not bad, considering.'

Yearlings came and went in the ring and the entry of number 20 crept closer. Jack Thomas's *sotto voce* commentary on each one continued thankfully diverting. When a dark, powerful-looking bay appeared, it provoked something like ecstasy in the old vet.

'Good God, look at the body on him! He's a racehorse this minute.' His voice became disappointed as the bidding began. 'He's making poor money for something that's out of a good mare. Great second dam too.' He gave a small chortle and rubbed his hands together. 'There! He's going up now. Scandalous to be talking about less than a hundred thousand for him. His grand dam is by Northern Dancer. You'd weep blood if you saw an animal like that going for anything less than a hundred thousand.'

He scowled at the auctioneer, at the crowd in general and sank deeper into the tweed coat. The bay, to Flora's relief, went for 110,000 guineas.

'Jack, I think I'll go see how Luke's getting on.' She moved to get up.

'Stay where you are.' The vet's raspy voice was firm. 'I'd a word with him before I came in. He's got everything in working order. Best to leave him be. He knows what he's doing.'

Flora, uncertain but on balance thinking he was probably right, sat down again. The vet suddenly leaned forward, hands on his knees as he gave a small groan. 'God, but this lad's a tragedy. He's small. His fetlocks are too long. Look at the way he's going back on them.' He stabbed the catalogue with a hard, brown finger. 'All that and he has the brilliant breeding. Just shows how you can lose in this business. But because he's bred in the purple the buyers will take a chance on him anyway.'

Flora got up. 'Be back in a few minutes, Jack,' she said. 'I can't *not* see what Luke's up to.'

253

She found Luke parading the grey yearling in the outside, preliminary ring. He'd never looked more like his father; eyes distant, face closed except when he looked at the horse. The colt was reassuring too. Even among the other stunningly turned out parading yearlings he looked what Ned would have called a 'topper'.

When Luke and the grey came abreast of where she was standing Luke loosened up enough to give Flora a half-grin.

'He looks fine,' she said. 'Everything all right?'

'He's looking great,' Luke said, 'and he's going to do well. Stop fussing, Flora.'

'Right.' Flora, with a last look, went back to her seat by Jack Thomas. By the time Luke appeared with the grey she had composed a carefully impassive face. Jack Thomas, demonstrating a heretofore unhinted at sensitivity, remained silent.

'We've a seriously good colt here,' the auctioneer began his patter, 'lovely head . . . look at that head . . .'

Luke seemed frighteningly young. But in charge. The colt was behaving himself. Not a bit skittish. Flora's palms were sticky. She sat absolutely still, only her eyes moving as she followed the boy and horse around the ring.

'They're interested,' Jack Thomas, breaking his silence, spoke in her ear. His stale cigarette breath was, in the oddest way, comforting. Flora couldn't see how he knew that anyone was interested. There had been no bid so far. She watched the spotters. Nothing there either, not a sign. 'Look,' Jack Thomas was patient, 'as a first foal there's nothing positive, or negative, about him. He'll do all right. His second dam was a good horse.'

There was a bid. Then another. Flora tried frantically to see where they were coming from and failed. The spotters were fast, she couldn't read them the way the auctioneer could. A jump of 5,000 guineas brought the price to 20,000 guineas.

'That fella's bidding for someone,' Jack Thomas said. 'I don't know who he is though.'

254

The price jumped again, then again. The colt was now on offer for 27,000 guineas. A spotter, Flora saw him this time, indicated a buyer close to where they were sitting and the price jumped by another 5,000 guineas.

'Might see a bit of real money now,' the vet all but rubbed his hands together, 'unless of course the buyer's a crooked bastard. If he's straight you're into the big time, Flora.'

The buyer was straight and he wasn't playing games. He outbid the Japanese when they eventually joined in, and paid 51,000 guineas for the colt.

'Not bad.' Jack Thomas gave Flora's knee a friendly squeeze. It was the most overt demonstration of pleasure she'd ever seen him make. 'Not bad at all,' he repeated.

'Who bought him?' Flora fought an urge to jump in the air, throw her arms around the vet, yell aloud. The question, the fact that she hadn't seen the buyer and couldn't quite believe in him, kept her feet on the ground.

'English trainer, I'd say,' said Jack. 'If he's who I think he is your grey'll be all right with him. And now I need a smoke and I need a drink.'

'Right,' Flora laughed, 'I'm buying.'

She checked on Luke who was pleased but playing cool, then bought Jack Thomas his drink in the bar.

'You did well there but you've two still to go, so don't go getting too cocky now.' He raised his glass.

'I needed to make something on him.' Flora looked rueful. 'We'll still only break about even, if that, because of the injury to the bay.'

'Aye. I was coming to that.' The vet took a long drag on his cigarette before taking it out of his mouth and studying the tip. 'I suppose you've given some thought to the upsets you've been having at Kimbay?'

Flora didn't answer him immediately. When she did she went for the jugular. 'I have. Is there something you want to tell me, Jack? Something I should know?'

'There is. Got a bit of information the other day that shocked me, I might as well be honest. Don't know what

255

conclusions you've come to yourself, but I knew you were worried. Sweeney is too but he's the kind prefers to bury his head in the sand about these things.'

'Jack,' Flora leaned toward him and fanned the smoke out of his face, 'if you don't tell me whatever it is you've on your mind I'm going to empty this drink . . .'

'All right, all right.' He signalled the barman for another round. 'It's this. I met a man the other day, on Saturday it was, at Punchestown, and he told me he'd heard Kimbay was earmarked as the site for one of those leisure complexes. In fact he went one further, said you were ready to sign on the dotted line, that Sweeney would be forced to sell out.'

'It's not true!' Flora felt as if she'd been kicked in the stomach. 'You must know it's not true, Jack. How could you even listen—'

'You should be damn glad I listened.' The vet frowned, white head bristling. 'It's like I was telling you earlier, Flora. You have to talk to people if you want to keep in touch in this business. Keeping too much to yourself isn't a good thing at all. Thing is, he's not the only one talking about Kimbay. There's a rumour been going the rounds for some time now, about things going wrong. I'd be inclined myself to think some of your upsets were helped along.'

'I heard some talk during the summer,' Flora said slowly, 'but then I thought it had died down.'

'Only because you didn't put yourself in the way of hearing it again. And Sweeney talks to no one. There's a pair of you in it . . .' He gave a disgusted grunt and lit another cigarette.

'Listen, Jack, all this talk is pure mischief-making.' Flora, making her point, jabbed her finger on the table between them. 'All that happened was that I was made an offer and turned it down, flat. Not just once, mind, but twice. Now – either the person who made the offer is stirring the shit for his own reasons or someone else is using it to make things difficult. All that matters here is that I'm *not* selling my share of Kimbay.'

256

'I know that. But you'll have to do something about the talk, Flora. It's going on for too long now. It's not good for the yard. Makes it look like you and Sweeney are at war. I've no love for the man but that kind of thing's bad for the yard.'

'But what the hell am I supposed to do?' Flora spoke through her teeth. 'If I protest I draw more attention to the talk and give it credence. If I say nothing then it just goes on.'

'You can take it easy for a start.' The barman brought their drinks and the vet became prudently silent while he paid him. 'It's my opinion, Flora,' he began softly as the man left their table, 'that the man you refused didn't take no for an answer. My man gave me a name, said a fella called Victor Mangan told him he'd be moving in on Kimbay sooner rather than later.'

'Did he indeed.'

Shock robbed Flora of anything else to say for a moment. Victor Mangan had been subtle up until now. His name had never been bandied about publicly, nor had his interest in Kimbay. He was going public for a reason, she was sure of it. She wished she just as confidently knew what it was. 'What would you do, Jack, if you were me?' she asked.

'I'd seek out Mangan. Have a word in his ear. Threaten the courts if he didn't watch what he was saying. Ruining a person's livelihood's no small matter.'

'Maybe that *is* the way to do it.' Flora could see Jack Thomas carrying out such a threat, effectively too. She wasn't sure she could do it herself. But his suggestion made perfect sense. 'And maybe I'll do just that.' She checked her watch and stood up.

'You'll only have yourself to blame if things get worse.' The vet walked morosely beside her back to the sales ring. 'And it won't stop at talk, you know that. I've seen this kind of thing happen before, Flora. Buggers like that don't stop. They're capable of going on for years, tormenting people whose lands they want until they give in out of

257

exhaustion and lack of heart for going on. Deal with it now, Flora. Before it goes any further. It's gone on long enough. Don't do a bloody Hamlet on it.'

'I won't.' Flora squeezed his arm and he looked embarrassed. 'And thank you, Jack. You're the motivation I needed.'

She *had* been a 'bloody Hamlet'. She'd known and done nothing but talk about the situation. She hadn't even listened and watched well enough, as she'd said she would. After today she would act, do something positive.

The afternoon was productive. The filly sold for 25,000 guineas and the colt for 18,000 guineas. Together with Flo Girl's winnings it meant they were making their way out of the woods. A new brood mare might even be on the cards; definitely an extension to the isolation unit.

A clear run was all they needed to make things really go. Flora would deal with Victor Mangan and see that they got it.

Chapter Twenty-Three

Flora compromised on Jack Thomas's advice about dealing with Victor Mangan. She knew the developer, he didn't. She felt fairly sure any threat of hers about legal action would be followed by a counter action for slander on his part. And he could win too. He'd been clever and he'd been 'civilized' in his dealings with her. It would be hard to prove he'd behaved otherwise with others. Or so she argued with herself. In her deep heart she suspected she was being cowardly, that she was simply backing off from direct confrontation.

Her compromise was to telephone. She would warn, rather than threaten, him.

He was honeyed charm on the line. But she was prepared for this.

'Flora! What a nice surprise! And congratulations on your win with Flo Girl. Wonderful pictures of her in the paper.'

'Thank you, Victor.' She tightened her grip on the receiver. 'I'd like to talk seriously for a moment, if you don't mind.'

Surely the chill on the line must be her imagination? Ignoring misgivings and forestalling intervention on his part she rushed on, briskly businesslike.

'It's been reported to me, Victor, and by someone I trust absolutely, that you've been giving the impression I'm agreeable to selling my share of Kimbay. You *know* this is not true and I must ask you to correct the impression. And *not* to give it at any time in the future. As I'm sure you appreciate, such an impression is not at all helpful to the yard.'

'Hold on, Flora, stop right there.' The amused tolerance in his voice set her teeth on edge. She was raving, it said, needed to be calmed down. 'I don't know who you've been talking to but I assure you I have never said you will be selling the yard. I may be guilty of wishfully discussing the suitability of Kimbay and its lands for my casino complex – but no more than that, I assure you. I'm sorry, Flora,' his voice became quietly sad, 'that you've been upset but I must say I'm surprised you would think me capable of that kind of unethical behaviour.'

'What I think is irrelevant, Victor.' Flora was crisp. 'My concern is with the reality of widely circulating rumours that I'm about to sell out. I would like you to put it on record, categorically, that you are *not* buying Kimbay. Otherwise –'

She stopped. She hadn't meant to issue a threat. He was too slippery, too clever by half for her to be able to prove anything against him.

'Otherwise what, Flora?' His voice was still soft, persuasively gentle. And quite menacing. She knew he could sense her backing off, her lack of commitment to the gutting procedure of law. She cursed him, silently, and went cautiously for broke.

'Otherwise, Victor, I'll be obliged to take legal advice. Such talk is seriously detrimental to my businesss.'

'Is this an accusation, Flora? Are you accusing me of deliberately damaging the business of the yard?'

Her mouth was dry. That was exactly what she was accusing him of. But if she couldn't prove it, and he pushed it to court, what would happen then? Visions of a vast damages bill, of enormous compensation awards, of the incalculable harm to the yard all loomed monstrously in front of her. She hedged.

'I'm saying that things you're reputed to have said are doing that, yes.' There, she'd said it. But carefully, like a lawyer. She felt less resolute than she had been, though, and knew again that he sensed this.

'I wish, Flora, that this misunderstanding hadn't happened between us.' His tone had become magnanimous. 'I accept, absolutely, your decision not to sell. Always have – though I still think it's a mistaken one.' He was making her feel like a recalcitrant child. She wanted to hang up but knew she must regain her ground, make her point strongly again before cutting the connection. Only she couldn't think how to put it, and he went on.

'It saddens me that you have these hideous suspicions about me.' He sounded sincerely and gently outraged. 'I have far too much regard for you personally to want to misrepresent any discussions we may have had.'

But he had. Misrepresented discussions. She knew he had. Jack Thomas would never have come to her, especially in the way he had, with information he wasn't positive about. Thinking about Jack brought back some of her earlier confidence.

'Believe me, Victor, our discussions *have* been misrepresented. I'm satisfied that my information is accurate. The rumours may be the result of a momentary indiscretion on your part, but I would be glad if you would take greater care in future.'

'I assure you, Flora, that I have always been careful in anything I may have said about Kimbay.' The menacingly soft tone sounded in her ear again.

'Not careful enough, I'm afraid.' Flora felt her patience stretch, a sense of panic descend.

'It may be,' he sounded thoughtful, 'that a conversation of mine has become twisted in the telling. As you'll understand, Flora, one talks with friends and colleagues about one's dream ventures. It's in the nature of the beast to dream aloud. You must talk, surely, about your own and your father's dream of owning a great racehorse?'

Flora, aware of the emotional pull of what he was saying, said nothing. She didn't indicate, with either sigh or murmur, that she'd heard what he'd said. In the silence he went on.

'I have naturally spoken about my one-time dreams for Kimbay. But purely in the context of a dream lost. I was obviously misunderstood, perhaps deliberately, who knows? Who will ever know? It's a tricky old world we live in, Flora, unfortunately.'

So, that was to be his line, his defence. Very plausible

261

it was too. 'Very tricky,' she agreed. She knew now for certain, in her gut as well as in her head, that he'd been spreading disquiet and at least implying she was about to sell.

But she had so little to go on. Hearsay and instinct weren't enough. Still, maybe this phone call would put an end to it all. Maybe now he would realize that she wasn't going to be either worn down or discredited out of her commitment to the yard.

'I hope there can be peace between us, Flora, in spite of this little misunderstanding.' He had injected a smile into his voice and she marvelled at his vocal range. She thought nastily of asking if he'd ever had stage training.

'Perhaps, like peace, some things are past all understanding,' she said instead, keeping her tone neutral. 'But I do hope this conversation has sorted things out.'

In the yard, later, she had another thought. What if, and just supposing, Victor Mangan was telling the truth? Who then was behind things? Who was causing mischief for the yard? And what would she do if things went on, if niggling, undermining problems continued, with her never sure which troubles were everyday bad luck and which maliciously intended to disrupt? What then? That sort of no-man's-land would slowly wear her down. Better the devil you know, she thought, and almost offered a prayer that Victor Mangan was the devil behind some, at least, of the yard's problems.

Flora didn't tell Shay about telephoning Mangan. She didn't want him growling again that she was imagining things and she didn't want to have to tell him the source of her information either. He would be scathingly dismissive once he discovered she'd been motivated by a chat with Jack Thomas. So she kept it to herself and didn't even mention it to Daisy. Afterwards, she would wonder if telling them would have made a difference. But then the business of living, she reminded herself, was an imprecise science. A daily gamble.

*

A long winter settled in quickly after that. The months before Christmas served up unusually cruel weather. November brought icy mornings and leaden afternoons as the days got shorter and shorter still.

Flora had always quite liked the dramatic changes of this time of year, but never so much as now. The sharp air and wintry smell of wood burning, the early falling, mysterious dusks, all brought tingles of pleasure. After five winters in the city she found herself of a mood to appreciate the splendid, sharp colours thrown up by the diamond glitter of morning frosts and, as the weeks went on, rediscovered a joy in the special brilliance of orange cotoneaster berries at the ends of white, frost-covered branches.

Never before had her own countryside's beauty meant so much to her. Nor, she suspected, would it ever again. This winter was special, a reflective time in her life and a period when she found herself glad to be alone. By cutting links with the hunt she had ensured herself this quiet time and felt her introspective mood a positive thing. It allowed her just to be, to come to terms in some way with all that had happened in the nine months since her father's death, both to her and around her. She had changed, she knew, but wasn't sure how, exactly. What she did know was that she felt more sure, that she was, as the French would say, more at home in her skin.

As if sensing her need, visitors were few during those months and didn't stay long. Fintan and Ollie visited sporadically and Melissa came not at all. Sophie rang regularly but, busy ghost-writing a book for a singer, was tied to the apartment and work. The money made the sacrifice worth it, she said. Victor Mangan might have fallen off the planet for all she saw or heard of him.

Serge phoned every other day and they planned a skiing holiday together in January. Flora half dreaded the prospect, with memories of how their last skiing holiday had ended still very much alive. She would have preferred to stay the entire winter, without break, at Kimbay but found she couldn't explain adequately to Serge the peace and retreat she was enjoying so much.

The money from the sales and Flo Girl's winnings went into the yard and seemed to disappear. Some of it at least was visible in their investment in an agreeable and valuable brood mare, and in the extended and repaired isolation unit. Flora had a phone installed in her bedroom, too, and more effective central heating put into the house. Demands from the bank accounted for all of the rest but Kimbay was, as the year drew to an end, in slowly improving shape.

Flo Girl was wintering well at Fairmane, in the capable care of Timmy Mulligan and Lorcan for the most part. Depending on how well she wintered, her first race of the coming season would be in mid-April at the Curragh. The Athasi Stakes was a mostly fillies race and would be a way of gauging how she'd fared over the winter.

Matt Hopkins, with the end of the flat racing season, had taken to travel and spending time away. From Marigold Flora heard tales of his movements between Deauville and Newmarket, his trips to Hong Kong, and even of a visit to Australia. From Shay she heard that it all had to do with money-making ventures. The trainer was buying for owners and involved in consultancy work.

'He works as a pin-hooker,' Shay said. 'Not many do it as well as Matt. He buys foals for others on spec, in the hope that they'll turn into valuable yearlings. Needs a really good eye, and Matt's got one of the best. He's a powerful judgement too.'

Flora didn't want to know about his travel arrangements but Marigold, increasingly bored at Fairmane, told her anyway. 'Now that he's hitting sunnier climes la belle Isabel seems to be turning up all over the place again. Must be great to be free as a bird, come and go as you please.'

She had come into the Fairmane yard to talk to Flora and stood shivering in a short denim jacket. 'I bet he marries her,' she said. 'She's got pots of old money she could put into this place.' She pulled a face at the bleak façade of the house. 'I'll bet that's his plan.'

'I doubt it,' Flora said. 'I don't think that's the way he operates.'

She was surprised how sure she felt about this. Arrogant, vain, limited in his understanding of women – Matt Hopkins was all of those things. He used women, too, when they allowed him, for gratification and amusement. But she couldn't see him exploiting a woman, a man either, for money or gain. She sensed in him an essential, dignified honesty that would not countenance such a thing. Marigold seemed to feel differently, however.

'Don't be so sure,' she said darkly. 'There's not a man alive won't take what he can if he thinks he'll get away with it.'

Flora shrugged. It was really none of her business.

In obscure atonement for not having come home the year before, Flora spent Christmas with the Sweeneys. She even, disastrously, cooked them a goose dinner. The concentration needed for this act meant that the festive part of the season passed busily, and without too much time in which to miss Ned, or Serge.

It was early in the new year when Marigold's sexual activities became of avid interest to everyone at Kimbay. Flora was the last to discover what was going on, on a day when she noticed Shay agitatedly looking for Luke.

'He's probably dropped down to the gate lodge for something,' she attempted to calm him down. 'What is it you want him to do? I'll –'

'No, you won't.' Shay was snappier even than usual. 'He'll do it when he gets back and he'll do it into the night if needs be.'

Flora knew better than to argue with him. She thought of going in search of Luke but instead mentioned his absence to Daisy later in the office. She was nakedly unprepared for her reaction.

'That's it,' Daisy hissed and reached for the phone. 'He either ends this thing or by God I'll, I'll –' For the first time in Flora's memory words failed Daisy. Unable to think of a fate evil enough for her son she began to dial what Flora saw was the Fairmane number. It rang for a long time. When it was answered Daisy snapped, 'Put Luke on,' and continued to hold grimly onto the receiver, fingers drumming on the desk as she waited for her son to speak to her.

Flora, filled with a worry that Daisy might combust, stayed in the room. She also wanted to know what was going on.

'Luke? Get back here *now*.' Daisy's voice was like splintered glass. 'You've got a job here, your father needs you.' She took a deep breath and let it out in fumes as her son said something on the other end. 'That's enough,' she interrupted. 'Your rights, for now, are here. And so are your obligations. If you're not back in fifteen minutes, flat, I'm coming over. So if you want to avoid the consequences of *that* you'd better leave now.' She replaced the phone with a slam that made Flora wince and take a step backwards to the door.

'Coffee, Daisy? Or tea maybe? Want something stronger?'

Daisy, unmoved and unsmiling, leaned forward heavily and put her head on her hands.

'God above, Flora, but that boy's pushing me to the limit. They time it, those children of mine. If it's not one it's the other getting at me. They're on and off, like a pair of switches. Luke was so easy before this. I should have known it was coming, of course. Maybe I should have paid more attention to him.' She gave a sigh so deep it lifted several papers off the desk.

'Well, everything's as clear as mud to me now.' Flora sat down. 'Care to fill me in on what's going on around here?'

Daisy looked surprised. 'Surely to God you know, Flora? The birds in the trees know . . .'

'Well, I don't,' Flora snapped, annoyed at the implication that she had her head in the sand – even if it was true.

'Luke's having an affair with Marigold,' Daisy spoke wearily. 'Or I suppose that's what you'd call it. He can't keep away from her. He's with her night and day, mostly at Fairmane on account of Matt being away so much. God knows what she's teaching him. My poor baby . . .'

Huge tears rolled down Daisy's face. Flora watched them, paralysed at first and unable to move. She found herself shocked that Daisy had actual tears to cry. Daisy was the rock they all leaned upon, a wiper of tears, not a cryer. But she was weeping now, making no attempt either to stop or even mop the tears as they poured down her cheeks and sidetracked into her mouth.

'Daisy, oh, my dear Daisy.' Flora's throat constricted as she put her arms around her. 'He's not a baby and he's just letting you know that. You haven't lost him either. Marigold's only an adventure, a life-passage. Come on now, you know I'm right.'

In her arms Daisy felt hopelessly huge. Her body at first couldn't seem to stop shaking but it did at last, coming to a halt in great shuddering gulps. Flora stepped back and tidied her hair for her, not an easy job. Daisy's face was a mess, red-eyed and unfamiliar-looking.

'Well, now, that was a fine thing,' Daisy, rubbing fiercely at her eyes with tissues, muttered half to herself. 'Woman my age. I wouldn't tolerate that kind of behaviour from anyone else. Crying never solved anything.'

'It lets go of tension, though,' Flora said mildly, 'and that's not a bad thing.'

'Now, then.' Daisy squared her shoulders. 'That's *that* over with. You won't see me crying over that lad again. I'll just have to hope that this is something he's going through and that he'll be himself again when it's all over. When she ditches him.'

'Had to happen,' Flora said. 'He had to discover sex. I'm sorry I didn't notice what was going on. What I *have* noticed, though, is that he's got taller. And he's becoming quite handsome too.'

'He is, isn't he?' Daisy spoke softly, a sad, loving smile touching her face. 'But a boy doesn't want to know his mother when the testosterone starts acting up. Shay won't mention a thing to him, only give him more work in the hopes of tiring him out.'

'Tell me about it,' Flora requested. 'When did it start?

267

And what's so terrible about him having an affair with Marigold anyway? She's older, got a bit more experience – nothing wrong with either of those things . . .'

'God knows how long it's been going on – more than a month, anyway.' Daisy blew her nose noisily. 'And it's not her age I mind so much, it's more the type of person she is. She's a lifetime older than Luke and that's not just me being protective. Her hold over him is all to do with sex, I know it is. A mother can see that much, at least. He's with her every spare moment he has, and a lot of moments that aren't spare too. She's all he thinks about.'

'He does his work.'

'No, he doesn't. Shay's been covering for him.'

'He's seventeen, Daisy. He had to find out what it's all about sometime.'

'I know that. But why with her? God knows what tricks and contortions she's teaching him. He'll never be the same again.' Fleetingly, a look of sadness and loss crossed Daisy's face. It disappeared as she said, darkly, 'And what about AIDS?'

'Unlikely.' Flora was dry. 'But you're right about him changing, never being the same. It's called growing up, Daisy. Let him go.' Easy to be clear-eyed and calm when it's not your child, she thought, and hoped Daisy wouldn't throw this obvious truth back at her. She didn't.

'It's what sort of man he's growing into that bothers me as much as anything else.' Daisy was irritable. 'He threw aside that young stable lass Dymphna when the siren put her eye on him. God knows, Dymphna was a silly enough creature but I didn't like the way he did it. He's got cruel.'

Flora could have told her that Luke's propensity to be cruel was nothing new. She didn't. 'Sounds like he's obsessed with Marigold,' she said. 'He's likely to get hurt too, because I'm willing to bet that Marigold will get bored before he does. Maybe, if he's hurt himself, he'll be less cruel to women in the future.'

'Ah, Flora,' Daisy stood up, patting Flora on the hand, 'you're like your poor father. Always hoping for the best in things. And maybe you're right, too. Marigold's other boyfriend is still around, by all accounts, though not so much as he used to be. He's an older man, more what she needs. If he so much as clicks his fingers she'll drop Luke. Poor lad.'

'Maybe. Who *is* this man? Does anyone know him?'

'No one. He's not from around here.' Daisy looked at the wall clock. 'I'm going home now and if I don't spot Luke coming across the fields I'm taking the car over there . . .'

'Don't, Daisy,' Flora advised. 'He'd never forgive you. You'll just have to go with it, for the moment, until it cools down.'

In the following couple of weeks Flora saw for herself how often Luke was missing and marvelled that she'd not noticed before. He worked hard when he was at the yard, was often there before her in the mornings. On several occasions she saw him riding back from the direction of Fairmane. He looked cheerful and not in the least exhausted.

She left for Austria and the skiing holiday feeling that, after all, the break might be a good idea. Serge would pick her up at Munich airport. He'd wanted them to go to a different resort, certainly to use a different hotel. But Flora had said no to both suggestions. Staying in St Anton, going back to the hotel, would help lay another bit of Ned's ghost.

The obsequious manager had moved on and his place had been taken by a small, energetic Italian. He was a man so altogether convivial that his smile made breakfast in the dining room worth while.

Snowfalls over Christmas and the New Year had been heavy and skiing conditions couldn't have been better. On the slopes Flora was delighted to discover how fit she was, how quickly she got her ski legs. Serge, after a long Christmas and several weekends with Monique, couldn't wait to get to the freedom and thrills of the high slopes and Flora, at first, was happy to glide quietly down the pine-bristled lower mountainsides. It lacked the heart-racing, knee-shaking sensation of higher-up skiing but there was a relaxing pleasure in having a forever-blue sky overhead and the finest of powdery snow under her skis.

On her fourth day of this, and with only three days of the holiday to go, she came off the slopes and was sitting with a *Glühwein* and *Apfelstrudel* when a sense of outrage swept through her.

'What the hell is wrong with you, Flora Carolan?'

She knew she'd spoken aloud when the very bored waiter looked at her with interest. She pushed the *Apfelstrudel* away and glared at him, then up at the ice-draped peaks where they cut into the blue of the sky.

'Up there, Flora, is where the action is.' She was careful this time, kept her furious thoughts silent. 'So what are you doing down here? The role of the little woman sipping more *Glühwein* than she really wants while she waits for her man just isn't you. Not any more. You're a big girl now. Tomorrow, and just because you want to, you're going up there. Alone. Without a guide. You can do it.' She lifted her glass to the jagged mountaintops and drank. Then she beamed at the waiter and left him a large tip.

She didn't tell Serge about going up because she didn't want him to worry or try to talk her out of it. He really didn't need to know, she reasoned, where she spent her day's skiing.

It was tough and exciting as she'd hoped it would be. A pure skiing experience. It was also more strenuous and tiring than she'd bargained for and by midday she'd had enough.

A tight-faced Serge was waiting for her when she arrived down in the lift.

'You have been on the top slopes. Alone.' His anger was barely controlled. It shocked Flora. She had seen him angry before, but never with her.

'Yes, I have.' She looked steadily at him, willing him to calm down. 'Why are you so annoyed? Come to that, why aren't you up there yourself?'

'You didn't tell me. Which means you knew it was a stupid thing to do. And I am here because I saw you and

270

came down to wait for you.' His anger added a chill to the already cold air between them.

'So I've spoilt your day's skiing, have I?' Flora looked away from him, back toward the mountaintops. She hated what they were doing. I should just walk away, she thought, but knew it would solve nothing.

'My day's skiing is not the point.' Serge kept his voice low as passing skiers looked curiously at their taut, angry figures. 'You should not have gone up. Not without a guide. Not without telling me . . .'

'Why? Why shouldn't I do what I bloody well want?' Flora's composure suddenly gave. 'It's my holiday too, Serge, and how I enjoy it is my business. I can ski wherever I choose and I do *not* choose to toddle down slopes that are beneath my ability. *I am responsible for myself*, Serge. So you can please stop treating me like a child.'

'Then you must stop behaving like a child. You are being stupid, Flora.'

'*Don't* call me stupid. It is *not* stupid to take responsibility for myself. It *is* extremely stupid of you to patronize me like this.' She wanted to turn on her heel but knew that the ski-boots would have made a farce of such a move. Instead she ground her teeth and dug her pole into the ground between them. It stayed there, upright and wavering a little in the soft snow. Serge, looking at it, gave a short laugh.

'You are right, Flora. Your decision to kill yourself or not must be yours. Just as you made your decision to run Kimbay. You have changed, *ma chère*,' he touched her flushed cheek with his gloved finger, 'you are becoming *formidable*. Another Monique in my life.' He leaned over quickly, touched her mouth lightly with his. 'It is a pity to fight,' he said, 'when we have much better things to do.'

They spent the last days of the holiday together almost all of the time. They did not talk much and Flora knew that Serge did not feel the need to. She wanted to talk herself, to tell him that he was right and that she had changed. But such a conversation would have entailed telling him how

271

much she was enjoying being in charge of her own life and how their life together would have to take account of this. Foreseeing tension and misunderstanding she said nothing. She still hadn't spoken of it by their last evening when, standing in awe of a sunset behind the mountains, Serge asked her what she was thinking about.

'About the mountains,' she said, 'and about littler things, too. I'm not sure . . . nothing really. Do you have a saying in French about making mountains out of molehills?'

'No. I don't think so. Tell me and I will know.'

'It's about what the shadows spread by the setting sun can do. How they can make molehills seem like mountains and make the ant appear a monstrous elephant.'

'It is saying that things need not be as important as they seem?'

'Exactly.' She turned to him, smiling. 'And that's what I was telling myself as I looked at the mountains.'

He put his arm around her waist and drew her to him. 'It is a wise saying,' he said. 'I will remember it in America.'

'In America? You're going to the States again?' Flora turned to look at him and he touched her hair and smiled.

'Yes. I must. For two months only. I have to consolidate the business I have been building there. Better I go now than later, when we are married.'

'Much better,' Flora said.

'It is for us, *ma chère*. I will eventually look after all of this from the Loire. That will be my job when we marry.'

Walking back to the hotel Flora asked, 'What will be *my* job when we marry?'

Serge stopped, took her face in his hands and looked at her seriously. 'Your job, Flora, will be to be happy.'

Turning to wave goodbye as she got on the plane next day Flora remembered that moment. Happy was not something she could honestly say she'd felt during the holiday. There had been moments of ecstasy in bed and there had been the gratification of being with Serge for a whole week. But there had been a peculiar unease, too, a feeling that she wasn't being altogether true to herself. The old, wonderful acceptance of the way things were between herself and

Serge had gone. She wanted, more and more, for him not only to accept the person she was but also the person she was becoming. And it was no good her pretending to herself that it didn't matter, trying to convince herself she was making a mountain out of a molehill. It *did* matter. A lot.

Maybe they should have gone to the sun, not come back here so close to the anniversary of Ned's death.

She felt happy now, though; now she was going home.

Chapter Twenty-Four

The days drew on to the end of February and dawn began to come earlier through the window of Flora's bedroom at Kimbay. Winter was passing and her father was dead a year.

And, twelve months to the day they'd gathered in the small churchyard to bury him, Nessa produced a healthy foal. Flora, spotting signs that foaling was imminent, had spent a couple of exhausting nights on bi-hourly visits to the mare. But Nessa, true to her quiet, dogged personality, pre-empted attempts at interference and foaled alone in the small hours. Her colt foal had found the udder and was already sucking when Flora arrived at the foaling box for a 6 a.m. check.

'You clever girl, you.'

A surge of relief warmed the morning cold from Flora's bones as she hunkered down to check the foal's swallowing movement. This little half-brother of Flo Girl was strong, and he was healthy. He'd been able to find the udder unaided. He would be dark, a definite bay and not a bit like his half-sister. It was a lovely coincidence that he'd been born on the anniversary of her father's burial.

'This one's for you, Ned,' Flora said aloud, but softly. 'I'll keep him, see what Matt Hopkins can do with him.'

The trainer called at Kimbay later in the day. He'd been back at Fairmane a couple of weeks but this was his first visit – which was either, Flora thought, a case of talk of the devil or another coincidence in the foal's short life.

'I was thinking about you earlier,' she greeted him cheerfully. 'We've a new arrival that I might just keep for training.'

Leaning on the half-door of the box the trainer studied

the foal. On his face was a tan which was fast fading and a shadowy stubble that was almost, she thought, a trademark. His hair was too long again, and, from where she stood sideways on, she could see how the corner of his mouth lifted good-humouredly. Maybe it always had. Or maybe he had something to be particularly pleased about these days. She thought, briefly, about asking him, but didn't. For one thing, she wasn't sure he would tell her.

Her well-honed instinct for self-preservation was the second reason she kept quiet. It was best, she felt sure, to keep a healthy distance from the trainer. Their relationship worked best on a neighbours-doing-business level.

'Ned was buried a year ago today.' She said the words to fill the silence but he looked at her quickly, as if expecting her to be tearful. 'Seems to me lucky, him arriving today.' She smiled. 'Fortuitous, you might say.'

The trainer smiled too, and resumed his study of the foal. 'I knew the funeral took place around this time,' he said. 'I hadn't realized it was the actual date.' He gave a small, throat-clearing cough. 'Birth of a foal always lifts the heart a bit.'

Flora stiffened. Was he saying that her decision to keep the foal was a purely emotional one, and therefore wrong? Or was the remark simply a reflection of how he felt himself? He was still smiling, and she decided to take the remark at face value.

'Shay tells me you're an expert judge of foals,' she said. 'What's your opinion of this fellow?'

'Bit early to say,' he was businesslike, 'but the signs are good. He's strong, good sire, useful dam, going-to-be-brilliant half-sister. Certainly you should think seriously about keeping him.' He shoved his hands into his pockets and turned away from the box. 'His half-sister's the reason I'm here. Looks like Flo Girl's wintered well. I came over to talk about her racing schedule with you, hopefully to get your approval.'

He refused a coffee, even to come into the house, so they discussed Flo Girl's future on the short walk to where he'd parked his car at the front of the house. He walked quickly, swinging his car keys impatiently, and Flora had almost to skip several times to keep up with him.

'As I've always said, I don't want to overrace her,' he said. 'Three races this season and that's it. We've already agreed she'll run in the Athasi Stakes in mid-April.' He raised an eyebrow and Flora nodded, silently. She wished he didn't seem to think her agreement a personal triumph for him. 'Prize money isn't great – about 10,000 guineas. But I'm putting her into the Irish 1,000 Guineas in mid-May. Winnings there are around 110,000 guineas. That'll pay a few bills if she wins.'

Flora wondered whose bills he was thinking about – Kimbay's or his own.

'What chance has she got?'

'A good one. Depends, of course, on how she does in the Athasi. I'll be putting her into the Derby too.' The last was almost an aside as he opened the car door. Flora caught her breath.

'What sort of chance has she got *there*?'

'A good one. I wouldn't enter her otherwise. Do I have your approval?'

'Go ahead,' Flora said.

She had to step back hurriedly as the car did a spinning, gravel-spraying turn and headed down the avenue. She stamped an impotent, furious foot. 'Bugger you,' she said, 'and your rudeness. If you weren't so bloody good with horses . . .'

She left the thought unfinished and looked across the fields to where she could hear the dejected bleats of an early lamb seeking its mother. A fine mist had started to come down, making ghostly shapes of the trees. Not so ghostly, though, that she couldn't make out Luke's form when a horse and rider became visible, riding fast from the direction of Fairmane. While the cat's away, she thought, and continued to watch as he came closer.

Luke's visits to Fairmane had come to an abrupt halt a few weeks before. His unwillingness to talk left everyone wondering if this had to do with the return of Marigold's boss or with the end of the affair. His moody moroseness, his sleepless-looking eyes and refusal to communicate with anyone but the horses made Flora incline to the latter view.

Daisy suffered with him, cooking his favourite meals and daily making herself available for his confession. The food went untouched and a glowering 'leave me alone' was as near as she came to hearing what had happened.

Luke was close now, and slowing down. Flora was taken by surprise when, instead of riding for the paddocks and on toward the yard, he pulled his horse's head around and came in her direction. She waited while he rode right up to a nearby fence and called to her.

'Visitors on the way, Flora. I invited them. Hope you don't mind.' He dismounted, tied Jumbo loosely to the fence and vaulted over.

'Do they have names, these visitors?'

Watching him approach it seemed to Flora that he was growing at a daily rate of half an inch. When he stopped in front of her their eyes were level. He grinned, uneasily but with a sort of jubilation too, and she knew instantly the visitors had something to do with Marigold. What victims love can make of us, she thought, and had a longing to protect him from the young eagerness of his desire.

'Marigold's one of them,' he confessed. His face was flushed but that could have been from the ride. 'She's never seen Kimbay, you know.'

'Yes, I know that. She told me so herself, some time ago. Why's she coming now, and who's she bringing with her?' Flora smiled what she hoped was a welcoming smile.

'Well, really she's bringing this friend of hers over.' His gaze met hers, defiant but unsure too. 'His name's Ciaran Watson and he was over at Fairmane, banging on about how he'd like a ride since he was in horse country. There's nothing he can ride at Fairmane, no one for him to ride out with either. So I said he could come over here, that I'd arrange something and go out with him.'

In the entire year she'd been back Luke had not spoken so many sentences to Flora. His vulnerability, his desire to please Marigold via the medium of obliging her friend,

277

were painful to behold. Flora wondered if the friend was the same one Marigold had spoken about months before. Surely even Marigold wouldn't expect one boyfriend to entertain another, and in her presence? Or would she?

Flora smiled reassuringly into his strained, blanched face. 'Hope the mist coming down doesn't put him off,' she said. 'Shay's leading out a couple of yearlings with Dymphna so I'm not sure what's available for him to ride. Take Cormac if you have to.'

'Thanks, Flora.' He turned to go and Flora, unable to control a mischief-making urge, called after him.

'Daisy's in the house. I'm sure she'll be glad to entertain Marigold while you're gone . . .'

'Jesus, Flora.' He turned, kicked at the gravel irritably. 'Do me a favour, will you?' His face was nakedly pleading. Looking at him Flora wondered if the emotional turmoil he was going through would, in the end, make him more compassionate or simply more manipulative. At the moment, it seemed to her, he was verging on the manipulative.

'Depends.' She was cautious.

'Keep my mother off Marigold's back while I'm out, will you? It's just a small favour, Flora. I'll do the same for you some day.'

'Doubt I'll ever need you to do exactly *that*.' Flora grinned. 'But I may extract payment in kind. I'll do my best to keep them apart, can't do any more than that. And stop worrying, Luke. The worst that can happen is that Marigold will leave.'

'I know,' Luke said. He looked desolate.

Marigold and her friend arrived up the avenue within minutes. While Flora walked with them around the side of the house to the yard, Marigold, looking wonderful in tan-coloured leather, made the introductions. Ciaran Watson was approaching middle age and it suited him. His square, smiling face would have been bland but for a certain character and humour stamped on it by age. If his expensive, brand-name country casuals and year-old BMW were anything to go by, he had money too. Flora felt sure he and

Marigold were an item – or had been. He seemed, some-how, exactly right for her. Poor old Luke, she thought, this isn't his league at all.

'Lovely place you have here,' Ciaran Watson said and Flora knew her impression of blandness had been right. 'Wonderfully relaxing part of the country.'

'We take it for granted, I'm afraid.' She matched his careful politeness. 'Luke tells me you're keen to take a ride?'

'If it's not an inconvenience.' He smiled, looking with a lazy deliberation around the yard. 'I appreciate your kindness.'

Flora wondered what line of business he was in. There had to be more to him than this courteous exterior. Luke appeared leading Jumbo and an impatient-looking Cormac.

'Hope I'm not taking the lad from his work.' Ciaran Watson looked apologetic, and Flora smiled, shaking her head. His tone when he mentioned Luke had been patron-izing – but then he was probably old enough to be the boy's father.

After they had left for the ride Marigold watched Flora mix food for several gossipy, but obviously bored, minutes. She stopped the nonsensical chat quite suddenly and asked, 'What do you think of him?'

'Think of who?'

'Ciaran, of course. Did you like him?'

'Seems a perfectly polite and nice middle-aged man.' Flora spoke slowly and without looking up. 'Is there any reason why I should give him more thought?'

'Well, no . . . Except that he's the man of my dreams. The one I told you about, remember?' She was glowing, her fair curls full of a newly-washed bounce and her eyes alight with life and fun. She looked innocent and knowing and irresistible. Poor Luke, Flora thought, and could foresee nothing but pain and humiliation in store for him until he got over his infatuation. She hoped he hadn't been smitten by anything more lasting. Like love.

'Ah, yes, I remember you mentioning him all right.' Flora wrinkled her nose reflectively. 'But I thought you'd found a dream closer to home since then?'

'God, Flora, don't be stuffy. It doesn't suit you. Luke was a bit of a fling, that's all. Ciaran's – well, he's a man, isn't he?'

'Tut, tut, Marigold.' Flora shook a disappointed head. 'Are you admitting you haven't managed to make a man of Luke? His mother's worries have all been for nothing at that rate.'

'If I'm nothing else I'm discreet about my lovers.' Marigold assumed a haughtiness. 'And since you're being so stuffy, Flora, I think I'll go up to the house and wait for the men in my life there. It's bloody freezing here anyway.'

She turned, bouncily, to go and Flora said, 'I wouldn't go up there, Marigold, if I were you. You'd be *much* safer waiting out here – even in the event of a thunderstorm you'd be safer here.'

'Why?' Marigold halted suspiciously. 'What's going on in the house?' She wrinkled her small nose, bunching freckles together and looking comically cute. The woman can't help it, Flora thought, she's a natural-born coquette – and she's also wasting my time. In some annoyance, and by way of a hint that she had work to do, she began to compile an overdue list of foodstuffs they needed.

'Daisy's going on in the house,' she told Marigold, shortly.

'Oh.' Marigold was silent for long seconds. 'I suppose she thinks I'm not good enough for her son?'

'Something like that.'

'And I suppose she thinks too that her son's pure as the driven snow?' Marigold's voice trembled with indignation. 'Well, let me tell you—'

'I'm not interested.' Flora's voice, cutting Marigold short, was a splinter of ice. 'And I'm very busy. You can wait where you like, Marigold, but I've got work to do. All I can say is that your chances of survival are much stronger out here than they would be alone in the house with Daisy. It's up to you.'

Marigold, sulkily, sat on an upturned crate. Flora worked busily, calculating quantities, figuring where corners could be cut. Marigold, apart from a few sighs, was considerately silent for about ten minutes. Flora, calculations finished, looked over at her with a conciliatory smile.

'Cold?' she asked. 'How about shoving on a pair of wellies and an anorak and giving me a hand with the feeding?'

'Wh-aat?' Marigold recoiled in genuine disgust. 'Feed the horses? You can't be serious.'

Flora was, but Marigold wouldn't be persuaded. Instead, and miserably, she followed Flora around as she did the job alone, feeding the few horses left in their boxes.

'I wouldn't have thought, Marigold,' Flora said as she fed and checked a mare she intended having covered the following week, 'that Luke was your type at all. Not that it's any of my business.'

'You're right, it's *not* any of your business.' Marigold was grinning, good humour restored. 'But our little fling has obviously exercised your mind, anyway.'

'Not half as much as it's exercised Daisy's,' Flora said. She peeled off the gloves she'd been using. 'She doesn't much fancy the notion of her son as a toy-boy.'

'I'm twenty-five, not fifty.' Marigold was tart.

'Luke's seventeen.'

'And I'm the Whore of Babylon, is that it? Corrupting the virgin youth of the county—' Marigold's flash of anger evaporated. 'Anyway, Flora, I didn't figure you for part of the moral majority.'

'It's not the morality so much as the wisdom of the liaison I wondered about,' Flora said.

'Well, then, you'll be glad to know that I've seen the error of my ways. Luke and myself are no longer . . . involved. We're just good friends, of the purest kind.'

'Sounds fun,' Flora said.

When he got back from his ride with Luke, Ciaran Watson seemed in no hurry to go. He walked around the yard, paying flattering attention as the boy explained how things worked and discussed various animals with him. Marigold, cold and fairly dancing with impatience, eventually dragged him away. She was laughing, her arm through his, as they went through the arch. Luke, rubbing down the horse he'd been riding, didn't even look after them.

He knows, Flora thought. The penny's finally dropped. Poor, poor Luke.

This time round Flora attacked the mating season with confidence. The raw, exposed and insecure woman of a year before seemed to her a stranger, someone she'd known briefly and quickly walked away from. She was familiar now with the form of most available stallions and chose the ones she would use based on a combination of knowledge and a dash of gut feeling.

It was later in the week of Marigold's visit, as she was leading a mare she'd had covered out of the travelling box, that Shay came up to her with a longer than usual face.

'Better take that mare straight to the isolation unit,' he said, 'we've a 'flu virus in the yard. Two animals down with it since you left this morning. Pretty virulent strain too, according to Thomas.'

Flora listened to him aghast. A virus could strike at any time, she knew that. But they were so careful always, and kept such a clean yard. It was bloody awful unfair that one should hit them now, in the middle of the mating season. When things were going so well. Unfair too that they'd managed to avoid it last season when a deliberate attempt had been made to infect the yard only to fall foul of mother nature's worst this season.

'I don't understand where it came from,' Shay, brow furiously corrugated, muttered beside her as they walked the mare to the unit.

Jack Thomas was in the main yard when Flora and Shay got back there. He'd dropped in several times during the day and was doing a check on the two animals with the nasal discharge.

'You're going to be damned unpopular with stallion owners for a while,' he said to Flora as she came up to him. 'They won't want to know about any mares from Kimbay until you're well rid of this thing.'

'The foal . . .?' Flora had been afraid to ask until now.

'Don't worry about the foal,' he said. 'He's full of antibodies from the colostrum. They'll keep him infection-free. You're *sure* there were no strange animals in here recently? Or that you didn't bring the infection back from another yard?'

'Definitely no to your first question, though I can't be a hundred per cent sure about the second.' Flora shook her head.

'The first animal to come down, your father's gelding – was he out of the yard at all?'

'Only for exercise . . .' Flora stopped, horrified at a thought which had just come into her head. The shock of its implications churned her stomach and for a moment she couldn't continue.

'Go on.' Jack Thomas was curt. Shay was looking at her with a more than usually taut expression on his face.

'Well, a friend of Marigold's, fellow called Watson, took her out for a ride the other day. It occurred to me . . . could he have been carrying the infection?'

'He could. And by Christ he did. It was no accident either.' Shay's voice was harsh, his expression bitter. He looked squarely at Flora, a fierce anger behind his pale eyes. 'I can tell you how he did it, too,' he said, 'because it happened right under my very eyes.'

'That's a serious charge, man. Are you sure you can prove it?' The vet was raspier than usual.

'I don't need to prove it. I saw what he did. That evil bastard brought the virus into the yard. I'm sure of it. This outbreak is no accident.'

'Tell us what happened, Shay.' Flora was surprised at how calm she sounded. She didn't feel calm.

'You'll remember I was out exercising a few animals that day?' Flora, remembering, nodded. Jack Thomas listened intently as Shay went on. 'Well, Luke and your man Watson rode up to us. They talked to us a bit and Watson said he hadn't ridden in a while, that he was enjoying it. Well, we were moving fast out there and he dropped behind, veered off a bit to the west of us. When I looked back he'd got off and was fiddling with the stirrups. We slowed down to wait for him and when I looked back again he was at the horse's head. Luke called to him and he got back up and followed us.' He thumped a knotted fist into his palm.

'Go on, man,' Jack Thomas was nodding his head, as if he knew what was coming.

'When we got back to the yard I saw him fondling another animal. At the head again.'

'Well?' Flora frowned, suspicions rampant, but not truly understanding yet how the thing had happened.

'We'd two dirty noses this morning. The horse Watson was riding and the one he fondled here in the yard.'

'You've another two now,' Jack Thomas was grim. 'The new mare and Jumbo are infected.'

'Great,' Flora fumed, 'bloody great. But what are you saying, Shay? Are you saying that Ciaran Watson somehow deliberately infected the first two animals?'

'It's as plain as the nose on your face, Flora, what the man's saying. And he's right.' The spectacle of a solidly united Shay and Jack Thomas at any other time would have afforded Flora amusement. Now all she could see was that they both knew something and were keeping it from her.

'*What* is as plain as the nose on my face?' she snapped.

'All it takes is a rag, or cloth of some kind, impregnated with the virus.' The vet was patient. 'You hold it over the animal's nose, get it to breathe in the infection. Easiest thing in the world to spread an infection, if you've a mind to.'

'That fellow had a mind to, all right.' Shay's mouth was a thin line. 'I blame myself. In the normal way I'd have been watchful of anyone turning up like that, out of the blue.' He looked at Flora and she saw embarrassment as well as anger in his face. 'But because of Luke and the business with Marigold I put my better judgement behind me. Didn't want to alienate the lad any further.'

'It's to do with what we talked about before,' the vet said to Flora. 'Phoning that bastard Mangan wasn't enough. Only made him draw in his horns for a while. I told you he

284

wouldn't go away. His kind never do, not until they get what they want.'

'Looks like you were right.' Flora avoided Shay's gaze. She couldn't avoid his probing question.

'Who did you phone, Flora, and what the hell have you and Jack talked about that I don't know?'

She told him then, about phoning Victor Mangan and why. 'You thought I was imagining sabotage when I talked to you about it,' she reminded him. 'Do you still think so?'

'I don't.' Shay cleared his throat. 'And I'm apologizing, Flora, here and now, for doubting you.' He held out a hand and Flora took it. Their shake cemented a trust that had been a long year in the making.

'I'll talk to Luke,' Shay said, 'see what he has to say for himself.'

'I'm certain Luke has nothing to do —'

'Don't think he has either,' Shay was brusque, 'but he's got a responsibility in this thing anyway. He's too big for a kick in the arse but by God I'm going to point out a thing or two to him.'

'And I'll call to see Marigold,' Flora said, 'get an address for Watson. Then I'll talk to Jarlath Maguire, see what he thinks our chances of a prosecution are.'

'Not good, is my opinion,' Jack Thomas said grumpily. 'You should have moved when I told you, back in October.'

'I'm slow,' Flora said, 'but I'm sure. And I'm learning to do a lot of things I wouldn't have done back then.'

Chapter Twenty-Five

Flora took action first thing next morning, driving as early as was feasible over to Fairmane. She telephoned beforehand to make sure that Marigold would be there and, when her voice came on the line after several rings, hung up without speaking. She wanted her arrival to be a surprise – an unprepared Marigold might be more forthcoming.

She herself was unprepared for the wan, tired-looking woman who let her into the office.

'Hello, Flora.' Even her voice had a flat quality. 'Do you want to see Matt? He's upstairs somewhere.'

'I came to see you, actually.' Flora closed the door behind her. She was glad Marigold was alone. She had been unsure how she would deal with things if the trainer had been in the office.

'What did you want to see me about?' Marigold's tone continued dull, uninterested. She wasn't wearing make-up, the first time Flora had seen her without it. The result was an older-looking Marigold, showing all of her twenty-five years. Apart from a scarlet scarf which tied back her hair she was dressed completely in black. Her eyes were curiously pale without the make-up and, in spite of her bored tone, watchful.

'I wanted to talk to you about Ciaran Watson, for one thing.' Flora, towering over the other woman, felt like a bully. She lowered herself onto the desk and folded her arms. She still felt uncomfortably looming, but reminded herself that the other woman was an able manipulator and not at all the delicate creature she seemed. Marigold's eyes slid towards the door.

'Don't even think about it.' Flora was dry. 'I'm not here to be messed around with, Marigold. I want information and unless you've got something to hide I can't see any reason why you shouldn't give it to me.'

'Don't you threaten me, Flora Carolan.' Marigold's features froze. 'I don't have to tell you anything I don't want to. And I can leave this room any time I want to.' Her petulance was waspish.

'If you leave I'll follow you,' Flora spoke lightly. 'We're going to have this conversation, Marigold, and whether we have it here, at your mother-in-law's or out in a field is up to you.'

'Better tell me what's on your mind so.' Marigold shrugged and threw herself into the armchair by the empty fire.

Flora crossed her legs and studied the tips of her boots. She was trying not to feel sorry for this strangely fragile Marigold, owner of a pale face and washed-out eyes. A small inner voice reminded her that today's waif would be tomorrow's temptress.

It was Marigold who broke the silence. 'Well?' she demanded. 'I don't have all day, Flora. I *do* have a job to do, you know.'

'Of course. I'm sorry.' Flora met her eyes. They were coldly defensive. 'I'd like to know why exactly you brought Ciaran Watson over to Kimbay.' It was bluntly put, she knew, but as Marigold herself had said, they didn't have all day.

'Because he wanted a ride. He couldn't ride any of the horses here.'

'Not even Matt's own Setanta?'

'He was afraid Setanta would be too strong for him to handle. Look, Flora, if it was such a big deal you should have said so at the time. Luke—'

'We'll leave Luke out of this, if you don't mind. And the big deal came afterwards. Truth is, Marigold, I got the definite impression Ciaran was quite an accomplished horseman. He was certainly well able to handle the stroppy mare Luke gave him.'

'Is there a point to all this, Flora, or is it just that you're enjoying the sound of your own voice?'

'There's a point all right. And why so defensive, Marigold? The point is that it seemed to me a fun ride wasn't a burning need with Mr Watson and that he might have had an ulterior motive.'

'What a pile of old shit.' Marigold got up and walked round the back of the desk, giving Flora a wide berth. She sat down and Flora turned on the desk to face her. 'What possible interest could Ciaran have in Kimbay? You don't even keep racehorses there.' She pulled open a drawer, took out and emptied the contents of a make-up bag onto the desk. She snapped open a mirror.

'Exactly,' Flora said. 'So perhaps you could tell me why your Mr Watson was so interested in Kimbay?'

'He wanted a ride, that's all.'

'I don't think that's quite all, Marigold.' Flora hardened her tone. 'Thing is, we've got a viral infection sweeping the yard. We also have proof that Ciaran Watson deliberately infected a couple of animals while he was at Kimbay. I want you to think carefully about those two facts, and the implications for both you and Mr Watson. Because I'm not going to let the matter rest.'

Flora was banking on Marigold's not calling her bluff. If she questioned her claim to have proof, Flora would only be able to push things so far before revealing how circumstantial the evidence was.

'It's nothing to do with me.' Marigold had begun to make up her face, beginning with mauve eye-shadow. Quickly, skilfully, she built up a protective mask, every flick of wand and pencil putting her further behind a barricade. Flora went in for the kill.

'It will have a lot to do with you, Marigold, when the case comes to court. You're a material witness. You could save yourself an awful lot of bother by squaring with me now.'

'To hell with you, Flora. To hell with all of it.' Marigold's eyes glittered in their made-up sockets. 'Ciaran's not a fool. He'll know how to deal with you lot.'

'Right, girls, what's this all about then?' Matt Hopkins,

cool and curious, leaned against the jamb of the open door. 'Anything I can help with?'

'It's all right, Matt.' Flora spoke hurriedly, annoyed at herself for not having turned the key in the door. 'Marigold and I can sort this out.'

'You're here, Flora, so it concerns me. Now, who'd like to explain?' He looked from one to the other of them, his expression questioning and expectant. As if we were schoolchildren, Flora thought, and misbehaving ones at that.

'I think perhaps Marigold and I will go elsewhere to finish our chat,' Flora stood up, 'if you can spare her for twenty minutes, that is?'

'Well, I don't *want* to go elsewhere.' The childlike qualities in Marigold's face had been taken over by a steely calculation. 'What's going on here, Matt, is that Flora's accused a friend of mine of deliberately bringing a 'flu virus into her yard. She's threatened me with court.'

'Mind filling me in a bit more?' The trainer left the doorway. He kept his eyes on Marigold as he stood in the middle of the room with his hands in the pockets of his leather jacket. 'What friend are we talking about here?'

'No one you really know.' Marigold tossed her head and loosened the scarlet scarf. Her hair fell free and bouncy and she was, all at once, her old, invulnerable self. 'But believe me, Matt, the whole thing's the most incredible nonsense. Flora's absolutely mad.'

'Well, up to a point I'd agree with you.' The trainer grinned, ignoring Flora. 'But in this instance I'd at least like to know what her grounds for suspicion are. Are we talking about your Mr Watson, by any chance? I thought he'd departed the scene?'

'He had, but he came back.' Marigold spoke in a rush. 'He called to see me here and when he said he fancied a ride Luke said he'd fix him up at Kimbay and he did.' She threw a look of injured innocence Flora's way. 'Now she's accusing him of—'

'I heard that bit.' The trainer's voice was sharp. 'We'll deal with the number and kind of your callers later,

Marigold, but for now I'd like to know if there's any truth in Flora's accusation?'

Marigold's face flared with righteous indignation and, as she started to speak, Flora turned to face the trainer. 'Please, Matt, I'd like to deal with this myself. There's a lot more going on than you realize and —'

'I'm not a fool, Flora.' The blue eyes flashed a sudden, cold anger. 'Yours isn't the only yard in the area to suffer mischief, remember? Though your horses do seem to be the target. If there's something going on I want to know about it. Marigold, I want an answer to my question, please.' He stood waiting, gaze unflinching on the by now half-heartedly defiant face of his secretary.

'How do I know whether he meant to do it or not?' Marigold's voice became bitter. 'I haven't seen him since then. Heard from him either. But that's men for you, isn't it? All the bloody same. They take you, use you and off they go.'

'We'll save the philosophy for another time, *if* you don't mind,' Flora snapped. 'Are you saying that you think you were used by Watson as a way of his getting into Kimbay?'

'It's beginning to look that way.' Marigold was sullen. Then words began to tumble out, hopeless and bitter all at once. 'He asked me months and months ago to bring him over there, when I first met him. Said he'd never actually been on a stud farm, stuff like that. He was really keen and he seemed to think I was a regular visitor to Kimbay and could just drive in with him. When I told him I'd never been there myself he sort of went off the idea . . .' She shrugged. 'He went off himself soon after that. Just stopped calling.'

'So you began to amuse yourself with Luke?' Flora asked.

Marigold shrugged again, more eloquently this time, but didn't answer the question directly.

'He phoned last week, first time in months,' she said. 'He said he might call some time. I knew the only way to get him to come, definitely, was to tell him I'd arrange for him to visit Kimbay. I dreamed up the plan about the ride

290

and got Luke over and', she looked at the trainer with despairing pique, 'the rest is history.'

Matt ran a hand through his hair. 'Christ, Marigold, how could you be so stupid?'

'Because I love Ciaran,' Marigold said.

In the small silence she sat still as a stone. The make-up could no longer do anything to hide the drained energy and lack of life in her face. Or in her voice, when she said, 'And it was all for nothing because he's gone and I know he won't be coming back. I don't know where he is. If I did I'd be with him.'

Wordlessly, Matt Hopkins went to the drinks cabinet and poured a large whiskey. He handed it to her and she took a long, slow drink. 'Thanks,' she said.

'You've left something out, Marigold, haven't you?' The trainer poured another drink and looked questioningly at Flora. She shook her head in refusal.

'What do you mean?' Marigold was gathering the make-up back into its bag.

'The bit about letting him in to free Flo Girl last August?'

Marigold zipped the make-up bag and gathered an anorak off the back of her chair. 'I'll be off now.' She stood. 'I don't suppose there's a job for me here any more. Not that it matters. It's got bloody boring anyway.'

'*Did* you let him in to free Flo Girl?' The trainer hadn't moved and he spoke very softly. The question seemed to fill the room and Marigold looked at him with real apprehension.

'Yes,' she said.

Neither Flora nor the trainer tried to stop her leaving.

'You've lost a secretary,' Flora said. Matt Hopkins didn't reply. He watched Marigold from the window as she crossed the yard and disappeared round the side of the house.

'Suppose I have. She was good, you know. No feel for the animals but a great head for figures.' He shrugged. 'Poor Marigold.'

Flora said nothing. Marigold had betrayed him, his

trust and the job he'd given her. She'd betrayed Luke and she'd betrayed Flora. And still she knew what he meant. Marigold herself had probably been used and betrayed most of all. She had risked her all and lost.

'So. Now we know who did it – but *why* did he do it?' Matt Hopkins turned a moody gaze on Flora and she felt immediately too close to him. She moved restlessly around the room, feeling the ceiling too low, the walls too close, wanting to get out of there but knowing she owed him an explanation.

'I think, Matt, that it has to do with a land developer fellow named Mangan who wants to buy Kimbay.'

She took a deep breath and explained to him, as briefly as was decent, the story of Victor Mangan's interest and her slow suspicions and ultimate telephone call. 'I was stupid enough to think that would be the end of it. It was all I could do because I've no actual proof he's been directly, or even indirectly, involved with any of the problems we've had at Kimbay. We don't even know that Watson was working for him, though I'd stake my life on it. I'd stake Kimbay, come to that.' She gave a wry grin.

'It would have been helpful if you'd told me about this months ago.' The trainer drew a long breath and glowered at her. Flora met his gaze steadily.

'Why?' she asked. 'You wouldn't have believed me. You'd have thought I was imagining things. Shay did. Now he believes me and now so do you. But now we have proof in the shape of Shay's observations and we've Marigold's testimony. Though I doubt either will be of much use legally.'

'Don't be so sure I'd have disbelieved you, Flora.' The trainer shrugged. 'Thing is, where do we go from here?'

'*We* don't go anywhere.' Flora spoke slowly, her gaze fixed on the trainer without really seeing him. 'I'll deal with this, in my own way. Mangan will behave for a while now, once he knows we're aware the virus was planted. That'll give me a bit of time.'

She left almost immediately after that, ignoring the trainer's attempts to get more information, politely and

292

firmly refusing his offer to help in some way. She could handle this her way. What was more, she wanted to.

It was three long weeks before the yard was completely free of the virus. Luke, during that time, worked like a man driven, arriving pre-dawn and prowling late at night too, checking and rechecking boxes, food, locks and anything that moved. No one tried to stop him and no one asked him why. That he was working out guilt, disillusion and pain in his own way was obvious to everyone. All they could do was hope it worked for him.

In the evening of what was the first relatively routine day at Kimbay since the beginning of the outbreak, Sophie rang.

'They tell me spring has sprung.' She was laughingly good humoured, a world away from the months of dark mornings and watchful nights at Kimbay. 'I'm told that birds are singing, buds are budding and all the rest of it. I've no evidence that any of this is true so I thought I'd pay a visit to my country contacts and check it out. Any chance of a bed?'

'Get in the car, now,' Flora ordered. 'I'll line up the birds and whip out a few green bushes. When will you be here?'

'Tomorrow. I'll come tomorrow,' Sophie said.

She arrived in the late afternoon and climbed out of the car pulling a vast, rug-like coat about her. What Flora could see of her looked wonderful – exuberant hair, glowing skin reassuringly radiating the old, rakish good humour.

'Good God, Sophie,' Flora tried to catch some part of her friend that she could hug, 'what's with the Siberian gear?'

'Case of hoping for the best and preparing for the worst.' Sophie pulled two large bags out of the back of the car. 'I plan to *walk*, Flora, and to abandon booze and all things carnal for the next three days. Think you can put me up under those conditions?'

'Sounds a bit radical. We'll take it a day at a time,' Flora said, 'see how it goes. What in God's name have you got in these bags?' She simulated collapse as she took one of them.

'Warm clothes. Boots. A few bottles – for you, of course. Are there no strong men to help us around this place?'

'This is an equal opportunities and equal workload organization,' Flora laughed, 'you carry your own bags. I hope you're hungry. I've made us some food.'

While they sat, comfortable and catching up over a salmon quiche, it came to Flora that Sophie could not have arrived at a better time. It was more than fortuitous, in fact; it was a godsend. She told her so.

'Victor Mangan', she said, 'has resurfaced.'

'Mmm.' Sophie nodded, unsurprised. 'Never thought he'd gone away. Tell me.'

Flora did, in detail. Halfway through Sophie reached for the bottle of wine and poured herself a glass.

'There's a time and a place for everything.' She excused herself. 'And this is definitely a time for a drink.'

'Ciaran Watson has disappeared,' Flora wound up, 'almost as if he'd never been. No one I ask seems to know anything about him and the guards can't help unless I want to prosecute. Trouble is, I'm up to my neck in work at the moment, trying to catch up on the three weeks lost when we had the virus in the yard. And Flo Girl has her first race of the season in a few weeks.'

'So you want me to see what I can root up on Watson?'

'Would you?'

'Yup. But he's obviously the messenger. What you really need to do, Flora, is shoot the boss – and I think I can set that up for you. Your Victor Mangan is a slippery and doubtful operator, no question about it. I've gathered some low-down on his activities. Very questionable, a lot of it, and just about this side of the law. I got diverted by that wretched singer and her book but I'll get back on his case straight away. We'll decide what to do when I've got the full picture. There's bound to be something we can hang him on. Rein him in, so to speak.'

'Sophie, you're great. You get me the information and I'll take it from there.' Flora sighed with satisfaction. 'Everyone's on guard at the moment so he won't do anything for a few weeks, at least. After Flo Girl's race would be a good time for me to make my move. Think you can give me the dirt by then?'

Sophie said she could and Flora changed the subject. She hadn't the slightest doubt that Sophie would turn up what she needed on Victor Mangan. What she was less sure of, but would sort out, was how she would use it, effectively, to remove him as a threat to Kimbay.

'Feel like a walk?' she asked when they'd finished eating. Sophie looked apprehensively at the sharp blue sky beyond the kitchen window. 'Seems a bit drastic, plunging into the beyond so soon after getting here. Maybe when I get acclimatized. We'll go tomorrow.'

'Up, get your boots on,' Flora was having none of it, 'tomorrow might rain. An hour's walking will shake some of the winter out of your bones.'

'An hour!' Sophie looked at her aghast. But she got the boots, pulled them on, groaning. 'You're so *robust*, Flora. Not a bit like you used to be. You make this walk sound like punishment. I want it to be gentle and meandering and . . .'

'Up,' Flora said.

They were on the return lap of the walk, a brisk forty-five minutes later, when a wheezing Sophie asked, 'Is this what you substitute for sex these days?' She was pink-faced and breathless. Her legs, she'd already complained, were suffering tormented spasms. 'You look so – so bloody awful *healthy*, Flora. You've become a nun. Or is there something going on I don't know about? An obliging country lad on the side, maybe? Come on, you can tell Auntie Sophie.'

'Nothing *to* tell, I promise you.' Flora grinned. 'Just plenty of clean, country living.'

'Can't last. That kind of faithfulness just ain't natural.' Sophie shook her head in a gesture of mock despair. 'What I want to know, Flora, is if Serge deserves it? Does he?'

'Absolutely,' Flora said.

'Mind you,' Sophie looked unconvinced, 'you were always inclined toward monogamy. Celibacy's only a step away from it.'

'Oh, shut up.' Flora increased her pace and Sophie, with a wail of protest, followed. 'What about you?' Flora asked. 'Any nice men on the Butler horizon?'

'There's been the odd diversion. Nothing memorable. But work's good.' She gave a relieved wheeze as the house hove into view. 'I've got a nice contract with a New York magazine to do Euro travel stuff for them. It'll get me away every so often. Other bits and pieces too.'

'Everything else okay?' Flora wondered, too late, if she'd been right to push Sophie into this walk. But surely, by now, she was fully recovered – from the physical effects of her fall anyway. Sophie, reading her mind, grinned.

'Are we talking here about my physical or psychological state? Because the one is wrecked and the other's great, thanks.'

Flora tried but Sophie was no more forthcoming. Recognizing a clam-up, knowing Sophie would only talk when and if she ever felt like it, she dropped the subject. They finished the walk in a silence broken only by Sophie's puffing complaints.

Sophie's company, her outsider's attitude to the stud and countryside, were like a warm breeze after the winter and spring. On the morning she left, Flora watched her pack with reluctance.

'Any regrets about decisions made?' Sophie looked up from stuffing her boots into a polythene bag. 'About staying here?'

'No.' Flora thought for a moment. 'I'm still not a hundred per cent sure where I'm going but at least I know where I've been. This last year anyway.'

'Oh?' Sophie waited.

'I've been growing up, ridiculous as it may seem. Bits of me that might never have been exposed have seen the light of day. What I'm saying is that I've found out more about myself than I ever would have in ten years of living the way I used to.'

'I take it we're not just talking fit calf muscles here?' Sophie sat back on her haunches, listening.

'They're a side product.' Flora grinned. 'No – it's more basic than that. Like I know now that I can make judgements and stick with things . . .' She trailed off vaguely. 'Things like that . . . You know . . .'

'Sort of,' Sophie said. 'The old Flora would have cut and run for cover when the going got rough. What made the equation different here, though, was the horses. Your father too, and wanting to do it for him. Does Monsieur de Maraville realize he'll be getting more than he bargained for in a wife?'

'Oh, yes.' Flora was positive. Then, 'Well, I think so.'

'Maybe you should tell him,' Sophie said.

Chapter Twenty-Six

The horses were parading for the Athasi Stakes. In less than fifteen minutes they would be running the Group Two over a mile of Curragh turf. To a horse they were sleek, graceful, honed to win. Flo Girl, high-stepping with a relaxed elegance, shone bright among the greys and bays. On her back, in Kimbay's red and green colours, Lorcan McNulty smiled faintly, with a cool that matched that of his mount, as he passed by Flora and Sophie.

'She's a beautiful creature, your Flo Girl.' Sophie's murmur was almost reverent. 'None of the others come near her in the beauty stakes.'

'True,' Flora said. 'But we're biased, you and I. And it's the running stakes that matter this afternoon.'

She was feeling slightly sick and more than a little cold. Her nervous chilliness wasn't helped by a sharp shower of sleet beginning to whistle across the Curragh plain. The sick feeling wouldn't go, she knew, until the race began. 'I feel terrible,' she told Sophie. 'Owning a racehorse should be more fun than this.'

'Wait'll she wins, brings you home all that lovely money,' Sophie said, 'you'll feel a lot better then.'

The cold had made Flora plump for the practical warmth of a long and elderly sheepskin coat. She'd covered her options by wearing a stretch black lycra dress underneath. If Flo Girl won it would be perfect for the celebrations. If she didn't the sheepskin had a certain coverall dignity.

Sophie, with more *savoir faire* than racetrack wisdom, had come dressed in the Carolan red and green, coat and dress respectively. Her hair colour for the day almost exactly matched Flo Girl's chestnut.

The horses moved out for the start of the race and the sleeting shower stopped.

'Let's go,' Flora said.

Matt Hopkins joined them in the stand. He was charming to Sophie, apologetic to Flora for having been tied up earlier. He betrayed no feelings of tension, no worries about the race to come.

'She's ready for battle,' he said as the horses were loaded into the stalls. The crowd became quiet. The race was announced. The stalls opened.

This time Flo Girl shot forward and took an immediate lead. For seconds she was a glorious flash, lengths ahead of the pack. Then they caught up and horse and jockey were swallowed into the thundering, headlong gallop of the race. When the field spread out and broke up Flo Girl was still running comfortably with the leaders. She stayed there, well placed to take the lead, as they came to the last furlongs.

Flora hadn't even noticed the horse which came streaking up on Flo Girl's inside. She was just suddenly and unbelievably there, passing her out, powerful and dark and taking the lead. Flo Girl tried, valiant and pushing, and the gap between them narrowed. The rest of the field fell behind. It had become a two-horse race.

The crowd roared and the dark horse passed the finishing post on the nod, a bare head in front of Flo Girl.

Flora kept her binoculars trained on horse and jockey, saw how Lorcan wheeled the filly in, patting and talking to her. They were all right then, both of them. They'd run a great race and come a good second. Flora felt only joy, no disappointment at all, and a warm relief that it was over, that horse and jockey were all right. It came to her, intuitively and with absolute clarity, that this was but one race in Flo Girl's racing career. She would run again, and again, winning and losing and carrying excitement with her in every race in which she took part.

In the winners' enclosure, when they got there, the tumult and steaming horses raised the freezing temperature. Flo Girl, snorting and blowing, suffered caresses with haughty tolerance. Holding laconic court Matt Hopkins advised journalists to keep an eye on Flora's filly. This, he assured them, would be her season. She was a Classic performer and she would be going all the way.

'Are you talking about a Derby win?' he was asked.

'You saw her run today. What do you think?'

The journalist agreed it had been an impressive performance, a good second placing, but – 'The Derby's a tougher race. Longer too – think she can maintain that sort of speed to win over a mile and a half?'

'Just watch her,' the trainer said.

On Monday, in the yard, Flora felt oddly restless. She found it difficult to finish things, found herself forgetting things too. It's the spring air, she thought, and it's because I'm still coming down from the race high.

She decided to take a few hours in Dunallen, stock the fridge, maybe buy herself lunch. In the supermarket the restless feeling persisted. She found it hard to make up her mind what to buy. In the end she threw in some frozen basics and decided to get out of the place, fast.

'Well, now, Flora! We didn't expect ever to see you shopping here again.' The woman who stopped Flora's trolley with a large, strong hand was middle-aged, tall and wide. Her red, smiling mouth was unkind and her eyes sharp. Marigold's mother-in-law had a lot to be irritable about, Flora knew, and her conversational style was famously quarrelsome. She wished fervently that she hadn't run into her and hoped the subject of Marigold wouldn't come up. On the whole she thought it unlikely that Marigold would have confided in Kitty Kennedy anything of the reason she'd left Fairmane.

'Hello, Kitty.' Flora smiled, wondering how quickly she could make her escape. 'Why shouldn't I shop here?' As soon as she asked the question she knew it was a mistake. It was like throwing fish to a seal.

'Oh, people were saying that now your horse is doing so well you'd be moving on to grander things.' The woman's eyes, under sharply pencilled eyebrows, were unhappily spiteful. 'Dunallen must be small fry to a woman talking all over the papers about owning a Derby winner.'

'Oh, I let my trainer do that kind of talking, Kitty. And my tastes are simple, really. As long as I can get porridge and free-range eggs I'll go on spending my millions here.'

'That's a relief to us all, I'm sure.' Kitty Kennedy sniffed. 'But I hear too that it won't be long now until you give up mucking out at Kimbay and become a lady of leisure with a rich husband. Italian, is he? The man you're going to marry?'

'French, actually. And I'll probably hang around dirty old Kimbay for a long time yet.' Flora knew she shouldn't let the woman annoy her but a surge of pure temper drove her on. 'The sad truth, Kitty, is that I'm perverse and stupid enough to like the mucking out work I do, and the people and animals I work with. Maybe you could pass that on to the "people" who seem to be so interested in everything I do.'

Flora felt herself doing everything in slow motion after that. She packed her shopping into the car, left Dunallen, drove to Kimbay and unpacked in an almost trancelike state. Her outburst at Kitty Kennedy had shocked her. She'd never done anything like it before. It wasn't so much *what* she'd said to the woman which had shocked her. It was more the passion she'd felt, the absolute belief in the simple credo she'd used to explain her life and the frightening feelings of inevitability about other things which it had released.

The feelings had been there a long time, waiting for her to face them. It had taken Kitty Kennedy and her silly gossiping to force Flora to look at a truth which she had known, but been unable to face, for a long time.

She couldn't marry Serge. She couldn't marry him because she couldn't leave Kimbay and he wouldn't come to live on the stud. She no longer loved him enough to give up her life for him.

She remembered the clear, warm feeling she'd had when first they met. There had been so much about Serge that she'd wanted, felt right about. She'd liked him being older than she was, that he was so secure of his place in the world. She'd known from the very beginning that he loved

301

her, that he would never let her down – exactly in the way she had known Ned would never let her down. She had relished Serge's confidence, the assurance that he was there for her, would be a security net when life went wrong. She had felt safe with him, and the safe feeling had allowed her to fall in love.

But she didn't need him like that any more. And, in not needing him, her love had become less.

It wasn't even that her love for him had ended. She still loved Serge, in the way she always had. It was simply that she did not want a dependent kind of love any longer. When Ned died he'd taken the security of his loving care with him. In its place he'd left her responsibility, duty, a chance to stand on her own two feet.

He had, in effect, left her his life.

Well, she had taken it and lived it and she was faced now with the consequences. She had subconsciously examined her life and made another, a life which was so much more worth living.

The consequences were independence, and choice. She didn't want to lean any more. She wanted to be in charge of her new life. Somewhere in the last, long year she'd moved on from the kind of love she felt for Serge, the kind of relationship they had. She didn't need a security net any longer.

Her independence had probably begun the day she'd decided to stay on at Kimbay. It had grown as other people grew to need her, as she'd come slowly to learn, and then care about, her work on the stud.

She would explain to Serge, as much as she could, in a letter. As a manner of doing things it was unforgivable, cowardly. But it would be far more unforgivable, infinitely more cowardly, to go ahead and marry him. And if she waited to do it face to face she would weaken and compromise and agree to give things more time. Which would not be honest or even fair because she knew no amount of time would change how she felt.

In her room she stood by the window and looked at the sky and scudding clouds. She had thought, living in

Brussels, that these skies were the thing she missed about home. She'd been wrong. The skies had simply been the manifestation of the quick vibrancy of life here. It was that, a quality of risk and immediacy, which she had missed.

She looked for a long time before she sat in the windowseat and composed a letter to Serge breaking off their engagement. As she wrote, the sun came out from behind the clouds, warming her face and lightening up the countryside. She hoped it would be shining for Serge, too, when he read her letter.

> I would rather not be writing this [she wrote], but it's the only honest thing to do. I want you to be happy. I want to be happy myself. I no longer think we can do it together. I have changed. You must know that I have changed. There is so much that I want to do now that I didn't want to do a year ago . . .

She was aware the letter was almost unbearably blunt. She didn't know any other way to write what she had to say. As she began to write again she imagined him raising the eyebrows on his fine, patrician face, the disbelief growing in his eyes. She didn't want to think about how he would be when he accepted the finality of her words.

> It's not that I don't love you, because I do. I just don't love you enough to leave here and live with you in France. Live with you anywhere that isn't here. I am telling you like this because I am so afraid that, were we to meet, you would talk me out of my resolve, convince me that I am wrong. And that would be no good, for as soon as you were gone, I would know, once again, that we must end things.
>
> Do you remember, in January in St Anton, when I spoke about making mountains out of molehills? I was thinking about all of this then, but in a vague sort of way. I told myself, and you, that my sneaking doubts weren't important. That they were only little hiccups and would go away. But they didn't and I know now that they won't.
>
> In a little while (I hope, I hope, I hope) we will be able to meet and talk and be the friends we have always been. When that happens I will return your beautiful ring. Be happy, Serge. I am so very, very sorry to hurt you like this.

She ended there because she felt she could say no more on paper. She didn't know how to say that she was, as much as anything, listening to a gut instinct when she told him she could not marry him. An instinct which told her she would never be happy with him now she'd got a sense of being her own person, got used to being in charge of her life. The Loire valley would be a prison after Kimbay.

Serge would get over her. His outraged pride would help him deal with the initial pain of rejection. There would be many, many hands willing to hold his, all of them smooth and comforting and many of them beautiful too. In time, because it was expected of him, Serge would marry the owner of such a pair of hands. He would be happy too, because he was a pragmatist and would want to take and build a life that suited him.

Maybe she would love again too. Her mother had loved twice, after all. And her second love had been her great love.

Flora went downstairs with the letter. She would go to Dunallen and post it straight away. Then it would be done and the consequences something else she would have to learn to live with.

In the hallway she met Daisy. 'Need anything in Dunallen?' Flora asked. 'I'm on my way to post a letter.'

'Must be urgent. You were there already today, weren't you?'

'It is and I was.'

They walked together to the car, Flora flicking the letter against her palm as they went. Daisy refused a lift down the avenue. She looked at Flora.

'Something on your mind?' She glanced at the letter. 'Nothing wrong, is there?'

'Nothing wrong at all, Daisy.' Flora drew a deep breath. 'Except that I've decided to stay on at Kimbay and I'm staying because I want to, not because it's something Ned wanted or because I feel I owe him or the boys or even the Carolan name. I'm doing it for myself and because the yard and horses matter to me. And because I like being my own woman, making my own decisions.

304

And,' she grinned, 'I want Kimbay to become one of the great yards.'

'I see.' Daisy began to gather her falling-loose hair back into its bun. 'I see,' she said again and this time she smiled too. 'It's the horses. Your father could never let go of them either. Well, I'm not surprised the bug's got you. Not surprised at all.' She gave her hair a final pat and stuck a pearly comb at the side. 'But what about that man of yours? Where's he going to fit into all of this?'

'That, Daisy, is something I've just worked out.'

'You're not going to do anything rash?' Daisy asked quickly.

'Yes. I'm afraid I am.'

When she got back from the village, and even though it was then darkish evening, Flora saddled up Cormac and rode out. It was soundly dark by the time she got back to the yard and the ride had done nothing to diminish the ache for what she had done. Even so, she knew she'd been right. The person she'd been when she had first met and fallen in love with Serge was gone. The person she'd become could never love him in the same unquestioning way. The marriage just wouldn't have worked. She owed it to Serge as well as herself to be honest.

She was sad and she was unhappy about what she'd done. But she had no regrets. She hoped she never would have.

Chapter Twenty-Seven

Investigating Victor Mangan had been every bit as interesting as Sophie had imagined it would be. She was by no me ns finished yet, but in the three weeks since she'd seen Flora she'd got a lot of information, and written it up with much lively reading about his close-to-the-wind dealings over the years. None of them had been illegal but a lot had been morally doubtful.

The weakness was that she'd failed to get any of his victims on the record. Victor Mangan dealt in bullying the elderly and the vulnerable and people like that did not, voluntarily, put their heads above the parapet.

Nothing of what she'd come up with would be of any use to Flora, either. Nothing before last night's tit-bit of information anyway. Handled properly *it* could be the one mistake she and Flora could use to hang him. Metaphorically speaking, unfortunately.

Sitting by the phone she considered the facts she'd got on the property developer.

The initial unearthing of dirt had been straightforward enough. Enquiries and searches in the Companies Registration and Planning offices had revealed his involvement in several well-timed and lucrative property deals and land coups. Further enquiries had shown a total lack of scruples on his part about the way in which he conducted business. The word on Victor Mangan was that he ruthlessly pursued, and got, what he wanted. He'd made column inches in the papers from time to time and some carefully phrased, awkward questions had been asked by watchdog groups.

But libel laws were stringent and he was exceedingly clever and nothing ever stuck. There was no law said he couldn't evict tenants when their homes became valuable. Buying up land which later became valuably re-zoned wasn't illegal either. Just good luck, as he said himself.

He was clever, too, in his choice of associates and Sophie had been unable to find anyone willing to go on record about business involvements with him. She had tried, God knows she had tried. But she'd persistently come up against the almost impossible barrier of honour among thieves.

Until now, and this most unexpected breakthrough. Sophie had discovered that Victor Mangan had had an affair with Melissa Carolan. It had gone on for eighteen months or more, and had only recently come to a graceless end.

Sophie couldn't believe it had taken her until now to find out. She should have sussed something long ago; there *had* to have been a link, someone who had tipped him off about the state of things at Kimbay. The acquaintance who'd told Sophie had done so almost casually, assuming she already knew. *Everyone* knew, he'd snickered, except the husband. Melissa's lovely nose had been put severely out of joint, he said, on account of she'd been quite brutally cast aside for the lissom charms of a nineteen-year-old blonde with a less complicated domestic life. Mangan's new love was wealthy too and it was entirely possible, Sophie's informant said, that the bachelor Mangan was finally planning marriage.

Which might make him vulnerable, Sophie thought. But then again, maybe not. Victor Mangan wasn't a fool and no one had managed to get at him before now.

No. Melissa was a much better bet. A woman scorned, and all that – though it wouldn't do to rely completely on Melissa's malice or desire for revenge. She might be fearful of implicating herself. If that happened then Sophie would find a way around such complications, persuade Melissa by other means to part with information. A worried Melissa, gently threatened with exposure, would almost definitely decide to be helpful. Sophie was a great believer both in just causes and in fighting fire with fire.

307

Melissa, when she answered the phone, didn't remember Sophie. 'Sophie Butler? I'm sorry, do I know you?'

'Only slightly.' Sophie was dry. 'I'm a friend of Flora Carolan. We had dinner together.'

'Oh. Yes. How are you?' Melissa didn't quite yawn. And Sophie didn't answer the question.

'I wondered if we could meet?' She was businesslike. 'I'm doing a magazine article on style, a sort of general, lighthearted piece on what people are wearing to lunch these days. I thought immediately of you . . .' She paused long enough for Melissa to take the bait. Sophie, from long experience, knew that only the high-minded or neurotically shy resisted publicity. Melissa was neither. 'It needn't take long – but if you're busy, please don't worry. I can always get—'

'Oh, I don't see any reason why not.' Melissa's offhandedness was unconvincing.

'Great.' Sophie was brisk. 'How about lunchtime tomorrow?'

Melissa found herself free.

Hoping to minimize the chances of their being seen together, Sophie booked a table in a quiet, solidly unfashionable Italian restaurant. She didn't want to risk a meeting with Victor Mangan, a regular on the fashionable-restaurant lunch circuit. Melissa was not impressed with her choice.

'It's not the sort of place I'd have chosen myself,' she spoke loudly, ignoring the waiter who pulled out her chair. 'I'd like you to note that in your article.'

'Fine, consider it done.' Sophie smiled agreeably. 'I chose here because it's quiet. We can talk uninterrupted. The food's excellent, by the way.'

They ordered. Melissa opted for a salad and, to Sophie's mild alarm, said a categorical no to wine. Sophie had rather hoped the relaxing effects of a decent Chianti would make Melissa talkative. For herself Sophie ordered smoked salmon tagliatelle with a bottle of Chianti Classico. Melissa just might be prevailed upon to indulge in a glass, or two.

While they waited for the food to arrive Sophie chatted

308

busily and took notes about why Melissa had chosen to wear an ivory pin-tucked dress and short black jacket for lunch, about the sort of restaurant she preferred and the people she would normally lunch with. Melissa was carefully voluble. Her beautiful face seemed to Sophie strangely immobile. She was reminded of the story of a Hollywood actress who, after a lifetime of controlling her facial expressions, died the proud owner of an unlined face in her fifties.

'Will there be a picture?' Melissa asked. Sophie had no difficulty lying.

'Definitely,' she said. The waiter arrived with their food and she put away her notebook, changing the subject.

'How is Ollie?' she asked. 'And your son?'

'They're fine.' Melissa spiked a piece of tomato. 'When do you think your article will appear?'

'Can't say really, I'll let you know as soon as I have a date. To be honest, Melissa, I'm more interested in another story at the moment.' Sophie, as if absentmindedly, poured Melissa a glass of wine. 'You might be able to help with it too.'

'I don't know,' Melissa looked bored, 'I prefer not to get too involved in things.'

'Oh, but this is something you were involved in for, oh, about eighteen months or so.' Sophie smiled, watching Melissa carefully. A small frown and greater degree of boredom were the only noticeable changes in her expression.

'Can't think of anything I've done for that time that might . . .' Melissa trailed off and shrugged. In slight but noticeable confusion she lifted the glass of wine and sipped.

Sophie pounced. 'You had an affair with Victor Mangan which went on for that length of time.' She was blunt. 'So I'm hoping you can tell me a few things about him I need to know.'

'How *dare* you!' Melissa's face turned chalky. 'This is completely outrageous! I don't believe what I'm hearing . . .'

Her eyes widened in alarm and the hand which held

309

her glass shook. Sophie guessed that Melissa was totally unused to straight talking. She was the kind of woman who demanded to be, and usually was, treated with delicate care.

'Maybe I should say it again,' Sophie began and Melissa, a trembling long-fingered hand trying to stop a sudden, nervously twitching cheek, shuddered.

'Don't. You're a real bitch. Anyone ever tell you that?' An ugly red flush crept up Melissa's neck.

'Yes. Many times.' Sophie was cheerful. 'I haven't always disagreed with them, either. So, now that we've established both of our credentials maybe we can get down to some *real* business.'

'But the magazine article . . .?' Shocked and worried, Melissa still clung to her hopes of publicity. Sophie softened.

'I'll fit it in somewhere,' she said. 'You know, Melissa, this doesn't have to be disagreeable. We might even find we can be of help to one another. Your ex-lover's been a bit of a shit to you, so I'm told.'

'People *know*?' Melissa's voice had become a whisper.

'That he dumped you?' Sophie shrugged. 'It's a small town and Don Quixote he ain't. Of course they know.'

'You haven't told Flora?'

Melissa was all at once urgent and terrified and Sophie knew the battle was over. Melissa was the kind of woman who craved attention and to be desired and to have the odd affair. Which was fine, all things being equal. But such women also, and invariably, wanted the cushion of a reliable, adoring husband in the background. Melissa had probably been managing her separate lives for years – with Ollie turning a blind eye as long she was discreet.

But all that had changed in the last few minutes. If Flora heard, and Fintan and the Sweeneys got to know too, then Ollie could not be relied on to continue compliant. Sophie knew she was right about this. Everything about the woman opposite indicated a fear that her world was about to fall apart.

She went in for the kill. 'I haven't told Flora, yet. And I probably never will, unless I have to.'

'Right.' Melissa sat up straight, pushed her plate and glass away and put her hands flat on the table. 'I want a black coffee and then we'll talk. Victor's a bastard anyway. I owe him nothing.'

The waiter brought them espressos.

'I need you to tell me anything you know about Mangan's interest in Kimbay,' Sophie said. 'And don't mess me around, Melissa. I know he heard about Ned's will and Flora's predicament from you. Ollie would *not* like —'

'You've made your point.' Melissa was cold. 'Just stick to what it is you want to know.'

'It's quite simple. What I want is some information we can use to stop that creep harassing Flora. I'm sure you can help, Melissa. A name, a conversation overheard, anything that might help.' She sat back and waited. She could see how the prospect of a little revenge was making Melissa feel better about things already. She could almost see the calculations going on behind the cool eyes, fixed concentratedly on the table.

'You'll have to believe me when I say I know nothing about anything that may have happened at Kimbay.' Melissa looked up, a small frown between her brows. Sophie was inclined to believe her. Mangan would never be stupid enough to involve Melissa — nor would he need to.

'I believe you,' Sophie said.

'But I *can* give you information which might pin him down on one or two other deals.'

Twenty minutes later Sophie had the names, particulars and contacts she needed to substantiate and make stronger the story she'd already written. There was more than enough for Flora to extract her pound of flesh, too.

Chapter Twenty-Eight

Flora sat and waited. She felt calm, very sure of what she was about to do. She crossed her legs and leaned back, watching customers as they came and went at the bar. There were a lot more than there would have been in a country pub at eleven in the morning. But then this coolly stylish café-bar was a celebrated haunt of the city's *beau monde*. They were probably breakfasting.

It hadn't been her choice of meeting place. She'd have preferred to rendezvous somewhere quietly unobtrusive. But Victor Mangan had been keen on this as a venue and she'd agreed. If he wanted them to be seen together then so be it. It could even be for the best – the parading quality of the place might ensure he kept on his best behaviour.

He was late but she wasn't worried. She knew he would turn up. He'd been breezily cheerful on the phone, full of confident predictions about Flo Girl's future and obviously sure that Flora had reached a decision about selling Kimbay. For her part she'd been non-committal, letting him think what he would, saying only that she had come to a decision and that it was imperative they meet. She'd been conciliatory in tone, friendly even. He would definitely turn up.

She was glad of these minutes to herself anyway. The morning had been hectic. She'd prepared herself the night before, going through the few papers Sophie had given her and putting them in a briefcase. But an early morning's visit to Fintan had taken longer than she'd bargained for. Her brother had then wanted to come with her to meet Mangan and she'd had to make him promise, on oath, to stay away. Even at that she'd left him unshaven and unsure on his doorstep, scowling in the early May sunshine and issuing advice as she hurried off. The subsequent rush across town in traffic had almost ruined her determined calm.

The minutes ticked on. At 11.20 she threw a longing glance at the bright street life, the sunny pavement tables. Maybe she could wait for him out there. At 11.23, as she'd almost decided to move, he arrived. She watched him make his way toward her, tall, lightly tanned, the picture of civilized urbanity. He nodded to some people as he passed, smiled at others. Flora wondered at the pecking order, what one had to do to merit a smile as opposed to a nod.

When he at last stood in front of her he smiled widely. 'You look wonderful, Flora,' he said.

He leaned forward and, for a shocking moment, she thought he was going to kiss her. But he merely nodded before slipping into the seat opposite. 'The summer suits you.' He looked at her, openly admiring her bare arms, her slim form in the long white linen dress. She hated him for his arrogance, his presumption that he had this right to assess her body. She fiddled with her wide black bracelet and looked at him coolly before signalling the waiter.

'Let me buy you a drink,' she said. 'What would you like?'

'Brandy,' he said. 'Will you join me? We must celebrate the rarity of this occasion.'

'I'll stick with coffee.' Flora gave the order.

When the drinks arrived she placed the papers from the briefcase on the table between them. His face registered surprise and she spoke quickly.

'I'm not here to talk about selling my share of Kimbay,' she said. 'But I *would* like to discuss some of your other property interests with you.'

He sat back abruptly and his eyes, for one revealing moment, sharpened and looked at her hard. Then he relaxed and draped an arm along the back of his seat. 'I'm sorry to hear you're not selling, Flora. But then that's your prerogative.' He paused. 'I must admit I'm fascinated, though, by your interest in other ventures of mine. Do you have a proposal to make, a plan of your own you'd like to discuss?'

313

'What I've got to say is more in the nature of a demand.' Flora touched the papers on the table, patted the briefcase. 'I've got copies of statements here which will substantiate what I'm about to say. The originals are with the journalist who did the investigative work. These statements', she separated two sheets of paper, 'have been made by two elderly tenants evicted by you from their homes of nearly twenty years. Quite legally, of course. But hardly fairly. You exploited their trust. Both of them understood that, after twenty years' tenancy, they would be entitled to new, longer leases on their apartments.'

He started to speak and she waved a silencing hand. 'They felt quite secure, even when you became their new landlord. What they didn't know was that if they broke their tenancy, moved out even temporarily at any point before the twenty-year end, they would no longer be entitled to a new lease.' Flora paused and took a long breath.

'But you knew. And you made it your business to buy up many apartments around the city with similar lease conditions. Always with elderly tenants. As their new landlord, and with just months to go on the twenty-year lease, you offered to paint and decorate their homes for the old people. You even offered them alternative accommodation while you did so.'

Flora had been looking at him as she spoke. His expression was one of amused tolerance but his stillness was reptilian. She shivered inside as she went on. 'When they returned to their homes and sought to renew their leases they found themselves ineligible to do so. Within months, weeks in some cases, you evicted them.'

Victor Mangan sipped his brandy and looked idly around the room. He put the glass down and drummed his fingers on the table. 'As you said at the outset, Flora, all of that was perfectly legal. What point exactly are you trying to make?'

'Only this, Victor.' Flora spoke slowly and softly. 'Those old people, and God knows how many lost their

314

homes to you, were too frightened to do anything at the time. But these two,' she picked up two sheets of paper, 'sisters who lived together, have been persuaded to tell their story. They have a young niece who is fond of her aunts and who is *very* keen to publicize their case.' She tapped the statements. 'But then you know that, Victor, because you've heard from her already.'

'She's a child. She knows nothing of the realities of life. I told her I'd have her in court if she—'

'She's eighteen; old enough to recognize moral depravity when she sees it. And now she has journalistic support she'll definitely be going public.'

'Then I'll have the journalist in court too.' His cold, controlled anger sat like a rock between them.

'You can try, I suppose,' Flora said. 'But you'd better get a damned good barrister. Some other of your dealings will be appearing in print too, one of which is quite definitely illegal. I'm talking about you getting insider information and buying land just before it came up for re-zoning.'

Victor Mangan finished his brandy and signalled to the waiter for another. He didn't offer to buy one for Flora. When it arrived he cupped the glass in his hands, swirling the liquid and speaking slowly.

'That's a very serious allegation, Flora, very serious indeed. I presume you're familiar with the laws of libel?' His face was quite still, and menacing. Flora separated another sheet of paper from those on the table.

'This is the statement of an out-of-work and aggrieved planning official. It contains dates and times of meetings, Victor, that you no doubt hoped forgotten. And the truth isn't a libel. All I'm presuming is that the law will protect the innocent.'

He gave a short laugh. 'How very naive you are, my dear.' He leaned toward her and there was no pretence now at either charm or urbanity. His expression was totally vindictive. 'If either you or the journalist in question, who I presume is Miss Butler, pursues this matter further you

315

will discover just how little the law protects people of no consequence.' He drew back. 'However, fascinating as all of this is, I feel somehow that there's more to come.'

'You're quite right, there is.' Flora was all at once feeling drained, wishing she'd opted for the brandy. She would have one later. A large one.

'It's this.' She put her hands on the table. 'If you so much as *breathe* the name Kimbay anywhere or to anyone again I'll go public about your offer and our subsequent difficulties.'

'Don't be ridiculous, woman. You don't have a shred of proof that your so-called difficulties had anything to do with me. I'm not an idiot, Flora, and I'm warning you that if you and your friend go ahead with this exposure stunt then you'd better be prepared for *real* difficulties.'

'Threats, Victor? You really should be more careful.' Flora stood up. She stepped back from the table and slowly removed her black bracelet. She turned it so that Victor Mangan could see the minuscule recording device Fintan had earlier fitted inside.

'It's been an interesting conversation, Victor. Together with the statements from the old ladies and the planning official's evidence, this recording of what we've talked about should help create a few difficulties for *you*.' She picked up the briefcase and slipped the documents inside. She snapped it shut. 'Thanks for the coffee. And now you really should get out into some of that sunshine. You're looking quite pale.'

The property developer didn't move. He had become grey and a muscle ticked convulsively in his cheek. One fist clenched and unclenched on the table as, low and vicious, he said, 'You bloody bitch . . .' He moved as if to get up and Flora, stepping away, raised an eyebrow.

'You can't win them all, Victor,' she said, and smiled brilliantly. She turned then, with a small wave, and made her way quickly, without once looking back, out and into the sunshine.

In the street she walked briskly in the direction of St Stephen's Green. She didn't slacken her pace until she reached the park railings and then she turned to scan the good-humoured teeming crowds she'd just come through. Victor Mangan wasn't anywhere among them. She hadn't really thought he would be.

Driving home, feeling quite lightheaded, she went over the meeting in her head. She'd covered everything she and Sophie had agreed on. Which meant that, with his threats on tape, Sophie's story had even more back-up. One of the morning papers had bought it and was ready to go with it within the week. Mangan would deny everything, of course, and scream libel. But the tape was bound to count for something and Sophie was adamant her sources would hold up. God alone knew how she'd got them.

And God alone knew what would come out in follow-up investigations by other journalists. It was in the nature of things that a story like this would run and run for as long as news could be squeezed out of it.

Victor Mangan wouldn't be pursuing property deals for a long time to come.

Chapter Twenty-Nine

The marquee transformed Kimbay. It stood in the field in front of the house, a palatial red-and-green-striped structure which made the house look small and gave the paddocks the appearance of a playground. In the bright, sunny daylight the myriad miniature bulbs strung between the trees and trailing across the garden and through the clematis looked like an insect invasion. At night, when they were turned on, they would become silvery will-o'-the-wisps, small dazzles of light creating a magical party mood.

That was Flora's plan anyway. She had decided, win or lose, that Kimbay was going to party on the night of the day Flo Girl ran in the Guineas. The invitations had been sent out, more than a hundred of them, the food had been organized and a four-piece jazz combo engaged to play the night long. Or at any rate until the last couple had danced the last dance.

It was the day before the race and the marquee and lights had just gone up. The animals, except for a nosy and intensely territorial Dipper, were keeping an uneasy distance. Shay was quietly disapproving but the twins, both of them, said they thought it time there was a 'bit of a thrash' at Kimbay.

Daisy was loud in her disapproval. 'What if the horse loses the race? What then?' she demanded. 'You won't feel much like celebrating in that instance.'

'I feel like celebrating now and I'll feel like celebrating then,' Flora retorted. 'I'm not going into mourning if she loses. Anyway, she *is* going to win. I feel it in my bones.'

'Your bones and your guts! You've become a great one for relying on your innards. What about using a bit of common sense? What if it rains tomorrow?'

'It won't. The sun's going to shine and we're going to win the Guineas and carouse until dawn.'

'Fine. But you should do it somewhere else. Not on your own doorstep. You're going through a crisis of some sort, Flora. It's making you behave as if you were Ivana Trump. A party'll attract hangers-on and parasites of all kinds to Kimbay. Your father never gave parties.'

'But my mother did,' Flora said, 'and it's been far too long. Do you know, Daisy,' she looked thoughtfully across the fields, 'that apart from the gathering here after my father's funeral there hasn't been a proper social occasion at Kimbay for nineteen years?'

'Nothing wrong with that,' Daisy said. 'Parties bring trouble. It's always better to let other people give them.'

'You won't be coming then?'

'I'll be there all right. Wouldn't miss someone else's party for the world.'

Flora walked through the marquee. The late afternoon heat through the canvas made the air heavy. A bee droned somewhere near her head and from outside the summery sounds of grasshopper and birdsong drifted through the opening. She felt sure it was going to be a good party. It was amazing how sure she felt about a lot of things these days.

Daisy, as always, had put her finger on something when she'd mentioned a crisis. Only the crisis was over and it had nothing to do with Flora thinking she was Ivana Trump. It was simply that she had, at last, come into her kingdom.

Serge had telephoned. The call had come late in the evening, two weeks after Flora had posted the letter. He didn't say 'I told you so', or remind her of the forebodings he'd had about her taking on Kimbay. He didn't talk either about his hurt or pain. It was a short call, dignified and *distingué* as everything Serge did.

'I am not going to persuade or argue,' he said. 'There would be no point in that, would there?'

'No. None at all I'm afraid. I'm so sorry, Serge, about everything. But it has to be this way, for me.'

'Yes.' She could imagine his shrug. 'But for me . . . I am not yet sure how things will be for me . . .'

And that was as much as he'd spoken of his hurt. Flora sought for something which would make things less painful, soften the reality of what was happening. She could think of nothing.

'It was a surprise, your letter,' Serge went on. 'But when I took time to think it seemed less so. It now seems to me that I was foolish not to have been prepared, not to have seen how your first life was reclaiming you.'

'How could you?' Flora said sadly. 'I didn't know myself, for a long time.'

'If I could change things, make it so that your father's will had never happened, then I would. But we have a *fait accompli* and I must live with it. You must keep the ring, Flora. It is yours now.'

'No!' Her cry was involuntary. She did not want this magnanimity, this selfless generosity. It was enough that she had hurt him; she didn't want a reminder of that fact sitting in her jewel box. 'I couldn't keep it,' she said. 'It belongs to your family, to Monique.'

'It is not the only ring in my family,' he laughed, briefly, 'and I would not care to give it to someone else anyway. I would like you to keep it. Perhaps then you will think of me when you wear it.'

'I will think of you anyway. Often.'

She had agreed to keep the ring. It would have been churlish, even cowardly, not to. Her discomfort was a small price to pay in the face of his need. And it was a very beautiful ring.

When he had gone off the phone Flora cried. Her tears weren't only for Serge, and his hurt. She wept too for the life she might have had, if only she hadn't come to know this one.

The Saturday of the Irish 1000 Guineas was a scorcher. The Curragh crowds jostled to fill the stands from early on and Flora, calmer by far than she'd any right to be, made her way through them to the owners' viewing stand. She was wearing a peach and cream polka-dot dress and a straw hat and was, according to a vibrantly clad Sophie, 'the irritating essence of collected cool'.

'Wait'll the race begins,' Flora said. 'That's sure to bring on a fit of the heebie-jeebies.'

It didn't. She felt quite detached as she watched the filly start the race at a gentle enough pace, almost as if she were on an everyday gallop at Fairmane. She didn't actually spot the moment when Flo Girl increased her speed, but quite suddenly saw how she was inching ahead, then further ahead still.

As the race went into the final furlongs of the dash for home the filly moved up to become the last of the four leading runners. The favourite, well in the lead, looked unbeatable. It was as the finishing post loomed, and defeat seemed inevitable, that Flo Girl from somewhere pulled power and speed. She passed the third and then the second runners. Fifty yards from the finishing post she caught up with the leader and for seconds before she passed him out they ran neck-and-neck.

She was a length and a half ahead when she went over the finishing line.

Flora, ignoring the hysteria around her, kept the binoculars stubbornly focused on horse and jockey. Flo Girl took quite a time to pull up and for a while it looked as if her incredible burst of speed would carry her halfway across the Curragh. But she slowed at last and headed for the unsaddling and winners' enclosures.

Flora and Kimbay were some 100,000 guineas richer than they'd been a couple of minutes earlier.

Kimbay when they got there was a riot of red and green flower arrangements, put in place by the caterers while the race was being run. The tiny bulbs were like fireflies everywhere, dazzling amid the garden's growth, flickering in the high trees. Flora walked through it all, greeting guests, ensuring they had champagne to toast Flo Girl, that the music could be heard, that the timid were not overlooked.

She gave silent thanks for the warm, clear evening and

the fact that, as it got darker, there would be a benign, cloudless moon and starry sky over them all. She couldn't have asked for things to be better.

But even as she mingled and sipped her champagne and accepted good wishes and felt the glow of it all she knew that things wouldn't always be like this. She had chosen a high-risk, hard-working life. Tonight was one of the perks. And by God she was going to enjoy it.

By the time everyone had finished eating, and the floor had been cleared for dancing, a huge amount of very good champagne had been drunk. Flora and a flushed Jack Thomas took the floor to the strains of the Curragh of Kildare. Ollie, with a demurely smiling Melissa, followed. Soon other couples braved the springy boards too, bodies jerking or blending with the music depending, and within minutes the dance-floor was crowded.

In time, and as the night went on, couples left the marquee and wandered under the trees or into the garden. Men alone stepped outside with glasses of keg Guinness and talked about horses, about that day's racing and other races to come. Fintan went on stage and sang and so too, at around midnght, did Daisy.

It was one o'clock before the party began to wind down. And still Flora went on mingling, a little tiredly now. She'd been doing it all night, flitting from group to group, on a high she didn't want to lose, not yet. The air in the marquee was heavy, weighted with the heat of dancing bodies. She left as the band went into an oldies medley and hummed to the strains of 'The Nearness of You' as she walked across to the garden. It was cooler there, and quiet. The music was a distant, drifting sound. She closed her eyes and went on humming, leaning with a sigh against the clematis-covered wall.

'Great party, Flora.'

She knew the voice and nodded, without opening her eyes. 'Thank you,' she said. 'I wondered if you were still here.'

'Did you? I thought maybe you were avoiding me. I haven't been able to corner you for a dance all night.'

'Maybe you didn't try hard enough.' Flora opened her eyes and looked, smiling, into those of Matt Hopkins. His smile in the moonlight was very white and his hair inky dark where it fell across his forehead.

'I've never known you not to go for something you wanted,' she said. 'Would you like to dance here, now?'

She moved into his arms and it was as if this, like the events of the whole day and of weeks past, had been inevitable. They swayed together to the far-off music, moving hardly at all. Flora closed her eyes and leaned sleepily against him. His arms tightened around her and they tried out a few steps, moving in awkward unison on the uneven grass.

The music stopped and they swayed together again until Flora opened her eyes and looked around. They were in the middle of the garden, their moonlit shadows lying long and close across the grass.

'I didn't think you would stay.' The trainer spoke softly into her hair.

'I know you didn't.' Flora turned in his arms, looking up at him, knowing what he meant. 'You decided a lot of things about me at the beginning and you were wrong. About most of them.'

'I was?'

'Very wrong.'

He traced the features of her face with a finger. 'I wasn't wrong to want you. I'm not wrong to want you now . . .'

'No, nothing wrong with that.' Flora moved back a little, but not so far that she couldn't still feel him, touch him. 'Your mistake was in presuming I would want you, too, in the same way.'

'Didn't you?' His voice was husky.

'I wanted you, but not in the same way. I wanted you fearfully. You seemed too big a risk and I would have had too much to lose. You could hurt me too much.'

'And you don't want me any more?' His voice was jerky.

'I do. But now I'm not afraid of the risk.'

323

'Flora . . .'

'Sssh . . .'

She put her finger to his mouth and he was quiet, watching her and waiting. When she reached to kiss him he said, 'Flora' once more and then nothing for a long time. He pulled her tightly against him and to Flora his body felt both familiar and strange, as if she had come upon a new world and love that she had always known. She locked her arms around his neck and a delirious, abandoned part of her thought how much she wanted to go to bed with him, hold him into her naked body, make love for long hours until they came to a beginning of knowing everything about one another.

But another part of her hovered, unsure, watchful and self-protective still.

If she was to love Matt Hopkins then she would have to be prepared for a love which would be neither gentle nor safe. It would be turbulent, completely unlike any other love she had known. He would be demanding and he would not always be there for her, not at all like the love she had known from her father, or from Serge.

But still she longed for him, and for what they could have together. And she knew that by wanting to be sure of his love she was asking for the impossible. Even so she hesitated, stiffening in his arms. He immediately loosened his hold on her.

'I don't want to leave you tonight,' he spoke softly. 'Don't tell me to go, Flora.'

'I can't let you stay,' she said. 'Not tonight. Don't ask me to explain.'

He dropped his arms and stepped back from her. 'I've tried to keep away from you,' he said. 'I've tried not to think about you. Even when your engagement ended I didn't come near you.'

'Yes. I noticed. Only I thought you were preparing to marry the beautiful Isabel.'

He looked startled for a minute. 'Why did you think that?'

'Marigold . . .'

'Ah, Marigold.' He shook his head and smiled a rueful smile. Then he took her chin in his hand and raised her face to his again. 'I can wait,' he said, 'but not very long.'

They held hands as they walked back to the marquee together. It would happen, in time. Perhaps. When it was right.

Epilogue

Flo Girl won the Budweiser Irish Derby on a day which was rare for the perfection of its weather and racing conditions. It was warm but enlivened by a small, fresh breeze. The ground was hard but not, thanks to rain earlier in the week, too hard. The sun, in an endless blue sky, shone from early morning on the searing green of the Curragh's wide acres.

With all of this the odds were still stacked against the filly. She was running in a race dominated by colts and colt winners, and against the winners of other Derbys. Her jockey, though excellently capable, was less experienced than most of his colleagues. She had not been favoured either, and the racetrack cognoscenti had been condescending about her chances.

The filly, they said, had 'a touch of class' but was 'something of a circus horse'. She was 'fast, but a bit green'. She would never be able to 'maintain the pace over a mile and a half'. And her jockey, according to the same sages, was 'good, improving all the time but not yet Derby material'.

Flora, accepting the trophy afterwards, felt weightless and unreal, as if it were all happening to someone else. It seemed to her that she was floating overhead in a bubble, part of a dream fantasy from which she would awaken to find herself in her bedroom at Kimbay.

As if from above she saw the woman who seemed to be her lift the trophy aloft, laughing and triumphant. Below the podium and all around the woman were the faces of people the real Flora knew and loved. Except for her father, everyone who mattered was there.

One face stood back a little, smiling, watching her.

When the woman lowered the trophy the face moved through the crowd and came close, kissing her on the mouth.

The bubble burst and Flora reached for the wonderful reality of Matt Hopkins's hand. Holding it she smiled with joy and for all the possibilities to come.

'We did it,' she said, and he nodded, grinning, at the trophy.

'Want me to carry that for you?' he asked.

'No, thanks,' Flora said. 'I'd prefer to do it myself.'